I0773151

Sagavis

Text Copyright © 2024 SL Thorne,

ISBN: 978-1-961615-17-5
Imprint: Thornewood Studios

SAGAVIS

By S. L. Thorne

DEDICATION
&
ACKNOWLEDGMENTS

This book was once part of Midnight and Amber. The conclusion, in fact. But together, the book was just too big without increasing the size and I'm one of those for whom all books in a series must be the same size. Hence, all my books are in the same trade size. And as the page count as one book would mean no hardbacks....

So, here you go. The end game. Where everything that has happened before has vamped up and come to a head. This is the top of that last hill. You know, the one on the roller coaster where everything up til now was just bunny hops and a few easy loops and shimmies. And then there you are, sitting at the top of the highest point, looking down into a 200 foot drop down a chimney into the deep, dark ground, and you know... you know what comes next. The screaming, twisting turns and loops that will rattle your teeth and make your heart race.

The first chapter of this book is that hill, folks. Buckle up. Cause it's about to get wild!

A special shout-out to my 'sister', Laura. Without whom, this cover would be lackluster at the very least. You can thank her lovely wife Tresa for the clarity and legibility of the back cover blurb.

<u>TABLE OF CONTENTS</u>

POLITICS AND SHADOW PLAYS

THE SQUARE

KIN

THE PLAGUE STONE

ALL HELL

END GAME

I

Politics
And
Shadowplays

ONE

Landros was sitting on the sofa in the front room, oiling his leather armor, salvaging the damaged shoulder and trying to figure out a way to put more protection there without reducing his mobility.

Lark drifted in, slid her arms around him from behind, and kissed his cheek. She took a deep breath. "Mmm," she sighed. "Always loved smell of leather. Especially new leather."

He leaned back, kissed her, and noticed that she had put on the blue dress he had brought from her wagon, the one he had bought her less than a week ago. She had not worn more than the borrowed shift from the temple or one of his shirts for the three days she had been here. She had also put on her jewelry. "Going?" he asked, feeling an uncomfortable pull inside at the thought.

"Have things to be doing, life to lead," she said softly, letting go and coming around to stand in front of him. She set her pack down for a moment. "Is not like will not see me. Know where I live. ...And where I work."

"I know," he breathed. He had known that before. It still had not kept her from disappearing on him. But, to think about it, how much of that was his fault? She had not known where to find him, and he had known exactly where to find her. He pulled her down into his lap, his hands resting on the Romeri's ample hips. "Are you sure you are up to working again?"

She touched the tip of his nose with a playful finger, "Are you not also ready to *do* instead of sitting about?"

He had to admit that she was right; he had known this day was not long in coming and had not really expected to be able to hold her here. He reached down to the floor on the side of the sofa, felt for the sword belt he had lain there. Catching hold of it, he handed her the short sword and scabbard. "Here, I want you to take this. I noticed you have not replaced your scimitar yet, from the fight with the succubus, and this will.... What?" he asked as she gently pushed it back at him, shaking her head.

"This blade is useless to me. Do not know how to use. Thank you, but.... have looked for scimitar, even sabre would do, though not so well. But all swords are sold to army, and blade-smiths have no time to forge special. I... I will have my brother get one for me when see him next."

"And when will that be?"

She shrugged.

He took her hand. "No, that is not good enough. You said yourself that you might have stood a better chance in the warehouse if you had had a sword. I do agree that if you have never used a short sword, your knowledge of the scimitar will hurt you. But you cannot go about, especially not at night as you must, without something. There are monsters in the streets. I've been hearing from the servants here that almost every night, something strange is reported, some mythical creature or well-known monster. It is more dangerous than ever out there."

"But is nothing to be done...." she protested.

"Not true," he said. He set the sword aside and wrapped his arms around her. "I know someone. He... collects things. The more unusual, the more he likes it. An exotic blade like a scimitar is something he just might have. Would you wait at least until I can set up a meeting?"

She shook her head. "Have errands to run and boy to teach fiddle. Is daylight," she said consolingly. "Is not so dangerous now."

He thought for a moment and decided not to say anything about the fireballs or the warehouse incident that nearly killed her occurring in full daylight. She knew that fact as well as he did. "When will you be done with Dane?" he asked.

"Should start just after lunch is over and inn quiet. Maybe hour or so."

"I'll meet you there. Then, you and I will go to my friend's and find you a scimitar. Do you have anything unusual to trade for one? If you don't, I might."

She smiled, thanked him for the offer. "I think can find something." She slid off his lap. "Now, be good boy. Will see you then," she said, giving him a deep kiss.

Landros watched her gather her things and head out the door. Sighing, he went back to his armor and tried to rub her from his mind for the time being.

It felt good to finally be out and about. She took her time, strolling towards the temple mostly oblivious to her surroundings and the darker moods around her. Smiling at people, she hummed a soft little tune she had been tinkering with off and on for a year or more; did not even notice the strange looks she received for her cheerfulness.

The temple was her first stop. She went into the Maiden's House and asked the first person she saw where she might find Sister Rue. She was politely asked to wait. Thankfully, Rue was not too long in coming. She looked much more rested than she had the last time Lark had seen her. They hugged fondly.

"How are you feeling, dear?" Rue asked, sitting beside her.

"Better, many thanks to you and Landros." She reached down into her pack. "Brought book back. Thank you. Is wonderful. Many of stories had not heard before."

Rue took the volume, smiling, caressed the leather cover fondly. "My mother gave this to me when I told her I planned to enter the priesthood."

Lark laughed, "Book of love stories is hardly gift for one taking vow of chastity."

Rue nodded wryly. "I think that was the point. My mother had 'plans' for me in the marriage department. She was trying to talk me out of it."

"I see she failed," she commented.

"Good thing, too. The man she wanted me to marry has, well... the wife he did take has been here several times already for 'household' injuries. I somehow doubt that she is that clumsy," Rue said quietly. She took a deep breath, brushing all the gloom aside. "So much for true love, eh? No, I am quite happy here. This is where I belong. And if the Maiden *does* choose to send me a lover, then I will simply move next door. I hope you enjoyed the book?"

"Yes. Is well-read, I notice."

"That it is," she mused fondly.

"Was wondering," Lark began. "Is possible to see Keltree?"

The priestess nodded. "Certainly, and I am sure he would love to see you, but he has gone to his brother's house. Tell you what, I am going to stop by tomorrow. I go every few days just to make sure he's not doing anything stupid and is *actually* resting. Why don't you meet me here after noon tomorrow, and I'll take you with me?"

"Oh, would love that! Have been wondering how had fared." She got up and shouldered her pack, only slightly lighter for the lack of the book. "Oh, has been any luck discovering who was other man with Ebastion and Lulelani?"

Rue shook her head silently.

Lark heaved a sigh. "This bothers Landros. Which bothers me. Is obsessed with this; that and hooded person." She snapped quickly back into her cheerful mode and again gave the half-elven woman a hug. "See you tomorrow noon!"

Rue sat back and watched the Romeri girl practically bounce out of the temple. "Too much energy in that girl," she breathed. "Could certainly use some of that vivaciousness around here," she added, getting up and moving back to her rounds of patients.

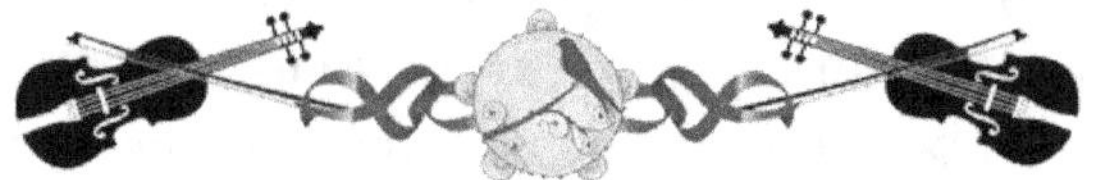

Landros heard the doorknob turn and looked up, hoping to see Lark breezing back in. The black-clad figure of his brother banished that hope, and he sullenly went back to work.

"I am surprised to see you actually here, brother," Portholus said. "I had expected you to be out and about on some secret mission again."

"Not this time." He set his armor aside and began putting his tools away. "Where have you been the last few days?"

"Oh, here and there," he mused evasively. "You know me." He slipped into the watercloset for a few minutes.

Landros went to the desk, grabbed a piece of paper, and jotted a quick note to his friend that he would be stopping by the shop that afternoon looking for a special item. He blew on the paper until the ink dried and folded it carefully. Tucking it into his pocket, he began gathering his things together, preparing to pay a visit to Colwyn to ask a few questions that had occurred to him.

He saw his brother leaning against the door frame with his brush in one hand, pulling long black hairs from it with the other. He looked pointedly up at him, asking the question without saying a word.

Landros crossed over, took the tool from him, and put it back where it belonged. He wordlessly went back to packing.

Portholus continued to stand there, smirking in his irritating way, while his brother did his best to ignore him.

"So, *why* is there long, silky, black hair in your brush?"

"Maybe because she borrowed it while she was here," he answered, trying to keep his temper in check. "I did not know you were so concerned about my grooming habits." He did not like being teased about Lark, especially by his little brother.

"She? No name, just 'she'?" he asked, moving to the fireplace where he tossed the hairs.

"I am not like you, little brother. I don't keep company with half the ladies in this town at once," he said curtly.

"This the Gypsy girl?" Scraps wandered in from the bedroom, saw Portholus, and ran over. "Hello to you too, little one," he said as the raccoon leaped into his arms, searching his vest for treats. "I am sorry, nothing for you today," he said. The raccoon sulked and jumped to the couch. He noticed Landros pointedly ignoring his question, so he tried a different tack. "Tell me about this girl."

"There is nothing to tell about this *lady*," he answered shortly, folding the blanket up and putting it into his bag.

Of course, he would not leave the subject there. "There has to be *something* to tell. She was here for several days, was she not?"

"She was hurt," he retorted. "I was hurt. We needed rest. She got it here. Again, there is nothing to tell."

Portholus smirked, amused by his brother's reluctance to discuss this mystery woman. "Maybe I should ask her?"

Landros rounded on him, "No," he snapped. "You will not go anywhere near her! Do you understand me?!"

Portholus looked deep into his brother's eyes, realization flickering across his own. He grinned in disbelief. "You're afraid I'm going to take her from you!"

"No," he denied, growling, "You heard what I said. You are not to go anywhere near her!"

His face softened. "You really are afraid."

Landros looked away, unable to look into his brother's face and lie to him, lie to himself. "Just stay away from her," he said quietly.

Portholus stared at his brother, incredulous. "You really think that I would take her from you?"

He did not even look up. "Yes." He paused for a moment, staring at the shirt in his hands before shoving it into his bag. "You have never had a problem with the ladies. Most of them fall over themselves and each other to get to know you. Yes, I have noticed it and have envied it. For some reason, this one has chosen me, and I do not want that ruined in any way. Just... Just leave this one be."

Portholus stopped him, made him look at him so that he could see the truth in his eyes. "I would never do that to you. She obviously means something to you. What, I don't know and I don't think you know either. But you have nothing to worry about, not from me. Why would I want to destroy what little I have left?"

He sighed, moved away. "Just leave her be. For me," he said weakly. He picked up his pack and hefted it to his right shoulder, as his left was still sore. "I have to go; I've got people to meet and things to do. Try and stay out of trouble, will you? Scraps, you coming?"

The raccoon hopped off the sofa and waddled across the floor, scrambling up his leg and into the pack on his shoulder.

"Landros," Portholus called. His brother looked back. "Just be careful with these humans."

"Don't forget to lock the door," he said as he left.

He had mixed feelings about his brother and Lark, and needed time to sort them out. His feelings for her had to be strong to pit him against his brother. He did not want to have to choose between them and did not know if he could.

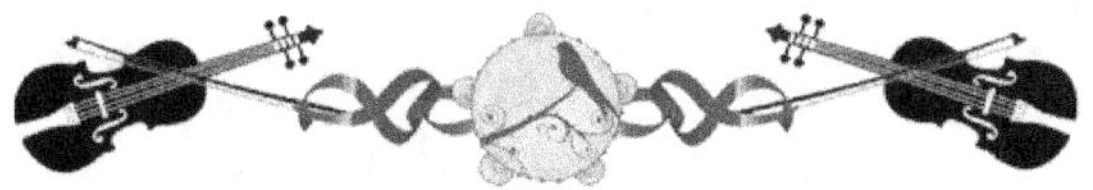

Lark entered the dressmaker's shop with Nightingale on her shoulder. Bianca came out of the back and fairly lit up when she saw her.

"I was beginning to wonder! Oh!!" she exclaimed, melting as she noticed what her customer was wearing. "Turn about for me, girl!" Lark laughed, spinning obediently. "I am *so* glad I never lengthened that dress! It is absolutely ravishing on you! Come on, I've got most of your others ready. And I need for you to try on the fourth for me. I was wondering what was keeping you! I thought, oh horror of horrors, what if you had gotten hurt out there when them fireballs came hurtling down? We're just so lucky it didn't hit us!"

Chattering away, she led her into the back room and took her bag. There was a young girl there Lark had not met before, who handed her a red dress. She was fairly pretty, with a round face and dark red hair.

"Oh! Where are my manners!?" Bianca exclaimed. "This is my niece, Sara. She helps me out when I get orders in. Wouldn't be as far along as I am without her help," she said, giving the girl a pat on the shoulder. The girl smiled demurely and began helping Lark change without a word.

Lark was almost overwhelmed by all of the attention but allowed the two seamstresses to pin her into the dress and tuck her up, put up with the poking and shifting of her body. When she turned to look in the mirror, she almost did not recognize herself. The dress was breathtaking. The bodice was daringly cut, showing a good bit of cleavage as well as giving her a bit of a boost. It was in a rich velvet of deep red with a latticework in gold thread embroidered all across it. The sleeves were long and billowy, of a nearly sheer red fabric akin to silk. She held out her arms for Sara to gather and tie the sleeves at her wrist, leaving a wide ruffle. The bottom half was in layers of subtly varying shades of red, the same material as the sleeves, but the panels curved from the waist, creating a spiral effect when she turned.

"Yes," Bianca sighed. "You were very right, dear," she said to Sara. "I *do* like the gold threading. I think some sort of trim at the hem, though. Something subtle. Maybe a spiral wrap of gold thread over a strip of velvet? Sort of like a unicorn's horn. What do you think?" she asked Lark.

She could not think of anything to say. "At this point," she said finally, "anything you think will look good will be gorgeous. Could not have imagined something so beautiful!"

"You'll probably need to get some red slippers to go with it, but that should not be too hard. It's not like there's a demand right now for dancing shoes."

Bianca and her niece made their adjustments and eased her out of the garment. She fitted herself into the two-piece blue one and was thrilled at how it looked and the way it moved with her. Tonight was as good a night as any to try it out, she thought with a smile.

"Beautiful work," she said. "Looks better than drawing."

"They always do, my dear. If they don't, I scrap 'em!" She made a tiny adjustment at the waistband of the blouse. "Bend back a bit, dear," she asked. "Hold that." She pinched the fabric together. "How's that feel?"

"Tight." She loosened it a tiny bit. "Better. Snug, but not cutting in half."

"All right, can you get it off without my letting go?"

In answer, Lark unfastened the front clasps and shrugged out of it. Bianca took the bodice over to a chair and began to sew the adjustment immediately.

She looked back at herself in the mirror and turned, moving in a slow, sinuous dance. She smiled. Just once, she wished she could have seen that dance in the woods through Landros' eyes. Perhaps the opportunity would avail itself for her to repeat the performance?

She felt a tug at her hips and looked to see Sara, who had yet to say a single word, unfastening the side clasp of the broad belt and sliding the skirt to the floor. She handed her a second skirt and a blouse, took the blue one, and folded it carefully. Lark dressed herself.

This skirt was the bright motley they had laid out together. It was beautiful. She missed her black and red calico skirt, the one that had been torn to near shreds by the pirates and the homunculus and his fiery mistress. This just about made up for it. The new vest fit better than her old one, especially after Bianca had her put it on inside out and pinned her into it. While she tried on the last outfit, Bianca stitched the front seams of the vest, making it tighter.

The last outfit was for everyday wear: a plain but vivid green skirt with no trim or markings or fancies, a simple white blouse, and a striking vest of a tapestried cloth in dark burgundies, browns, and golds with green accents. It was almost plain, but Lark liked it, especially with the vest not being designed to be so shaped, though it flattered her silhouette nicely.

Bianca bit off the last thread and gestured for her to put the red vest back on. She puffed and lifted and adjusted the blouse line and bust in a rather familiar but disinterested manner. When she finally stepped away and let Lark see, the vest did absolute wonders for her figure. Her breasts arched in soft mounds over the edges of the blouse, seemingly on the verge of self-exposure, but were actually far from it. Not to mention looking fuller than they really were.

She bent forward and looked up to check how much she showed. There was nothing to see. Nothing was revealed that could not already be seen when she stood straight. But, oh, would it encourage men to try! She wondered for a moment what Landros would think of it, whether or not he would be jealous of her taunting of other men. She brushed that aside. He knew what she did for a living. If he was not comfortable with it, then she could not be comfortable with him, as she would never be able to give it up. It was part of her.

Bianca was pulling the rose-colored suede laces loose, drawing Lark from her reverie. "That just about does it. I'll have the red dress finished by tomorrow, so you can stop back in and pick it up late in the afternoon."

Lark slipped out of the red vest, put the tapestried one back on, and buttoned it. The girl, Sara, handed her the rest of her new clothes, including the blue dress she had worn in, all wrapped neatly up in a black silk scarf shot with copper, silver, and gold threads. "There you go, dear," Bianca said. "Now, come back tomorrow for your last dress, and any time after that you need new clothes, hear?"

Lark thanked her profusely. "Are certain Landros paid enough? Surely...."

The woman began to shoo her out of the shop. "Now, none of that. I've already been paid, and he was most adamant about you not addin' one copper royal to my fee. It's all taken care of. Now, if'n you want something else, then we can talk laurels. If not, mosey on!"

Nightingale flew out the door, leaving Lark little choice but to follow. She thanked the woman again and turned down the street towards Colwyn's with her bundle clutched to her chest.

Landros was, at that moment, in Lord Colwyn's office. Neither man was very happy with the news he had just called attention to. "You can see why I have to ask the question, my lord?" Landros asked. "I know the source was dodgy, but it was so casually thrown out...."

The knight nodded and waved him to silence while he paced the room. Landros remained seated, staring into the fire, absently turning the copper ring on his finger. He did not know whether or not to believe what the hooded mage had said about the King and the Lord Mayor's responsibility in the siege. There was a great deal about recent events which bothered him. They had yet to identify the dead Falcon; not even Colwyn had known him, and there was nothing on his person that might identify either him or his purpose. Clearly he had been sent to investigate something. People were already trying to discover his identity without much success so far. Efforts were also being made to keep the luring of hapless adventurers to their deaths to a minimum, with similar results. Four others had already disappeared without a trace. No one he had personally known, but still....

Colwyn's voice snapped him out of his musings. "This is something that definitely bears looking into. There is far more going on here than meets the eye, and, as you have mentioned, I have long known that there is a traitor in the government, but not whom. There are spies everywhere, but what kind is the question? We already know they have magical aid... If only we had enough of a force to leave the city and make an outright assault, we might be able to break the siege or, at the very least, get someone out far enough to reach the king's ear."

"We do have the forces," Landros said suddenly. "We just have to convince them to give up their time and greed and safe little lives to go out there and do it."

Colwyn looked over at him. "And who might that be?"

"Think about it. The enemy has already seen it," he said, making noise of exasperation. "Twenty of those vital resources have already vanished or been killed. Others have been convinced to be less than helpful, if not outright part of the problem. There are still plenty more hiding about in places like Bayside."

"The trouble is convincing them," he mused as he realized of whom the elf spoke.

"You convince the mayor to make a speech in the square and put forth a call to arms. You encourage those who can to gather and outfit a unit, register them as irregulars, and get them out there on the field with the regulars, and we *can* make a difference. These are people with skills at fighting and skulking and strategies with the odds out of kilter. Better yet, they have the magic to help. Magic swords, small rings, minor spells, wands, little things that the army does not have access to and would never be able to get handed over to them, not without an out-and-out revolt. Some of those items are heirlooms, but useful nonetheless."

The Lord mused a moment, "Makes perfect sense. And no harm can be done in trying. This might also help us in other ways as well." He stopped pacing and stood straighter. "This was your idea, so I think you should be the one to present it to the mayor. You convince him. I will bring this to the Knight's Council. And between the two of us, we might just pull this off."

Landros hesitantly interrupted. "I... I don't think that's a good idea, my lord. I have this... difficulty in dealing with bureaucrats. I simply have not the patience for them."

Colwyn shook his head. "The Lord Mayor is not exactly a politician," he grinned. "You put the plan to him as you put it to me, and he will give you a fair hearing. Just leave a letter with his secretary up at the hall or, even better, at his home," he amended, thinking on his feet as he paced, "and an appointment will be set up for you. I think it best if this sort of idea comes from one of those you are talking about recruiting. Oh, and while you are in his office... any information you can gather, covertly or otherwise...."

"I understand," he sighed, standing as he realized there would be no arguing this. Accusations had been made. They had to be investigated. "Though I must confess I feel downright shifty investigating a man like the mayor for treason without harder evidence."

Colwyn gave him a clap on his right shoulder, even though he had to reach across him to do it. "How else does one gain hard evidence? And very often, it is just such a person. Saintlier men than he have assassinated kings. By the way, how is your shoulder? I remember you said something the other night about my picking the wing everyone seems to favor?"

"Oh, yes," he winced, rubbing his left shoulder self-consciously. "It is fine now, if a little stiff. Lately, every time I've been wounded, it's been to that left shoulder. I am beginning to wonder if it is not some flaw in my defense or attack strategies. I thought maybe, when you had some time, we could spar a bit? Help me figure out if that is the case, and if so, what can I do to correct it? A real fight is no time to be studying your moves to see if you are leaving an opening."

"Certainly. One of a knight's responsibilities to his squire is to teach him to fight. That you came to me a seasoned fighter has perhaps made me a little lax in that. I would be glad to help. When you are ready, let me know. Your shoulder probably needs a bit more rest and a little loosening up first. Now, out with you. You have things to discover and a traitor to root out."

"Yes, my lord," he said with a bow. He gathered his things and left.

TWO

Lark stopped by her caravan to put her new clothes away and repack her bag. She carefully folded the two-piece blue one and put it in with her violin and timbrel, adding appropriate scarves and accessories along with her brush. She looked around her wagon, thinking. Landros had said to bring something unusual. The only thing unusual that she really had was the wand he had given her so many months ago. She had tried it, but could never figure out what it was supposed to do. It had been in her secret drawer and so had not been stolen with everything else. It would not be an even trade, she knew, but perhaps he would have something else that interested her to make it even.

Adding it to her pack, she hurried out the door, stopping only to grab a pair of boots and put them on. She checked up on the horses, managed to catch Dolal and swung up onto his back. She galloped across the pasture towards the carriage gate, slowed down to a walk when she entered the stable yard. Lord Colwyn was there, waved her down even as the stable boy went to open the gate.

She pulled up and Colwyn caught the horse's halter, gave him an affectionate slap on the neck. "I see you are feeling better, my lady," he said jovially. "I hope you are none the worse for the abuse?"

"Am well, Lord Colwyn," she smiled. "In fact am looking much forward to working tonight."

"I was thinking I might do some repairs to the wagon, and the bird house." Nightingale piped up excitedly at this, making Colwyn laugh. "And I wanted to ask you before I just went and did it."

"Oh, you are too generous. Is not necessary," she protested.

"It is not a problem, really. If you are uncomfortable with me poking around your caravan just say so and I will curb myself. But," he added, "truth be known, I have some serious thinking to do and carpentry always helps me do it more clearly."

Lark chuckled. "In that case, help self. Am certain Nightingale would appreciate solid roof overhead. While at it," she added, leaning forward, "if birdhouse not enough, is drawer inside not closing right. Fix this, too?"

"Gladly," he laughed, letting go of the horse's head. He hesitated a moment, as if not wanting to say something he felt he had to.

"Yes?" she prompted.

"I realize it would be hard for you, but... sometime soon, at your convenience, I would like to speak with you about your ...misadventure. Perhaps there might still be some shred of important evidence that was overlooked?"

She took a deep breath, nodded. "If think will help find this hooded person, then yes."

He breathed a sigh of relief, and gave the horse a slap on the rump. "Thank you. Now go on, before you are late wherever you are going."

Lark rode out of the gate, wondering where men such as he were hiding in the world that her family had met so few, or if he was simply unique.

When she trotted into the stable-yard at the Cinnamon Tree, Ivaska came charging up to the big paint, dancing on his hind legs to try and reach her. She laughed, slid off the other side of the horse. Ivaska simply went under, jumped up and put his paws on her shoulders and licked her face. Dolal, now untethered, wandered on his own into the stable looking for something to eat. She managed to get Ivaska off of her, scratched his excited head and went inside once she was certain the horse was being taken care of.

Politics and Shadowplays

Lily was coming out of the pantry with a smoked ham in her arms when she came into the kitchen. She dropped it on the table with a thump and locked the pantry behind her. "I was wondering when you'd show up. How are you feeling?"

"Wanting to dance."

"Good. Folks around here been a bit edgy. It'll be good to have a distraction about. DANE!!" she bellowed up the back staircase. "He's been going absolutely nuts worrying about you, though."

A sudden thumping on the stairs heralded the small boy charging for the kitchen. He groped his way to the table, tripped over Ivaska. "Hello, boy," he laughed, thumping the great hound. "Aren't you supposed to be outside? Mama, you called?"

"Your music teacher's here," she said and set about pulling down spices to flavour the meat.

"Lark?!" he cried in excitement.

"Right here, Dane," she laughed. The boy found his way to her and hugged her, began almost as quickly to lead her into the main room to the great fireplace.

She just laughed and went with him, fished out the violin and, taking it from its case, laid it in his eager hands. She sat back, sipping at a mug of watered wine that Neneis was kind enough to bring her and listened to the boy play. He was a little rusty, but then, he had no violin of his own and therefore could not have been practising the last few days.

As he played, she made small corrections to his finger placement, showed him a few new tricks to get the strings to do what he wanted them to do, but for the most part, she left him alone and allowed him to play as he wished. He learned very quickly, feeling the instrument more than most students. There was not much more that Lark could teach him. Practice was what he needed now, practice and encouragement. A couple of hours passed quickly.

From the door to the street there came a clapping as Dane finished a spirited piece with few mistakes. The boy stood, and bowed, turned to his teacher. "Does this mean the lesson is over?" he asked.

Lark looked over at Landros, now crossing the room. "Yes, it does," the elf said. He took her hand, kissed it, smiled as she blushed. He held her at arm's length, to get a look at her new clothes. He raised his brow in appreciation. "I definitely like it. It's a little more plain than I'm used to seeing on you, but very becoming."

"Are doing very well, Dane," she said, without answering the compliment, pulled her hand away with a glare of mock embarrassment. "You need to keep practice. And remember, what you feel, you must play. What ears hear they will feel. To play passion, must feel passion and send through strings; To play sorrow, must feel sorrow and same. If you not feel what you play, audience will not believe you, and not pay attention, which means not pay," she added, rattling her tambourine.

"Is it like magic then?" he asked.

"Yes, is very like magic. But getting every note right but not feeling true, then is no good. Music fall flat. If you feel music inside you, play what you feel."

"I'll remember," he said. He began to put the violin back in its case, but she put a hand on his arm to stop him. "Ma'am?" he asked.

"No, you are not out of practising. You keep playing. Lesson over, not practice. I have errand to run. Will be back for tonight."

She set the case by his chair and, tossing her bag over her shoulder, sauntered out of the taproom with her hand in Landros's.

"How was your day?" he asked.

"Not bad. Have to say, Lord Colwyn is piece of work," she laughed. "Have feeling would rather be carpenter than lord."

"He is a very 'common' man, and in his position that is very uncommon. Hard to believe he was born in that house, practically raised to his position. This makes him perfect for what he has to do. He is very down to earth," he admitted. "Why? What has he offered to do now?"

"Is at very moment repairing Nightingale's house."

The bird chirped his appreciation.

"If I remember right, that thing needs repairs," he chuckled. "This way," he said, leading her down a side alley.

"What? Where we go?" she asked quietly.

"To my friend's," he evaded.

They walked hand in hand for several more blocks, not saying much to each other, but then, there was no real need. It was a pleasant stroll, until their direction took them up the back of Bayside and into less savoury territory.

"Is friend live here?" she whispered.

"No, he keeps his shop here. He lives further in."

"But if has so much... unusual... is not safe?" she protested.

"Oh, it's safe all right. He pays handsomely to keep it that way." He kissed her to silence any further protests and escorted her into a nearby tavern. "Stick close and mind your pack," he warned.

In response, Nightingale hopped onto the lip of the bag, and rode there daring any wayward fingers to stray too close.

He led her over to the bar, ignoring the patrons he wove through. He pulled an over-large brass coin out of his pocket and showed it covertly to the bartender.

The man nodded his head to a curtained entryway next to the bar. Landros tossed a thin silver onto the bar and led Lark through the curtain. It was dark back here, so she activated her pendant. There was a small door at the back of a narrow hallway at which they stopped. Landros put the brass coin into a slot by the door and let it drop. He listened carefully as the disc rolled down its chute and landed in a metal receptacle. There was a sharp clank and the door unlocked in his hand.

She gawked over his shoulder at the device as he led her down a narrow stairway, stopped half-way to retrieve his coin from a tray inset into the wall. "Is magic?" she asked, sniffing the air, found nothing.

"No," he answered. "A simple counterweight and balance. The coin comes down the chute," he said, pointing to a narrow slit just big enough for the disc. "Any thicker or larger and it won't fit. The coin lands on the plate, trips the lock. Too light and it won't trip the weight. Too heavy and it'll push the weight too far, springing a trap. It is all in very delicate balance."

"Is fascinating," she breathed, followed Landros further down the steps to a second door. As he put the disc to yet another slot, she asked, "Another lock? Is paranoid, this friend?"

"No, just paranoid," he chuckled. Lark gave him an odd look. He dropped the coin and a few minutes later, a small, withered human opened the door, ushered them in.

She looked him over, even as he gave her a close scrutiny. If he were not so thin and delicate seeming, she might have taken him for a tall dwarf. His eyes were bulgy and pale grey, his skin papery and mottled. There were only four or five flat grey hairs sticking up on the top of his head and his ears stuck out a bit on the sides. All in all he reminded her of a frog.

Landros introduced her. "This is Edis, collector of all things odd and himself the pinnacle of his collection."

"Hmmm," Edis mused, scratching his chin with a long, yellowed nail, making a horrible, dry scratchy sound. "She's worth collecting herself, I dare say," he mused. "Ah, well," he added, brushing aside the thought with a wave of his hand and moving into the shop as Landros pulled Lark protectively closer. "Let me see, I believe he said you were looking for a scimitar?"

"Yes," Lark said. "Have you one?"

He began poking through various things on the worktables and shelves in the room. Most of what he collected looked little more than junk. But every now and then he would move something that would release a waft of musty magic her way, filling her with curiosity and wonder. Half of it lay scattered on worktables in various pieces and states of repair.

The light here was very dim, except where her pendant reached, and the shadows were thick and heavy. "What do you want a scimitar for if I may ask?" he asked after a few minutes. "What's wrong with a short sword or an arming sword? Why so exotic a blade?"

"I...." Lark jumped as a black shadow leaped past her shoulder, just barely missing the mockingbird perched there. Nightingale ducked under the protective cover of her hair as the cat sulked off. "I learned on scimitar," she said, regaining her own composure, still trying to calm her familiar. "Is what papa taught me."

He glanced over at her, "So, she's as exotic as she looks," he mused, went back to his digging. "So why didn't papa give you one?"

She looked over at Landros, uncertain why she had to answer all of these nosy questions when there was trading to be done. He only shrugged, nodded for her to answer if she wanted to. "Was stolen ...by succubus."

Edis cracked his head on the bottom of a shelf trying to turn too fast to look at her. "Succubus?!" he croaked. "What dealings you have with a succubus?"

She sighed. "She was attacking my lover," she said flatly. "Someone had to do something."

"Yes, but you did not have to do it with just a dagger," Landros added.

Edis looked from one to the other of them, his eyes bugging more than normal. "Is this a regular occurrence?" he asked.

"In our line of work it seems to be," Landros growled.

"Is why I need sword," Lark explained. "Was almost killed other day because had only dagger."

"I see," he muttered, raising one stringy eyebrow. He began rummaging again. "Well, I only have one at the moment, and it's a real piece of work. Won't be cheap."

"Neither is what I have to trade," Lark said firmly.

"Oh? What have you to trade?"

Lark was careful about revealing too much before she had seen the goods. "A wand," was all she said.

Landros looked at her. She mimed an apology behind Edis's back. It was all she had. He squeezed her hand reassuringly, nodded to her. If this sword was as good as he was hinting at, it would definitely be worth it.

"What kind of wand?" the man asked carefully.

"Let me see scimitar," she said.

He looked at her from under his arm, grumbled to himself. Then went over to a desk piled high with junk and pulled out a bundle wrapped in old burlap. So, Lark thought, the old toad had known all along where the blade was, had just been feeling her out.

He unwrapped the cloth and held it out to her, still cradled in the fabric. "Special it is. Very special. Once belonged to some Northern T'car or Suntan or whatever it is they call themselves."

The sword had a tarnished silver hilt with a simple tapered cross piece curved in a swept 'S'. The grip was wrapped in dark leather with silver thread. The scabbard was of a polished teak with a plain silver cap and throat. Lark handed her pack to Landros and drew the sword. The blade gleamed like liquid silver in her hands and there were three tiny runes scribed just below the crosspiece. "Strength, courage, protection," she read, musing. "Good runes for blade." She could smell the faint mustiness of latent magic lingering below the heavy pungency of silver oxidation.

She hefted it, felt its light weight and perfect balance. She moved into a clearer area to test it, fell in love with the way it felt in her hand and moved through the air.

Landros watched her working with the blade, had to admire her technique. It was like an extension of her hand in one of her dances, under complete, precise and deadly control. The light from her pendant flashed off its surface like liquid.

"It likes you," Edis said.

She stopped. "It?"

"It?" Landros echoed.

Edis nodded, held the scabbard up, still by the cloth. "It did not like the man who brought it to me. It cut off his hand."

"Cheery," Landros mused.

"Is magic?" Lark asked, seeking confirmation as she slid it into the wooden case.

"Vaguely," he shrugged. "Now", he said, wrapping it up again. "Show me this wand." There was greed blatant in his eyes, and a look which said there would be no further information or questions answered until the trade goods were seen.

Landros held her pack for her while she rummaged through it and pulled out the wand. She handed it to Edis who took it over to a dim lamp, and, after rubbing some of the grime from the glass, examined the twist of white wood with its crystal tip.

"Any idea what it is?" he asked.

"No," she answered truthfully. "Priest who did examine said command word was 'Wherefore'."

"Hee hee!" he shouted suddenly, then remembered he had customers and sobered himself instantly.

"You know what is?" she asked.

"Have you used it?" he answered.

"No. Could not figure out how. Used command word, but nothing happened."

"That is because you did not use it all. Watch," he said.

He held the wand up and said firmly, "Wherefore cat!"

Suddenly, the tip began to glow, he waved it slowly over the piles of junk and followed the intensity of the crystal's light until it was nearly blinding, then winked out. He began to dig through the pile.

Lark giggled. "Not work," she said.

"What makes you say that?" he snarled, not stopping his rummaging.

"Because cat is over here, making second foolish grab for my familiar," she said, less happily. Landros grabbed the cat by the scruff and shooed him out of the room.

"Well, that may be so if I was looking for *that* cat. But I'm not!" He pulled out an armlet with intense joy. "I've found it, I've found it!!" he crowed.

"Found what?" Landros asked.

The man clutched it to himself protectively. "Can't have it! Not for trade not for sale!"

"I did not say I wanted it, just what was it? How come you asked for 'cat' and found 'bracelet'?"

"Oh," he said, a little sheepishly, then slipped the band onto his bony wrist. "Is cat's eye. Let's me see in the dark. Helps me find things without being found. Sewers are getting dangerous these days. Now, about this wand. I think I could find a use for it," he said evasively. "What else do you have to compliment it?"

"For sword?" she laughed. "I think not! Nothing else. Is wand for sword, even."

"Even?!" he screeched.

"Even," she said, taking the wand back from him. "You used already. Without asking, might add."

"I showed you how to use it!" he snarled defensively.

"And found something very valuable to you," she came back. "You need this," she said, waving the wand in his face. "I need that," gesturing to the burlap bundle. "Trade?"

He made a low noise deep in his throat which could have been a growl, made a pouting, 'I-*hate*-being-forced-into-this' face. But he jerked his head towards the sword and snatched the wand from her.

Lark laughed, put a hand on Landros's arm before he could do something drastic about Edis's manners. She perched herself on a relatively clear corner of a table and opened the sword on her lap. She ran her hands lovingly over the well polished wood casing. "Why is wood?" she asked.

"Huh?" he said, looking up from admiring his new prize. "Oh, it's a desert sword. Wood is more precious than gold."

"Tell me more about," she asked. Landros held out his hands to see it and she gave it to him readily.

"I wouldn't do that if I were you," Edis warned.

"Why not?" Landros asked almost arrogantly. He slid the blade halfway from the sheath, ran a gloved finger across the flat of the blade and along the edge to test the sharpness.

"Because it don't like men," he said flatly, just as Landros let loose a yelp when the blade slid through the leather and sliced his finger.

"I can see that," he mumbled with his thumb in his mouth. He handed the blade back to Lark. "Here, you hang on to that."

"Tell me what you know of blade," she said, smiling as she took the weapon. She bent forward, kissing his finger tenderly, glove and all.

Edis sighed. "I'll have to get back to you on that one. That its name is Quicksilver is all I know for certain. Everything else is just hearsay. Check back with me, or tell me where I can leave a message..."

"At Cinnamon Tree," she said. "Am found there most evenings."

"Lark," Landros warned. "I don't want you heading out this way alone. It's too dangerous."

She tossed the scabbard, caught it, "Not so dangerous as before."

He pulled her in close. "What am I going to do with you?" he growled playfully.

She grinned, slipped one arm around him. "Oh, don't know," she purred. "Toss me over shoulder and ravish me in meadow?"

Edis cleared his throat. Lark spun. Landros pulled her back against his chest, bent to her ear. "Be careful what you wish for, princess," he whispered.

"If you two are quite through? Anything else? No? Then off with you. I'll be in touch if I find something," he said, and began shooing the pair of them off down another passageway.

"Where...?"

"Shhh!" he hissed. "I don't want you walking through the tavern with new goods wavin' about. You're goin' out the back, and don't even try comin' in this way. It's a one way street."

Lark kept close to Landros. "Like said," she whispered. "Paranoid."

He laughed softly.

Nightingale peeped from under her hair, agreeing wholeheartedly.

After a few minutes down a dry, echoey, winding tunnel, they found themselves unceremoniously dumped on the street and the door slammed invisibly behind them.

She tucked the scabbard into her belt and walked arm in arm with him back to the Cinnamon Tree. She felt very content with his arm around her waist and the new blade at her hip. "Thank you for bringing me to Edis," she sighed happily.

"I'm rather glad myself," he said, his mind beginning to wander. He loved the smell of her, the feel of her, so comfortable beside him like this.

"Am sorry about wand, though. But was all I had unusual for trade that was not heirloom."

He pulled her closer, pressed a kiss to her temple. "Now, I don't want to hear it. It was a gift for you to do with as you needed. Besides, I'd say this sword is a hell of a lot more useful, *sesket*?"

"Yes," she laughed. The sound of that simple Romeri word coming from his very elven mouth struck a chord deep inside her, set her to thinking.

THREE

They entered the Tree through the kitchen, where Ivaska waited, tail thumping, for the ham-bone being pulled out of the stew. Lily sat them both down at the small table and placed a bowl of it in front of each of them, refusing to take no for an answer as she bustled in and out of the kitchen. Dane, sitting across from them, just grinned as he ate.

"I'm all warmed up," he said after scraping his bowl clean. "Can I play for you tonight?"

"We'll see," Lark said. She finished her own supper quickly and got up, tossing the empty bowl into the washbasin. She gave Landros a quick kiss and headed for the stairs.

"Where are you going?" he asked as she grabbed her pack.

"To change," she said simply. "What, you think I dance in this?" she asked with mock arrogance. "This for 'mucking about'. I have clothes for dancing," she added with a sly grin and sauntered up the stairs.

Nightingale remained on the table with Landros, pecking away at a crust of bread. He looked at the bird, "What is she up to?" he asked, not really expecting an answer and got none.

"No telling," Lily said as she breezed through.

Dane just continued grinning. "I don't know, but it jingles, whatever it is."

Heleda dropped the soup bone and shooed the dog outside, closing the door loudly behind him as she muttered something negative in his direction. She looked over Landros's bowl. "More?" she asked.

"No, thank you," he answered, putting his bowl and Dane's where Lark had put hers. He could have eaten more, but he felt distinctly guilty eating too well when he knew there were others in the city who could not afford even this meagre meal.

Impatient to be off, but curious as to what Lark's new clothes looked like and why she was being so secretive about it, he went out into the taproom and bought an Ale from Neneis. He went back into the kitchen and found himself an out of the way corner to wait. He was not about to leave without saying good-bye anyway.

He did not have to wait long. He heard her before he saw her, jingling faintly with every step. He looked up, saw her slim dark ankle glistening above bare feet, with a band of braided blue ribbons adorned with tiny bells tied around the left. This view was followed by bare, well-oiled leg, capped just below the knee with a cloud of sapphire silk. The blue skirts swirled about her legs, gathered by a broad belt set low on her hips. The belt was embroidered and sewn with tiny glass beads and strands of gold cording strung with tassels and more bells. Above this belt rose her bare, taut stomach, also oiled to a deep sheen.

Landros stared open-mouthed, unable to think as the rest of her came into view.

Her breasts were closely covered in tight, dark silk, draped with cording and bells and small tassels that hung from the bottom of the blouse at her ribs. The sleeves were diaphanous billows of blue. She wore her hair pulled back in the front and caught up in a garland of blue silk roses with streams of ribbons hanging past the opals in her ears. She was a complete vision. And for a moment, he was unsure whether or not he was simply seeing things, so like the costume she had conjured for him in the grove was this dress.

"That's... that's not going to melt away before the evening's over, is it?" he asked suspiciously when he could get his tongue to work.

Lark laughed. "Looks just like, yes?"

"Too much like," he almost groaned, tried very hard to keep from physically reacting to the sight.

"She came up with all on own. I told her nothing. So guess chose right?" she asked, sauntering across the kitchen towards him.

Before she got half way, he tossed a silver coin on the table, shouldered his pack and started for the door. "See you later, Lark," he said.

She looked absolutely crestfallen. What had she done? "What? You will not stay for dancing?"

"No, I will not stay for dancing," he said flatly.

"Why? You not like dress?"

He sighed, rested his head against the jamb of the door. This was not going to be easy. He looked up at her, saw the hurt look on her face and the sudden sense of self-consciousness wash over her. He dropped his pack and went to her, held her at arm's length. "No. I love the dress. *That* is why I have to leave. I... I have things I *must* do tonight. And if I stay and watch you dance ...in that, I will never be able to leave, and you will not finish your night's work and I think Lily would not appreciate that."

She began to grin, understanding suddenly why he had tried to leave so abruptly. It was not that he did not desire her, but that he desired her too much. She tried to press closer, to embrace him just for being himself, but he held her where she was. He reached over and pressed a kiss to her forehead, tried again to leave. This time, she held him back.

"You are going to get in trouble with Navarie again," she warned.

Growling to himself, he pulled her tightly to him, determined to punish her for tormenting him and enjoying it. He kissed her, long, deep, and promising. There was fury buried in his kiss, a knowing that this was going to haunt him as much as it was going to haunt her.

She felt as if struck by lightning. She was helpless in his embrace and would have it no other way. He released her lips, held onto her waist until she was steady enough that she wouldn't go tumbling to the floor.

He started again for the door, grabbing his pack. That had done it, though. He would *have* to visit tonight, want to or not. Behind them they heard a wooden bowl hit the floor. "Oh, my word!" Lily gaped.

Landros looked over his shoulder at the innkeeper, took in her stunned appraisal of Lark's new clothes. "My thoughts exactly," he replied and headed out the door.

Dane piped up, having heard his mother drop something and react uncertainly to something he could not see. "What? What?" he complained. "What am I missing?"

"I'll explain when you're older," Lily replied firmly, bent to pick up the bowl. "Lark, are you certain you want to go out there like that?"

"Why? Is that bad?"

Lily shrugged. "Could be. Coolie's out there. He doesn't stay long when you aren't performing, which is a mixed blessing."

Lark sighed. "I'll stay out of Coolie's way. Dane, would you go out and start playing something for me?"

The boy jumped up, "What do you want me to play?" he asked, taking the tambourine she handed him.

"Something slow and sultry."

"The Faerie Queen," he answered, nodding.

"Wait," she added, pressed the wooden sheath of the scimitar into his hand. "Put by your chair where I can grab quickly if have to, but whatever you do, do not draw yourself, all right?"

"Oh, all right," he sighed. "Ivaska!" he called.

The dog came trotting happily in through the door the elf had left open, bone firmly in jaws. Heleda about had a fit. "You better be taking that animal into the taproom!" she growled.

Ivaska slunk swiftly past her, following Dane obediently into the other room.

Lark cast a minor cantrip, shrouding herself in a veil of shadows to divert the eye and make herself mostly ignored. She followed closely on the heels of Lily as she hauled a heavy tray of plates into the other room, moving slowly enough her bells made little noise. She slipped into the shadows next to the great fireplace and behind Dane's chair. He ignored her, used to this trick, and got out the fiddle after laying the tambourine on the hearth's edge near Ivaska, and the sword where he had been told to.

Lark waited until he began playing, watched the crowd carefully. Dane struck a few notes on the fiddle to test its tuning and then began to play a haunting little melody that was one of the first pieces she had taught him. 'So,' she thought, 'that is what he calls Faerie Queen. Fitting.'

The crowd reacted to the music, as she had known they would, looking to the corner to see who was playing and what kind of performance to expect. Coolie was in his usual seat, at one of the tables nearest the hearth. His eyes narrowed as Dane began to play, looked around for Lark. After a few minutes, when it became obvious that the Gypsy was not here again tonight, he turned away, sullenly swallowing his ale. The rest of the crowd also returned to their conversations, only a few actually listening to the boy play, most more interested in their companions and the barmaids. Nightingale thoughtfully remained in the kitchen for the moment, knowing that to appear would be to give her away. Besides, there were unattended currants in the kitchen.

She waited a moment more, making sure her timing was right, then began to draw the smoke from the fireplace, collecting it into a roiling mass that quickly got people's attention. As soon as it was thick enough, and just before panic set in, she slipped into it, dropped her shadows and began to dance in place to the music. She let the smoke curl and condense around her sinuous body, making herself appear as if she had formed herself out of the smoke before letting it disperse. The crowd's reaction was just what she had been hoping for.

The taproom trickled into near silence, with only the clattering of cups in the background of the music, and the violin, and the bells on her hips and ankles.

She danced before the hearth, shaping the music with sinuous turns. She bore in mind Landros's earlier reaction, and his promise of being careful what she wished for. Her desires translated unconsciously through her body to her audience, who clearly understood what it was to desire something one could never have, to view and touch and taste some delight one can never keep.

Normally when Dane played for her, it was impossible to take over the music, to make it hers as she could with any Romeri fiddler, in part because he could not see her to be influenced by her. It came to her great surprise when she realized that the music had shifted to fit her mood, painfully sultry and full of unfulfillable desires and yearnings. The bells, she thought. It had to be the bells giving him a chance to read her in a way he never could before. She began to use them, send signals to him.

The applause was thunderous when she finally stopped, filled the small room almost unbearably. Ivaska barked in competition until Lark hushed him. Coins flew through the air. She laughed, snatched a few of them before they could land. It did not matter that they were only pennies. That there were so many in such troubled times meant a lot to her. She used a poltergeist disguised as a dust devil to gather them up and drop them into the timbrel.

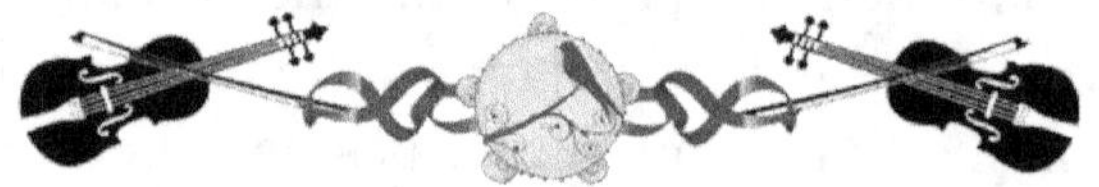

Landros stopped by his apartments, sat down long enough to write the letter that Colwyn had asked him to write and sealed it. He tucked it into his shirt and emptied his pack. Laying out the blanket, he summoned up a large, portable supper and carefully wrapped it in a plain linen cloth and put that into his pack. Gathering the last of his things that he thought he might need, he headed out again.

His journey took him first to the Mayor's house, where he left the letter with the maid who opened the door. As his lordship was currently at supper, she promised to give it to him with his evening brandy. Landros gave her a silver piece just to be sure.

Next, he headed to the poorer section of town, not quite Bayside in the way of criminal activity, but not far from it in abject squalor. He never understood why these places were always in the poorer neighbourhoods. Perhaps no one wanted a house full of screaming kids next door in the better ones.

The building he wanted was once a stately old home at the back of a good-sized yard. The sign on the gate, swaying in the wind proclaimed 'The House Of Lost Lambs' with the painted figure of a lamb in a shepherd's arms. Landros went around the back, clearing the fence with the aid of a well-climbed tree and quietly slipped in the kitchen door.

He tried to be as quiet as he could, lest he wake up any of the children who were probably just getting to sleep upstairs. He pulled the bundle of food from his pack and set it on the counter, taking up the carefully folded linen from his last visit from the sideboard. Just as he was starting to leave, he saw the flickering of an approaching candle.

A tall, middle-aged woman in a dressing gown entered the room, started when she saw him, then relaxed. She placed a hand to her chest, breathing hard. "Oh, my boy, you gave me quite a fright!"

"I'm sorry, Mother Zedia," he said politely with a small bow. "I dare say you startled me as well."

"You are early," she said, sweeping past him to get a small mug from the cupboard and a bottle of wine. "But I am glad I ran into you," she added as she poured a very small amount. "Saves me the trouble of having to find you."

"Oh?" he asked, leaning back against the counter. This was interesting. He hardly ever saw or spoke to the proprietors of the House, though they knew him. Occasionally he ran into one or more of the children. He seriously doubted that she even knew his name.

"Yes. Father would like to talk to you." She dumped a small packet of herbs into the wine, stirred it and put the bottle away. "Would you come up and see him? He's a bit ill, and I don't want him out of bed right now."

"Certainly," he said, opening the door for her. He followed her up the stairs to the second floor, still wondering what in the world this could be about.

Halfway down the hall they heard a faint giggling. "Don't make me come in there!" she warned. The giggling stopped instantly. "Here we are," she said softly, opening the door to one of the bedrooms.

Landros stepped into the small, cosy chamber. There was not much room to move around, every inch of space having been utilized by old furniture. The Mother crossed to the bed with a stately grace more appropriate to a noblewoman than a priestess in charge of orphans, and placed the cup carefully into the trembling hand of the older man in the bed. Landros sat down in the chair Mother pulled over for him and waited until he was ready to talk.

Father Mullen was a singular man, had been a well known adventuring priest in his youth, as Adrick and Rue were now. Landros had met him when he was first setting out on his own, still trying to find his place in the world while taking care of a younger brother along the way. Father Mullen had once given him some very sound advice and lent a hand with extricating his brother from some trouble he had gotten into. When he retired from active duty, he had asked the temple to open this place and let him run it. Rumour had it that it had once belonged to Mother Zedia's family before hard times had befallen and it became run down. Or that they had simply moved on to a better place in another city, and left this one to ruin. There was no telling the truth, and Zedia was certainly not going to. It gave the gossips something harmless to wag about, she said.

Father Mullen handed the mug back to Zedia and sat up further, made himself comfortable. "I am glad she caught you, my boy," he said in a gravelly voice. He turned his head, coughed, cleared his throat. He sounded terrible, and did not look much better. His once dark hair was almost wholly white now and limp with oil and sweat. The liver spots stood out more starkly on his shrunken skin than Landros remembered from the last time they had met face to face. "How is your brother? Still getting into trouble?"

Landros smiled, yielded to the pleasantries even though he wanted to get straight to the meat of things. "Staying out of it at the moment. Or at least getting himself out. You?"

He coughed. "Been better. You are doing well?"

"Well enough."

"Ah, impatient as always. Well, I'll get right to it, then." He gestured at Zedia to get her attention as she tended the fire. "Mother, go get young William. He is here tonight, isn't he? I thought I heard him a little while ago."

"Yes, I think so." She left the room as gracefully as she had entered it.

"Still have ears like a cat," Landros chuckled.

"Useful skill with children," he laughed, ended in a series of coughs. "I wanted to talk to you," he said, getting serious. "I understand you are....(cough)... asking questions in certain places. Low places and worse questions."

Landros started to say something, fully surprised by the revelation. He did not think he had been that obvious. Father Mullen waved him to silence.

"No, I am not thinking what you think. Young William saw you last week sometime. You were making some disgruntled noises, very unlike you," he said evasively. "Said he saw you finally get your head together with an unsavoury Northerner. Sometime after that, we heard that you and some friends of yours had gotten seriously hurt in an ambush by enemy recruiters, which is why William brought up the subject of your sifting through underworld trash."

The door opened, drawing their attention. Landros was surprised to see Billy waltz in, strutting like a peacock. He held out his hand to Landros. "Ev'nin', sir!" he grinned.

"First of all," Landros began, shaking the hand but not letting go of it, "what are you doing spying on me?" he demanded.

Billy turned at least three different colours trying to come up with a decent answer to that one. "I... well... were... I saw ya one day, down at th' Free Gillies and saw you's wif some ind'vidu'ls I knows is bad news. I knows one of 'em wot 'angs wif th' two I saws you wif and 'e was skulkin' about in back. I decided since I owe's you m'life, I oughter pay ya back. 'E didn't try nufin, but 'e was a-thinkin' it."

"What were you doing at the Three Gillies?"

"I was looking fer m' pa," he said firmly. "Kin' I hav me 'and back, sir? You gots a grip on ya!"

Landros let him go and sat back down. "What are you doing here?" he asked. "I thought...."

Billy shook his head. "'E up an' vanished 'bouts a week ago. Wif our ma' dead, Pa an' Thera's all I got..." Landros understood that position well, began to feel a greater kinship with this street-rat. "So, when Pa' didn't come 'ome two nights inna row, I brought Thera 'ere an' went lookin' fer 'im. I ain't found 'im yet, tho, but I ain't gonna give up, even tho 'e gets mean when 'e's 'ad too much. 'E's all we got."

Landros, mulled all this new information over for a few minutes. He felt a bony hand scrabbling at his back, turned to see Father Mullen trying to touch his shoulder to get his attention. "Yes, Father?" he said, coming closer to the old man.

"Talk with Billy awhile," he croaked. "He'll tell you more than you can discover on your own. Remember, he may be young, but he's invisible. There are things going on in this city that only the invisible ones can see now, and they are not going to come forward on their own. You have to find them and ask. There are bad omens on the horizon and we will not emerge victorious without using all our assets, not just the obvious." He sank back into his pillows, muttering to himself in-between fits of coughing, "Remember the invisible ones...."

Mother Zedia ushered both young men out of the room and down to the sitting room. She lit the lamp for them, picked up her candle again. "I have to go, I must take care of Father, and a couple of the younger ones have the sniffles. It was good to see you again, my son. And Father... Father wanted to see you himself before..." She cut herself off abruptly.

"Before what?" Landros asked.

She ignored him. "Billy, remember to put out the lamp before you leave, or go to bed, whichever you decide to do," she said, shielded her candle and prepared to go back upstairs. Landros stopped her with a gentle but firm hand on her arm. "Before what, Mother?"

She looked at him, her dark brown eyes hard and wet in the flickering candlelight. "Father Mullen is dying," she said bluntly. "There is nothing the temple can do. This illness is beyond them. He wanted to speak to you, to see you again before that time, something about when he was young.... Now, if you will excuse me, I have to go see to him.

Landros felt as if someone had just pulled a knife out of him. "Why didn't he say something?"

"Because he is a proud man. And a stubborn one."

He let her go, feeling as if his moorings were coming loose one by one and this was just another broken rope. "If you need anything, anything at all, do not hesitate to ask," he said. "You can leave a message for me at the Golden Cygnet or at the house of Lord Colwyn. I have a friend who is staying on his property who can get the message to me quickly. I'd like to know... before...," he could not seem to get himself to say the words, "if you can. I want to know regardless."

She nodded, turned and went upstairs.

He sat down, the better to digest the ill news. After a few minutes he looked up, saw Billy sitting there waiting patiently and remembered suddenly why he was here in the first place. "Tell me about this man you saw me with," he asked.

Lark was having a very good night, in spite of the verbal advances and long looks Coolie kept giving her any time she came near enough. She largely ignored him. She gave the boy a break every now and again, playing for herself so that he could help his mother if she needed him to. During one of these breaks, she played a haunting yet slow, passionate melody she had been working on. There was applause, but it was too mellow for this crowd on this night. They called for something more rousing.

She saw an empty chair, leaped gracefully from it to the tabletop, and began slowly, teasing. It was a song that Dane did not yet have the skill to play, but that she had been playing and dancing to since she was twelve. It did not take long to heat up and send her hopping from table to table to the bar where she finally stayed, dancing and fiddling without knocking over a single beer. Neneis completely ignored her, serving up his drinks regardless of her nearness or footwork. This, of course, made her skill seem all the greater to the absolute thrill of the mostly male audience.

It was a good night.

FOUR

Landros slipped in the back gate of Colwyn's estate, his mind reeling from the information Billy had given him. He headed determinedly towards the house, so focused on the light in the study window that he almost tripped over the stable-boy trying to get his attention.

He caught his balance, swearing in Elvish. "What?" he snapped, when the boy apologized but still tried to keep him from going to the house.

"I'm sorry, sir, but... that mattress you asked for. It's here."

He drew up short. He had completely forgotten about it. "Where is it?"

The boy pointed behind him. "In the carriage house."

"Thank you. I will get it myself, later. First I have to see your master." He brushed past the boy and went inside the house.

The Lord was writing at his desk, referring frequently to a map of the city and surrounding countryside. He looked up as Landros slipped in unannounced. On seeing the look on his squire's face, he set his pen down. He gestured over to the brandy decanter and Landros poured himself one without further encouragement. He tossed it down, swallowed hard and poured a second before he sat down in the nearest chair to nurse it.

Lord Colwyn waited patiently. Landros took a moment to find a place to start.

"I went to the orphanage tonight," he said flatly.

Colwyn nodded, still not sure what was going on.

"I spoke to Father Mullen, the proprietor of the place. I actually know the man from his younger days, so it was hard seeing him.... Father Mullen is dying, by the way. I don't know how much longer."

"Of what? He should still have several years left in him," Colwyn said quietly.

"Some illness. Mother Zedia said the Temple has no clue and can do nothing. But that is not.... One of the orphans there is one of the boys we rescued from the island a few weeks past. He had some very disturbing news."

He leaned back, watching Landros with hawk-like eyes. "Go on."

"Before Ashanda and her friends disappeared, Vanishti met with some unsavoury types and set up a meeting. This sort of thing is not uncommon in Bayside and not always illegal. A lot of adventuring work begins like that. But shortly afterwards, the whole party vanished. About a week later, Vanishti shows back up, is evasive about where he's been and his whole attitude has changed. He begins to negotiate for the same men he had negotiated with earlier, whom I suspect are agents of the hooded mage and the same people that tried to corrupt or kill me and my friends, and Lark and hers, and probably countless others in this city." He paused, sipped at the brandy.

"We know this," Colwyn said cautiously, encouraging him to continue.

"Vanishti had a shadow. A grey-haired elven woman dressed wholly in shades of dark grey. It is believed she is an observer for the enemy, possibly an assassin as well, sent to keep an eye on the 'recruiter/bellwether'. She slipped out of sight when Vanishti was killed and has recently been seen keeping an eye on someone else. Always the same person. If we can get someone who is good, and I mean REALLY good, to keep an eye on her, find out who she's watching, we might be able to track this back to the source."

Colwyn remained silent for a long while, thinking. Landros just watched the colours change in his glass against the firelight. "This is good information?"

Landros did not look up. "As good as it gets. There's no motive for truth or lies, but maybe hero worship," he added as an afterthought. "As for me, I am not much good to you any more as a spy."

Colwyn leaned forward. "You were never a spy, Landros. You were brought in because you are a good scout. You have found quite a bit of good, solid information so far.... why doubt yourself now?"

He leaned his head back against the chair. "Because no one in Bayside will talk to me now. Word among the enemy is out. Hood has seen my face. One too many times, I might add. Word is among his flunkies that I am not to be approached, I am not to be tangled with, but that anyone seen giving me information is under a sentence of death. That is why."

Colwyn got up and poured himself a brandy, paused to savour it a moment. "This boy ..."

"Billy."

"Billy. He brought you this information?" Landros only nodded. "How old is he?'

Landros shrugged. "Fifteen, twenty maybe?"

The knight looked surprised. "Big difference between fifteen and twenty, Landros. Either way he is hardly a boy now."

He realized what he had done. "I'm sorry. He is human. Maybe... maybe the age of your stable-boy."

Colwyn nodded, understanding the mistake. "I guess with elves there isn't much difference between fifteen and twenty. He is old enough to use as a spy, if he is careful and he is eager. If he gathered this information on his own, he is good enough to be this spy you say we need. Would he be willing to gather information on your behalf?"

He sighed, drank his brandy sullenly. "I don't like using him, but I do not see as we have a choice. He is ...one of the 'invisible ones'."

Colwyn perked up. "'Invisible ones'?" he asked.

Landros rubbed his temples, "It's something Father Mullen said tonight. They are the ones people ignore because they do not want to see them, or because they are not viewed as a threat."

The knight nodded. "We have a veritable army of 'invisible ones' out there if we are smart enough to use them. Do not worry, my boy, we will find some use for you. Perhaps as a general to this 'army'. I would suggest meeting him only at the orphanage as you have been. If he lives there, his going in and out will not be suspect."

"But what about me?" he asked sullenly. "Will my going there on a regular basis not be suspect?"

"My boy, you have been sneaking in and out of that place for months now and few are the wiser. No one will think any different now. Stop selling yourself short. And I'll make that an order if I have to." Landros could feel his gaze on him, but did not look up, simply drank the brandy in his hand. "You've done enough tonight," he finished. "Go get some rest."

Landros got up, swallowed the rest of the brandy and set the glass on the sideboard. "If you need anything, I'll be out at the caravan. I have some improvements of my own to make."

He chuckled. "Between the two of us, that woman is going to start complaining that her wagon isn't hers any more."

Landros looked at his lord with uncertainty in his eye. "I hope not. If she does not feel comfortable, she'll move. And here is the only place I feel she is safe."

"Go on, get some rest," he growled. "You've earned it."

Lark was halfway across the room when the fight broke out. It was nothing at first, just an argument between a pair of less than sober men, a pair of soldiers having a difference of opinion. She ignored it, knowing that Neneis would handle things if they got too far out of hand. When she heard the sound of a violin string breaking and the toppling of chairs and barking of wolfhound, she turned.

The fight was a close, furious tangle, and had already dislodged Dane, pressing him tight in his corner and in very real danger of getting hurt. Lark jumped onto the nearest table, taking the 'high road' to the fireplace. She used a poltergeist she had been playing with earlier to bring her sword, scabbard and all, leaping into her hands.

As she reached the last tabletop, she cracked the nearest of the fighters across the head with the wooden scabbard. The struck soldier reeled back, holding his skull and no doubt seeing stars. Lark ripped Quicksilver from the sheath, and jumped in between them, waving the blade dangerously close to the other soldier's face. The man watched the gleaming blade as if it were a snake that had suddenly risen up in front of him. Ivaska pounced on the first one who had sunk to the floor. He sat on him, growling, daring him to move.

"Am thinking party is over," Lark growled.

Neneis finally managed to reach the fight, picked the one up off the floor and rescued the other from Lark's tender mercies. He escorted the two of them, rather unceremoniously, out the door. She ran to Dane, set her sword on the floor next to him. "Are you...."

"I'm fine," he whimpered as she began to examine the reddening mark on his forehead and one under his chin where the violin had been resting. "But they broke it!"

She took the fiddle he pressed into her hands as his mother finally made it through the press and began fussing over him. Lark examined the instrument carefully. There was no severe damage, just a scratch or two where it had been struck and the broken string. Even the bow was in good shape, miraculously. "Is all right, Dane. Just string, which can fix."

He breathed a loud sigh of relief, began complaining about his mother's handling of him. "Momma, I'm all right!"

"All right? Look at you! You've got a knot on your forehead and a cut on your chin! There's no telling what else those bullies did to you!"

Lark put a hand on her shoulder. "Lily, calm, please. Are upsetting him. Will be fine. Is only where fiddle clipped him when they bumped him, and cut is from string. Will heal. Take into kitchen and give something warm to drink and will be better. I will come shortly. Am thinking show is over for evening."

Lily nodded, gathering her son up and shuffling him off into the kitchen, still fussing over him.

Lark set the stool upright again, praised Ivaska for his help with a scratch to his ears and put the fiddle back in its case. She picked up her sword, looked around for the scabbard. She saw something waving out of the corner of her eye, looked up and saw Coolie waggling it in the air with a self-satisfied smirk. "Ivaska, *guard!*" she said, pointing to the tambourine filled with money. The hound walked over and lay down with the instrument between his huge paws.

Lark went over to Coolie, determined to be dispassionate. "Thank you," she said, held out her hand for it.

He pulled it out of her reach. "Uh-uh," he chided. "This could have so easily been stolen. I did you a big favour by picking it up and watching it for you. I think I deserve some reward...." he said, left his sentence hanging.

"What have in mind?" she asked sarcastically. She knew exactly what.

"Oh, let's not be greedy now," he said, pretending to think. "Let's see,... a kiss? Something so sweet and simple? *Ah!*" he yelped in surprise as the scimitar flashed at his cheek and, like lightning, shaved a narrow strip from his beard.

"Was good enough? I think Quicksilver like you, there is no blood ...yet."

Glaring at her with a hard expression, he handed her the sheath without taking his eyes from hers. She kept her eye on him and her sword between them as she took the scabbard and backed a few steps away. Only then did she turn her back on him and sheath the weapon.

She picked up her tambourine and, with Ivaska at heel, went into the kitchen.

"I'm telling you, mamma, that's what I heard," Dane was saying. He sat at the table with a cup of sweetened milk in his hands, complaining as his mother tended the cut on his chin.

"Well, I don't care. I don't want you repeating it. It's dangerous talk."

"What is dangerous?" Lark asked, sitting down. Ivaska wandered out the door, happily aided by Heleda.

"Can I tell her, mamma? Please?"

Lily growled, walked away. "I give up!" she cried.

Dane sidled up, eagerly began filling her in. "The two men who were fighting, I heard what set them off. They were complaining that their orders made no sense. I think they were from different units, because they were comparing orders and complained that it seemed like the Mayor was deliberately weakening the defences of certain parts of the city, like the East gate."

She did not like the sound of this. "Dane, is serious. Mother is right. You cannot repeat this. Or at least choose carefully who you tell and where. Words like these are treason and dangerous. Tell you what, when you hear something like this, tell me, but only when I say is all right to tell. No one can be near to overhear, or you might be hurt because you heard too much."

His mouth opened in shock. "Would someone really hurt a blind boy? Just because I heard something?"

She ran her fingers through his golden locks, "Sweetling, is war. Is dangerous time. There are, and always will be, men who would hurt anyone or anything getting in way. Is why your mother is afraid of these words. These people not long ago stole twelve children, all younger than you, to feed them to demon in trade for help conquering city. Must be careful. Yes, there are times you must trust blindly, but there are equal times to keep mouth shut.

"You listen always, and you hear much because you say nothing and they assume you cannot hear or speak. Sometimes is best defence. But you hear any more noise like tonight, tell me need private practice and will make sure no one overhear us. Then you tell me. Is could save us all, some of what you hear. But have to be careful. Promise?"

He nodded. "All right, I promise. I think I'm ready for bed, though," he yawned.

"Come on," Lark said, getting up. "I tuck you in."

Landros was just making the new bed, finishing it off with a rose on the new, goose-down pillow when he heard his name being called. He opened the wagon door, looked out. Charging up the slope along the river on a barded warhorse was Colwyn, in full field plate, bellowing for him at the top of his lungs. Seeing Landros, he pulled the horse to a stop and threw him the reins to a second steed just behind him. "Grab your sword and mount up!" he ordered. "We have a breach at the East gate. We're hard pressed and need every fighting man we have!"

Swearing in Elvish, Landros buckled on his sword and jumped from the wagon to the saddle. "That's it," he snarled. "This war has inconvenienced me for the last time!" he growled. "It ends now!"

Colwyn actually laughed, a deep, hearty, almost mad sound. "That's the spirit!" he bellowed.

Landros did not find it funny. He had been deadly serious. This was the second time that the enemy had put a halt to his evening plans, and he was quite tired of it. He had reached the end of his patience, ...not that that was a long reach by any means.

Lark had changed clothes after putting Dane to bed, and came down the back stairs with her pack over her shoulder. "I'm telling you, he was interested something fierce! And if he wasn't Lark's sweetheart....!"

She stopped, listened to the two barmaids as they gossiped over the dishes.

"Are you so sure that was him?" the other girl asked.

"Huh! What other blond-headed elf do you know that keeps such a tight eye on that Gypsy?! You saw the way he was watching her!"

"I saw how *every* man in the room was watching her and he was no different," she humphed. "Especially in *that* dress! I'm surprised we got any attention at all!"

They fell silent for a moment as Lark heard someone enter the kitchen with what sounded like a tray full of dirties. As the door swung closed again, they resumed, lowering their voices. "I know. But he was watching her differently. He was ...I don't know, he looked positively jealous or pissed every time she flirted or looked more than an instant at any one man. He's a right charmer though."

'Landros, here tonight?' Lark thought. That could not be. She would have seen him, she was sure of it.

"He had his hands all over me out of the pretence of 'protecting me', he said, from the fight? But when things cleared up, he suddenly let me go. I saw where he was looking, and it was at Lark dealing with Coolie. I don't know what it was they were talking about, but he was stiff as a board, like a cat ready to pounce. He actually smiled though, when she cut him. Then went back to chatting me up! Like nothing had just happened!"

"That could not have been Lark's sweetheart. He would have torn Coolie a new ass, had he seen that."

Lark barely kept herself from laughing. The girl was very right about that.

"Coolie needs a new ass."

"Besides," the other maid continued. "I don't think her sweetheart is that tall."

Lark came down the stairs. "Evening, girls," she smiled as she set her pack down under the table and began counting the money in the timbrel. They fell silent instantly and hurriedly finished up.

Lily came in, dropped into a chair beside her, watched her count. She propped her chin on her fist.

"Rough night," Lark mused. "But good for money," she added.

"I think those louts cracked the table," she complained. "Thank you, though, for taking care of Dane for me. Sometimes I worry too much about him."

"Be careful being protective. Is hard I know with him blind, but ...is why I left home."

"Point taken," Lily sighed. "But he hears a lot he shouldn't."

She smiled. "Yes.Well, will not talk so carelessly now."

"Good. These are dangerous times, Lark. And, quite frankly, they scare me. I know we don't seem to feel it here, but... I can't keep the wolves at bay forever." She sat up, looked very grave. "Lark, we are friends, yes?"

Lark looked up at her, warned by the tone of her voice that this was serious. "Why?"

She took a deep breath, let it out after a moment, waited until the two maids headed back out into the taproom to finish up out there. "As I said, these are dangerous times. Fireballs going off goddess only knows where or when, monsters wandering the streets... if something should happen to me, or to the Inn, we will have nothing. Dane will have nothing."

"Neneis...." Lark offered.

Lily looked over her shoulder as if making sure her brother-in-law was out of earshot. She shook her head. "He is a good man, and he loves him, but... he is not the best person to take the care of a blind boy in hand. What I guess I wanted to ask is... if something should happen to me or the inn, and Neneis cannot take him... can I impose my boy on you? Can I trust that he will be in your care and raised right and allowed to make of himself whatever he will make? I know that there are a lot of women in your father's caravan, a large family can easily take care of one more.... I don't want him going to an orphanage like so many others will. He'll not be allowed to follow his music, or he'll be turned into a beggar, or... oh, who knows! I just want him looked after by someone I know understands him."

Lark put her arm around her. "Is not going to happen," she insisted. "...But if come to this, trust that I will take him, my clan will take him in. I can assure you they will not use, abuse or smother him. They will take care of him while teaching him self-reliance. In fact, if would not mind, might do him good to go with us for year or so. Apprenticeship, I believe is called? Learn things every bard must know. Lots of bad things are said of Romeri, but our clan is good and not like these fairy-tale gypsies. Even better, if can arrange, have him go now, be out of war and safe, even though you may not."

Lily looked up, eyes wide with the possibilities. "How could you get him safely out? It's nearly impossible....!"

She shook her head. "May take time to set up, but not impossible and perfectly safe. I would have to talk to papa, though."

Lily hesitated, fidgeted with her hands. "At least ask. I... I would have to think about this."

"Good. You think. I'll talk. Was good night," she said, sliding Lily's ten percent to her. "Eighteen silver not bad haul for siege, even if mostly pennies."

"Looks like more when in pennies," Lily smiled, pocketing the coins. "Maybe that dress was a good idea after all. Though I'm glad you are wise enough not to wear it home."

She grinned. "Not complete *pashaska!*" She pocketed her money and shouldered her bag. "Will leave Ivaska again?"

Lily shrugged as she headed out into the tap room. "Sure. He's already run off thieves twice this week. I'll see you tomorrow. Be careful going home."

Lark gathered up her things and her familiar and headed out to the stable. The stable hand, having been warned by the familiar's appearance, was getting Dolal out of his stall. Ivaska was sniffing about in the hay, bounded over to her. She scratched him fondly, but told him to stay here. He wandered over to the small pile of old straw under the chicken coop and laid down, grumbling.

As the stable-hand handed the horse over to her, holding her things for her so she could mount, he held her back a moment and whispered, "I'd be careful how ya go, miss. There's a long shadder over yonder with an eye on the stable-yard. I don't know what it's waiting for or who, but you might be seen as an easy target if it ain't picky."

"Thank you," she said, swinging onto the horse's back and settling her pack over his withers. "Will be careful."

She guided Dolal out into the yard and kicked him into a gallop. She saw the man as she passed by, a tall, pale fellow all in black, but she saw no more than that. Nightingale flew off, looping back to keep an eye on him. The man did try to follow, but slowed down and gave up when it became apparent she was not going to slow down. Nightingale then flew on home.

Lark did not like the idea of someone following her, tried to tell herself that he was simply a thief looking for an easy mark and thought she might be it, that he had gone back to his post and waited for someone else when he had given up. But she could not help the thought that he might be one of Coolie's friends. She was convinced he was the same elf that had been hitting on the barmaid, and had reacted badly when it seemed Coolie was in danger. No, this did not bode well.

It was not until she flew past the watchman on patrol in the upper district that she realized she had not slowed down at all since leaving the inn. She pulled Dolal up short, wheeled him around and returned to the watchman, hailed him.

He held up his lantern, looked up at her curiously. "Everything all right, ma'am?" he asked.

"Am sorry, did not hurt you?" she asked, leaning over her knee to talk to him.

"Nah," he said, shaking his head. He was fairly young, handsome, and flattered that a pretty young thing like Lark had actually come back to chat. Ever since that first night, Lark had had no problems with the city watch in this section of town. Orders had quickly trickled down that she lived here under the protection of a powerful noble. Some may not have liked it, but no one harassed her. "Is there some problem? What's the hurry?"

"Actually, might be," she said. "When left Tree, was man in shadows watching. Tried to follow. Do not know if he did, but if you see anyone skulking about..."

"What's he look like?"

"Tall elf, I think, blonde, fair skin, wears black. Have never seen before. There was also problem at Tree tonight, so he may not be only one come looking, *sesket*?"

He smiled wryly, "Someone not take no for an answer?"

"You could say," she said, straightening up. "Thank you. And sorry again!" she called, trotting off down the road.

The stable-boy sleepily opened the gate for her, having heard her coming. She entered the yard, looked towards the big house, saw lights still inside. "I know is late," she said, "but is master still perhaps taking visitors? Have important news."

The boy closed the gate, shaking his head. "No, ma'am. He's not home. There was a problem and he had to go. Took every man inna house with 'im."

"Oh," she said. "Could you tell him when come home, that will need to speak with him after breakfast?"

He nodded sleepily and headed off to bed.

Lark sighed, suddenly very tired, and trotted into the fields along the river to her wagon.

She dropped to the ground and pulled the make-shift bridle from his head in the same movement, did not even turn to watch him plunge into the river and up the other bank. In retrospect, she probably should have stayed at Lily's. She did not relish the idea of spending the cool night under the wagon. She most certainly could not sleep on her hard, bare bed. Nightingale did not even peek out of his house to say good night.

She dragged herself into the wagon, kicked off her boots and put them away, hung up her pack and violin. Something smelled off. She stopped, took a deep breath, aside from the faint smell of fresh wood and oil from the newly mended drawer, there was something else, something floral and something... elven. She turned, activated her pendant.

She gasped at the sight of the newly made bed, spread with a gorgeous new patchwork quilt and a pillow with a single violet rose on it. She picked up the rose, brushed it tenderly along her cheek, drinking in its sweet perfume. She knew where he got these roses, had seen them growing on the wood-side of the main house. So, Landros had been here, possibly even planned to spend the night, but no doubt the emergency had called him away. Perhaps, when everything was taken care of, he would be back.

She sat down on the mattress, noticed with a start that it was stuffed, not with wool, but feathers! She smiled, he was far too generous, this elf of hers. She set the blossom on the stovetop, in a small glass. Taking Quicksilver from its sheath which she set on the shelf where her mandolin once rested, she hung the scimitar on the hooks over the bed, undressed and crawled between the covers.

FIVE

Lark woke the next morning to an empty bed. It was not terribly late, but she still hurried to dress and pack for the day as she remembered there was much she had to do, beginning with her landlord. She shrugged into her new motley skirt and vest and tossed appropriate accents into her bag for the red one she planned to pick up that morning. Tying her hair back with the banded scarf, she tucked the rose at her temple, and rushed out the door and up to the house. She could smell a late breakfast cooking in the kitchen and knocked on the door.

The scullery opened it, brought her in, offered her something. Lark only accepted a slice of bread, which she shared with Nightingale and asked if it would be possible to see the Lord. The scullery gave her a mug of warm cider and disappeared for a brief moment.

"The maid'll go ask," she reported, coming back.

She had just finished the bread when the maid entered the kitchen and led her to the parlour. There was no one in the room when she entered, so she set her things down and sank into one of the large, overstuffed chairs. It was very comfortable. She snuggled into it, tucked her feet up under her and waited, playing idly with the mockingbird on her lap. She had him singing scales by the time the door opened and Colwyn walked stiffly into to the room.

She started to get up, but he gestured for her to remain seated. She noticed that there was a slight limp to his right leg and he moved slowly, as if every movement was pain. He stood with his back to the fireplace, letting the heat sink into his bones. "Ah," he sighed. "Now, what can I do for you?" he asked cordially. "Have you had breakfast?"

"Am fine, thank you, Lord Colwyn. Am here for business," she began.

He gave her a long look. "You aren't going to bring up the subject of rent again are you?" he asked.

"No," she said, shaking her head soberly. "Is serious."

He gestured for her to continue.

"Last night was fight at Cinnamon Tree. Was two soldiers. Someone heard what was argument and is not good I think."

"How bad is not good?" he asked, folding his arms over his chest.

Lark flushed at the gesture, politely looked away, telling herself that he did not know what that meant, that he was only gegenta. "Treason, though don't know whose. Said were comparing orders, complaining that orders left East gate weak. Am thinking one of these men was supposed to be on duty there last night, but…" she looked up, having heard a sharp intake of breath from the knight. His face was tight and pale, but he said nothing, waited for her to continue, but still kept his arms crossed. She looked away again, as if talking to the air. "Fight broke out when one said Mayor might have done deliberate, knowing made weak there. How could man of his skill not know?"

Colwyn moved stiffly away from the fire, paced the room in obvious irritation.

"What is wrong?" she asked, getting up and confronting him.

He took a deep breath, stood tall and looked her over, as if assessing whether or not he should enlighten her and how much. "The East wall was assaulted last night," he said. "Defences were very weak indeed. If there had not been a small garrison of men nearby, and I and a handful of other local lords not been able to get men together quickly enough…." He began pacing stiffly again. "Thank you for bringing this to my attention. This matter will be investigated."

He glanced back. "You would not happen to know the name of the two soldiers?"

Lark shook her head. "But might be someone at Tree who knew: Neneis, maids.... might ask."

"I'll take care of that, thank you. And if this *someone* hears anything else like this... I do not care what the hour, if you have to have me pulled from my bed, do it. Now, if you will excuse me?" he said, bowed over her hand and left the room.

She sighed, felt suddenly drained. Nightingale flew to her shoulder and tried to perk her up. She just stroked his breast, gathered her things and left.

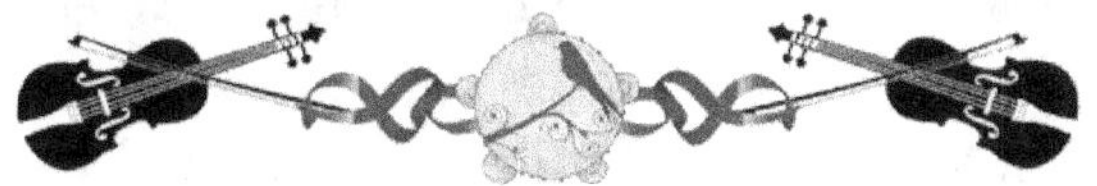

Landros felt like hell. He was sitting in a large room at the temple getting patched up again by a Matron's priest in blue robes. The blow to the side of his head had been healed already and all that remained of it was a faint ringing. His ribs were wrapped in bandages, having been unceremoniously kicked in the back by large man with the lower body of some hoofed animal. But whether that half was bovine, equine or goat, he had no idea. The priest was carefully sewing up a long gash on his thigh.

The fighting had been terrible. The single squad of soldiers guarding the East gate had been overrun in minutes. A secondary off-duty battalion, put in place as a precaution by the Magistrate, had not been enough either. If not for the irregulars and the local residents being close enough and able to send men, the gate would have fallen and perhaps the city shortly thereafter.

Adrick drifted by, helping here and there among the wounded, saw Landros sitting there so calmly and stopped.

Landros greeted him.

Adrick just stared in apparent shock, said to the priest mending his thigh, "What? You didn't have to get 'Snake-Eyes' to hold him?" he asked.

The priest looked up at him. "Nah. She stopped by, but we decided that would not be necessary," he grinned.

Landros scowled. "Are you quite through having your fun at my expense?"

"Yes, Landros," he laughed, "I think I am. I am glad to see that you had the common sense, however, to allow yourself the healing you need without a fuss."

"Common sense, your ass, my son," the priest snorted. "He had to be carried in. If he didn't get healing, he wasn't going anywhere."

"Now that sounds more like the elf I know, father," Adrick grinned. "I sincerely hope the enemy got the worst of all this?" he asked with a gesture that encompassed not just Landros but the other wounded men-at-arms around him.

"Oh, we gave 'em hell all right, brother!" called a nearby soldier. "Ain't nothin' left o' the raidin' party!"

Landros just scowled in his direction. "I'll tell you, though," he said to Adrick, "it was damned peculiar that there were just enough of the enemy to overwhelm both the regularly stationed guard and the rather convenient reinforcements. If it had not been for Lord Colwyn and Lord Periden's timely arrival...."

"Yes,..." he mused, lowering his voice. "I've been hearing that song all through the infirmary. What was the loss count for our side, do you know?"

"Too many," Landros answered sullenly, flexed his leg slowly as the priest indicated him to.

Feeling somewhat better but determined to be on his way, he tried to stand up. The priest pushed him easily back into the chair. "You aren't going anywhere, son," he said firmly. "Not until tomorrow. This patchwork will hold you until we can get rest enough to mend it the rest of the way. Until then, you bunk here."

"I can't, I have..."

"Nothing that cannot wait until tomorrow. Now stay put while I find you a bed." He stood up, towering over the two shorter men by a good head or more. He cracked his back, picked up his medical supplies and turned to go, adding an aside to Adrick, "And, my son, if he doesn't stay put, tie him down."

Landros was not happy. "Wipe that sadistic grin off your face, Adrick, or by your maidenhead I'll find a way to do it!"

The epithet stung Adrick visibly, colouring his mood a little darker than before. "How is your Romeri girl?" he asked sullenly.

"Well the last I saw her. With attacks coming in the middle of the night I have not had much time to spend with her."

"I see," he muttered. "Have you seen Lith since...?"

Landros shook his head. "Might want to look him up, check up on him."

Adrick nodded. A man dressed in a plain white tunic with a blue belt came over, checked Landros's injuries briefly to identify him, and helped him to his feet. "Come on, I've got a bed for ya," he said.

Landros allowed himself to be supported by the man, feeling every step he made as if someone was repeatedly stabbing his leg, again and again. Adrick grabbed his other arm and between the two of them, got him to a corner bed under a high window. When the other man had left, he turned to Adrick, "What's with the new robes? I don't remember seeing that one before. What branch...?"

Adrick sat down on the edge of the bed with him. "He's a volunteer. We needed some way to identify them quickly. We've had so many people milling about, looking for news on loved ones, or needing healing, we could not have them in their own clothes. We tried putting them in acolyte robes, but too many people kept asking them for medical help they could not give. So, we pulled those white tunics out of storage and threw in the blue belt so that no one recognizes them as actual clergy, but the clergy don't run them off for civilians. It's worked so far, and it seems to give them a feeling of importance, of being helpful, which is good for morale."

"Oh."

"Well, you get some rest. I do have my duties, even though schedules and order seem to have gone down the sewer drain."

"Hey, see if you can get me some writing paper and a pen or coal-stick. I need to write a couple of notes." Adrick hesitated. "It will keep me from wanting to get out of bed," Landros added.

Adrick began moving immediately. "I'll be right back."

"For a while," Landros finished under his breath.

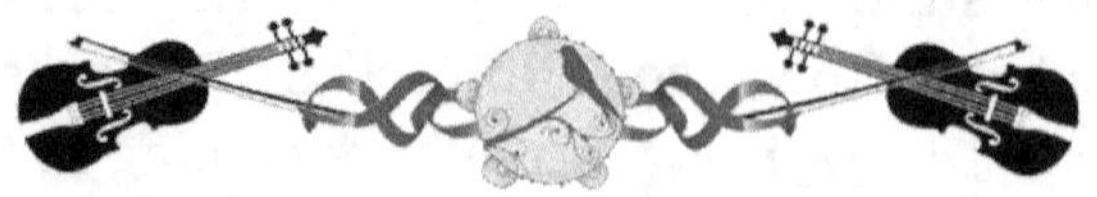

Lark was waiting on the steps outside the House of the Maiden when Rue finally came out to meet her. "Sorry to keep you waiting," she said, adjusting her basket on her arm. "It's a madhouse in there."

"I understand," Lark said, shouldering her bag and following her down the street. "Is busy. Hope not too many lost?" Lark did not mention her fears about Landros. He had gone with Colwyn last night, of that she had no doubts, but she had not heard from him, nor was he at home. She had sent Nightingale up into the room through the chimney with a short note and the smallest of Bianca's silk roses.

"Losses were heavy enough, though the injuries were worse. Our numbers of fighting men have been lowered considerably, I fear. Most of the wounded had severe arm or leg injuries, as if the enemy was trying to dismember as many as they could. I hate to say that they had some success. Fingers, eyes even, sometimes a hand or a foot we can rejoin if we get both pieces soon enough, and even then sometimes not without some permanent damage, but whole limbs we cannot do for."

Lark walked along quietly, trying to put herself in a better mood than she had begun the day. Before long she was humming the tune that she had not quite ironed out yet. She played with it, trying to remember some of the modifications she had made last night.

"That was a sweet little melody," Rue commented when she stopped.

"Not done yet. Have words, but cannot make fit."

"Oh? I did not know you wrote songs."

Lark shrugged. "I don't. But once in while I get one buzzing 'round wanting voice. Have one been working since was twelve, still not completely happy with."

"I like this one. You will have to sing it for me when you have it done. Here we are," she said, climbing the steps to a house-front in yellow and brown.

A woman answered Rue's polite knock, tall, and willowy. Lark was taken in by how beautiful she was. Her eyes were a brilliant shade of green, flashing in the sunlight, which made her upswept braids appear as a halo of fire around her fair face. "Oh, Rue! Please come in!" she said cheerfully. Her voice was strong and mellow, easily the voice of a mother still young enough to be so breathtaking.

Lark followed Rue into the house, which was immaculate. The Sister handed the woman the basket and allowed her to take her cloak. "Vanessa, this is Lark. She is a friend of Keltree and I."

"Oh yes, we've met," she smiled. "We crossed paths at the bedside, though we did not get to talk much. Navarel spoke of you quite a bit upon her safe return. I still cannot thank you enough for bringing her back to me! Can I take your bag?"

"No, thank you. There are things in to show Keltree," she said. "Am sorry, but ...Navarel?" she asked, confused.

A small, familiar voice came from the stairs. "That would be me," Navarie sighed, skipping a few steps as she came down. "Hello, Sister Rue. Hi, Lark! Uncle Keltree's out back."

Rue looked up at Vanessa, "Not doing anything I hope!"

"Oh no," Vanessa smiled graciously. "That is expressly forbidden. But he likes to sit out there and brood. Can I bring something out for you to drink? I am afraid I haven't much in the way of proper guest service...."

Rue put her hand on the woman's arm. "Do not you worry for us, water would be fine."

"At least let me bring you some tea," she offered.

Rue sighed. "All right, but here...." she said fishing something out of the basket Vanessa still held. "Put this into Keltree's cup. It will help with his stomach pains."

"Thank you," she said. "Navarel, would you take our guests out to see your uncle?"

"Yes, mamma," she smiled and took Lark by one hand and Rue by the other and led them out to a small porch.

Keltree was sitting in an old chair with his legs stretched onto the rail in front of him staring out at the wild flowers filling the edges of the small yard. He looked up as they came out and immediately put out his pipe. "Navarie! Tell me you brought your old uncle that hammer?" he pleaded. The girl ran to him and he put his feet down and pulled her onto his lap.

"No, silly," she giggled. "I brought company, though. Something you CAN have."

Keltree looked up as Rue and Lark stepped out into view. "Lark!" he exclaimed. "Lands, girl! I thought you'd plumb forgotten all about me!"

Lark laughed, set her bag down and allowed him to kiss her hand. "No, just... had other things," she said. "And once you leave temple did not know where to find you!"

"Navarie, hop up and let me go get them another chair," he asked as he gestured for them to pull over the other one on the porch.

She did not move. Lark hopped up onto the rail instead. "Is all right. Is fine. Rue, you sit."

The priestess did not sit just yet, but put Keltree through a thorough prodding. "Getting better," she said. "Still having those stomach aches?" she asked.

"No," he said.

"Yes," said Navarie.

"Keltree?" she asked in a chiding tone.

"All right! Yes, but they are not as bad any more. And only when I eat certain things." Navarie gave him a long, warning glare, her little fists on her hips. "And do certain things."

"Well," Rue said, standing up, "maybe in a couple of weeks I'll let you get around to mending that back fence."

"And the fourth step from the top, and that squeaky cabinet in the kitchen...." he rattled off.

At that moment, Vanessa came out with the tea. "That squeaky cabinet keeps you honest," she said. "Lark, are you sure you're comfortable up there? I can get you a chair."

She laughed. "No, am fine, really."

"Suit yourself." She served the tea. "I am sorry there is no sugar, but I have to save it all for Keltree. The herbs for his stomach are too bitter otherwise, and its the only way I can get him to drink it."

No one complained. Lark watched him the whole time his sister-in-law was outside until she excused herself to go back to her mending. The way he watched Vanessa confirmed the suspicions she had earlier confided to Landros. He flirted shamelessly with every woman he met, but only to ease the pain in his heart at being in love with his brother's wife. She could not help but wonder what kind of stormy courtship that must have been, or if he had not met her until after his brother had won her. She was a bit curious to meet Keltree's brother, to see the man that could turn her eye from a man like him.

"Please, Rue," he was saying. "It won't be a strain, just a little hammering. My brother's a mason, not a carpenter. I mean, look at that fence!" he complained.

Rue sipped her tea patiently, "You aren't a carpenter, either, remember? You are an, oh what was it?"

"Thrill-seeker and would-be dragon-slayer," Lark offered.

"You forgot story-teller," he amended with a hurt tone. He made a face as he drank his tea. He thought about it for a second, then tossed it down like whiskey, set the cup on the window ledge behind him. "So, I understand you've been up to quite a bit," he said to Lark, hefting Navarie so she was more comfortable for him.

"Yeah," Navarie injected. "How are things with your elven friend? He finally come around?"

Lark actually flushed, smiled to hide it, "Yes, he… 'came around'."

"Good," Keltree said. "Good."

The afternoon sped by in pleasant conversation. Rue and Lark both were careful not to tell him how bad things were actually going outside the gates. No mention was made at all about last night's attack, and the shadows were growing long when they finally left. As they parted ways a few blocks from the temple, Lark thought she saw a shadow across the street, following her; but when she looked, it was gone. She remembered the man from the stable-yard the night before and, hand not far from the hilt of her scimitar, hurried towards the Cinnamon Tree.

Tonight was much quieter. There were fewer patrons to come in, and those that did came mostly for the food. Lark settled for softly fiddling, working on her song and telling fortunes from her corner table. Her fortune-telling brought her more attention than anything else, and eventually she gave up on playing, allowing Dane to practice.

Many people wished to know what the future had in store for the city and themselves. Some were not happy to discover that they could only ask a single question, but they accepted her response that it was bad luck to ask twice the same night. "Tomorrow", she told them.

She was disturbed by some of her readings. There were far too many endings tonight. Out of curiosity, she did a casting for herself. Her path was rocky, with a lot of near misses, but it ended in *gyfu,* the partnership. She sighed, decided to pack up early.

It was only midnight when she bundled herself up in the new cloak she had bought from Bianca that morning, and walked home. The night was cool, but not uncomfortable yet. There had not been enough sun lately, with all of the smoke in the air from the bombardments, and things had remained cooler than was seasonal. The streets were quiet and uncomfortably still, the silence occasionally broken by the distant echoes of footsteps.

Coolie had not been seen at the inn tonight, which did not make her more comfortable about walking home. She wished she had thought to ride out this morning, but it was too late to change that choice. Every shadow she saw was Coolie lying in wait for her until, after too many starts and false threats, she stopped worrying about it altogether.

As she turned down the lane towards the upper district, she heard something further down the street, off to the right. She hesitated, listened, debating whether or not to investigate or go on home. Nightingale flew off, asking her to wait.

There was light around the bend, he said, and flew to the source. Lark began running towards that source less than a minute later, her sword in hand. As she turned the corner two streets up, she came upon the scene of utter chaos. A small patrol of watchmen were desperately engaging a huge, winged, lion-like beast with serpent tails and viscous fang-filled jaws. One of their lanterns had broken and the oil had spread in a flaming puddle in the street. The shutters of the houses along the road remained tightly closed, though there were two men, in hastily donned trousers under their nightshirts, battling the beast with an old sword and a fireplace poker.

Lark dropped her pack and doffed her cloak, bade Nightingale to keep an eye on it. She carefully went around the side of the beast, staying back for the moment. Whipping up a quick little poltergeist, she had it pick up one of the discarded lanterns which had gone out instead of bursting into flames, and doused the creature's wings with the oil. From there it was a simple trick to jump a spark from the fire to the feathers.

The creature howled with rage and pain as its wings burned to cinders in less than a minute. It leaped over the head of the nearest man, raking him with his claws and running, still aflame, further up the street where it dropped and rolled in the wet gutter. They gave chase to it, Lark severing the snapping, serpent's tails and using the poltergeist to toss them, still writhing and alive into the oil burning in the road.

Between the six of them, the beast was killed in short order, in a blind panic and unable to effectively fight back because its mane had already caught fire. Lark made the filthy water leap from the gutter and extinguished the corpse.

It was not until the head was set at least four feet from the rest of the body did they stop long enough to look at each other. One of the men in his pyjamas was holding onto his shoulder where the beast had clawed him deeply, turned self consciously away when he realized that there was a woman there. Lark let him, said nothing out of politeness. Everyone but Lark was scratched up and hurt in some capacity. One of the watchmen was looking pale and greenish, having a nasty looking bite from one of the tails.

The highest ranking member of the watchmen, a sergeant, turned to the two civilians and thanked them for their help, took their names so that 'they might be properly recognized and rewarded for their bravery'. Lark he tried to ignore completely.

She paid it no mind, turned instead to his paler companion, looked at the bite on his arm. He winced, tried to pull away, but she easily held him. He was weakening fast. Lark made him sit down, then laid him back on the street and pulled her knife out. Before she could do anything, the other watchman grabbed her wrist and man-handled her to her feet, dragging her away from him.

"Wait! *Pashaska*! Is poisoned. Is dying! Let go!!"

The sergeant came over, "What the hells?!" he bellowed.

"I caught her trying to stab Davin!" he grunted, still trying to hold onto the struggling girl.

"Saving him, you *pashaska*!" she screamed. "Look at him!" she yelled at the sergeant.

Instead, he moved to help his man restrain her. She kicked out, trying to get loose. He back-handed her, clamping an iron manacle on her wrist while she was still reeling. Nightingale flew in, pecking and flapping and scratching until the private's flailing fist managed to connect with him and sent him careening to the street in a daze.

The shout of the wounded civilian called their attention. "Martin!" he yelled to his neighbour who was up the street, using Lark's discarded cloak to put out the fire in the road. "Go get your wife!! He's been snake bit!"

The man dropped the cloak and went running into one of the houses. Lark continued to struggle, now with desperation, as they tried to grab her other wrist and get it close enough to the first to bind it as well. "I help you, this how repay?!" she growled almost unintelligibly. "May your narrow-minded stupidity only cost you!" she spat. She was only inches from the second manacle, began a shrill keening that was not unlike a banshee's wail.

A woman in a blue dressing-gown came running down the street, dropped to her knees beside the stricken man. She looked around her, saw Lark's dagger where it had fallen and grabbed it, began to do what Lark had tried to and was arrested for. Luckily, the private noticed and called it to his sergeant's attention. "What's she doing?" he asked.

"What I tried!!" Lark snarled, kicking out and finally connecting, managed to free herself. The sergeant, however, maintained his grip on the second cuff and pulled her up short by the chain.

"I have done all I can," the woman was saying. "He is in the hands of the Old One now, if she will let him go or keep him. If this had been done sooner, I might have been able to...." She looked over at the commotion behind her. "What is the problem?" she snapped.

Lark seized the opportunity to plead her case, leaning back, still straining against the sergeant's leash on her. "I tried to cut out poison, Mother," she said, noting the holy symbol of a closed hand around the woman's neck. "This... *gosho*... stopped me!"

She got up, crossed to them. She grabbed a hold of the taut chain between them and just held it. "Why have you arrested her?" she asked the sergeant calmly.

"This gypsy harlot comes out of nowhere at the end of the fight and next thing we know she's leaning over one of my men with a dagger in hand, a man who had been standing not a moment before!" he growled.

"This *Romeri*," Lark spat, "was here for whole end of fight. *I* was one who burned wings! *I* was one who cut off tails and threw into fire!"

"If you were part of that fight, then how come you ain't hurt like the rest of us?" the private snapped.

"Maybe," she glared, "because am quick enough to stay out of way!"

"*Enough*!" the priestess said loudly. "Young lady, tell me exactly what you did and were going to do."

Lark kept her eyes on the sergeant. "Was going home. Heard shouting and come to help. Saw fight and drew sword. Used magic to catch wings on fire with oil from lantern. Helped chase down and cut off tails and help kill. Then saw him pale and unsteady. Looked at wound and saw snake-bite. Since *I* cut off tails knew were real snakes, with real heads and real poison. Were still alive even after cutting off. Made him lie down so poison move slower, and so could cut out wound."

"What would you have done then?" she prompted.

"Then would have tied off arm above bite and tried magic to save life. Am not so good with healing magic, but have saved lives before with, so would have tried. Most certainly would have gotten him to temple or priest. I know not much of healing arts, but I know snake-bite, how to dress for real help."

The woman took all this in and then turned to the sergeant. "Let her go," she ordered, letting go of the chain.

"What!? You haven't got the authority to order me to...."

"I most certainly do," she said. "Oh, not direct authority, but I know people who do. Refusing to admit you needed a woman's help to kill a monster is one thing, arresting her because she showed you up is another. Now unlock those manacles!"

He stood up straight, tried to look down at her. "She assaulted two members of the Night Watch. I can arrest her for that alone!"

"If I were her, being attacked and arrested for trying to save a man's life, I'd have assaulted you, too," she snapped. "Now uncuff that before I bring this matter to your superiors. I don't think you want to have to explain to your private over there how you almost killed him should he pulled through this, which he *might not*, thanks to you two!"

"I haven't got the key," he said imperiously.

Lark felt her heart jump.

The woman's eyes narrowed.

"It's true, Mother," the other private said. "We don't have the key. Only officers have keys."

"Not problem," Lark said arrogantly. Now that she was not struggling and could think straight, she remembered that she did have a way to unlock these things. She drew a small glowing rune on the surface of the manacle, small enough that it could not be identified easily from their distance. The lock sprang open and the manacle swung free and empty in his hand.

The sergeant did not look happy and Lark couldn't care less. She rubbed her wrist, noticed a thin reddened mark along the base of her hand where the iron had cut into her during the tug-of-war.

"Thank you, Mother," she said. But the woman turned away from her with a barely civil acknowledgment and began inspecting her neighbour's wounds.

Lark picked up her dagger and walked away from the whole scene, beginning to shake. She felt a despair creeping up on her, which she deliberately turned to anger to keep herself from breaking down completely. She picked her familiar up, still sitting dazed on the side of the road, checked him out carefully. He was bruised and battered, missing a few feathers. She spread his wings, checking his pinions. His left wing would not open fully, not without a reflex jerk and a small chirp of pain.

Lark was furious now. She began to swear under her breath in Romeri. *"Until you mend the error of your ways, may bad luck follow all your days,"* she hissed.

She took the scarf from her hair and carefully wrapped Nightingale in it, making sure he could not move his wings and hurt himself further. She picked up her bag, wrapped herself in her scorched cloak and carried Nightingale home.

SIX

Landros's day was not going well. He had been up most of the night with pain in his thigh, tossing and turning feverishly. He had been singularly unhappy at having been cooped up in an infirmary, and even the long letter he wrote to Lark failed to cheer him. Before breakfast he had seen a healer and was on his feet again by the time the meal was served. Before he could go about getting his own breakfast, he was informed that he had been healed first thing at the request of the Lord Mayor, who even now, was waiting to speak with him in his office at the City Hall.

He hurried off, Lark's letter still in his pocket. Even though he had been urgently summoned, he was still asked to wait in the hall outside the Mayor's office for half an hour. By the time the door opened and the Magistrate came out, red-faced and irate, Landros was ready to leave. He did not wait to be invited, but walked into the office unannounced and closed the door behind him.

The Mayor looked up, stood, gestured for Landros to have a seat. "I'm sorry to have kept you waiting, but he can be very long winded to no purpose. It is amazing how long it takes that man to say absolutely nothing," he sighed. He began to fish through his desk, came up finally with the letter that Landros had dropped off the night before. "Now," he said, reading through it again, "would you care to elaborate on this?" he asked, handing it to Landros across the desk.

Landros glanced at it, to refresh his mind on exactly what he had already said, and set it back on the desk. "Last night," he began, getting up to pace so he could think and work the stiffness out of his leg, "we nearly had a breach of the east gate. A week past we had a severe assault on the North wall. Both of these attacks were fended off by a blend of regular soldiers and civilian help. People like me. It is obvious that the regular soldiery is not sufficient, nor can the city afford to conscript and feed the majority of the male populace of this city. However, it has occurred to me that it would be not only wise, but economical, to recruit adventurers and trouble-seekers like myself as irregulars, letting them collect, feed, arm and care for their own small units which can then be used to break the siege. We have the equipment, some of us have the money, and most of us have the inclination to do this sort of thing, yet would not care to enter the regular army because of disciplinary differences and after-war repercussions."

He finally stopped pacing, looked over at the Mayor who sat thinking. "Your suggestion does have some merit," the man said finally. "But what incentives will be necessary to convince this adventurous population to do this? From my experience, though available for anything exciting and dangerous, they usually expect some reward for risking their lives."

Landros put his hands on the back of the chair, leaned forward. "If you do it right, none will be asked. If they could band together, their numbers would at least equal that of the current army. With their magic and skills we can end this and discover for ourselves why the king has not sent us aid or word. All of us are suffering because of this damned siege! A lot of them have already lost people important to them and stand to lose even more. If you put out an official call to arms; allow those who can afford it to front groups of irregulars, gather and command them; give them the semblance of authority while letting them feel they are the heroes coming to rescue the town, and you'll have your army. If they can sign up as irregulars without fear of still remaining soldiers after the crisis, you will gain more response and a higher morale among the men. Even among the women. There are some females out there that are pretty damned good in a fight."

The mayor began musing to himself. "Let them feel they have captains who are one of their own, that they have authority while being able to give them orders. And responsibilities," he added. "Responsibilities carry more weight and loyalty than orders. Something you want to do is always more important than something one is ordered to do. Yes, I can see how this will work."

"The enemy has already seen this possibility," Landros added.

The mayor looked up, "Oh, how so?"

"Some of these adventurers have already been subverted or slain."

"Oh, yes, I remember. Yes, I will have to give this a bit more thought, put this into terms that both the Council and the populace will understand and be stirred by, and then present it to them. After that, we will see. I think it will go over well, though." He gave rueful grin. "As long as they do not have to pay for it."

He rose, shook Landros's hand. "Thank you for bringing this to my personal attention," he said. "These are troubled times in which we do not know who to trust. I will do what I can with this and pray the city has the wisdom you do."

Landros walked out of the office feeling very glad that the Lord Mayor of Portswain was not a bureaucrat.

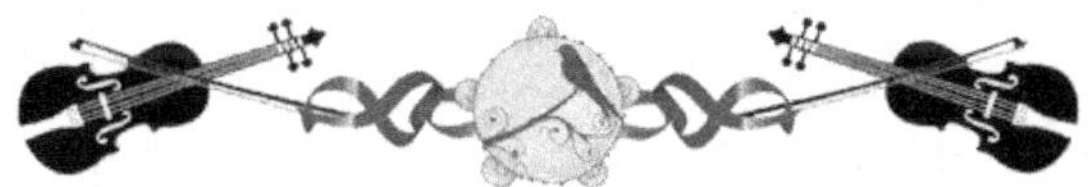

Lark was in a thoroughly foul mood. She had taken Nightingale down to the temple, asking for Rue. Only to be told that healing was not available at the moment for pets or wild animals no matter what price she offered, and that, no, she could not see Rue. When she had pressed the priest that this was more than a mere bird, but a familiar, and that his pain was her pain, he was kind enough to set the wing and bandage him for her, but refused to do more.

She went back to the caravan. The grass was starting to change colour beneath it, so she scouted out a new place to park it. It took her nearly an hour to find and catch the horses and hitch them up; let them go again once the wagon was where she wanted it. She began to tidy up the place, finding whatever she could to keep busy and her mind off of last night and this morning. She carried a bag of her clothes to the river, deciding that it had been too long since she had done her own laundry. She kilted up her skirt and rolled back her sleeves, wading in to the shallow end of the river.

The act was mindless and calming, though something was still bothering her. She could not quite put her finger on the problem. All she knew was that an ill wind was blowing, and nothing good lay ahead.

She waded out of the water, wrung out and hung her laundry on the lower branches of the tree. She heard a noise above her and looked up, saw a raccoon watching her curiously. "Hello," she said. "Hope you have no mind to stealing clothes."

The creature scampered quickly down and jumped into her arms with a joyous screech, which of course upset Nightingale. she laughed as the raccoon licked her under her chin, chattered happily at her. "Well, hello, Scraps. Did not recognize you from so high up!" She calmed her familiar. "Settle, Nightingale. Is friend." She sat down on the river bank with the animal in her lap and leaned against the tree, running her nails through his thick coat. The action did more to soothe her than she realized.

Scraps was in heaven. He rolled over onto his back in her lap and began kneading the air with his paws and purring when she began scratching his tummy. She got up after a while, went back into the river to finish her washing. Scraps sat on the bank and watched her. After a bit he waded in himself and went fishing. He caught a few large minnows, but not much else would come that close to the shallows with her working there. She hung the last of her things on the tree, checked the dryness of the others.

She heard a bell behind her, looked to see Scraps fishing a ribbon with a bell tied to the end of it out of the river. He brought his prize to the shore to show her.

She bent down, wrung the water out of the ribbon for him. "Must have escaped one of dresses," she mused. "Well, you find it, you win it," she said and tied it loosely around his neck.

He chattered happily at her, flicked it to make it ring.

"Welcome," she said, stood. "Now, I have to dry clothes."

She summoned up a small wind, strong enough to dry them quickly, but not hard enough to blow them off the branches. A stronger wind blew up behind her, a cold, evil wind not of her summoning. She turned, stared across the fields. She saw nothing, but even the horses were on the move, heading towards the safety of the stables. Lark grabbed her clothes, wet and all and hurried to the caravan.

Landros hung his soggy cloak behind the door and began peeling off his wet clothes. He wanted a hot bath something fierce, but with the lightning storm outside, he did not dare. He took his clothes into the bathroom, draped them over the edge of the tub to dry. Grabbing a towel, he dried himself off as best he could, wrapped it around his waist and went into the bedroom to light a fire. He laid the wood in the grate and began to spark the tinderbox when he heard a scrabbling, and a strange ringing up the chimney. Just as he was about to grab a candle and look, a bundle of dirty black fur dropped onto the top log and went rolling with it out onto the floor.

"Scraps!" he grumbled. "I warned you about mucking about in the chimney!" The raccoon looked up, soggy and sooty, and chattered. Landros almost laughed. "Com'ere, you," he said, dropping his towel over the wet animal and picking him up. He sat down on the floor with him, rubbed him dry and relatively clean. There was a chirring complaint from inside the rough fabric and, finally, a grey and black face peered out.

Something tinkled. He looked down, saw the ribbon running around Scrap's neck and the trailing bell on its end. He fingered it. "Now where'd you get this?" he asked. The raccoon just grinned at him, snatched the bell away, rang it. "Oh, let me guess..." he said, and tried to take it off.

The raccoon leaped out of his lap and ran under the bed. "Well at least someone's been able to see her!" he called, and grudgingly went back to lighting the fire.

Once it was crackling merrily away and he began to feel elven again, he picked up the towel from the floor and looked at it. It was filthy. "Oh, the laundress is going to love this!" he growled, throwing the towel into a corner and getting himself some dry clothes.

Lark stared sullenly out at the rain. It had not stopped for two days and, sooner or later, she was going to have to brave it. She had eaten the last of her stashed food and had no more wood left to burn in the stove. She was absolutely miserable.

Nightingale was not much happier. He felt like a pet bird whose flight feathers had been clipped. Not to mention feeling like a perfect target for any hungry cat that came along.

Lark had enough. She threw her red dress into her bag along with a couple of other necessary things and grabbed her cloak. She put up the hood, making a nest inside of her hair for Nightingale. He refused to hop onto her hand, gave her a negative chirp and looked away. "If you want to eat, best come with me," she said.

Grudgingly, he climbed onto her finger and allowed her to put him inside the hood. She grabbed her bag and, taking a deep breath, darted out into the rain.

Landros had enough. Two-and-a-half days of sitting around watching the rain fall had brought his patience to an end. He got himself together, threw on his cloak and headed off to Colwyn's. If he had any luck in this world, maybe Lark would be out there. If not.... He did not want to think about that. Things might end up broken if he thought about that. He shouldn't be thinking about her at all, or so he told himself. He could not have her, she could not stay with him, would not stay, so why bother?

The rain pounded on his hood, soaking him through to the skin. He found himself headed, not for Colwyn's, but more towards the Cinnamon Tree. Well, maybe she had gone there and stayed. It would not hurt to check, certainly. And if she was not there he would head on to Colwyn's.

When he stepped into the taproom, the barmaid looked up, smiled and sauntered over. "Come in, brave soul! Can I get you something hot to warm you?" she asked.

"No," he said, shaking his head. "I was wondering if Lark was here?"

She shook her head sadly, "No, sir. I'm afraid not. Haven't seen her since the rain started. Haven't seen hardly anyone since the rain started."

"Thank you," he said, and, tipping his hood to her, turned and left without another word.

To Colwyn's then. A little more water could not make him any wetter than he was, that was for sure.

Three blocks away, he saw a cloaked figure up ahead and across the street, walking steadily through the rain, hood up and head down, much as he was. He stopped, watched the figure, closely. There was something familiar in the way it moved. It came to a street corner, tipped its head back a bit to get its bearings. A slim, dusky hand came out of the cloak to hold the hood up enough to see without letting the rain in. There were three bands of gold dangling from the wet wrist.

Landros was certain it was her. He ran across the street, not caring that the water at the gutters came halfway to his knees. He caught up to her, grabbed her, and pulled her in close in the shelter of a nearby doorway.

Lark gave a startled shriek, tried to pull her scimitar before she realized who had just seized her. Oddly enough, it wouldn't budge, but by then it was an irrelevant point.

Peering in under her hood, just to be sure he had the right woman, Landros kissed her without a word.

She felt as if she had just been pulled, half-drowned, from a deep river. That kiss was like a breath of air to her. Unfortunately, Nightingale was not so enthusiastic about the handling. He began to fuss rather loudly, making noises that sounded more like a squirrel's bark than a bird's call.

Landros pulled back, looked in on the bird. "Hello to you, too, my feathered friend. Shall we get in somewhere out of the rain?"

"Was going to Tree," she said.

"I just came from there, and I think it would be an excellent choice."

She looked out into the rain, which seemed to be falling harder, obscuring visibility more than eight or nine feet. "Is raining," she said.

"I noticed," he chuckled, brushing aside a lock of black that was plastered to her cheek.

Taking her hand, they ran out into the downpour. She laughed as she tried to keep up without jostling her bird too much.

They almost missed the building in the heavy curtain of water, but they finally found their way in and Landros took her cloak from her.

"Found her I see," the barmaid said sassily. She took their cloaks and hung them to dry on the pegs. "Fire's lit, and I don't think you'll find too much in the way of trouble getting a seat by it. I'd mind the dog, though," she said and sauntered into the kitchen.

Lark went immediately to the fire with Landros close behind. Seeing her dripping wet like this, in that red motley skirt, reminded him much of that first night... was it really three months ago? Ivaska gave her a very enthusiastic greeting, pushing her over until she was sitting in front of the hearth with him. He licked the elf as well, when he sat down beside her. She laughed, tried to fend off the beast long enough to untangle Nightingale from her hair.

When she set the wet bird down on the hearthstones, Landros saw the bandage and splint on his wing. "What the hells happened to him?" he demanded.

Before she could say anything, Nightingale began hopping about squawking and chattering and doing a very rough pantomime of the incident that almost had them both laughing, but for the seriousness of the matter.

Lily came out of the kitchen to investigate the uproar. "Hey! Good to see someone out and about on such a miserable night. What's his problem, besides his wing?"

"What happened to wing, and fact could not get healing for him."

"Which you are about to explain," Landros said.

She sighed, not wanting to dredge this up again, but knowing the look on Landros's face she would have to, or this evening would be far more miserable than it was.

Lily pulled up a chair.

"Is happen night before rain start. I stopped to help three watch and two men kill winged lion beast. Not in my neighbourhood," she added quickly. "Down road from there." She went into the tale, trying to stay as emotionless and succinct as she could. When she reached the part about the aborted arrest, she wrapped her arms around herself, shuddered and not from the cold.

Landros felt a heat rising up inside of him, a heat not born of the fire next to him. He laced his fingers in the scraggly fur of the dog, trying to keep from saying anything before she had finished. Rest assured, though, someone would pay for this.

"Nightingale tried to stop them when they grab me and was hit. How broke wing." She looked up at Landros, saw the tightness in his jaws, the hardness in his eyes and the redness of his face and knew what he was thinking. She reached over and set a hand on his arm. "Please," she begged, "no make more trouble. Have enemies enough now. If you cause them more trouble and embarrassment, will find something legitimate or inarguable to chain for."

He looked in her eyes, saw the fear there. He had not missed that she had said 'chain' instead of 'arrest'. How well he knew her fears in that department. He pulled her tenderly to him, "Lark," he said. "*Simara Ellinoia*, you cannot let these sorts of things go undealt with! If you do, they will only see that they can continue to harass you and not suffer for it."

"Please!" she insisted. She was bordering the hysterical. The watchman had been unhappy enough when the Priestess had threatened to tell, goddesses only knew what he would do if that threat was actually carried out, especially after he had complied with the demands. "He did what was supposed to. He let me go! Mother said she would not tell if he let me go! If you do something...!"

Landros sighed. "All right, Lark, but this is the last time I will allow something like this to happen without acting. You would not allow me to take care of the thieves, and you will not allow me to put a stop to this unfair, bigoted treatment of you that nearly got you arrested."

"Is over," she insisted. "There is nothing to stop now. Is done!"

He gave a growling sigh. "The next time something like this happens, you tell those crows that you have powerful friends, and then start naming names. You tell them that you are a guest of Lord Colwyn Abberwood and you are subsequently under his protection. He is a very influential man with a seat on the council, so if nothing else, they will have to investigate your claim."

Lily stirred behind them. "Lark, I'm sorry. Some of the people in this town are less open-minded than others. They fear what they do not understand and cannot control." She got up. "Well, seeing as I don't think I'm going to get any other customers tonight ...again... can I serve the ones I do have? Something hot to eat? Something strong to warm you? A hot bath?"

"Food is wonderful!" Lark chimed, remembering the bareness of her cupboard.

"I'd be interested in that bath," Landros said without taking his eyes from Lark. Yes, a bath was just what they needed to melt away the nastiness of the past several days.

Lily headed for the stairs, "A bath it is then!"

"Can I help you carry the water?" he asked.

"No," she chirped cheerfully. "But thank you. I'll get you when it's ready, and then bring your supper to the room."

He turned back to Lark. She was warming her hands at the fire, starting to shiver. Ivaska moved out of her way, tired of being dripped on. "Cold?"

She just nodded.

"I'd offer you my cloak but I'm afraid it wouldn't do you any good," he chuckled, pulling her close to warm her. She settled her back against his chest, leaned her head on his shoulder. Unfortunately, that position gave him an incredible view of wet white silk and olive skin. He gave a soft groan, buried his face in her hair. That only made things worse. She was wet and steamy now, her scent permeated everything and the long, bare throat so close to his lips was more than he could resist.

He began to kiss her shoulder, soft and slow, worked his way to her neck. She gave a shudder, an involuntarily reaction to his warm breath against her cold skin. He kept going, pressing soft, silent kisses in the hollows of her ear. She leaned back against him, completely at his tender mercies and revelling in it. He tilted her chin his way, kissed her long and deep. His hands began wandering as he pulled her closer to him, down her clothed thigh and up again, under the fabric, slow and stealthy. She was warming up quickly.

"All right, you two lovebirds, not in my taproom!" The sound of Lily's voice made both of them jump like a pair of adolescents caught in improprieties. "Upstairs, both of you!" she ordered. They hastened to obey, Lark trying not to giggle. "And don't come back down until you've got it out of your system!"

Landros stopped on the stair, looked back. "You don't want that room back, do you?"

"Go on, Git!" she answered, shooing them up the stairs. She grabbed the bird who was trying to hop after them, took him gently into the warm kitchen. "Oh, no you don't. They need a little nesting time and you are not welcome."

It did not take them long to shed their wet clothes and sink into the steaming water. It was probably the most delicious feeling Lark had had in months. She could not remember when a bath had felt this good. The elf sitting behind her who could not seem to keep his hands to himself did not feel so bad either.

After a minute, and the heat of the water and the fire began to seep into his bones. He settled back, just content to hold her in his arms for a while. But damn it! if she just wasn't so ...so ...so *sagavis*, this would not be so hard, letting go of her.

He started as the door opened, held Lark back against him and ready to sink beneath the water as Lily brought in a tray heavy with food and wine and set it on the hearth.

She bustled out again without a glance or a word their way. But Lark saw the grin in her eyes as she walked passed, knew she was secretly happy for them. What Lily did not understand was the misery this relationship was going to eventually cause. The only possible outcomes were either a broken heart or a broken family.

Landros could sense a dark mood slipping over her. He did not understand it, but feared that it had something to do with the war and the way she had been treated a few days ago. He began to take measures to banish those thoughts, whatever they were, from her mind.

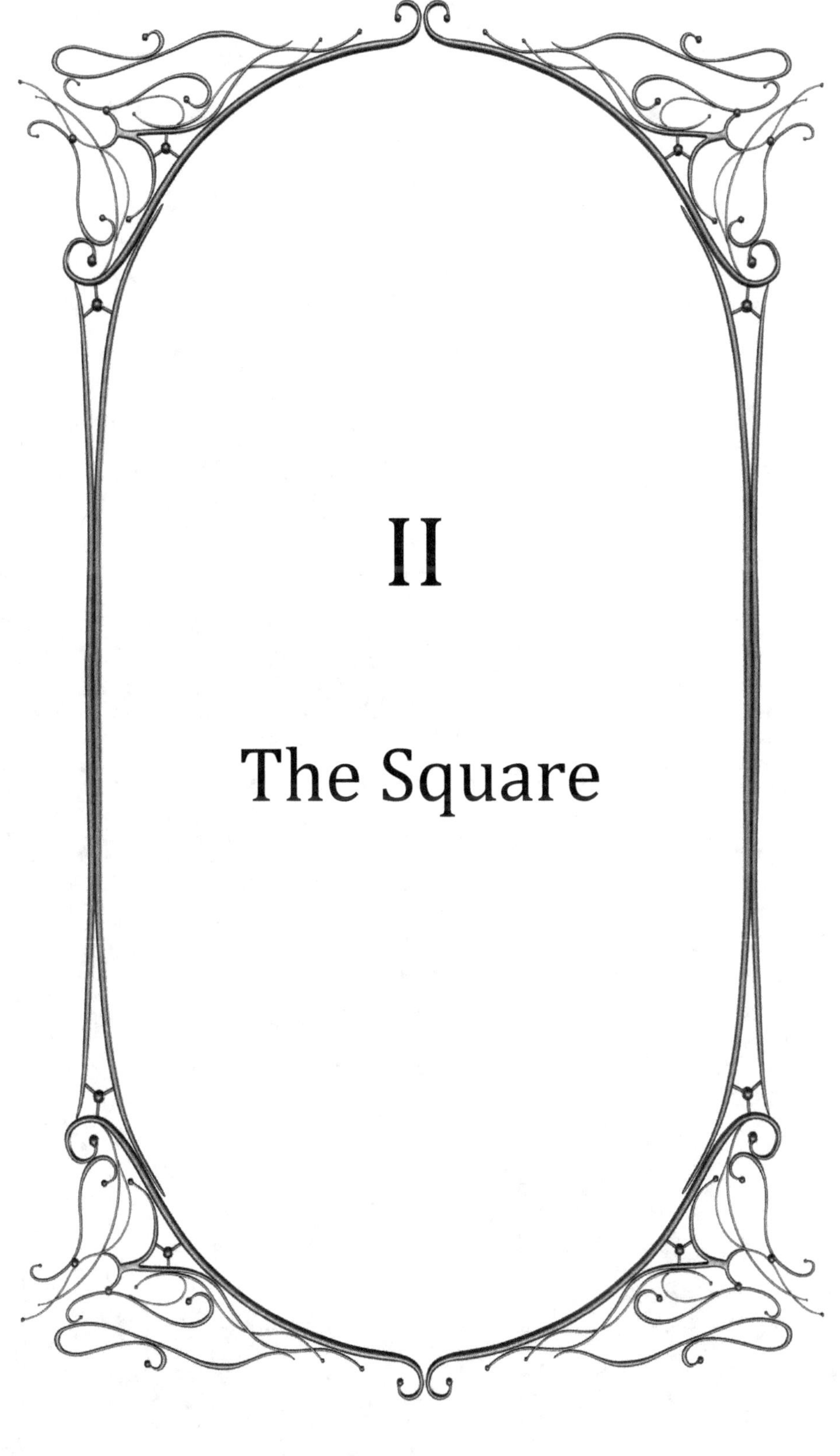

II

The Square

ONE

No sooner the weather cleared, Lark and Landros went for a walk. After four solid days of rain, the streets were still flooded and the temperature ranged wildly from steamy days to frigid nights. The sewers were full. The river was threatening to over-flow its underground banks and the streets in those places where it ran above-ground. The sun was shining, making the city rather humid, but after being cooped up by torrential rains for so long, nobody really cared.

Criers had been sent out, wandering the streets ringing their bells and bellowing "Hear Ye!" At the street corners they would stop and announce their message to all who could hear before moving on to the next. They stopped to listen one of them as the young man came near enough to be understood.

"Hear ye! Hear ye!" he rang, his voice not unlike that of the bell in his hand. "His Honour, William FitzWaller, the Lord Mayor of Portswain requests the presence of the people in the Town Square at midday for an announcement of great importance! Hear ye! Hear ye...."

"Wonder what is news?" she mused as they wandered away from the corner and the crowd.

"I think I know," he commented.

She glanced over at him. "Oh? Care to enlighten?"

Nightingale, clinging tightly to her shoulder, added his two cents.

Landros shook his head. "No. I trust the Mayor will explain better than I could. ...If I'm even right."

She left it at that, walked content beside him. "Is nearly midday, perhaps should go now? Get good places so can actually hear and understand?"

"That is a good idea." He turned them down a side street, cutting past the crowds slowly beginning to think the same.

It did not take them very long to get to the square, but even then it was quite crowded. She saw a ledge on the second floor of the stone building near them that over-looked the platform. Footholds were easy, as time and riots had worn away the sharpness of the corner. Gesturing for him to follow, she kilted up her skirts and scaled the wall to the ledge. Several street kids had already found the perch but, at the urging of the oldest of them, they tipped their caps and scooted down to make room.

Landros was not comfortable at all. It was nothing like a tree, whose branch could be straddled for security. The balance was all wrong. Lark, he noticed, did not seem to be having any problem with it whatsoever.

It was not long before there was movement by the edge of the square. The City Hall building had a large apron platform extending from the columned portico for just such purposes. The Lord Mayor was coming up from the crowd, not from inside the building. He paused on the steps, shooed off two guards who were trying to follow him. He stood alone and tall on the platform, in simple clothes with only his gold chain and medallion of office as adornment. He waited patiently until the crowd fell silent, then he began to speak.

Lark, without looking, slipped her hand into Landros's.

"My fellow citizens," the Mayor intoned, his voice carrying easily across the square. "I come to you in dire times. As you know this city has been under siege for several months and may remain so for several more. Our armed forces are small. A great many of you have volunteered already, entering the soldiery and the city watch. For your initiative and courage, I salute you. Many of my advisors tell me that the citizens want to try to break this siege with a full assault. You are tired of the monsters and the raids and the rains of fire and stone from the sky. We all are. No one wants this to end more than those who have suffered from it. And I tell you we are **all** suffering.”

“Tell us something we don’t know!” someone shouted. The crowd rippled with murmurs of assent.

The Mayor nodded. “Very well. We have three choices. We can surrender and be ruled by an unknown government, for unknown purposes to unknown ends; or we can wait it out, falling eventually, but only after greater hardships, maybe being rescued by outside forces as of yet unheard from.”

“You mean the king?!” someone sneered

Yeah! What about the king?!”

“Where is the king!?”

The shouts rang out across the square like a wave. The Mayor waited it out. When all was silent again he answered sadly. “I can honestly tell you that I do not know where the king is, or what is keeping him. I can tell you that I feel in my heart that it must be serious indeed if he has not yet arrived by late Autumn. Provided word reached him within a month of the siege, which is not unlikely if news travelled quickly, then he should have been here by now. And, even if it moved slowly, we should see relief soon. But, in spite of numerous scouts sent out and messengers sent, none of which have returned, we have no news either way. For all we know, we are not the only city under siege.” The crowd began to murmur again. The mayor continued without raising his voice at all, and the whispers hushed and listened.

“But we cannot count on the king in this. *If* he arrives, it will be because the Three will it. This is something that we have to do ourselves. If we fall, it will be because we gave up. Not because the king did not care and did not come. An enemy that can sneak up upon us so quickly and thoroughly no doubt can stall the king long enough to bring about the downfall of a single port city."

"Why haven't they crushed us already?!" someone asked.

"Yeah?! **With the size of their forces and that mage, why don't they just teleport their army into the square and be done with us**?!"

"It frightens you, doesn't it?" he asked. The crowd fell absolutely still. "To think that the enemy could overwhelm us at any time? That they are that strong and we that weak? But that is not what frightens me. What frightens me, and what should scare you most, is why they have not. Think about it. If they can and haven't, *Why*? Why not let loose their hordes upon the walls and the streets and take us by force? Why waste their resources picking at us as they have? I have no answers for that. But I have had ideas, and *that* is what frightens me."

"Landros," Lark said quietly. "I do not like this...."

From somewhere in the front of the crowd someone said something, then said it again, louder even as Lark realized the truth of it. **"They want the city in one piece**!"

"*That* is what I fear," he continued. "Why they want it in one piece is a mystery I do not intend to discover the hard way. We must not wait for them to wear us down, to make us willing to surrender just for the relief it will bring. We have a third option: a frontal assault; break this siege once and for all. But it cannot be done with the forces we have.

"Yes, I have been told by my advisors, and frequently, that I have the right to draft every able-bodied male citizen of this city into the army and order them as I please. I could do that. But I won't. We cannot afford it. I could, rightfully, take the food from every table within these walls, leave your children to starve to feed that army. But that I will not do, either. I will not take from you. I will not destroy this city in order to save it. It will save itself or it will fall because that is what the city wills. If we are to survive this, we have to work together, we have to give up everything that we can spare or we all will fall. Yes, I can send press gangs out to round up soldiers and supplies, but that would waste precious resources and send a message to the enemy that we are weak, desperate, and unwilling to fight for what is ours."

Silence reigned.

"What I am standing here now to ask you, each and every man, woman and child, is to give what you can give, of yourself, of your stores. A proposal has been made to permit those who have the resources to gather and back troops of irregulars, men and women who are under their control, but whose Captains will take orders from the army. These men and women can use whatever weapons, magic and supplies which are available to them, with no further obligation to the city military once the war is over. It is believed that these irregulars, being volunteers, will fight harder, having more reason to fight than because they have been told to. That the wealthy of the town will be backing them allows the burden on the city to support them to be lightened, and the tax upon the people's resources to be eased.

"Those of you who are interested in commanding, assembling or backing such forces, see Marshal Calais inside City Hall as soon as you can. The details will be posted in the usual locations around town. Those of you who are interested in participating, but do not desire to or cannot meet the requirements of command or support, see Sergeant Tibbs outside the barracks. Once again, this city will survive or fall based on what you decide in the next two days."

As he stepped off the platform, the crowd went up in a roar. Lark stood up, tugged on Landros to head down. One of the boys grabbed her arm, shook his head and pointed down at the street. **"Too much a press!"** he shouted over the din. **"You come wif us! We gets ya down!"**

She nodded, helped Landros to stand up while keeping his balance on the foot and a half wide ledge. The boys walked the edge and around the corner, and the two of them followed. The boys jumped down to the roof of the next building at the rear of the first, gestured for them to keep up. She looked back at the elf and laughed, slipped her hand out of his and jumped, landing light as a cat on the other roof. He waited until she had moved out of his way and jumped himself, landed solidly, but on his feet.

She put her hands on her hips and looked him over admiringly. "Am impressed," she purred.

"Hey," he shrugged, slipping an arm around her waist, "I'm an elf remember? I'm perfect."

"Come on, ya two lovebirds," the oldest boy growled. "We gotta git goin'!"

Lark just laughed as she overheard the smaller of the boys, with his head close to the third, whisper, "They's not gonna go all kissy face on us are they?"

Landros could feel the heat rising in his cheeks and pulled his hood up to hide his flush.

The boys shimmied down a hole in the roof that led down to a dark room. The oldest struck a candle-stub and went down a rickety stair, through a maze of ancient rooms into a cellar. The two other boys moved an old wine cask and crawled into a hole in the wall behind it. The littlest one went in first and disappeared.

The oldest turned to their guests. "I cain't carry th' light in here...."

"I can make light," Lark said.

The boy shook his head. "No good, ma'am. We know th' way only in th' dark. You go on in, mind yer heads. Follow little Timmy, he'll call off th' turns."

She looked at her lover, shrugged and crawled in. Landros hesitated. He looked at the boy holding the candle. "So where are we going?" he asked.

The boy grinned, "You'll see, Gen'ral. You'll see."

'General?' he thought as he got onto his hands and knees and followed Lark.

The tunnel was narrow indeed. An adult of any size would have severe problems following any of these kids into these tunnels. As it was, even with his slight build, he was brushing the sides. He could feel other turn-offs in the dark, tried to count them.

Finally, they emerged into a large, natural cavern lit by torchlight and rusty lanterns. There were rough beds all along the walls with ratty blankets and not a few rats. There were broken bits of furniture and roughly repaired cast-offs rigged to 'make do'.

The older boy went over to one of the many tunnels that ringed the chamber and bellowed "TERRI!!!"

He then pulled one of the chairs from a crate table and offered it to Lark. Not to be rude, whether she wanted to or not, she sat. Landros quickly took up station behind her with one hand on her shoulder and another on his sword hilt and waited.

A few minutes later, a half-elven girl, maybe fifteen or so, came out of the tunnel and confronted them. She and the older boy carried on a short, low conversation after which the girl came up to the pair, sized them up almost rudely.

Finally, she stuck out her hand to Landros. "Welcome to the warren, General," she said.

Landros took her hand, noticed she had a firm grip for a girl. "Why do you keep calling me General?" he asked.

She laughed. "Because you are." She turned away, stuck two fingers in her mouth and blew a shrill four note whistle. "General, meet your army," she said with a flourish.

There came a rumbling in the tunnels, a hurried scrabbling that echoed through the chamber, getting louder and louder. Kids began to spill out into the room, all ages, all sizes, all kinds. They stood about, staring at the pair of them wide-eyed. A few minutes later, Billy sauntered in, brightened at the sight of them. He strode up, bowed to Lark, kissing her hand gallantly, "Princess," he said. "'ow do, Gen'ral?" he piped, shaking Landros's hand.

"Billy, what the devil is going on here? Who are all these children and where do they come from?" Landros asked, not letting go of his hand.

"We live 'ere ...when we needs ta. Somma us, ain't gots no uver place an' somma us comes 'ere whens we needs a place to crash, or gets away from th' bigguns. We are th' invisible ones. Well, parts of 'em anyways. Th' riff raff an' castoff's a' society's ills! Ain't we, mates?" There came a cheer from the thirty or so odd kids in the room. The echo made it sound like there was a lot more. "This 'ere's our Queen, Terrisera. She looks af'er us an' keeps us outta trouble."

"Which ain't easy with you lot," she growled and pushed him playfully out of the way. "Billy has told us you need information. He has also told us that you feed the orphans at the Lambs on a regular basis and have often been a champion to the children of this town. We appreciate this more than you can know. Therefore we have elected you our general and intend to help you fight the enemy. We understand you would never let us out on the actual field of battle except as drummers and bandage haulers..."

"Not even then," he said.

She glossed over that. "...So we intend to fight where we can, here. We know something's up and we *will* find out what. Just like we knew what the Mayor was planning before today's announcement. When we do, we'll send our reports through Billy to you at the House of Lambs, or send a message of some sort to set up a meeting."

"How many are there?" Lark asked.

"Enough," she smiled. "More than enough. All want to help."

Landros decided that if he was going to do this, damn it but he was going to do this right. "First off, someone get me a map of the city," he said and strode over to the nearest wall without a bed under it and checked it out as a hanging surface. If the nails were long enough, it might work.

"Yous finkin' what I fink yous finkin', Gen'ral?" Billy asked.

"Maybe," he mused.

Billy nodded and promptly disappeared. By the time someone came up with a map, he had reappeared with an old, soft-wood board, taken probably from some ancient crate in some forgotten warehouse. He took some rusty old nails out of his pocket and pounded the board into the wall with a block of wood, and then pinned the map to it with four crooked stick-pins whose origins Landros was not about to ask.

Lark just sat in wonder at the hustle and bustle about her, trying not to laugh at the children playing at soldiers and inducting each other. There was an argument about to break out in a smaller group about who was going to be what rank. She came over. The sight of her standing over them with her hands on her hips shut the whole group up, except for one who insisted sullenly, "But she started it," he pouted.

"Well, I am to finish," she said. "Now, let see. Have only one general. Do not need two. Have privates, need lots of privates. Need Sergeants keep privates in line," she said, ticking them off on her fingers. "Then is Corporal, Captain, Colonel, Major and …that is all."

"That's wrong," one boy said, crossing his arms sullenly.

Lark popped his elbow. "Uncross those when talking. Is rude." She turned to the rest of them, wagging her finger the way Rosita always did to her little ones. "From now on, anyone I see doing this, I ignore. Is means 'want to be left alone.' So do this, and I leave alone. *Sesket*? …Do you understand?"

They nodded sullenly, "Yes, ma'am."

The boy uncrossed his arms and stuffed his hands in his pockets instead. "Now," she finished, turning to him. "How is wrong and what is right?"

He pulled his hands out and began ticking them off. "It goes private, corporal, sergeant, lieutenant, captain, major, colonel and general. There's others in there, but them's the basics."

"How do you know so much?" someone poked him.

"My dad is a Lieutenant. I know these things!"

"Enough!" she snapped. "Now," she continued when she had their silent attention, "I think to begin, rank should be by age and experience. *As you prove yourself*," she said, raising her voice over the shouts of complaint, "or disprove yourself, promotions and demotions be in order, *sesket*?"

"Sounds perfectly reasonable to me," said Terrisera from behind Lark. "Better yet. Maybe the General should pick his colonels and they their majors and so on, whoever's left is a private and will be assigned one place or another."

There were mumbled complaints from the younger kids, but nothing serious. They trotted off to get the attentions of older, more influential children, hoping to get better ranking than private. "You are good with them," Terri said. Lark shrugged. "Well, Colonel..."

"Oh, no!" Lark said, holding up her hands. "Am not to be drafted into this. Will be partisan, but no ranking me! Keep me out."

"All right," she shrugged. "You can be our standard then," she grinned.

Lark sighed, "Do not know which is worse. Actually, have someone might wish to be party to this. Is good source of information. Hears things from loose tongues. No one pays attention because cannot see, think as well cannot hear or speak...."

Terri nodded. "Dane of the Cinnamon Tree. We know him. He and his mother both have a kind heart. Yes, he would be good. But he cannot be a private. Maybe..."

"Maybe no rank," someone taunted. "Maybe just call 'im The Bat! He can be our spy!"

Lark laughed. "All can do is ask."

"And all he can say is no."

She looked the girl over. "How old are you?" she asked.

Terri shrugged. "Fifteen, sixteen, somewhere in there. Why?"

Lark chuckled. "Not much younger than I, but difference seems..."

"So great?"

"*Sesha*. So great."

Terri sat down on one of the beds. "I grew up fast. I had to. Pop sold me to the whorehouse when I was twelve. Too many girls. They started me as a scullery, but I slipped out the kitchen door and ran off. A lot of the poorer girls I know come there of their own will, thinking they ain't got no other recourse. But I wasn't gonna be that way. I knew if I tried, I could make something of myself. Yes, I stoop to petty thievery from time to time, stealing bread and things to trade for things. Some of these street-rats pick pockets, or beg, or just scavenge. Sometimes we sell information. We take care of ourselves."

"Are all of these without homes?" Lark asked, indicating the children all around them.

Terri shook her head. "No, very few actually live here. The warren is a place for them to come when they need to, for most of them. Those two over there?" she said, indicating a boy and girl playing at jacks in a corner, no more than eight. "They come down whenever their pa's been drinkin', hiding from him. Others just crash here when they are too tired or too far from home. There are some runaways, some orphans. Those that're too little I send to the House of Lambs. Like Billy's sister. Lots of them just come down here for the companionship, something to belong to, someone to play with, a safe place to be. They keep me company. Marthen, over there, was one of us once," she said, indicating a burly youth perhaps a little older than Lark. "He apprenticed himself to a blacksmith about four years ago. He's getting married soon, he says and may even get the shop when his master dies. Did real good, does good by us."

"You are ranie in your way. Queen of little Romeri."

She smiled. "You could say that."

Across the room, Landros was busy dividing the map into sections and assigning them to four "Colonels" or "Cardinals" as they had begun calling themselves. Before too much time had passed and the top staff had been briefed, everyone had a code name of a sort. The four oldest had ceased to be mere Colonels. Now they were The Cardinals: The East, West, North and South Winds; which suited them fine, and Landros finally went with it. They were an information network after all, not a real army.

Billy was dubbed the South Wind, in charge of Bayside and the docks. A tomboy named Felise was chosen to be the West Wind, in charge of most of the upper and larger residential districts because she knew a lot of the kitchen help and gossips. Her mother was a laundress and she was always sent to pick up and deliver things. A long-legged, lanky boy by the name of Tamlain (who fancied himself a piper) was given the title of the East Wind and charge of upper Bayside and the merchant district. The title of North Wind was given to a small elven boy with the unlikely name of Mouse. The North part of town encompassed Tent Town and warehouses, a place he'd been crawling about all his short life.

Landros gratefully handed the reins over to the Cardinals and their queen and, taking Lark by the hand, retreated to a corner pallet to breathe. He put his arm around her shoulders and pulled her close. "I think my Lord has bitten off more than I can chew," he sighed, watching the activity in the chamber.

"Who would have thought such place would exist below?" she sighed. "That have organized does not surprise, but is lucky this place, this warren."

She closed her eyes, content in Landros's embrace with the happy sound of children around them. Behind her closed eyes, she saw the chamber, saw something else besides this den of street-rats. It was like song in her heart, this vision, an epic ballad moving through her soul like a dragon through the sky.

She saw a nest of them curled up in the centre hollow, a great mother earth dragon and her brood of young, slithering in and out of the tunnels around them. Then she saw something evil creep in, a miasma sent by something ungodly to choke the young and burn out the heart of the great mother. She became as stone, sank into the earth with the last of her brood and vanished. The evil came, faceless and black, seeking something powerful that the dragon had left behind. But the evil was driven out yet again by something, someone. In her eyes, Lark saw the cavern empty, bare to the walls, but painted and ornate. A rune was etched over each entrance save one, the one from which Terri had come. That one was labelled for the Wyrd, the unknown, the Silent Oracle.

Beside him, Landros felt her shudder, looked down and noticed her eyes were closed. He held her tighter, "Are you all right?" he whispered.

Lark just set her hand on his arm reassuringly and got up, walked over to the nearest tunnel, her eyes still closed. Landros followed her, confused, uncertain whether it was a nightmare or a vision that held her, that moved her.

She ran her hands over the rune above the tunnel, saw it clearly in her mind's eye: Wyn, the rune of joy. Opening her eyes, she saw an almost non-existent impression of the same rune. It was so worn away that only her fingers knew the difference. She knew what these runes had been placed here for, as protection among other things, like directions. She knew also that she must re-mark the tunnels, lest the evil get in again, and destroy all of this, find what it had killed the great dragon for. The hooded mage was part of this evil, of that she was certain. Whatever it was that mage was looking for, it must not be found.

Lark reached up and touched a place on the wall. She could see with an inner eye where the sigil began, but all Landros saw was cold, bare rock until she began to trace the rune. It lit up with a cold blue fire, scoring the stone and leaving a blackened mark behind.

He recognized the shape as the constellation she had pointed out to him once as joy, the sign she was born under. Lark moved away to the next tunnel, closed her eyes a moment and traced another, burning this one as well. Now he was thoroughly confused, though he did not dare break her concentration to ask. She seemed to be choosing the runes with care, never the same one twice.

By the time she had done the third one, the children had noticed and watched, fascinated. She stopped in front of one of the tunnels, looked at it curiously then passed it by, not marking it at all, went on to the next. When she was done, Lark stood back, turned, made sure that the tunnel she had skipped was the only one without a mark, then moved to the centre of the room.

She had to move a few crates, but she found the spot she needed. She slipped out of her shoes, planted her feet and raised her arms. A humming vibration began beneath her soles, ran through her body: the beating of the dragon's heart, faint, but there. She began to call upon it, drawing the power into herself and out again, connecting the runes one by one to each other and to her with every pulsing breath.

Landros stepped back, and the children flattened themselves against the walls. The woman looked like a wind witch standing in the middle of the room, hair a living mass of black tendrils and her skirts the wings of some great creature. They could feel and hear the vibrations about them, and the runes on the walls began to glow again one by one. Landros felt a sudden panic, not knowing if she was doing this or if she was yet again the victim of something more powerful. Something kept him from moving towards her but he could not say if it was something external, fear or plain wisdom.

As abruptly as it began, the glow and the wind faded. She tried to maintain control, to keep the power flowing, the heart beating, but she could not hold onto it. The heartbeat slowed, weakened and the power holding her up suddenly gave out, the song ended.

He felt himself move before he realized why, caught her just before she hit the floor. He sat down with her in his lap, the children swarming around them. He tapped her cheek, shook her, looking her over for signs of injury. "Lark! Speak to me, little one! Please!"

She moaned in response, opened her eyes. "Hello, my Kestrel," she purred. She looked around, saw the scores of little faces peering down at her and laughed, remembering one of the tales from Rue's book. "Why do I feel like princess rescued by fairy king?"

He just kissed her, grateful that she was all right enough to make jokes.

"Mmm," she sighed. "Is reason enough to faint. Maybe I faint again..."

"Lark, this is not funny. What in the name of the nine hells happened? What did you do?"

She sat up, pushed her hair out of her face. "Do not know. Was guided by something else. I know was right. Did everything right. Could feel her all around, but... I must have weakened myself with runes, was not strong enough to do both. Another time." She saw the worry still in his eyes and smiled, caressed his face tenderly. "No, is not possession, my general. Is something else. Better. Am weak, but am fine. Will be doing no magic tonight, is certain," she chuckled wryly.

Landros picked her up.

"What are you doing?!" she laughed.

"Taking you home," he said shortly. He turned, looked around, trying to find a way out.

"No. Lily's," she said. He looked at her. "My things are there," she said. "And is food and bed if needed."

He looked at her, thought for a moment, looked deep into those eyes and... "Fine, Lily's then," he said reluctantly. "Now how the hells do I get out of here?"

The children giggled.

"Well, first of all, General, you have to put her down," Terri said. "There is no way to walk out of here. All ways are through the tunnels."

"Am fine, my kestrel. Can make my own way out," Lark protested. She brushed her fingers along his cheek, looked at him so tenderly he suddenly had no inclination whatsoever to let her go or deny her anything. With great reluctance, he set her on her feet, but did not remove his hands, in case she was not steady enough. "Thank you," she said, giving him a light kiss.

"Then ya follows me!" Billy chimed. He proudly led them to the tunnel marked Wyn and crawled in.

Landros insisted that Lark go ahead of him, in case she fainted or weakened she would not be left behind unawares. She teased him that he just liked the view better.

This trip was more twisting than the first one, took more turns and ran more steeply. Finally they emerged into a high part of the sewer and walked the ledge beside the slowly subsiding river of sludge to a grate opening a short distance away. Billy stepped to the other side of it, made a grand gesture. "Ta-da!! One ladder to th' Cinnamom Tree, at yer serfice! Just two blocks over i'is! See you at th' Lamb t'night, gen'ral?" he asked with a sharp salute.

"It depends on a meeting this afternoon." He returned the salute, shook the boy's hand. He climbed the ladder first, made certain that the coast was clear above, and then helped Lark out. Billy had been right. They were in an alley not two blocks from the Cinnamon Tree.

Lark slipped her arm around his waist and walked with him back to the inn. Ivaska greeted them enthusiastically as they entered the stable-yard, nuzzling and pushing at them for attention. They went up the back stairs to their room where Lily had laid out their spare clothes on the bed, folding the shirts and pants.

Landros began throwing his things into his bag. He turned, saw Lark slipping out of her clothes and stopped cold, feeling very warm all of a sudden. When she reached for the red dress lying on the bed he stood up. "Just what in the name of the Abyss do you think you are doing?"

She looked over her shoulder at him. "What, you wish me to entertain tonight like this?" she asked, turning to face him and spreading her arms with the dress still in hand. "Will certainly get attention, but am not certain want to deal with what kind."

He crossed the room in two strides, swept her up into his arms and dropped her, rather unceremoniously on the bed. Before she could squirm away, he pinned her there with his body. "Now see here, Princess," he said, ignoring her giggles and squirming to get loose. "I want you to stay here and get some rest. If you don't want to stay here, I'll take you back to the wagon and tuck you in myself. But you overextended yourself in the warren and you need to recouperate."

She lay still then, staring up at him with a pout on her face. "But if *want* to dance?" she asked.

He tried to ignore the bare leg sliding sensuously up and over his. "Lark, I mean it. I don't want you fainting in the middle of a room crowded with hungry and drunken men."

"So," she said, beginning to move her other leg against his inner thigh, ever so slowly. "How are you to keep me in bed? *Sesket*?"

"I could always tie you. That scarf you always keep on your head can restrain much more than just your glorious hair."

She felt a flush and a tingling wash through her at that threat, a tiny wave of nervous excitement. She did not show her reaction, parrying the remark with one of her own. "Besides, you have meeting. You have report of your army to give. You have real army to sign in for."

He just looked down at her, startled, her naked legs completely forgotten. "How do you know I intend to join the irregulars?"

She just smiled softly, inevitably. "I know you. You cannot stay out of this. You will not join regular army, but this? This I think was your idea."

"How?" he asked. He could not remember having mentioned it to her.

"It smells of you," she shrugged, lifted her head up enough to press her cheek against his neck, nuzzling her way between his shirt and his shoulder. "Like this," she purred, nipped.

A shock went through his entire body with that bite. What was that she said about not working any magic tonight? he asked himself. He kept her arms pinned, but it did not stop her from arousing him. He pressed his forehead against the pillow, moaned into her hair, "Lark... *Ellinoia*, please... don't...."

"Don't what?" she asked innocently, moving from his shoulder to kissing his throat, up by his ear.

To his surprise, he realized that she was actually purring. "That... is an odd action for ... a bird-lover," he stammered.

He could feel her smile against his throat. "All women are in their basic nature feline," she rumbled.

"Lark....," he warned, feeling himself reacting to the subtle shifting of her body beneath him. "Stop..."

"Why?" she asked.

"Because," he said, lifting his head from the pillow and away from the intoxicating fragrance of her hair. "It makes me want to do *this*..." he said, pressing a deep, long, weakening kiss to her mouth.

After a minute or so, he came up for air, "And I don't have time for *this*..." he said and kissed her again. 'Ah, the hells with it,' he thought, rolling onto his side and pulling her close against him.

TWO

When Lark came down stairs finally, it was early evening and the customers were beginning to gather. Landros said his farewells at the top of the stairs and headed off to Colwyn's via the back door. Nightingale fussed at her from the hearth, complaining about having been left behind the whole morning and locked out the whole afternoon. She just laughed at him, stroked his feathers and fed him dried currants.

She was feeling languid and loose, ready to dance for the sheer joy of it. She was dancing even without music as she wove between the tables, chatting occasionally with people she knew. Spinning, she turned to head back to the fireplace and slammed into Coolie.

He bent near her, inhaled deeply, sneered, "You smell like a man."

Irritated by his possessive audacity, she leaned closer, took a few light sniffs of his garlic sweat and beer-stained shirt. "Funny. You don't," she said softly and whisked past him.

Determined not to let him spoil her evening, she began with a riotous melody, one so fast she could not really dance while she played it. The fiddle was practically smoking when she was done. The applause filled the small room, then faded down again to the murmurs of conversation, and Lark began to play something softer and more quiet.

At the back of the tavern some movement caught her attention. She looked up, but by then, whoever it was had slipped outside and disappeared. There was someone sitting at her corner table by the fire, someone who was coughing and sniffling and sounded very under the weather. She decided to find another table farther away to tell her fortunes in.

It was late when she changed clothes and left the Tree. The moon was already high in the sky, so she had no fear of shadows sneaking up on her tonight. She would see them coming provided she stayed in the open. She stopped to play a bit with Ivaska before bidding him a good night and telling him to stay put and guard well. Watching him bed down by the chicken coop, she turned to go and found herself suddenly swept up in a giant bear hug by a large man.

She shrieked. Nightingale fell from her shoulder and fluttered awkwardly to the ground. Lark tried to pull the scimitar, but it would not draw. Then she realized that it was only her brother and settled for pounding her fists on his broad shoulders.

"You beast!!!" she laughed.

From the second floor, Dane's window opened and Lily leaned out. "Lark, are you all r...? Oh, hello, Ox!" she called. "Try and keep it down, will you? You'll wake my guests!"

"What guests?" Lark mocked as her brother put her down. Lily just laughed and closed the window. "Ox, you give fright!" she growled, slapping her brother's chest. "Be glad this get stuck or would have been skrrrrtt!" she said, drawing the sheathed blade across his gut.

"Maybe should oil it?" he taunted. "Let me see," he said, holding his hand for the sword.

She shook her head. "Would not be wise. Blade does not like hands of men," she said. She pulled on the hilt, was surprised when the sword slid out as if it were oiled silk. "Is strange. I guess comes out only when want to." She showed it to her brother, held it for him while he examined the blade without touching it.

He gave a low whistle. "Is nice. Where you get?" he asked.

"*Odd little man in underground shop,*" she said, shifting to their native tongue. "*Traded wand for. Was very good trade, I think.*"

"*What happened to yours?*" he asked as she sheathed the blade and retrieved her complaining familiar from the flagstones.

"*Succubus stole it. Don't ask,*" she laughed tiredly. "*Is better not knowing. Walk me home?*" she asked. "*Have shadow am thinking.*"

"*Can I ask you again to come home, Illyana?*"

"*No, you cannot.*"

"*Then I will walk you home, little sister,*" he sighed, began walking with her out of the stable-yard. "*After all, you have moved, and I know not where you have moved to.*"

She smiled. "*You will like new place. Is nice, is safe.*"

"*Good.*" They walked a few minutes in silence. "*What is wrong with Nightingale?*" he asked.

"*Some idiot watchman broke wing. Is fine. Will fly soon. For now is just grumpy.*"

"*And why is dog I give you living with innkeeper?*"

Lark sighed. She had not relished the question, though she knew it would have come eventually. "*Is loan. She feeds and employs me. I loan her dog to watch chickens. Lot of thieving lately. Am safe and watched where am, so dog not needed. And gets fed well and lot of attention with Dane and stable-boy to play with. Am fine. When leave city, he come too. Besides, I eat eggs he guards. So in way is still watching me.*"

Ivan grumbled to himself, but knew better than to argue with his sister's logic. "*So, Gruma said you wanted to see me?*" he said, getting right to business.

"*Yes,*" she sighed. "*Is about blind boy, my fiddle student.*"

"*Oh?*" he asked with an arch of his brow.

"His mother is worried. Things are getting... odd around. She worries that uncle cannot take him if something happen to her or to inn. His father passed few years back, so without mother he has no one. He would not be good for orphanage."

"What are you saying, Yani?"

"Am saying have promised to care for him. What am asking is to talk to father for apprenticing. She said she would think, but I believe is best. Want to ask if papa will take boy in for year. You heard him. Is good player. But mother is too protective and knows this. Is old enough now to learn self-reliance. And with siege and war and other nastiness going on, is better he is there and not here."

"And you, Petrovna? Are you not safer there than here?"

"Am happier here," she said and left it at that.

Ivan wisely did not say another word the whole way to the upper district. He looked around him in nervous curiosity once he realized what part of town they were in. *"Should we be cutting through here?"* he asked. *"Will not Watch think we are up to no good?"*

"Probably," she grinned, turned to walk backwards so she could watch him, *"But dare not do anything about."* Nightingale gave a short 'so there!' chirp, which made both of them laugh.

They heard a whistling up ahead, saw a swinging light. The bearer stopped, held up the lantern to get a better look at them. "Halt!" he called. "Who goes!"

She laughed, kept her eyes on her brother. "Evening, lieutenant!" she called, certain that it was the young man she had almost run over with Dolal a few nights ago.

"Miss Lark?" came the answer. Ivan's eyes grew wide. She was not sure if it was with surprise or displeasure. The lieutenant closed the distance, bowed when he recognized her. "Ah! It is you! Forgive me, I thought, seeing you not alone... that you were someone else."

"Is all right. Are doing job. This is brother, Ox."

"Evening, sir," he said, tipping his hat to him. "Well, I've got my rounds. All's quiet so far, but never know... Have a good night, miss, sir," he said cheerily and went, whistling still, back to his rounds.

As soon as the man was out of earshot, Ivan grabbed his sister's elbow and began walking her down the street. *"What was that all about?! Do you want to get us both arrested?"*

She jerked her arm free. *"For what?"* she laughed. *"Walking up street?"*

"Yes! In case you don't remember, girl, you are Romer! That is all they see, his kind, and to them Romer is thief!"

"All that *one sees,"* she seethed, angry now, *"is pretty girl who lives on this street! Yes, some of his peers do think like this, but not all. If we wish to be treated otherwise, we should expect to be treated otherwise. Now, do you wish to visit caravan or not?"*

He stared hard at his sister. Lark knew what had to be running through his mind. How much of a gegenta was his sister becoming? Finally, he nodded and allowed her to lead him to the gate of Lord Colwyn's manor. Before she could get the gate open enough to let them both in, the stable boy came running out. He skittered to a stop when he saw her.

"Oh," he said with disappointment as he opened the gate. "I thought you was the master."

"Is Lord Colwyn gone?" she asked.

He nodded. "Lord's council meeting. He was awfully anxious about it. Good night!" he chirped and trotted back into the stable.

Ivan frowned as she set off towards the house. She just shook her head, certain what he must be thinking. She cut around through the garden and into the woods before she activated her pendant. Nightingale gave a happy chirp when the caravan came into sight. "Was hurricane through here some time ago. Ripped up wagon pretty bad. Lord Colwyn is friend of friend and allows me to live here. Even fixed wagon when needed."

"I see," he said and not without some displeasure in his voice. "You have cultivated some powerful friends, Petrovna."

She sighed. "In these times Romeri need powerful friends. Will you be staying night?"

He sat down on the tail of the wagon. "Since you invited me..."

She raised an eyebrow. "What, Jena getting soft?"

"No, Jena gave me daughter," he grinned.

She threw her arms around her brother with a squeal of delight. "Am so glad for you! What is name?"

"Anjenia Ivanova," he said proudly. "Will be singer no doubt. Has strong lungs." She perched beside him after settling her familiar into his birdhouse. "Have other news, as well," he added, pulling out his pipe and packing it.

"Oh?"

"Yarmine is getting married."

"Is about time she quit giving that poor boy chase-about!"

"He finally pinned her down, literally. Told her: marry me or let me go, but will not get up until you decide."

She laughed. "Always romantic, Gregor."

"Whatever works," he shrugged. "It would be good for marriage and clan if you were there."

She thought a moment, looked up at the moon hanging in the sky above them, partially obscured by clouds. It was nearly full. She gauged no more than a few days. "Is close."

"Yes," he said. "Will begin in two nights."

"Come back for me," she said quickly, an action which was not lost on her brother. "Day after tomorrow."

"A lover?" he asked, lighting his pipe.

She looked at him with her dark eyes, trying to fathom how he had guessed or deduced that fact. No man had ever been known to have the sight, though occasional gifts weakly manifested themselves. "Is rude question, Petrovich," she told him and went inside the caravan.

Ivan sat outside, smoking his pipe, and thinking.

She gathered up blankets for her brother, knowing that her refusal to answer had told him what he had wanted to know. She did not care, she, at least, had not admitted it, and it *was* a rude question. Brother or not, that did not give him the right. Besides, if he knew he would probably try to chase him off, like he had every other boy who had ever been interested in her. Not that Landros would yield to such things. It would no doubt start a fight that neither could win.

If he knew that her lover was gegenta, he would probably tell their father, who would more than likely order her forcibly dragged back. That, or issue her the ultimatum that she feared, that had kept her from giving herself fully to her handsome young elf. She was not certain she could choose between her family and her lover.

She went back outside, drop ped the blankets beside him. "Here. Is comfortable under wagon. Have slept there myself once or twice," she said.

"Thank you," he answered.

She crouched beside him, gave him a small bag of coins.

"What is?" he asked, confused by its chink and weight.

"Money. Have favour to ask."

"Yes?" he said, looking up at his sister, his face lit only by the soft glow of his pipe.

"Little boy I tell you of, is good player, but needs practice. Cannot always leave my fiddle... The local instrument maker lost his shop to earlier attack, his hands... are ruined now. Cannot get new fiddle here. Need you to find me one and have no trade goods. Anything serviceable will do."

He pocketed the bag, nodding, though reluctantly, it seemed. "You are giving much for this boy," he said. "This gegenta."

"I like him, and is good player. Besides, owe his mother more than can repay. Goodnight."

She went back inside the wagon, not really wanting to stay outside longer than she had to, afraid of the questions her brother might ask. She went straight to bed, aware of him out there, smoking on the tail for a long while.

Landros sat in the chair of his Lord's study, dozing as he waited for his return. He was startled awake by a voice asking the question, "I take it you've heard the Lord Mayor's speech?"

"My Lord?" he asked, snapping to consciousness from dreams of a pair of sultry, dark blue eyes.

"Let me guess you got very little sleep during the rains," he grinned.

Landros felt a flush beginning around his ears. "Something like that. I did hear the Lord Mayor's speech, and I have other news for you."

He told Lord Colwyn of the underground and the warren, though not how to get there, and of the small army he had 'inherited'.

"General, huh?" Colwyn chuckled.

Landros rubbed the back of his neck in embarrassment. "Not by choice, sir, but I am afraid so."

"Amusing, but useful. Have you yet to sign up for the irregular army, then?"

"No, sir, but I intend to."

"Good, I don't want you to. I'll need you in my own forces."

"I do not mean to be rude, my Lord, but I have plans you might want to hear."

Colwyn looked up, saw the intense look on his squire's face and sat back. After a moment he gestured for Landros to go on.

"You remember when we went out to rescue the children that there was the matter of a wild elf who helped us and died in the confrontation with the succubus?"

"I remember something of that nature, yes," he grinned, remembering also how he had met his squire.

"Well, his chief made a promise to me, and I to him. That tribe is outside of the enemy forces' circle of influence." He stopped there, waiting for it to sink in. When he saw the look of enlightenment on the lord's face, he went on. "If I can get out there, I can get them to help and have a complete, *real* army at our disposal, *at the rear* of the enemy."

"Are you certain they will put themselves at risk?"

He nodded. "They are plagued by the enemy as well, though not so openly. They have already made a promise to me I intend to hold them to. All I have to do is get out there. And for that, I will need some priestly help."

Colwyn sat quietly for a long time, and Landros let him think. After a while he got up and began penning a letter which he signed, sealed and handed to his squire.

"Take this immediately to Father Orlin at the matron's house. Make sure that no one else sees it. After he's read it, explain your plan to him and do what he tells you. I'd suggest going prepared to stay, in case you have to. I would guess the city will be prepared to launch a counter-attack within about two weeks or so."

"Two weeks?"

He sighed. "It takes time to move an army. And if we move slowly enough, we can move without being noticed and prepared for. The council has decided that to gather quickly is to be noticed, as well as ill-prepared, and the mayor agrees."

"Won't going now wake the good father up?"

He shook his head. "He is something of a night owl. Go, you've stalled long enough," he chuckled. "And may the goddesses watch over you."

Landros slid the letter into his pack and started for the door, but the knight's voice called him back. "Doing this doesn't get you out of my unit," he chuckled. "You'll just be one of my commanders."

He sighed, nodding and took his leave, headed into the woods, rather than the gate. First things first, he thought. He could not leave for potentially several days without telling her something, or at least leaving her a note. He was already packed for long travel, had everything he thought he would need in his bag.

He saw the caravan just up ahead, trotted across the grass to it, hoping she would be there. He had a stolen rose in his hand as he silently slipped up the steps. The scent of her struck him the moment he opened the door, sweet poison. She was getting to be an addiction, he realized. He quietly went to the bed, sat down on the edge and just watched her sleeping for a long moment in the swathe of moonlight drifting in through the open window. He caressed her cheek with the rose, watched her slight, almost feline reactions to the touch, sensual even in her sleep.

After a brief moment, and a murmur or two, she opened her eyes, stared dreamily out the window up at the moon, then turned and started as she saw him. "Landros!" she cried softly, the smile melting its way across her face.

"Hello, princess," he said, kissed her. She clung to him, unwilling to end the kiss or the embrace, and, truthfully, neither was he. It was a long moment before he was able to pull away. He rested his forehead against hers, unwilling to end the contact even that much. "I have to go," he said painfully.

"Now? Why? Cannot stay even night?"

"No. I have to go immediately. You remember Savaren's people?"

"Yes," she said hesitantly.

"I have to go find them and prepare them for the battle. I do not know if or when I will be back, and I have to go now. I did not want to disappear without a word to you, or a kiss." He caressed her cheek with the back of one finger, memorizing her face, as if he could forget those lips.

"Be careful," she whispered, lacing her fingers in the soft curls at the back of his neck. She tilted her chin up, kissed him again.

It was the last kiss he would permit, otherwise.... "Farewell, Illyana, *simara ellinoia*," he whispered, laying the rose against her cheek and reluctantly moving away.

Lark just lay there as she watched the patch of light from the doorway grow and fade, taking him away from her. She rolled over, facing the window and the moon and just let the tears fall as she cradled the rose to her cheek. She was aware that he stopped and bade a farewell to Nightingale, who had poked his head out of his house to find out why she was suddenly so sad.

THREE

Landros bore his note to the temple, insisted upon it going into the hands of the priest for whom it was intended from his own hand and no other's. This, of course, annoyed the clergy who were actually still up at this hour. Finally, they led him to a small study/laboratory somewhere deep within the temple web complex and left him there. He recognized the elderly priest immediately as the one who had teleported them out into the woods the first time. He seemed to have an inordinate amount of energy for someone of his age as he turned and welcome Landros in.

"What is it that I can do for you?" he asked.

Landros held out the letter, waited while the man read it.

After reading it twice and muttering to himself in a tongue Landros was not familiar with, the priest got up and began poking around his shelves, pulling out references and maps and other books seemingly at random, muttering to himself all the while.

He looked up after a few minutes, as if startled to see him there. "Why are you still... oh, never-mind, my fault. I cannot do this yet, have to investigate probabilities, probe current preventatives, et cetera," he said with an absent wave of his hand. "Go to bed, I will have an answer or a transport for you come morning or so. Yes, yes, go on," he said, leading Landros out the door of the study and calling to a sleepy acolyte who happened to be in the hall. "Gevin! Take this elf to a cell and give him a bed. I will send for him in the morning or sooner if I need him! I have work to do like a fever and I want him close!" He turned to Landros, "Go on, get some sleep, my son. I'll let you know when I'm ready, when I need you. Won't be any time to lose when I am!"

With that he left him in the care of the acolyte and disappeared back into the room, closing the door behind him. He growled to himself and hoped the man was not as insane as he came across.

Lark got up rather early the next morning, took her brother to Lily's for breakfast. He did not say much to her at all, but promised that he would return to get her for the full moon. After he left, Lark gave Dane his violin lesson early, teaching him a new song. She found her mind wandering through out the lesson. Something was disturbing her, but she couldn't figure out what. She was just... restless, uneasy.

She laid out her clothes for the evening in the small room Lily apparently never rented out. Laying the bright red gown on the bed, she felt rather plain in the simple, solid colours she had chosen to wear, but was not really in the mood to be bright and flashy. She shouldered her pack and trotted downstairs, merely waving to Lily as she headed out the door. She noticed, out of the corner of her eye, that Dane was entertaining a young friend in his corner.

Landros was already awake and pacing his cell when the acolyte came to summon him. The timing was good, as he was about to lose what little patience he possessed. He was taken immediately into Father Orlin's study. "I cannot do it," the man said the moment the door had closed behind him.

"I'm sorry, what was that?" Landros asked, not quite sure he had heard what he thought he had.

"I said it cannot be done at this time. You see, there is something out there preventing us from teleporting in and out. Otherwise we'd have help by now. I was able to break through it once before, but it has since been fortified and it will take me a while to figure how to breach the defences, and then I cannot be certain of getting you back and out again. No, it is best that you wait until you are ready to go and closer to the actual time of the attack to give the enemy more things to think about than this breach and allow you time to gather some extra forces from here within the city walls."

He held up his hand to forestall any complaint the elf had been about to give. "For whatever reason, my son, it cannot be done *now*. I will keep attempting, and will notify Lord Colwyn the moment it is possible." He handed Landros a sealed letter. "Please ferry that to his Lordship and tender my personal apologies. And to you, my apologies for wasting your time last night. I hope you slept well enough?" With that he turned back to his bubbling bottles and apparatus, seeming to have forgotten the elf was even in the room.

Landros turned and quietly left, saved his fuming for later. Absent-minded though he might seem, he needed this man's good will in the future if he were to successfully reach the wild ones outside of the city in time to mould them into a rear flank. He stalked his way across the city, returned to Colwyn's house to deliver the letter, and perhaps get some breakfast. Maybe Lark would still be at her caravan and a picnic might be arranged. Yes, that would soothe his raw nerves quite nicely.

Lark wandered through the town, not really seeing much. Somewhere in the marketplace, she found herself softly singing Romeri wedding songs. Possibly it was because of her father's daughter's upcoming nuptial, but she was not sure. She was in a very strange mood, teetering between delirious happiness and abject misery. She did not even notice that the goods she was passing by were shabbier than usual and that food was becoming a more valuable currency than gold. Nightingale, perched on her shoulder, piped something about being followed, about some dark shadowed figure that always seemed to be behind them. As Lark turned to look, her arm was grabbed by a passing urchin who used her as a brake as he turned to her.

"Lark!" he cried, laughing madly while he tried to catch his breath. "Goddess but I's glad I found you!"

"Billy! What is?! Someone chasing...?"

Before she could finish her question, he shook his head violently. "No, Rog sent me! You 'members th' dwarf wha' 'elped us onna rescue?"

"Yes, I know Rog," she said, pulling Billy off to the side of the road, out of traffic. "What is wrong?"

"Don't know really. 'E pops outter one o' tha sewer links an' sees me 'bout to 'ead fer th' warren. 'E tells me ta go gets ya and not to spare me 'orses! Didn' say why, jus' ta get ya and quick."

"Where is?" she asked, re-shouldering her bag.

"Foller me," he said and taking her hand, began weaving in and out among the crowd.

He led her to the back of a secluded building, double checked to make certain that no one was observing before sliding open a grate in the alley. "Go on first. I'll pass yer things down."

Lark handed him her bag and her bird, which surprised him.

"What? 'e can't fly?"

"Not for while. Wing broke," she said and slid down into the open grate. She hung for a moment, waiting until her eyes adjusted before she dropped down into a thin layer of old water. She was suddenly grateful she had put on her boots that morning. She called softly up for Billy to drop her bag, caught and shouldered it. A few seconds later, a long string was lowered with the bird clinging awkwardly to the end of it. She chuckled, collected him and stepped back to get out of Billy's way.

He dropped down beside her, and, with the string tied to the grate lid, tugged it back into place. He took her hand and led her through the sewer. It took a little while, but her eyes finally adjusted to the dimness and she was able to see enough to avoid the deeper channels and some of the debris scattered through the tunnels by the recent floodwaters.

Five minutes later they were turning down a wider, oddly dryer branch where Rog sat waiting for them. He jumped up, met them halfway. "Not followed?" he asked Billy.

Nightingale answered him instead, chirping a negative response.

"Thanks," he grumped, not terribly sincere. "All right, kid, thanks, ya done the job. Lark and I'll take it from here," he drawled and started to lead her off down the tunnel.

Billy cut in. "Oh, no, sir! I's comin' wif yas!"

"Like Hells, boy," he growled. "Too dangerous!"

"I 'appen to be a full Colonel in th' un'erground army, fank you very much!" Billy snapped.

"Enough!" Lark snarled, jerking her arm free. "I go nowhere with neither until know why!"

Rog sighed, turned from the boy and lowered his voice to confide to Lark why he had sent for her. "I saw something down here I think is significant. I need you for two reasons: One, as a secondary witness; and two, as someone what knows the rune tongue as it relates to magic."

"Runes? Thought you read...."

He shook his head. "I read the *tongue*, but when the runes are used as symbols, fer magic not communication, it might as well be human scratch!"

"I see," she mumbled. "Where?"

"This way," he said and started to lead her away again. He stopped and waved Billy off as he tried to follow them. "You back off, boy!"

Lark laid a hand on Rog's arm. "Let him follow. If hangs back enough, if we get into trouble he can find us help and quickly. He knows these tunnels better than you, my friend."

Rog humphed and grumbled, but said nothing more and began to lead them into the dark. Lark paused long enough to remove any jewellery she had on that might give her away and followed, tucking them into her pack.

The stable boy cheerfully waved to Landros as he came in, informed him brightly that the master was not in today, but that he would be back in the afternoon.

"Has Lark left yet?" he asked.

"Yes sir," he piped. "Her an' her friend."

"Friend?" he asked, somehow certain he was not talking about the bird.

"Yeah, the man what she brought home with her last night. Big fella! Gypsy, I think."

Landros felt a small spark of jealousy at the news, stifled it. He had not remembered another person in the wagon and she had not mentioned anyone even as she tried to get him to stay with her. So, where had this person been when he had arrived? He handed the boy the letter. "Here, see that your master gets this."

He turned and left, headed for the Cinnamon Tree. It was possible that was where Lark might have gone, perhaps even with her Romeri 'friend'.

They tramped quietly through the tunnels, Lark eventually having to bend over to keep from hitting her head while Rog padded on, completely oblivious. The tunnels became dryer here, somewhat more airy and less foul. She noticed another smell in the air, something that she could not notice before over the heavy, hot odour of decay: Magic.

Rog slowed down, gestured for silence before creeping closer.

The stench became stronger the farther they went. Lark could not remember ever smelling magic quite so foul and evil before. Even the demon circle had not been so... oppressive. Nightingale danced nervously on her shoulder, though he did not make a sound.

They rounded a corner, saw light ahead and Rog stopped, pressed back against the wall, gestured for them to do the same. The tunnel had gotten taller here, enabling her and Billy to stand up again. She pressed flat against the wall and felt her head tip back through a hole. She turned quickly, noticed a small square cut in the stone behind her and peered in. It looked out over the room on the other side, and she was horrified by what she saw.

The chamber was roughly pentagonal in shape, with sconces in each of the corners. In the middle of the floor was a pentagram, pegs hammered into the tip of each point. To each peg, a woman was chained, kneeling inside the points, facing the walls; harlots by their dress and the heavy paint upon their faces. Some of them were no longer young.

In the centre of the pentagram was a large cage containing five huge birds of a type Lark could not identify from her position. They flapped about, but made no sounds that would identify them. Then a robed figure blocked her view, began waving its long, bare arms and chanting in an androgynous voice. There was a horrendous stench, and squawking and screaming suddenly filled the room. She covered her ears to block it out, but still could hear the din driving its way into her head. It was all she could do to keep from screaming herself.

There was a sulphurous explosion and all was quiet again. Then the robed figure moved, and she looked up to see five harpies flopping half-conscious on the floor. The remains of their torn shifts hung about their necks, revealing, dirty, pendulous breasts that smelled sour even from across the room. Their vulture-like bodies were filthy, caked and coated with grime, blood and offal. Their hair hung in scraggly, matted locks as they looked about nervously, trying to get their bearings, their mouths open and panting as a panicked hawk's might.

Beside her, Billy craned himself up on his toes to look, and immediately pulled back. She handed him Nightingale, tried frantically to think of a spell she could use that the mage could not steal from her, when there came a deep, resultant "**FOOM!**" from inside the chamber. When the smoke finally cleared, the room was empty save for a few dirty feathers and scraps of cloth. The lights went out and even the mage was nowhere to be seen. After a few long minutes, Lark judged it safe to enter the room and cautiously crept around Rog.

It was not a solid chamber, she discovered. There were columns separating each "wall" on which a bowl of burning oil was placed, no longer lit, and a passageway disappeared off into the dark behind them.

She lit the room with her pendant, trying to keep it shielded as best she could. She bent to examine the marks on the floor and the walls. "Are these runes wanted me to see?" she whispered.

"Yeah," he answered, poking around behind the walls, looking for signs of the magician or his/her egress.

"Cor!" Billy hissed. "That was th' mage from th' island!"

Lark stood bolt upright. "You've seen face?"

"Yeah, but, it wavered, ya' know? Never really th' same face ev'r' time you lookt. I knows 'at voice tho'!"

Landros was strolling unhappily from the Cinnamon Tree and a scant breakfast. For some reason, his gut was giving him all sorts of hell and it had nothing to do with what he'd eaten. Something was wrong, or was about to go wrong, he just knew it. The last time it had reacted this strongly, was just before Nightingale had dropped out of the sky into the temple courtyard indicating Lark was in deep. Before that, it was just before his attack in the alley, and before that, when the siege had begun. There was something very not right about the morning. He squinted up at the sky, at the low hanging cloud-bank. That he could not find Lark troubled him.

Something caught his attention in the clouds, something that flew without grace or real competence. It grew slowly larger until he was able to make out the hideous figures of five grotesque harpies. They flapped, clawed and screeched at each other. By now, people in the streets around him had begun to notice something was amiss. No sooner the figures were recognizable, people began to run, screaming for the nearest shelter. This of course, alerted the attention of the harpies who, spoiling for a fight, swooped down screaming with delight.

Landros pulled his bow, nocked an arrow and let it fly. It struck its mark, but the creature did not fall, merely staggered in the air and tried to pull the arrow from her putrid breast with her claws. A second arrow found the heart of another harpy and she fell like a stone, hitting a young man running for cover. He kicked the carcass off of him, rolled over, retching from the stench. Landros got off two more arrows before the creatures were too close for the bow and drew his sword.

He was not the only fighter in the street battling the foul things. A watchman and a pair of civilians took up the fight with the remaining three harpies. Even some of the street children were helping, throwing rocks at them from safer distances, ducking into small places the harpies could not follow when pursued. The first one Landros had hit, attacked him, still clutching at the arrow with one claw. The smell of her as she beat against him with her wings was vomitous, and he was suddenly grateful that he had only had a small breakfast of bread and cheese and had foregone the greasy sausages. Batting her claws aside, he split her breast upon his blade, flung her off with a violent swing and turned to hack into the back of another one pursuing a pretty young woman past him. The running woman fell, screaming, covering her head, but he struck the harpy before she could attack the prone figure. The bird-woman rounded on him, screeching unintelligibly.

A second swing beheaded the beast, spraying him with hot, foul blood. He turned, searching the sky, making certain that the young woman was protected. The last two harpies were taken down by the other fighters and by sling-stones from the urchins, who gave Landros a smart salute and promptly vanished. He turned to the woman, helped her to her feet. She was stunningly beautiful, and clung to him, weeping in terror.

"It's all right, my lady. They are dead. There is nothing left to fear," he said.

She looked up at him with pale blue eyes and he realized that she was elven. Her silky, pale brown hair was caked with blood and tears and dirt from the street where she had fallen. She drew herself up to her full height, a scant few inches shorter than he, straightened her clothing as best she could. He found himself staring at her, inexplicably drawn to her soft, ivory skin and the smooth, high curve of her cheek. There was some cloying and intoxicating scent about her that was beginning to arouse him.

"I must look a fright," she fussed as she straightened herself out.

"You look beautiful," he found himself saying, oblivious to the people beginning to mill about now that the danger was over. Scavengers were deciding whether or not the harpies were edible, and a squabble over one of the corpses erupted unnoticed behind him.

Then he heard someone nearer shriek and exclaim, "I know that woman!" He turned, saw someone pointing to the harpy on the ground at her feet. "That's one of those harlots down at Marcel Street!"

"Are you sure?" someone asked her.

"I've seen her countless times when I've gone there hunting my husband!"

"I... I am trembling," the elven woman said, drawing Landros's attention back. "I... feel somewhat faint...."

He caught her before she collapsed, though she struggled to remain conscious. With a growl to himself and his luck, he swept her into his arms and carried her back to the nearest inn or tavern, which happened to be the Golden Cygnet.

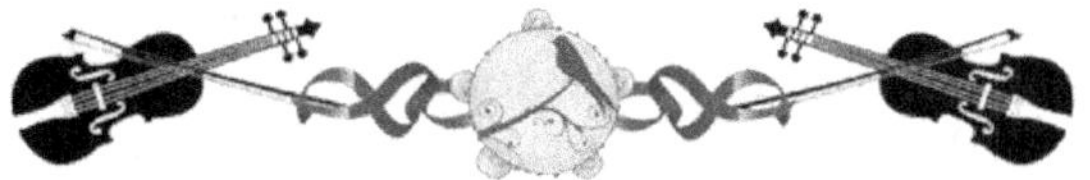

"Lark, what do you make of this?" Rog called softly, beckoning them over to a narrow stand on which was perched a book.

It was a heavy, leather-bound volume, easily a hand's breadth thick, with flimsy ribbons, yellowed with age, marking several places. Lark opened the tome, was startled to see the picture of a basilisk on the left hand page, with a list of ingredients, a diagram of the pentagram on the floor with several runes in various places, and a listing of creatures on the right. She flipped to one of the marked pages, saw the creature she had encountered in the street. The page read 'Chimera'. The 'recipe' on the facing page contained the proper markings needed on the pentagram and the objects needed within it to create the beast, which, according to the book itself, exists nowhere but within the fanciful imaginations of man. The recipe called for a large feline, a bird of prey, and a trio of vipers.

Lark flipped to the next ribboned page; saw the makings of the flock of harpies which called for large predatory or scavenger type birds, and an equal number of women, preferably of foul temperament and questionable disposition. There was even a note at the bottom stating that use of virtuous maids or matrons for the spell would produce something more akin to swanmays than harpies; which was possible with only slight alterations in ingredients and rune placement.

Lark was flipping to the next ribbon, to see what was planned for the next 'random' attack when she heard a loud crack and turned just in time to narrowly avoid a lightning bolt which splintered the stand and sent the book flying. The mage, once more hooded and gloved, stood at the far side of the room, preparing a second spell.

"I have you at last, gypsy!" the mage spat, the voice dripping with the kind of venom only a woman's voice knows. "What shall I make from your bones? A skeletal centaurette? A sphinx? Or whatever monstrosity I can splice together? You seem to like patch-work!"

A lightning bolt cracked from the mage's hand, impacted Lark full in the chest. She felt her heart stop, her breath fall short as she hit the wall behind her. She tried to draw her scimitar but her hand would not obey her. Everything swam before her eyes. She tried to call forth a spell, but could not get the breath to speak the words, much less draw the strength to channel the magic. The column beside her toppled, and she moved before it could hit her, though she seemed to move in slow motion. Another bolt struck her, and her world exploded.

FOUR

Lights flashed all around her, swirling, attacking, buffeting her about as if she were a mere dandelion puff in the wind. Things began to solidify slowly, the lights to condense and combine until they were a bonfire and then scattered. Smaller lights became lanterns hanging on hooks outside a ring of brightly painted wagons. There were people all around, watching the dancer in front of the fire.

She did not recognize anyone, though the roofs of the wagons were red, marking them as Rushavska. A door opened in one of the wagons, and she noticed, in that last moment, the bird house hanging from the eaves. She saw herself, though much older, in more sombre colours, leave the wagon and walk out into the woods. She followed, curious and confused. Just outside of the wagons' range, the woman who was Lark turned and started at seeing her younger herself. The dark eyes narrowed. They were cold and hard, heavy with the weight of being Ranie.

"Has mother sent you for me?" she asked.

"I do not know. I... I think I am dead. But I cannot be...."

The woman shook her head. *"No, you cannot be."*

"Where... where is Landros?" Lark found herself asking.

The woman tilted her head curiously, as if trying to put a face to the name. *"Oh, that elf. I gave him up,"* she said casually. *"I had responsibility to family after all,"* she added, almost defensively.

Lark shrank back into herself, away from this cold, hardened woman who was her. She recoiled from the thought of becoming this creature who lived only for the clan she guarded with nothing left for herself.

She felt something pulling at her, and gladly yielded. Anything to get away from this dark, unwelcome future. She turned, ready to embrace whatever darkness was there rather than follow this path. She found herself suddenly in the arms of her mother in a field filled with wildflowers and butterflies, partly ringed by a stand of protective birch.

She hugged her tightly, held on longer than she knew she should; was not surprised when her mother gently disentangled herself and pushed her to arm's length. It was an act which told Lark that she was not dead yet, but hanging somewhere in between, for it is never well for the living to embrace the ghosts of the dead, no matter how well meaning.

"Daughter, what have you seen?" she asked gently.

Lark looked over her shoulder, though the Romeri camp was gone. *"Nightmare,"* she answered.

"And what do you think made that nightmare?" she asked.

Lark sighed. *"I think she gave up something very precious and very rare and has regretted it ever since. But why did I see that?"*

"Because you need to make that choice," she said tenderly.

She looked back at her mother in shock, at the face that was just as she remembered it. *"What do you mean?"*

"I will show you."

Lark looked around, surprised suddenly to find herself in the taproom of a tavern she could not quite place. It was busy, but not overcrowded. Then she saw Landros enter with a young elven wo-man in his arms. *"When...?"* she began.

"Now," her mother answered.

"Oh...."

He set the woman down at the nearest table and left, returned quickly with a goblet of wine which he gave to her. She seemed quite weak. Lark looked her over carefully. She was bloody and dirty, as if she had fallen in the streets, and Landros himself was covered in blood. The harpies, no doubt. But Lark saw that, under the muck and grime, she was incredibly beautiful. She stared so long and so hard at this woman who could not take her eyes from Landros, that she began to see through her.

Coiled in her breast was a viper, a ghostly serpent which unwound itself just enough to strike at him, trying to poison him. She looked at him, saw after a long moment, a soft, pliant armour surrounding him. An armour of pain it seemed; an old pain. She herself had already encountered this armour, had felt the spikes it could sprout if it felt it necessary. She also saw a weakness in its surface, a dent if you would, a worn, patched place. Something had breached it, or was about to....

Her vision was disturbed by the sudden closeness of the woman to him, feigning weakness so that she could get near enough for the serpent to do its work.

"*Are you all right?*" he asked her. The cadence of his words had an Elvish ring to them, but somehow Lark understood them.

"*I am now,*" she whispered, and kissed him.

She saw the serpent coil around him and rear back to sink its teeth into the back of his neck. She reached out and grabbed for it, hoping it was as much a ghost as she was and therefore solid to her. She made contact, wrestled with the surprised serpent. It managed to free itself, but now she had its attention instead of him, which suited her fine.

Landros, meanwhile, gently untangled himself from the woman, "*My lady....*" he began with obvious embarrassment.

"*Rocilianesianta,*" she purred.

"*I am sorry, Rocilianesianta, I....*"

The woman drew back a little ways, obviously hurt, drank sullenly from her wine, stared coyly into its depths. "*She must be incredibly beautiful, this elven girl,*" she said. The serpent made another strike for him, bit into Lark's hand instead. The bite hurt, but the venom did nothing to her. She continued to fence with the snake, keeping it from obtaining any kind of grip on Landros's armour even when she missed.

He was momentarily confused, then answered, "*She is not elven, but yes, she is very beautiful.*"

There was a surge of triumph in the woman, though her mortal face did not show it. "*Oh, a mere dalliance then. I may have a chance after all,*" she purred, coming closer again, close enough to make fending off the snake difficult for Lark without reaching through people.

Landros shook his head. "*I am not my brother. I do not 'dally' with women.*"

She sat up; even Lark found herself paying more attention. "*Of course it is. It will last, what? A couple decades? One, if you leave once the 'bloom is off the rose', depending on her age now. Fifty years at most if you can stomach living with a crone.*"

Lark could feel an anger beginning to burn in him at these words, and waited to hear what he might say in response. This, of course, was what the woman wanted, to distract them both. Lark knew it the moment she took her eyes off the snake, but she could not help it. She burned to know his answer. The serpent sank its fangs into Landros's armour and clung there. She was helpless to remove it, or to try. All she could do was stand and listen as he stood, moved away.

He gave a polite bow. "*We are elven, and therefore do not understand the ways of the short-lived. That does not make them any less worthy of love because we do not understand them.*" With that, he turned and went upstairs, dislodging the serpent without ever noticing it was there.

She laughed as the woman fumed, was surprised when she turned her glowing-coal eyes on her and the serpent raised its head and spoke to her; but Lark did not stop laughing. "You are dead, gypsssy!" the serpent hissed. "The only way that you will hhhaave hhim isss in the sshadow realm.... and even then...." Then the serpent was laughing, as if it knew a secret Lark did not. But at the moment, she did not care.

"Be that as may be, Longtooth," she chuckled, "but Love will find Love's own way."

The tavern faded around her, and once more she stood with her mother in the field ringed partly by white birch trees. This time, her grandmother was there, and it was her grandmother who spoke.

"*You must choose now, Illyana, between your place within our clan, your power as Ranie, and your gegenta lover.*"

"*Why? Why must I choose?! And why now?!*" Anger replaced her earlier humor, married to an inexplicable grief.

"*Because you must, my child,*" she said, as gently as she could. "*You are dead... and it will take power to bring you back. Power only Ranie has.*"

"*My ring...*" she began.

"*Is only reason you are still between, my little bird,*" said her mother gently. "*And you are not alone in that place you have died.*"

"*You could not elude this choice forever,*" Gruma added.

Lark felt something within her rebelling again. "*Are you saying that I must become Ranie or die? Is that it?*"

"*No,*" her mother said. "*There is moment in our lives when we come into our true power, usually at critical time. Before that can occur, choice must be made, choice of how that power will be used and why; which, in turn, chooses type of power and its strength.*"

"*But I am not ready! I left because I did not want that yet, though you and father both wanted that mantle thrust onto me!*"

"*Your father wants you to be what* he *thinks Ranie should be, and that is not man's place,*" her grandmother said. "*That is why I permitted you to leave, to become that which you are destined to become, to find yourself. But hour of choosing is upon you, Mahril, and so now you must choose.*"

There was a great sadness in her ancient voice, though Lark had no time to process that. She felt the world outside of her reeling, felt her connection to another place slipping slowly, an effect, she guessed, of remaining too long in the realm of shadows. Therefore she would have to choose and soon, or the choice would be irrelevant. She looked to the edge of the woods, saw the shadowy image of the woman who was supposed to be her and shuddered. No, she would die before she became that cold creature, that heartless being that reminded her too much of her father. But there was still her responsibility to the clan. Self-sacrifice was noble enough, but was the price too high? And was she willing to pay it?

"*I have sister,*" she said suddenly. "*Sister who is young, but who is still growing, who may come into her own power, who may take Romeri lover and love well and acceptably. If I leave, our clan will not die, will perhaps be even better served by Ranie who is not dead inside. Therefore I choose Love, whatever pain, agony or hell that brings me to. Mama, I'm sorry,*" she said, turning to her. "*But I follow your lead, though that leads me away from home. I would rather be weak gegenta witch than powerful but hollow Romeri sorceress. I will choose sedentary love over empty life on road. I must trade one love for another.*"

Something happened then, an opening within her. A woman stood before her, of timeless, ageless beauty. Her mother and grandmother stood on either side of Lark, forming a triad. She felt suddenly part of a great cycle, felt the power that flowed continually in circular, familial motions from old to middle to young. Lark knew then, who the woman in their midst was, knew what was happening and what her place was in all things, and, above all, what she had chosen.

"*Mahril, Mahren, Magruma,*" she breathed in awed reverence as the woman reached out and touched her forehead.

"Welcome to your power!" the goddess said.

She felt a surge run through her body yet again, like the lightning but different, wholesome, ecstatic. She felt a tugging begin, pulling her back to her body, a pulling *at* her body. Lark opened her eyes to find herself staring at the pocked, smoke-stained ceiling of the chamber, being discreetly dragged out of the room between a gap in the walls opened by a fallen column. She tilted her head back; saw Billy tugging at her arm little by little while keeping his eyes on the combatants beyond them.

Nightingale, sensing her return to consciousness and her desire not to attract attention just yet, gently pecked at Billy's shoulder, on which he was currently perched. Billy looked up at him, annoyed, then felt Lark's fingers tap his wrist. He nearly jumped out of his skin.

She rolled onto her side, still trying to be as quiet as possible, and got to her hands and knees. Across the room she saw Rog and the mage locked in mortal combat. Rog had gotten too close too quickly for the mage to cast spells at him, having wasted all his or her concentration upon Lark. She stood, feeling strong and confident and fearless. Was she not her clan's Mahril, the Maiden? as her mother had been the Mahren, the Mother, and her grandmother was the Magruma, the Grandmother? Every Ranie was each of the goddess's aspects in her season. Lark knew she was still not ready yet to take over from her gruma, knew that her clan was not ready for her, but she was still a Ranie. She felt the power and the knowledge surge within her, protective.

She gestured for Billy to step back out of the way and strode fully into the room in spite of his attempt to stop her. She stood there for a moment, in the centre of the pentagram, waited until the mage realized she was not lying dead on the floor, and smiled. Rog looked up, saw her and his jaw dropped open. The mage took advantage of his momentary distraction and kicked him backwards, out of the way.

Lark said nothing, did nothing, as the mage gathered up the energy in the room and prepared to hurl it at her. "You should have stayed dead," the mage growled in a deep voice.

She did not flinch as the ball of eldritch energy shot towards her, nor did she dodge. Instead, she merely lifted her hand and drew Eolh in the air, a rune which glowed with a warm fire and hung there before her. The energy ball struck the rune and erupted around it, dissipating in a brilliant, but harmless display of light and electricity.

"My turn," she said sweetly. She twisted sideways and began to draw another rune in the air, this one on a horizontal plane, Sigil, the lightning bolt. "Is for Savaren," she said softly, and whipped the last line of the rune towards the mage like a sling. A bolt of lightning formed from the rune and shot straight for the mage, was not completely dodged.

Rog, very wisely moved sideways out of range.

Lark fired again, "Is for children you stole," she intoned as the mage scrambled to cast some kind of protective magic.

A bubble-like shield went up around the black robes, shimmered, but yielded to the incoming lightning. This time the mage was thrown back, toppled a column, though it seemed that the shield had softened the blow some. The mage staggered, tried to cast another, more offensive spell.

Lark struck again, "Is for Ebastion and all others who died because of you."

The bolt again found its mark, some of its potency leached out by the shimmering bubble which seemed to hold and maintain the power for itself. As the mage fell, scrambled to escape, the hood fell back, revealing flat, oily, dark grey hair slicked back close against the head, but a mask remained in place, still obscuring the mage's gender and race, the shape of the head was too androgynous.

Lark drew one last Sigil without noticing the fine traces of dust that were beginning to filter down from a ceiling overstressed by the energies being released beneath it. "And this one..." she said. "This one is for me!"

This bolt struck the mage full in the chest, caused a backlash within the shield as the mage tried to strengthen it. Before Lark could do anything else, she felt two pairs of hands grab her from behind and pull her from the chamber. Off balance from being dragged backwards by both arms, she stumbled and fell. She found herself quickly buried under the protective bodies of both the dwarf and the boy as an explosion rocked the tunnel and the vile chamber just beyond them collapsed in on itself. When the dust finally settled, they got up, helped Lark to her feet and Billy began to lead them out of the tunnels.

Lark felt the power which had welled up earlier subside with the need for it. It was still there, though dormant now. A strange high possessed her, a need, an urge that cried for expression. She yielded to it, dazed and hungry for any purpose or guidance. They passed by numerous tunnels and sewer exits, headed no doubt, for the one they had come in through. As Lark brushed wordlessly past one set of rungs embedded in the wall, the desire to exit here seized her, and she yielded without a thought.

Below her, she heard Rog call to Billy, "Where the hells does this one go?"

"Pops out near th' temples I fink," Billy answered. "Hey, Lark!" he exclaimed, looking back and realizing why he had been asked the question.

"Let 'er go," Rog said. "She probably needs the healin'."

She was only vaguely aware of footsteps on the rungs below her as she moved the sewer lid and climbed out onto the street. People swarmed out of the way, leery of anything coming up out of the sewers.

She found herself facing the gate to the main Temple of Three, nearest the House of the Old One. She walked in, climbed the steps without hesitation, noticing very little on her way to the main altar. No one tried to stop her, though one or two tried to offer assistance which she ignored. She stopped at the offering plate, just under the statue of the goddess, offered forth a small, reverently bold prayer and, having no money, laid one of her rings in the plate.

Without a word or an acknowledgment of an approaching priest's stunned murmur of thanks, she walked away, letting her newly awakened urge lead her to a secret side passage connecting this hall of offering to that of the Matron. This time she laid a bangle in the plate, offered her thanks and left without waiting for question, thanks or offer of aid, short-cutting yet again to the Maiden's hall to repeat the process. Then she left the temple through the Maiden's gate.

She was manic, bordering on madness as she moved through the crowds. She headed purposefully towards her destination, though she had no real idea where she was going.

Landros was sitting in the taproom of the Golden Cygnet, drinking from a deep mug of weak ale and trying to fathom why the unknown, drop-dead gorgeous elven woman had suddenly come on to him, and why in the whole of the Abyss had he brushed her off, especially when the reasons he gave were not guaranteed. He heard someone push violently through the doors, looked up and saw Lark glancing about, wild-eyed.

He stood. She saw him and crossed immediately, seized his head in both hands and pulled him into a deep and hungry kiss. The elven woman was that easily banished from his thoughts.

The few people in the taproom began to cheer, giving shouts of encouragement, especially when Landros found himself sitting in his chair again and Lark had yet to let go. There was a desperation in the embrace that felt wrong somehow. And he smelled ozone. He disentangled himself with difficulty, saw the scorch marks on her blouse, the charred and frayed edges of her vest laces, the dirt and other smudges on her face and hands, and the wildness in her eyes. She smelled like a lightning struck tree.

He stood, ignoring the jeers of the taproom's denizen's, held her at arm's length long enough to assess how badly she had been hurt. "Goddess!" he swore. "What in the nine hells happened to you?!" he demanded, feeling a panic beginning deep in his chest.

She just smiled, looked into his eyes as the mania slowly began to ebb and she was once again her own master. Her voice was a bit hoarse as she answered, "I got religion," and reached for another kiss.

A wave of dizziness swept over her as he picked her up in his arms. "No, am fine," she protested.

He turned to the nearest employee, a young scullery boy who doubled on errands. "You, go straight to the temple and get Sister Rue! Tell her to bring her herbs and be quick!" He turned to the bartender who had come out from behind the bar to investigate. "Ben, send me up a bath, a stew and a bottle of strong wine."

"I'll do what I can," the man replied.

With that, he turned and trotted up the stairs to his room two at a time, completely ignoring Lark's weak protests.

He opened the door, whisked her into the bedroom, ripped the covers back with one hand and set her on the mattress without a word. Scraps, who had been asleep between the pillows, chattered his protests and waddled away to find a quieter place to sleep. Nightingale arrived on the window, watching Landros with amusement even as Lark watched him with love. That he was fussing over her so desperately told her everything she needed to know about how he felt about her, that and his earlier resistance to the succubus.

"Am fine, love. Am Mahril now. All is well."

Landros started at the word Mahril. It was very similar to an Elvish word for maiden, usually used only when referring to *the* Maiden. She must have hit her head, he thought, began tucking her in.

Rue called from the open door, "Landros? Lark?"

He crossed to the bedroom door, surprised. "That was fast! What'd you do? Teleport?"

She shook her head. "No, I followed her from the temple."

Landros felt his fear shift to anger. "She was at the temple?"

"Yes. She came in without a word, dropped a gold bracelet into the offering plate and left. Word is she left something in everyone's plate, one on each altar."

He crossed the room and seized Rue by the shoulders. "And YOU LET HER GO!?"

"Landros!" she exclaimed. "Let go and calm yourself!" He released his grip immediately, took a step back. "She seemed out of it, but otherwise healthy, and she did not ask for healing," she answered, straightening out her robes. "Besides, Mother Mylenai would not let us stop her. She told me to follow her, but not to interfere. The goddess has her own plan for that one," she snapped, pointing to the other room. "It is not for me to second guess that, nor for you! Now if you will get out of my way I will go and see what, if anything, is wrong with her!"

As Rue brushed past him, he grabbed her arm, looked up into her eyes, just slightly above his. "When I asked her what had happened, she said she had 'got religion'. I will want to talk with you about this 'religion business' when you are done," he ground.

She jerked her arm free without taking her eyes from him and went into the bedroom, slamming the door behind her.

"There is nothing wrong with me," Lark croaked.

"Except maybe your voice?" she said with a raised brow. "Let me be the judge of that."

"Nightingale flew," she cracked with a smile as the bird sailed down to land on her knee.

Rue smiled back and nodded as she would to a child. "Yes, I know. Billy handed him to me outside the temple. I spared a little spell for him. It's getting too dangerous for him to be grounded. Now be quiet and look at me."

FIVE

Landros paced the room outside. Water bearers arrived with the bath water, filled the tub silently and left. The scullery left a tray with a bowl of thin but steaming stew, a dusty bottle of old, red wine and a pair of goblets. He kept thinking, getting nowhere, wondering what in hell's name Mother Mylenai had to do with all of this.

Rue finally came into the room and sank down onto the sofa just as Landros was closing the front door.

"Is she....?"

"Fine," she breathed.

"Fine? She thinks she is a goddess! What do you mean fine?!"

"Goddess?" Rue asked, leaning forward. "What makes you think she thinks that?"

"She said she was Mahril now, Mahril...."

"Is the Maiden, I know," she nodded. "It is quite common for some cultures to refer to their priestesses by a derivative form of the goddess's name: Mother, Grandmother, Sister. If you think about it, the high priestess is in a way the earthly representative. A minor avatar, if you will."

Landros could not shake a sense of foreboding that explanation suddenly evoked. He began to pace again. "What happened to her? Did she say?"

"Apparently she was struck by a magical lightning bolt," she said, propping her elbow up on the back of the sofa and resting her head on her hand.

"Lightning," he repeated.

"Yes, lightning. Several times."

He exploded. **"What kind of damned religion lightning bolts their followers**?!"

She got up, tired, stood in front of him with her hands on her hips. "Why don't you go ask her? Instead of standing here yelling at me?" With that, she snatched up her small medical bag and headed out the door. She paused in the door-frame, "Let her take a long, hot bath, let her soak a while. Feed her and let her rest. She'll be fine in the morning. How I don't know. She took two lightning bolts to the chest," she added as she closed the door.

Landros, regaining his composure, went into the other room. To his irritation, Lark was standing at the window entertaining a pretty little bluebird which Nightingale seemed to be trying to im-press. The bird flew off as he approached, snatched Lark up and put her back onto the bed. Nightingale complained vociferously and flew off after his friend.

"Landros...." she complained in a tired voice.

"Do you want food or bath first?" he asked. His tone told her nothing she said would be heard until both events had occurred to his satisfaction.

"Will you join?" she asked.

He thought a moment, picturing her and him in a hot steamy bath, "Food, yes. Bath, no," he said sternly.

Lark sighed. The beast she had met on the Andromeda was back. She got up, or tried to. Landros put his arm out and stopped her. "Bath," she growled, waited until he picked her up and carried her into the bathing room.

She insisted on standing to undress herself, tossing her singed, dirty, sewer-mucked clothes at him. She managed to get her skirt onto his head and slipped into the steaming water before he could get it off. He took the clothes into the other room, dropped them into a corner to be dealt with later. He pulled a shirt out of his chest of drawers and brought it back into the bath room. She was nowhere to be seen.

"Lark?" he called.

Just as the panic was beginning to rise up in his throat again, she came up out of the water, pushing her wet hair back out of her face. "Hmmm?" she mumbled, looking up at him. "You say something?"

He sat down on the stool beside the tub, let all the held air leak out of his lungs. "No," he said.

Lark shrugged and sank back in the water, savouring the clean heat after the cold stink of the sewers. Landros just watched her bathe, calming himself as she soothed her own tired muscles.

"Mmmm," she murmured. "Should have eaten first. Now am sleepy."

Landros moved the stool to the head of the tub, began to wash her hair for her, gently massaging the muscles of her neck and shoulders. She relaxed even farther. After a few minutes of this, she jumped.

"What?!" Landros cried, afraid he had hurt her.

"Was... fell asleep," she admitted, half turning to look back at him, her cheeks rosy from the steam. She quickly slipped under the water, rinsing herself completely and stood. "Should get out. Stay too long and will pickle."

He wrapped her in a thick towel, dried her off himself. She leaned languidly into the caresses, savouring the attention and the tiny expressions of caring. She did not know if he realized them as such, but to her they were endearments nonetheless.

When she was dry, he handed her the shirt, which she coyly slipped over her head and pulled down to cover her nakedness. She made no moves to lace up the front however, let it hang tantalizingly open. He did not say anything about it, but tried to keep his eyes away. He carried her back into the bedroom, laid her on the bed and tucked her in, propping up the pillows so she could sit up. Then returned to the front room and brought back the tray of food.

Scraps was sitting politely on the bed next to her, leaning back against the pillows as if waiting for supper to be brought to him as well. He laughed, which made her look over to see what was amusing him. She tickled the furry little thief, chasing him off the bed long enough to eat her food in peace.

Landros sat down on the edge of the bed, drank a glass of the wine as he watched her. At least she had a good appetite, he noticed. When she was done, she shared the heel of her bread between the bird and the raccoon and Landros took the tray, but insisted she finish the wine. It was very good, and he had to wonder where the proprietor had been hiding it.

He set the tray outside the door and returned to tuck her in.

"Am fine," she protested.

"Rue said you needed rest," he insisted, "so you might as well get comfortable. When you are feeling better, and are up to the task, you can tell me what happened. Perhaps in the morning."

"Perhaps now," she said firmly, grabbing his wrist and pulling him down to sit beside her. "*You* get comfortable. Is story should hear, not that Billy will not give full report later, and I wish to hear his side. Only remember so much."

"What was Billy doing in the fight?"

"Don't know. Did not see all fight. Only saw him dragging me out of way when came to."

"What was Billy doing with you in the first place?"

"He led us through tunnels. Was supposed to hold familiar and stay back, run if was trouble and get bigger help." She shrugged, "Guess did not listen to orders well. Now you going to listen or no?"

Landros sighed, sat down beside her, rubbed the back of her hand tenderly.

"Had gone wandering this morning, out in marketplace when Billy came to fetch. Said Rog was in sewer and asking for me and only me. So went with him." She filled him in quickly, and the closer she came to her experience beyond, the more excited she became.

Landros found it disturbing. She was describing being struck by lightning with the excitement of a fanatic.

She felt the tension in his hand, pulled it to her lips and kissed it, looked deep into his honey-golden eyes. "Yes, think came close to dying, but not dead. ...Had my initiation, might say. Am now Ranie! Cannot deny it any more!"

Landros felt his heart slam against his ribs and stop beating. Being Ranie meant she would leave now, that she would go away and lead her clan as she had always been intended to do.

"Have no caravan, true," she went on, oblivious to his pain, "but Ranie no less! Know what is mean now, 'Ranie', what Power means and is, where is come from!"

"I suppose I shall have to find a way to get you back to your clan," he said, feeling himself grow very cold inside.

She kissed him suddenly, surprised him by laughing. "Silly, Kestrel. If desire to leave this place, could walk out of bedroom door and be outside of city. All ever needed was to ask mother to come home and Gruma would send gate. No, is not mean am going to lead Rushavska clan. Not yet. That am still not ready to do. Not while Father runs things, or Gruma remains even partly in this world. There would be more conflict than is good for caravan. So, for now, am without caravan, like prince without kingdom, but who is no less prince, but, like that prince, subjects equal power. No, am not leaving. For moment, *this* is my caravan," she purred, and, taking his face gently in hand, kissed him.

He felt suddenly comforted by those words, though 'for the moment' seemed to deny everything else, but at least for that 'moment' he was content. Maybe with enough time.... As he stood, something else she had said clicked in his brain finally.

"Wait. You can gate out of here at any time? Even the man who 'ported us out to find the children can't just do that anymore. How? Why didn't you..."

She pulled him back down to the bed. "Shhh," she soothed, smiling. "Is not so easy. *I* can do nothing of sort. Even if knew how. Message to my Gruma, it takes. She sends gate. Is small, and different magic, so slips past siege barrier. So, no, cannot use to get army outside. I do not know rules, but know there are rules."

Getting his hopes under control, he got up and went back into the bathing room, fetched his brother's oils from the small cabinet where they were kept. He went back into the bedroom with the bottle in hand. "I think it is time you rested," he said and tugged the shirt off over her head.

"Thought you said rest?" she grinned as she looked up at him from underneath static charged hair.

"I did," he said and gently but insistently rolled her onto her stomach. She gave a tiny yelp as he poured a small amount of oil into the small of her back. "Sorry, I did not have time to warm it."

She looked over her shoulder at him, her nose twitching with the sharp aroma of the juniper oil. As he began to rub it into her skin she felt a sudden, forced relaxation overcome her. She dropped her head down onto the bed, her hands under the pillow as she moaned.

Scraps trotted up, sat down on her pillow and watched curiously. After a few minutes, he began to mimic Landros, rubbing his tiny fingers through Lark's hair, massaging her scalp. She suppressed a giggle, and Landros chuckled. After a few minutes of this, Scraps became bored with the exercise and wandered off in search of leftovers.

As his hands caressed the back of her neck and shoulders in long, powerful strokes, she found it harder and harder to remain awake enough to enjoy the massage. Apparently he realized this, for he suddenly growled, "Stop trying to fight it and just sleep."

"But is feel so good. Don't," she moaned, "want to miss... every... moment...."

"The whole point of this is to put you to sleep," he replied.

"Oh," she murmured. That was the last thing he heard from her. Before he had reached her feet, she was out. Not wanting to leave the job unfinished, he completed the massage as he would have had she remained awake before covering her up with the blankets and seating himself in the nearby rocker.

He sat in the chair by the fireplace long afterwards, listening to the crack and pop of the fire. He watched her intently, her face turned slightly towards him. She had a different kind of beauty when she slept, something that made you not wish to disturb her peace, a childlike innocence.

'I have to be crazy,' he said to himself. 'Lying there is a human who has begun to enchant a heart I thought would never feel again. Why?'

His more suspicious side answered, playing the devil's advocate, trying to find logical, though pessimistic answers. 'Could be any reason. Could be a ruse. You could be no more than a source of protection. She is a Romer after all, and to a Romeri any non-Romer is merely someone to use.'

'Then why is she here?' he asked that niggling side of himself. 'She came asking for nothing, just to be here. Rue gave me the impression she thought Lark had been led here. Look at her, she sleeps so peacefully. She has to be content.'

'Content that she has the best of you?' he asked himself. 'Ahhh, be wary of falling for her. Loving her could be a tragic mistake. She is not only a Romer, she is human. They have short lifespans and do not take love as seriously as elves do.'

'But, perhaps because of that short lifespan they take it more seriously?'

'Letting the girl in could be a mistake,' his mind insisted, tried to tighten the armour against the sleeping angel.

'Not letting her in could also be one. She has managed to stir up feelings that have been dormant for too long. Maybe it is simply time to start feeling again?'

'How do you know?' he argued. 'What is she feeling? Do you know that? She may feel nothing at all for you. You could very well be just another mark, or someone to enjoy for the moment and forget as soon as she is gone.'

He sighed. 'Maybe, but maybe as well I can win *her* heart. She just admitted she could have left here at any time. She chose me over others more powerful and more wealthy. After introducing her to Lord Colwyn she still comes to me, not to him. If I were just a source of security and wealth she would have turned to Colwyn as soon as my back was turned. Obviously, I provide her with something other than wealth and security, something hopefully only I can give.'

He sat back, brooding, covered his mouth thoughtfully as he leaned on the arm of the chair. 'She is so beautiful lying there,' he thought, as if that one thought outweighed everything else in the world.

He looked up out the window, realized that he had been watching her purely by firelight. He did not want to go, to leave her, but night had fallen and he wanted answers from Billy. He steeled his resolve, forced himself to get up and walk out the bedroom door.

Once the inn was behind him it was somewhat easier. He strode out into the night, a bag of food slung over his shoulder, feeling strangely good about the world in general. She had been hurt and she came to him, not seeking healing, not seeking help, but because she wanted to see him and had not wanted to wait for aid. If she were elven he would have an inkling as to what that meant but, being human and Romeri, it could mean anything, everything or nothing.

It was a pleasant night, in spite of the distant rattle of combat. He kept his eyes open for possible attacks, or more wandering monsters, even though he had a feeling that Lark had unwittingly destroyed the source of those monsters, or at least had buried the means to make them. He shuddered thinking of those five women who had been transformed and murdered. He felt that the mage had murdered them as if his hand had held those swords. Or was that *her* hand? He shook off that train of thought as he opened the back gate to the orphanage and slipped quietly into the kitchen.

He was surprised by the number of candles that were lit in the house. It was late, but it seemed that there were quite a few people up and more adults than this house normally held. Billy slipped into the kitchen as Landros was trading sacks. The boy put a finger to his lips and, taking a candle from a drawer, led him down into the root cellar to report.

No sooner was the door securely closed and the candle lit, Landros laid into him.

"Do you want to explain to me what the hells happened down there this afternoon?!"

"Sir?" Billy asked, startled.

"You were in the sewers this afternoon. There was a fight. Lark came straight to me after getting out and I want to know what happened down there!"

Billy began to fidget nervously. "I seen th' dwarf crawl outta one uv th' tunnels. 'E was too close to th' warren, so's I was gonna leads 'im away. 'E tells me ta go gets Lark and be quick abou' it! I went an' gotter. 'E'd foun' this place uv magic an' wanted 'er to tell 'im what i's for. Tha' hooded person, th' mage? was there an weavin' a spell-like, see? When 'e was done, was these 'arpies an' then they's all vanished. We went in to take a look see. Rog foun' 'is book on makin' monsters, i' looked like. Lark were lookin' it over, then suddenly tha' mage was back and shoots 'er wif a bolt a' lightnin' from 'is 'and! She knocked over a column when she fell, an' th' mage 'it 'er again! Rog was able ta get close enough ta fight 'and ta 'and. I snuck aroun' back a' th' wall an' tried ta drag Lark outta th' fight while Rog 'ad th' mage occupied."

"Why didn't you leave immediately to go for help?!" he growled. "You could have gotten yourself killed and no one would have known one way or another what had happened!"

"Wha', an' leave th' lady down in th' fight ta git killed if she weren't all ready? Wha' you take me for?! A coward?" he exclaimed indignantly. "I wa'n' about ta take on tha' mage, I ain't stupid! But I wa'n' gonna leave a lady 'urt!"

Landros looked at him, still angry, but controlled himself. "No, you are not a coward, but if the lady and you and the dwarf had been trapped, then we would not know how to find any of you. From now on, all soldiers of the underground will travel in pairs. That way, one can go and get help if needed. Understood?"

Billy nodded, though sullenly, "Besides," he added, "she sudd'nly gets up and goes after th' mage, throwin' lightnin' o' 'er own! Brought tha bloody roof in! Rog an' I barely gots 'er out in time! I don' fink she even noticed th' cave in! But," he added, changing his tone and reaching into his shirt, "I gots this while she was beatin' up onna mage." He opened up a large piece of paper, showing it to Landros against the candle. "It was inna small back corna' near where's I was trying ta get Lark out frough."

Landros turned the paper over, recognized it as a rough map of the city. On it in various places, were deliberate ink marks. "I'll take this to Lord Colwyn, see if he can make out quite what these may correspond to," he mused. "It is obvious these are marking something. Is this all you recovered?"

Billy shrugged with a grin. "No, sir, but tha's already been divvied up, your gen'ralship, sir! I'll be gettin' th' princess 'er share sometime soon!"

"How about my place tomorrow morning," he said. "I don't want her disturbed tonight. She needs her rest."

Billy just grinned, saluted and disappeared into the shadows of the cellar. When Landros raised the candle to see where he had gone, he saw a barrel board swing back into place and no other signs of the boy.

He growled to himself and tucked the map away. He went back upstairs, returned the candle to its drawer and left for Colwyn's.

As it turned out, the knight had already gone to bed after a very long and tiring series of meetings of the Lord's Council. Landros decided that what he had to tell him could wait until morning. Besides, there was a gorgeous, nubile young woman asleep in his bed.

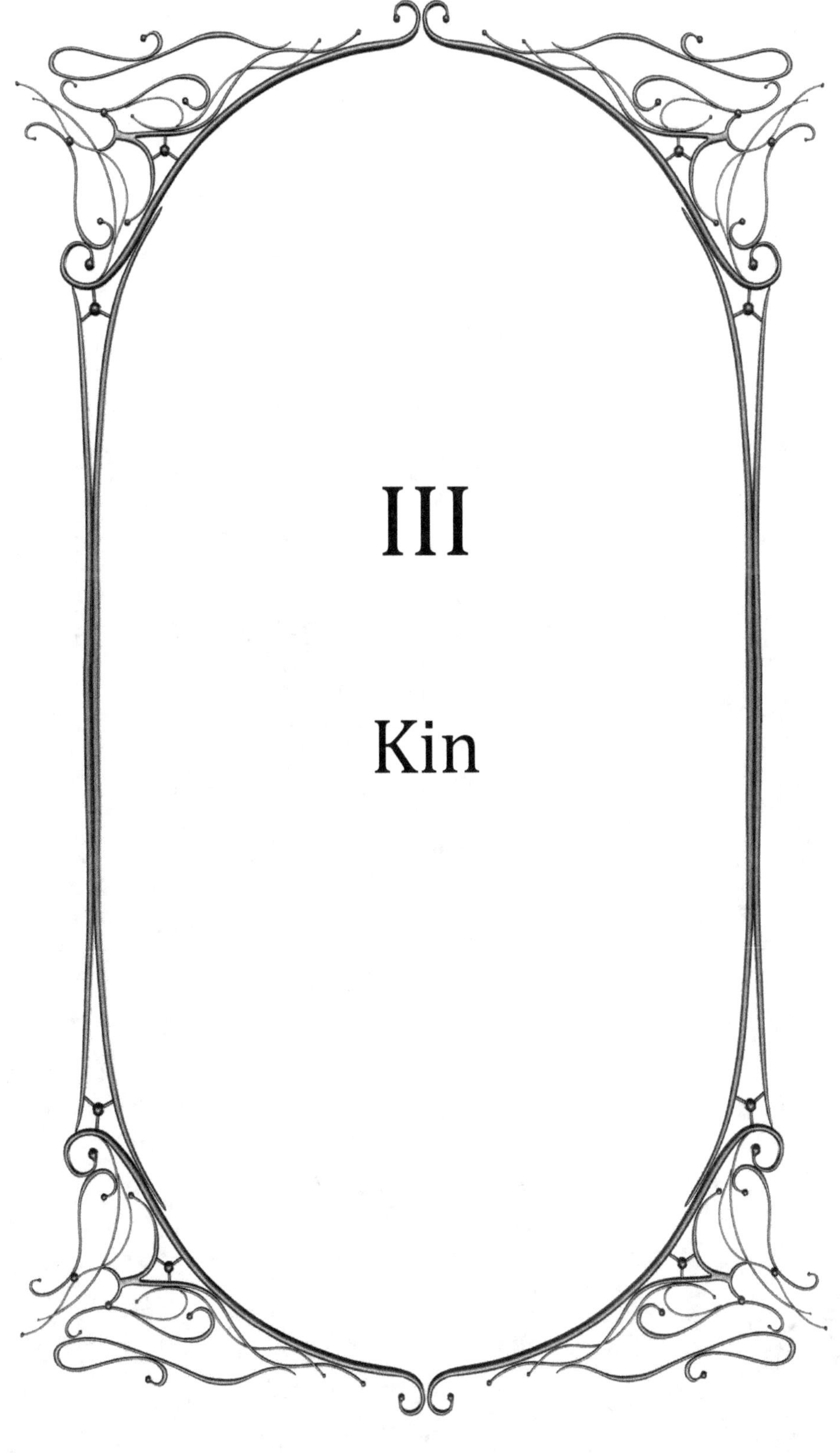

III

Kin

ONE

Lark awoke the next morning to find a note on her pillow:

> Have gone to make a report and to run a few errands. I will be back very soon, so please do not disappear on me again. If you desire breakfast, just ask the staff to send something up.
>
> Landros

She sat up, looking over the note again, admiring the handsome elvish flavour to the script. Scraps was curled up just under the blanket next to her,no doubt having immediately filled the warm spot Landros had vacated. She ruffled his ears gently, which made his tail twitch a bit, but did not seem to wake him. The shirt she had been loaned after her bath was hanging on the bed post beside her and she snatched it up, slipping it on.

Nightingale, who was dozing on the mantle in the other room, warned Lark that the door had opened and that Landros was not the person who had walked in. She bade him to keep out of sight.

She listened intently, worried by the fact that the man made no noise as he crossed the floor. She looked about hoping for a weapon close at hand, saw nothing but a dagger on the night stand. The bedroom door swung open as she snatched it up, and she saw a man all in black, hidden beneath a deeply hooded cloak. She felt her blood freeze as she realized he was the man that Nightingale had seen trying to follow her out of the inn some time ago. In fact, he had been tailing her for some time now. She scrambled upright, curling one foot under her and the other bent, ready to spring away should she need to, and keenly aware that Landros's shirt was the only thing she had on.

As if surprised to see someone actually in the room, the man started to draw his own sword. He stopped, looked her over with a hint of amusement and sheathed his blade. Scraps suddenly jumped from the bed into the man's arms, began chattering an enthusiastic greeting that knocked back the man's hood.

He was elven, slightly taller than Landros, and slimmer, more wiry. His hair was a darker gold bordering on brown, but his features reminded her very much of her lover, especially when he smiled. Though there was a bit more... arrogance? snideness? to him. She could not place quite what it was about that smile that disturbed her.

When he spoke, his voice was huskier than Landros's, with a harder edge, though still apparently well-suited to silky words and pretty phrases. "Hello to you, too, little one!" he laughed with surprising genuineness. "I see you have learned a new trick! Picking pockets!" he added in admiration as the raccoon came up with a small pouch of dried apples and leapt to the bed with his prize. He watched the animal curl up next to Lark's unconsciously well-displayed, bare leg and gave her another look-over that left her shivering.

"It seems that he has taken a fancy to you, my lady," he said, unfastening his cloak and throwing it on the chair. He eyed her still tense grip on the dagger, grinned, apparently amused to no end. "You will not need that," he said, gesturing to the knife. "But if you feel you must have a weapon, you could go for the blade above the mantle in the other room."

She just continued to stare at him. What did he take her for? she thought.

"Oh, that's right, you'd have to pass me to get it, wouldn't you? How stupid of me. Here," he said, unbuckling his sword belt and tossing the scabbard lightly onto the bed just inches from her knees. "Though you will need neither blade. I never set out to harm a lady."

Scraps watched the exchange as he ate, disturbed by the obvious tension between two of his favourite people, but not enough for it to spoil his appetite.

Lark watched the elf ease himself into the chair and rock it back, steepling his fingers, watching her intently with eyes like wild honey. She tossed the dagger to her left hand and drew the sword with the other in a single motion. The elf raised an eyebrow.

"Really," he began. "Am I so much a threat, pretty one?"

"You have been following me," she said in a slow, steady voice.

"Ah!" he exclaimed, leaning back more comfortably and resting his left ankle on his right knee. "You noticed. And so I have, so I have."

It disturbed her that it did not seem to bother him that she had noticed. "Why?"

"Why?" he chuckled, as if the reason should have been obvious. "Have you not noticed a resemblance? Do I not remind you of someone?"

She said nothing, continued to glare at him cautiously as he struck a vain pose intended to call attention to his features.

He sighed. "I do apologize for startling you, sweet lady, but I had rather expected to be sneaking up on someone else." He stood, gave an expansive, sweeping bow. "Allow me to introduce myself. I am called The Bold, Portholus the Bold. Rogue by profession, scoundrel by the grace of the goddesses, at your service. And you, my dear, are Lark, the lady whom my brother has spoken very highly of. I had hoped we might meet face to face, but had not expected it quite so soon."

"Does not explain why you follow me," she said threateningly.

With a mocking smile, he tried to lower the tip of the sword with two black gloved fingers. He seemed somewhat disconcerted when the blade would not move. "Is it not obvious? I desired to find out more about you and had promised my brother I would 'stay away from you'. So, instead I have watched. And I must say, I like not all of what I see. Especially your taking a Gypsy man home with you last night," he added casually.

"What relatives I invite to my wagon is no business of gegenta," she snarled.

His face seemed to relax. "Ah, a relative. I hope for my brother's sake that you are not lying to me." Before Lark could get actively ruffled, he held up a hand, "Before you say anything, I would you hear me out. I know of your Gypsy heritage, and I know your kind do not 'dally' with those not of your nomadic race. Any dealings you have with non-Gypsy are purely for profit, whether honest trade or trickery. If it is money you seek, my brother has none. He spends much of what he does have on the children and the poor. He is also currently struggling to gather funds to arm a force of troops to aid in the war effort, something he has been working on for some time. If I had funds myself, I would give everything to him, for he has been nothing but supportive and loyal to me, his younger brother. There are no jewels or riches to be found here." He paused a moment, but not long enough for Lark to lay into him as she so desperately wanted to do.

"If you seek to cause him harm in any way, know that you will not succeed. Though it is not always apparent, my brother, in my opinion, is destined for much in this city and in this land and I will do whatever I can to see that destiny comes to pass. My brother could be one of this city's greatest heroes, a true knight, if he chose to do so. I feel that this may never happen since he seems to have such a dislike for the pomp and circumstance that surrounds human knighthood. But he has a heart and soul purer than any knight I have ever met. It is a shame that knighthood can not be awarded on that principal alone, as it is among elven-kind."

Portholus picked up the poker and stirred the fire, looked over his shoulder at the still-seething woman struck dumb by the force of her rage. "He believes that he is in love with you," he said.

She felt something else strike her with those words, that moved her to a different kind of silence.

"The fact that Scraps likes you is a point in your favour, but *I* am still concerned. I have watched you for several days now, watched you work crowds of leering men, flirt and tease. I can tell you that your behaviour leaves me wondering as to your intentions. My brother is all the family that I have. I do not know if he has told you what happened to our family."

Lark's eyes were unreadable. She had known something had happened to Landros to build that suit of armour she had seen while in the shadowlands, but not what. Portholus did not stop to give her time to dwell on the revelation.

"That will be for him to tell or no, but I will tell you that you have his heart in your hands. I suggest you walk very softly with it. Breaking that heart could destroy him and if you chose to do that, I would suggest you put your affairs in order, because I *will* come for you and seek retribution for what you have done. If you truly care for him, tell him soon or leave and allow him to heal."

His gaze on her was cold and hard, belying the fanciful, gay and charming exterior he affronted, more in line with the sharp black clothing he wore. "He wonders how he could have been so fortunate to have attracted the attentions of such a lovely creature as yourself, and in that respect, I too wonder, for you are a very lovely young woman indeed. But be that as it may, there is much you do not know of my brother, and I will not let you hinder him in the slightest."

There was something familiar in the way the elf stood and postured. There was a protective concern overlaying the threat, leaving her no doubt that he would make the attempt to carry it out regardless of what it might cost him. She had seen a similar posture on his brother, though with slightly less arrogance.

He threw his cloak over his shoulders, fastened the simple sterling clasp. "If your intentions are honourable and true, then I offer my sincerest apologies for offending you. But if they are not, then I will hunt down and exterminate every member of your family from the face of the earth, and I have a very long life *and* the patience to do so. He would give his life for you right now, and do whatever it takes to protect you. Do not take advantage of him or you *will* have me to deal with.

"Heed my words well, my lady," he added and closed the bedroom door behind him.

By the time Lark got off the bed and opened that door, the front one had already closed. In frustrated anger, she threw the sword across the room, watched it clatter uselessly against the wall. She then threw herself down onto the sofa, staring at the dead coals in the fireplace and sulked.

A few minutes later, after Scraps had crawled into her lap in an attempt to soften her mood, the door opened and Landros walked in.

There was a hint of nervousness in his smile as he gazed at her. "You look better in that shirt than I do," he mused. "But, maybe you might prefer this instead?" he offered, unwrapping a new set of clothes. The blouse was white, ruffled at the throat and wrist, and the skirt was a pastel swirl of rainbow colour. "I hope it fits," he added as she drifted over.

"Is lovely," she said without conviction, taking the dress and heading for the other room.

He took her hand, kissed it. His eyes scoured her face for some explanation of the sudden indifference. Her odd behaviour made him wary. "Was my brother just here? I passed him on my way in, but he merely waved and went on without a word. I had wanted the two of you to meet. He can be a bit headstrong, I'll admit, but I hope you like him."

Lark looked into his eyes, saw the worry born of love in them and knew what Portholus had said about Landros had been true. But there was no joy in her heart right now, only far more problems to be solved. "If was who said he was, then yes, was here." She started to move away again, intent on getting dressed, but he pulled her close.

"Lark, what is the matter? Did he say something to upset you? Tell me what is wrong," he begged.

She pressed a light kiss to his lips. "No. What is matter is not for you to solve or deal. But rest easy, will be dealt, and hopefully soon." With that, she left him alone and slipped into the bedroom to change.

His mind began to race in manic circles. Something had obviously occurred between those two and he was damned if he knew what. He turned to put his things away and saw the sword lying on the floor. He picked it up, recognized it as his brother's. Something had *definitely* happened. Judging from what Lark had said, she was not about to tell him, so he would have to ask Portholus. He had to get his sword back to him anyway.

Lark spun in from the other room, the rainbow skirts flowing around her. The lightness of the colours set off her dark complexion well. She was obviously making an attempt at being cheerful, but there was still an undercurrent of ...something. Before he could comment, there was a knock on the door. Growling, he ripped it open, doubting seriously it was the person he wanted to take a piece out of. Portholus would not have knocked.

He was surprised to see Billy standing there, all grins.

"Mornin', Gen'ral!" he piped with a tip of his ragged cap. "Th' Lady still in residence?"

Landros stepped out of the way. "Come on in, South," he sighed.

Billy strode over to Lark, hat in hand and bowed flamboyantly. "Top o' th' mornin', Princess!" he crowed. "Rog an' I 'ope sincerely yer 'ighness is well? Was a nasty set you took yestid'y, ma'am, tho' equally nasty what yous dealt," he added, leaning in with a grin and a conspiring tone.

"Am well, Cardinal, thank you. But is not well you should go about calling me 'Princess'. Are dangers in strangers knowing."

The look on the boy's face was almost comical. "You mean yous a real... yous real roy'lty? I...I only fought... coz Nav'rie called yous... like a faery tale, a nickname... not 'at yous...." He dropped to his knees in front of her, staring at the floor as he wrung his hat in his hands. "F'give me, yor 'ighness...."

Lark looked across at Landros, and he was glad to see real merriment in her eyes again as she made Billy get up off the floor. "Please, Cardinal. Is supposed to be secret," she said.

"Oh, right," he said, nodding. "Royal enemies an' all."

She sighed, "You come for reason?" she prompted.

"Oh right!" he exclaimed, reaching into his ratty jacket and pulling out a pouch which he placed in Lark's hands. "It's yor share a' what I managed to snatch below from 'at side room whiles you were strikin' 'at mage. We divvied up once we gots to a safe place an' I tol' Rog I knew where ta find ya'. An' I did! Figgered if anybody knew, th' Gen'ral would. An' 'ere ya are! An' there ya go! An' I finks I'll be goin' now!" He made another deep bow, saluted Landros and dashed out the door.

She sat down on the sofa and carefully spread her skirt on the cushion beside her. With Nightingale perched curiously on her shoulder, she dumped the bag onto her skirt. She was overwhelmed by the cascade of coins and jewels that tumbled out. She looked up at him, her eyes wide. He sat on the floor at her feet and helped her sort and count the money.

She sent Nightingale to get her a small pouch from her bag. She knew what was going to come of this money. She also knew that Landros would never take it from her, so she would have to be sneaky. When Nightingale returned, she counted out a hundred of the bright golden laurels and put them into the pouch. This she tied to her belt to give to her father's daughter as a wedding gift. The rest she would leave behind for her elf. There was only about five hundred in other coinage there, but a substantial amount of gems that they guessed from size and clarity to be easily a thousand laurels just by themselves..

Nearly two thousand laurels, she thought. That should arm and feed at least a hundred men.

They put the money back into the bag and tied it off. "Well, Lark," he said, "It looks as if you are now a rich woman." It worried him that she might very well no longer have need of him, no desire for him.

She pushed the bag aside. "Is only money. Would have been better if had found something tradable, something more useful. Hordes of gold only breed desire for more gold, and gold you cannot eat. It can be worn, true, but.... Is not in my heart."

She was getting depressed again, now that the initial delight and surprise at the sudden windfall was over. He kissed her hand, idly caressed her knee with his other. "Will you please tell me what is bothering you?" he asked. "If there is something I can do...."

She shook her head. "No. Can only make things worse. Is Romeri thing. And I have to leave you."

That stopped him cold. His eyes drifted to the bag of gold lying on the sofa beside her. He felt his heart beginning to ice over with dread. Gently, he felt her fingers on his chin, tilting his face to look up into her eyes.

"Moon is full tonight, so I must go..."

He shook his head, not understanding, afraid his brother had really screwed things up for him. "What does a full moon have to do with your leaving? What, are you a werewolf?" he asked, not feeling the joke in his heart.

She half smiled. "No. Thought I... no, had not time to tell. My father's daughter, Yarmine is getting married. Romeri weddings we hold on full of moon. Feasting and dancing will last three nights, with actual wedding at moonrise of second day, when moon is truly and wholly full. My brother came to get me night before last, but wanted to warn you first. And when you came to caravan, woke me so sweetly, had completely forgotten. Was unhappy next morning when woke and remembered." She brushed her fingers tenderly along his cheek with a sad smile. "Is so much easier to remember things when you are not so close."

"How did you know I had not left yet? I did not even know that until I got up that morning," he said, confused.

Her sad smile deepened, had a tiny hint of mischief. "I saw you when I walked shadow-world. I knew where you were, saw you speaking with succubus."

His hand seized hers. "Succubus?" he said. "You saw me with a succubus?"

"*Sesha*," she nodded. "Was elven woman. I think you rescue from harpy? Both were covered in blood. I saw her kiss you, watch whole exchange. Was trying to charm you, but I fended off her serpent."

He took both of her hands in his, controlled his anger at the deception of 'Rocilian'. "How did you know she was a succubus? Are you sure?"

She nodded calmly, undisturbed by his panic. "I saw serpent living within her, which tried to bite and infect you with her venom. Spoke with serpent after you leave her. Was no doubt. Not same kind as on island, but in mortal guise."

He vowed to himself that he would kill that woman if he ever saw her again.

She recognized the murderous look on his face and kissed his forehead. "Do nothing rashly, lover," she said. "Is possible she took form of innocent woman to tempt you, someone with form you might find more attractive than mine. If you do see same woman, do nothing unless she tempts you again. Like as not, she will not even remember you. Or serpent could have possessed. Has happened before. And worry you not of me. I will return when moon begins to wane again, and then we must talk."

She kissed him, soft, tender and sweet, burning away the raging thoughts of the succubus that had tried to steal his heart and use him. He deepened the kiss, wrapping his arms around her slim, but full young body, and pulled her down to the floor with him. Not knowing if she was coming back, he'd be damned if he let her leave with just a kiss. Perhaps, if he was skilful and lucky, he might leave her with a memory she would not soon forget.

Lark left him dozing on the wolf pelt rug in front of the empty fireplace. It was well into the afternoon judging from the sun slanting through the window. She took the bag of gold into the bedroom with her. Throwing her things into her pack, she tossed in another hundred of the coins and penned a quick note. She looked about for a place where he would not see it immediately, but would find it sooner rather than later. She decided to set it on the hearth, tied the note to it and stepped back.

She felt a presence behind her, turned to see Landros standing sleepily in the doorway, watching her. She crossed to him, slipped her arms around his waist and laid her head against his bare shoulder, hoping he had not seen what she was doing.

"Leaving?" he asked softly.

She nodded. "Brother will be waiting and I have things to get together. Was going to wake you when I was ready. No sense you moping while I pack." Not that she had much here to pack. She disentangled herself from his embrace and tucked her scimitar into her sash. "Will try to get as much food as can carry to bring back. Preserved stuff: salt meats, dried fish, preserved fruit, apples, that sort of thing."

"Do what you can," he murmured. "Find out what you can."

She shook her head. "My family are not in Tembia at moment. They are way up in Alphasia. If no word has reached king's ears, no one there will know any more. And we do not camp near gegenta habitations for weddings. Other clans might, but not the Rushavska."

She shouldered her pack, gave the sleeping raccoon one last stroke and scratch and then drifted past Landros into the other room. "Three days?" he called as she crossed to the door.

She looked back over her shoulder at him, "At very least. Will try not to stay too long, but... have responsibilities," she sighed. "Look after horses for me?"

He nodded and she looked away, closed the door behind her, unable to bear the pained look on his face any more.

By the time she had packed up the few things from the caravan she would need and returned to the Cinnamon Tree, dusk had fallen and Ivan was already waiting for her. He was drinking a beer while having a conversation with Lily. She looked up when Lark came into the room, nodded knowingly. She crossed over, gave her a hug. "Enjoy yourself, kid. Stay safe."

"Will talk to father about Dane," she said as Lily continued past, delivering her tray of food and drink.

"Took you long enough, Petrovna," Ivan smirked, draining his beer. "Must have been some farewell."

Lark deliberately ignored the remark and turned to say good-bye to the boy. Only when she was completely ready did she return to her brother and let him lead her out of the tavern.

Landros waited until nightfall to go looking for his brother. He had a pretty good idea where he might be found. He walked down to the outskirts of Bayside to a seedy little tavern with a worn-out sign board depicting a mangy tomcat with a torn ear. It was called The Stray. He thought it extremely fitting as he opened the door and cast about, looking for his own stray.

Finally, he sighted his brother lounging in a corner with a wo-man wrapped around him. His long, elven fingers were dancing in-appropriately across nipples which were only just concealed by her overflowing blouse. There was a great deal of whispering and gig-gling going on over there.

Landros made his way across the crowded room, pausing only once to pound his fist onto the top of a pickpocket's head and stopped in front of the table. He just stood there, arms crossed over his chest, waiting until Portholus looked up at him from the wench's ample bosom.

He looked up into the expressionless face of his brother and promptly whispered something to the girl who pouted, but got off his lap and meandered away. He rewarded her pout with a firm slap across her ample rump, growling, "Later!"

"Come with me," Landros said, not wanting to do this sort of business inside the tavern. Without another word he stalked outside and waited on the side of the building next to the alley.

Portholus followed, apprehensive, but not unduly nervous. Still, he was surprised when Landros suddenly grabbed him and slammed him back against the wall. *"What the hell did you say to her*?!" he snarled in Elvish.

"What are you talking about?" he began, trying to be nonchalant.

Landros shook him. *"Lose the flippant attitude. I told you to stay away from her! What the hells did you say to Lark?!!"*

His expression changed instantly, though still somewhat startled. *"What did she tell you?"* he asked with surprising calm.

"Nothing! Only that it was a matter she had to take care of and would on her own. Now I want to know what you did to upset her!?!"

"I upset her?" he asked.

"Yes, you upset her! So much so I could not even get her to smile! It's like you drained the vivacity out of her!"

"I will talk with her again, if you wish," he sighed.

"She left," he growled, letting him go suddenly.

"She left? What do you mean she left? I did not think she would just pack up and go without a word."

Landros glared up at him. *"What* did *you expect?"*

"Not quite this. Though maybe it is for the best?" he offered.

Landros pulled the note out of his shirt, waved it in his brother's face. *"And what about this? What did you tell her about my needing money for the war?"* he growled.

Portholus looked the note over, written hastily but still clearly legible. It said simply:

For your War efforts.
~Lark.

He looked numbly up from the paper.

Landros continued fuming without breaking a step. *"She left that note on my hearth with a bag of gold and jewels worth several thousand laurels! She never even bothered to get the gems appraised!"*

Portholus was visibly at a loss for words.

"Your explanation had better be a damned good one! I did not want her to leave, but she claimed she had to attend a wedding. I would have told her of my war-related plans in my own way and in my own time! Now I have to find a way to give this money back to her," he growled.

After a moment, Portholus got himself back under control and stood straighter. *"Yes, brother, I had a few words with your lady friend. I am sorry if she decided to leave, but if what I said to her was the cause, then you are better off without her. I did not approach her intentionally. I went to the apartment looking for you, and surprised her. As to what I said to her, that is between the lady and I."*

Portholus stood steadfast in the face of his brother's rage. They stared at each other, neither willing to yield. Finally, to keep from hitting him, Landros turned and walked away.

"Why couldn't you just leave well enough alone? Now I do not even know if I will ever see her again!

TWO

Lark was set upon by several small children the moment she set foot within the encampment. She greeted them, laughing as they were shooed away by their mothers who had a more sedate reception for their leader's eldest daughter. Lark's father had chosen an open field for the wedding site, with a clear running stream flowing through it and an ancient orchard nearby. It was a nice camp, plenty big enough for two caravans and the score of other, smaller ones who happened to cross the path of either clan on route and who followed to join in the celebration. A wedding was time for all Romeri to celebrate and enjoy life and the blessings of renewal.

Petrov Tetsarovich Rushavska was a late middle-aged man, somewhat paunchy, but still very muscular and active. His moustache was thick and still black, as was his thick, curly hair. His flashing black eyes took everything in as he sat drinking with Gregor's father. He wore simple clothes, the same dark green trousers Lark always remembered him wearing, tucked into the tops of his black boots; a new yellow silk shirt worn without laces and a red velvet vest hung open that Rosita had embroidered with gold ribbon. His single golden earring jangled as he turned to observe the commotion. He stood, excused himself from his guests and came over to welcome his children.

He embraced Ivan first, with a back slapping hug that had always reminded Lark of a pair of bears. Gratefully, when he turned to her, he was far more gentle, kissing both her cheeks and drawing the two of them back to the fire to introduce them around.

"This is Ivan, my oldest, and his sister, Illyana," he said.

Victor, Gregor's father, nodded knowingly. "Danine's eldest daughter. Yes, I can see it in her face. And in her body. She is thin like her mother was."

"She dances like her mother, too," Ivan said proudly.

Lark, uncomfortable with all the attention suddenly, begged out of the conversation on grounds of going to visit the bride.

Yarmine was delighted to see her, regaled her with the whole story of how Gregor had gotten her to agree to all of this, while her mother and mother-in-law to be made adjustments to her dress. It was pretty, one she knew Yarmine would wear for years after. The bodice was a dark blue suede with sleeves of fine yellow linen, and a blue skirt overlain with gold lace.

She listened to her half-sister chatter for several minutes before wandering off to visit her grandmother. The entrance to her barrel-shaped caravan was open, only a curtain of beads blocked the entrance, allowing a semblance of privacy while permitting a refreshing breeze to blow through. Lark seated herself on a stool nearby and waited. She idly toyed with the laces on her vest, undoing and retying them to make certain they were tight enough and would not slip the knot.

Beyond her, Yarmine's two brothers were circulating the camp, collecting the gifts for the bride and groom, announcing in loud voices the amount of gold given as it was received, but only after multiplying it by a hundred for luck. As they gravitated her way, Lark tossed them the pouch she had brought. They bowed, thanked her and wandered off, only to shout a few minutes later, louder than before the surprised sum of ten thousand laurels!

She only had to wait a few more minutes before a couple of young men with yellow scarves around their necks hopped out of the wagon and disappeared into the growing crowd. She got up and went inside, sitting down on the many silk-covered pillows across a low table from the old woman wrapped in a dark purple dress with red and gold beading.

Ruby was easily in her eighties, with the soft, withered face of the ancient. Her eyes were a sightless white with heavy lids. They had an unnerving habit of staring into a person, of reading their soul in such a way that no secrets seemed left. Lark waited until she spoke.

"Your mother says hello," Ruby said.

"Hello, mamma," she whispered.

"Would you get me some tea, Mahril," she said, gesturing to a cup and a pot on the small stove behind Lark.

She got up without a word and poured the cup of tea, adding the usual spoonful of honey. She set it in her grandmother's hands, still strong and unshaking in spite of her great age.

"Surely you have not come for me to tell fortune, ranie," she said, sipping at the warm tea.

"No, Gruma, I have not. But have come for advice. Have taken very big step and do not know what to do now."

"You are ranie. You will do what needs to be done for your caravan," she said firmly.

"But I have no caravan...." she began.

"Your caravan does not move, no," the old one cut in. "But is ever-changing still. Your caravan is that which you chose to protect when you crossed over. Is what you crossed over for, why are still breathing. Your choice will dictate what you do now."

Lark sighed. Somehow she had known she would get no answers here. "Does father know?"

"Know what?" she retorted. "That you are ranie or why you are ranie?"

"Either."

"Your father may notice something is different with you, but who with eyes would not? But as far as your lover is concerned... if he knew, you would know he knew. He will not give you up lightly. You mean far too much to him."

Lark nodded, knowing she had chosen the hardest road by far.

"Go on now, festivities will begin soon and you will be expected to perform."

Lark rose, crossed the short distance to the door and stared out at the raucous camp sprawled beyond the beads. She sighed one last time, put on a joyous face and stepped outside.

Landros was not happy. It was bad enough that Lark was gone, bad enough that he was not convinced she would return. Now he had been summoned to the Magistrate's office. He was not alone. Adrick and Lithgorin, now a stone-faced young elf, were with him. Landros looked across at Lith, knew the pain he was feeling, knew it would be decades, if not centuries, before the elf would be able to feel again.

As they approached the office door, they heard the sounds of an argument. When the sergeant guarding the door opened it, the volume jumped to near painful levels for the three of them. They stepped inside. Keltree was in a full shouting match with the magistrate that ended the moment the three of them stepped into the room. Both men were red-faced and fuming, but the magistrate had apparently won for now.

The magistrate turned to Landros and his friends, gestured for them to close the door and approach. He looked behind them, as if to make sure there was no one else coming. Satisfied, he sat in the only chair and began without any preamble whatsoever. "Just east of Bayside there is an empty building where Danhaven here has brought me word that some treasonous rats are meeting. I want you to go in, break up the meeting, kill or arrest as many of these vermin as you can and bring back heads, tails and whatever else you can uncover. There are spies and friends of the enemy in this town and I want their necks stretched publicly. The people deserve their revenge from these evil men who would sell us street by street!" He handed Keltree a piece of paper and folded his arms across his chest.

Keltree handed Landros the paper. "You might want to pick up a couple more strong arms before heading to this address. I cannot go with you, as I have not yet been released for combat."

Landros took the paper, looked at the address and the figure of seventy laurels each written there. He wondered why Keltree was so pissed off about this whole mission and what the argument had been about. He looked over at the magistrate. "If you know for certain these men are committing treason, why don't you send in a troop of the Watch or the army? Why pay us seventy gold apiece to do what they should do as part of their job?"

Keltree's colour heightened, his jaw tensed as he answered. "Because the Lord Mayor is suspected of being involved. Men under his command would, whether intentional or otherwise, warn him or those involved. It is best if freelancers do it, in any case. That way there is no reason to doubt the findings," he grudgingly admitted.

Landros did not like this, but to refuse would be to give the magistrate some reason to doubt his own loyalty, and he was committed to truth. Perhaps it was time to find out what that was, one way or the other. He stood, shook the tall man's hand.

"Wish I could go with you," Keltree said, leaving it obvious there was something else he wanted to say but could not in front of the magistrate.

"I understand," Landros answered, and gestured for his friends to follow him out the door. Keltree walked them out.

Once they were away, Keltree kept his voice low. "I do not know any more than you do now. The rumour is pretty strong about the meeting. It is the Mayor's involvement I doubt. But we have to know for certain and this sort of this *does* fall under the magistrate's jurisdiction. What choice have we but to go through with it and what happens will happen?"

"Do you have any idea of the layout of this old house or how many will be there?"

Keltree shook his head regretfully. "I am afraid not. They will probably be in a room where the light will not show outside, somewhere in the centre of the house, a small upstairs room or the basement."

"I can case the place in relative silence," Lithgorin injected softly.

Keltree nodded. "Good. As to how many there are... I would guess at around twenty or so. But be careful, there might be an individual or two known to dabble in magic." He then shook hands with all of them and took his leave, muttering to himself about this whole thing being 'a nasty bit of business'.

"We are going to need some more muscle." Landros said, turning to his friends. "Anyone know where to find Barak?"

Lith nodded. "He's down at the Sleepy Dragon."

"Good, that's on the way. Anyone else you can think of?"

"What about that dwarf who came with us to get the children? Rog was it?" Adrick asked.

"Good idea. I'll take care of getting him and meet you down at the Dragon."

"What about Lark?" Adrick added. "We might be in need of her talents."

"She is unavailable," he said flatly and walked off.

He fumed to himself. Adrick *had* to bring her up, didn't he? It wasn't bad enough what they were up to. He stopped at the edge of the square, took a deep breath of the cool night air, tried not to wonder what Lark was doing at the moment.

He saw something small dash through the shadows a short distance away, gave the short, trilled whistle he had taught to all the army kids. As he began walking a little way down the street, a boy fell into step beside him.

They walked casually side by side. Landros spoke to him in a low voice. "I need the dwarf named Rog. The South Wind might know where he is. I need him at the Sleepy Dragon and that is where I am going."

The kid gave a short nod and disappeared into the nearest alley. Landros kept walking, taking a leisurely stroll towards the seedy side of town.

By the time he appeared at the Sleepy Dragon, Rog was already leaning against the wall by the door. They nodded to each other, and Landros went inside. The Dragon was understated tonight, no where near as rowdy as it was known to be. The name itself was a joke, as it was bragged in Bayside that the Dragon never slept. Barak was finishing up his drink while Lithgorin bent near his ear, filling him in briefly. They nodded when they saw Landros and he went back outside to wait with Rog. In the meantime, he quietly filled the dwarf in.

"You up to it?" he finished.

Rog spun the hammer in his hand idly, "Yeah, I'm up to bustin' a few heads. When do we leave?"

At that moment Adrick and the others stepped out into the night. "Now," Landros said, and the small party of friends began what they tried to make appear to be a casual stroll from tavern to home.

They waited across the street from the old house, in an alley shooting dice. It was the kind of neighbourhood where this activity would not be entirely out of place if kept to the shadows, which is precisely why they were doing it. A handful of coins changed hands frequently, giving the appearance of heated gambling for any observers that might happen along. No one was really paying attention to the game.

After about twenty or so rounds, Lithgorin showed back up. "They are in a room on the first floor. A large dining area, I think. I can't tell how many there are, but there are more than a few. A couple of guards, but they can be taken out quickly and quietly. They strike me as fairly lazy and not on the ball. I slipped right past them."

"Why didn't you take them out?" Barak asked.

"Because I did not want them to be discovered before we came charging in. The only way out of the dining room is the large front doors and the kitchen, but the kitchen door is blocked off by a section of the roof that caved in on the kitchen side. I was able to get into it another way and overheard some of what they were saying. It ain't good. The Mayor has ordered the guard on the Eastern gate cut in half, putting those men to guard the North wall over near the breach. The people in there are being sent to replace the relocated guards as false 'civilian' reinforcements and are to open the gates sometime around midnight. If all goes according to plan, the city will be overrun by dawn."

Landros stood, passed Barak his dice back. "All right, Lith, you head back in just ahead of us. Take out both guards. Think you will need help, or can you get both of them without the other sounding the alarm?"

"I think I can handle it. It's not like they're back to back or anything. Like I said, not on the ball."

"Good." He turned to the others, "We give Lith just enough time to take out the guards, then we assemble outside the room and kick the door down. Adrick, you have any spells that might help us take them out without killing them?"

He nodded. "I think so. I don't know how many it'll take out, but, if you give me one clear shot..." he said, hefting a small glass bottle he pulled from his robes. "They'll be sleeping like babes."

Landros nodded. "We'll stay back 'til the smoke clears, take out whoever's left. All right, now just be as quiet as you can going in. Adrick, the minute the fight's over, you run for the watch to round these mongrels up."

As they broke from their tight huddle and slowly began to cross the street several paces after Lithgorin, Landros heard movement from further back in the alley. He hung back, turned to investigate when he heard the soft signal whistle come from an iron balcony above him. He looked up and saw a scrawny-looking girl watching him with luminous eyes.

She gave him a smart little salute and whispered. "Ev'nin',

General. Corporal Cat's-eye, an' I heard ever' word."

He nodded, returned the salute. "Very good, Corporal. Report to your Wind and then to Lord Colwyn. He'll take care of things from there."

She gave another salute and disappeared inside the building. Shaking his head in amazement at the children's endless resourcefulness, he quickly crossed the street to the house and slipped inside.

Lithgorin had dispatched the two guards with embarrassing ease and they stood before the dining room door waiting for him. On an even count, Landros, Rog and Barak kicked the door in and stepped back, giving Adrick room to throw his bottle. He chanted his prayer, holding forth crossed fingers and his medallion in the other hand. A thin green smoke exploded from the shattered bottle, shifted to sinuous tendrils that coiled around the necks and faces of the startled men within, forcing its way into their mouths and noses. Twelve of the twenty individuals around the table sank to the floor in an unconscious heap. A couple of them were trying to force their way through the kitchen door with no success.

They stepped into the room to engage those who remained as the smoke began to clear. A bolt of something came from across the room, struck Barak in the right shoulder. He howled with surprise, but hefted his blade and waded into the room once he realized the wound was not as serious as it had felt.

Landros charged in, found himself face to face with an attractive human woman wearing men's clothing and a black, studded leather vest. She held a wand in her left hand, her right tightened upon the hilt of a rapier.

"It would be a shame to kill such beauty," he said, though remaining wary. "Surrender now and live, or fight and die. Your choice."

She raised the wand and hissed something under her breath. She was quite startled when nothing happened. Cursing, she threw the wand aside and drew the rapier, began circling.

He did not permit her to get around him. He was not stupid. She was obviously trying to get to the door, believing herself more than enough to handle the priest guarding it. Her sword lashed out, was mostly parried, but slid down his blade to sink into his left shoulder. "Not again," he growled, and threw himself into the fight.

It took him a moment or so to get the feel of her weapon, to be able to shift his defences and attacks to work around the rapier's lighter weight and faster speed. Both of them took a few cuts, but nothing serious, until her blade broke. She flattened herself against the wall, swore profusely, nursing her badly injured hand. Then suddenly, a grin flashed on her face, a foreign word slid across her tongue and she vanished altogether!

Landros swung wildly, slicing through the air where she had been and the immediate vicinity. It was just that, empty air. He heard her laughing somewhere behind him, turned to try and find some evidence of her passing, in the blood on the floor if nothing else. There was nothing. Then Landros saw the man on the other side of the now overturned table raising a crossbow aimed at him. He dodged to the left, tucking and rolling to the floor, springing back to his feet in a crouch, sword at the ready. An eldritch bolt screamed into the melee from the doorway, echoed by the unexpected cry of the woman who faded into view and collapsed onto the floor, struck dead by both the crossbow and the magic bolt.

Rog finally reached the bowman as he was reloading, caved his head in with his hammer. Within moments the fight ground to a halt, the survivors on their knees with their hands up, weapons on the floor in surrender. Barak and Rog ushered them into a corner of the room and held them there at sword point while Landros and Lithgorin searched the papers on the table for harder evidence. Adrick, as he had been requested, ran for the watch.

Lithgorin busied himself searching the bodies, living first, then the dead. Rings, necklaces, money and anything paper or anything which might identify them was confiscated and set on one of the chairs.

Landros examined the papers on the table itself. He felt his blood beginning to boil. In his hand were once-sealed orders from the Lord Mayor himself, giving the irregular troop lead by Maveen DeLaSkintz orders to relieve the Sixty-third at the East Gate before midnight. Accompanying these papers were less official orders, though no less authentic, to open the gates just after midnight, to admit the army waiting outside and aid in the quick, stealthy and complete take-over of Portswain.

He stared, stunned, at the papers. "This cannot be true. These have to be forgeries! Something does not feel right here!"

Lithgorin came over, having collected everything from the bodies, with a letter in hand. It was from the Mayor to the dead woman. He handed it to Landros without a word.

The missive was a personal thank you from the Lord Mayor to Commander DeLaSkintz for her loyalty and sacrifice in volunteering to lead a troop in these desperate times. It went on to say that he had special plans for her particular group which would be detailed in a separate, sealed letter which would be hand-delivered soon. The seal on the bottom of the letter seemed authentic enough, and seemed to bear out the other evidence on the table.

Rog piped up, "We gotta turn this in. Let th' Council a' Lords decide."

"Let's take this back, insist the Magistrate call a council and present this to them, not to one man." Lith suggested. "The Council... let the Council decide. They are his peers, not us."

Landros nodded, numbly began collecting the papers and putting them carefully and safely into a nearby satchel.

Lark took her turns dancing and fiddling for the assembled clans. The bright yellow doors of the Bravida stood out by the firelight, contrasted sharply with the red roofs of the Rushavska beside which they were parked. She wandered from campfire to campfire as everyone else was, mingling and sharing the food and drink and joyous celebration.

She did not feel the party as keenly as she would otherwise have. The last wedding she had attended was much like this one, only then she hadn't been mooning over a gegenta. She sighed. It had to be barely midnight by the clock in Portswain, but she decided to go to bed anyway. She found herself a feather-bed that had been thrown under her brother's wagon for whomever and curled up under the quilt. It was not long before she found herself sandwiched in between various smaller cousins and nieces. Lulled by the heavy, regular breathing of the children and the warmth of their bodies, Lark finally slept.

The sun was already high in the sky when the camp began to stir again. Strong coffee was brewing over the renewed fires, its aroma rousing most of the camp with the promise of the breakfast that would follow, for those who had the stomach to eat anything.

Lark wandered listlessly through the camp, only acknowledging the most insistent of well wishers, accepted a small cup of coffee from one of the Bravida clan. She did not stay to chat long, but wandered off again as soon as her host's attention had been drawn away. This time she walked with her arms folded, guaranteeing her privacy. She was thinking, but unfocused. Her mind was cluttered and clouded. Something was wrong in Portswain and she knew it, but there was nothing she could do now, not for two more days.

She wandered into the nearby apple orchard, only a field away. Drifted beneath the canopy of ivory and pink blossoms that fell like snow all around her when the wind blew too strongly through the branches. It was a warm, beautiful day, but Lark found she could not enjoy it. Some of the children had followed her, were playing games among the ancient trees. A few of the camp dogs chased after them, barking playfully.

Lark hummed quietly to herself, working out a song that had been bothering her all night, had been nipping at her creative heels for a few days now. She leaned back against a tree, tilted her head up to stare into the branches overhead. The sky glinted like blue jewels through the leaves. It was a truly beautiful day. A shame she could not enjoy it, or the peace and tranquillity that filled it.

Some of the children tore past her, ignoring her in their games because she very obviously wanted to be left out. Watching them run, she saw her oldest brother, Ivan, entering the orchard. He was not looking at her, but it was obvious to her that he was covertly watching her, waiting for her to take her arms down so he could speak to her. She decided not to and turned to watch a pair of bees buzzing from flower to flower on a low hanging branch next to her.

After a few moments, she heard her brother speak to the children in a loud, deliberate voice. "If you see my sister, Illyana, tell her that her father wishes to speak with her."

Lark sighed, began walking back to the camp. She was getting hungry anyway.

THREE

Landros was in a foul mood. The raid on the East Gate had been neatly foiled. The army had turned back after seeing the gate well-lit and bristling with spears, arrows and ballista. His left shoulder was still sore from the stab wound, but he had refused healing, as usual. Besides, the pain helped him keep his mind off of other things. He had brought the evidence, as requested, into the meeting of the Council of Lords that had been summoned with surprising swiftness. He said nothing, not trusting himself to speak, let the papers speak for him.

Lithgorin retold what he had overheard before the attack and the prisoners confirmed him. It had also been presented, by the Magistrate, that some of the captive and dead traitors, were actually criminals who had been released without his authority, perhaps for this very task. He even produced the pardon and release papers, signed and witnessed in the Mayor's own hand.

A witness was produced, a lowly aide who, having been privy to the Lord Mayor's private chambers and offices. He confessed to suspecting the Lord Mayor of similar unspeakable crimes some weeks before, but having been afraid to speak up, not wanting to believe what had been said. This aide brought forth confirming evidence from the Mayor's own private safe.

Through all of this the Lord Mayor sat silent, watching one person and then another. When the room had at last fallen quiet, the next highest ranking Lord in the room stood and addressed the accused, asked what he had to say for himself.

Landros found the Mayor's words confusing, as their weight and conviction seemed to belie everything that had just been said about him.

"Under the overwhelming weight of such evidence, there is nothing I can say. That it could be believed of me that I would do such unspeakable things, grieves me deeply. Still, there is nothing for me to do but to turn myself over to the mercy of the people, and pray that the Goddesses in their infinite wisdom see fit to reveal to us the truth before it is too late."

Even to Landros, who was no seer or truth-sayer, something did not seem right. He chalked it up to disbelief that such a great hero as the Mayor had been to this city could turn against it so quickly and so completely, and dismissed his unease. He collected his weapons at the door and left after that. He had volunteered to give up his swords on entering, lest he do something rash and hot-headed, like trying to kill the mayor outright.

The tavern in which he sat now, mulling over all of this, was virtually empty. It seemed that the entire town was in the square witnessing the judgment that had taken the Lord's Council the entire night to pass. Landros had been in this tavern drinking since he had left the Hall.

Lithgorin and the others had met him there earlier, had divided the treasures they had recovered and been allowed to keep. There had been little enough money taken from the traitors. What they had been paid by the Magistrate came to far more. Landros had not even wanted that. It felt too much like blood money to him. When Barak had suggested they dice for the three items found, he had thrown the bones without even looking at them, a gesture which suddenly and painfully reminded him of a certain dark-eyed Romer. When he had won first pick, he chose an ornate little brooch that had been taken from the dead woman. He had pinned it to his shirt to keep from losing it, thinking, if he ever saw Lark again, that he might give it to her, and got up to get a drink.

Before walking away, as Lithgorin was trying to make up his mind: the ring or the wand, Landros had pointed to the ring and said, "I'm pretty sure that one is a ring of invisibility."

Now it was early afternoon and Landros had emptied almost an entire barrel of ale on his own and wasn't the least bit drunk, much to his frustration. He wanted to get completely torched, to keep from having to think about the horrors around him, the betrayals, and where those thoughts would inevitably lead him. Damn it, but a man had to have something to have faith in! And if nothing else, there was the faith that if you drank enough, you got drunk, and when you got drunk, the world washed away with sobriety. Now he couldn't even trust in that any more.

"Oh, hun!" the barmaid cooed next to him as she refilled his mug. "My soul, but you ain't put away more booze than any man I ever seen! You've drunk enough to put a giant on his ass, much less a man yor size!"

He looked sullenly up at her. She was pretty enough, if a bit over-weight and over-worked, with flaming red hair that hung about her face in tight, frizzy curls. No doubt she was over-used, too. "You have a problem with my size?" he growled.

"No, darlin'," she countered, giving his shoulder a friendly pat. "I like ya right nice. Quite a handsome fella, but ev'r'body knows, th' bigger a man is, th' more he kin drink without fallin' on his face. 'Cept fer dwarfs a'course, but they's a bit diff'rnt somehow. You've drunk enough to put a whole clan of dwarfs under th' table! Sure you shouldn't eat somethin'?"

"No. I want to get drunk! Maybe if I don't eat, I'll stand a better chance," he growled.

He noticed the barmaid move away, acknowledging something or someone else behind him and turned, saw Colwyn staring balefully down at him. Landros looked away, glaring into his cup before draining it.

The knight turned a chair backwards and sat. He stared at some invisible point on the table in front of them. It was a long while before either of them spoke. "Have you been to bed?" he asked.

Landros just shook his head.

"No food, no sleep and a tun of ale," he mused. "Landros, if you aren't drunk now, you never will be."

"Then I'll drink something stronger. This is half water anyway. Red!" he shouted, half-turning to try and find the barmaid. She was nowhere to be seen. He and Colwyn were completely alone in the bar.

"No, I think we've both had enough. It's all over, Landros. It's time for bed," he said. He stood, taking him by the arm and pulling him gently to his feet. "Besides," he added in a lower voice, "you are already beginning to get surly and even drunkenness is no excuse for unknightly behaviour."

Landros did not argue. He grabbed his cloak and sword and left the bag of gold he had been paid that night on the table for 'Red'. He followed the knight through the city streets without a word. Colwyn lead his horse, preferring to walk with his squire in silence.

Landros was thinking, trying to figure out why he had been unable to get drunk. Goddess knew he had consumed enough alcohol. He had even tapped into his little white jug to no effect. It was frustrating. He had never been resistant to alcohol before. In fact, it was not ten years past that he and Portholus had gone out and gotten him roaring drunk, much to the ache of his head come morning. Hells, even earlier that day, he had felt the beginning of a drunk coming over him, but that had ended shortly after Lithgorin and the others had joined him.

Then it dawned on him. His head had cleared after pinning the brooch to his shirt!

When the moon rose that night, the entire sprawling campsite gathered in the open field under the twilight sky. Old Ruby stood around a brass basin beside Lyuba, the Bravida ranie who was well into her middle years and heavy with child. Lark had been bade to stand beside Lyuba, making the trio complete: Magruma, Mahren and Mahril. The bride and groom stood before them, flanked by their respective fathers and the oldest of their brothers.

Lark held out a silk scarf, shot through with gold threads and beaded tassels, held it over the basin and called upon it blessings of health, strength and vitality of the young couple. Then she dipped it into the herbed water within the basin and passed it to the Mahren. Lyuba took the scarf in her agile hands and, holding it over the basin, called the blessings of faith, fertility, and binding love, then dipped it as well before passing it into the withered hands of the Magruma. Old Ruby held up the scarf, intoned upon it the joys of grandchildren, the gifts of wisdom that comes with age and the years in which to achieve it.

Dipping it once more into the water, she handed one end to Petrov, the other to Victor. She held onto the centre of it for a moment longer, then let it go.

Victor turned to face Petrov. *"Brother you are to me now, as our children become one family. I give you my greatest treasure, my son, Gregor Victorovich Bravida,"* and so saying, he gave his end of the scarf to Petrov.

Petrov turned now to the happy couple who stood staring into each other's eyes, right hands clasped tightly. *"Yarmine Petrovna Rushavska, my daughter, my joy. I who helped give you life now give you a husband. Take him in love, be faithful, be obedient, be happy."* Petrov then lay the scarf over their clasped hands, wound it carefully around their wrists and up their arms as far as it would go, letting the ends dangle. He set his hands on their joined ones. *"Now you are one, both blood of my blood, daughter and son."*

As he released them, Gregor pulled Yarmine to him by their bound hands and kissed her to the roar and delight of those watching. Music was struck and as the triptych of ranie moved to a nearby fire, a group of children jumped up and, joined by scarves of their own, began dancing around the happy couple who were still clinging to each other and laughing.

The three ranie sat alone at the fire beside Old Ruby's wagon. They said very little between themselves, concentrating on the fire and their chanted prayers, tossing the occasional herb into the flames for blessings according to their dominion. Revellers brought food and drink for them, left it silently beside them before slipping off to rejoin the party. This was to ensure the blessings wished upon the marriage and to appease those of the shadows who would wish ill upon the young couple. This night, like the first day of their lives, was their most vulnerable.

It was near midnight when the young, unmarried men gathered around the couple, cleverly distracted Gregor long enough to get Yarmine away from him. They formed a barrier between the two, keeping him from reaching his new wife. With a coy smile, Yarmine removed the flowered wreath from her head that signified her maidenhood and tossed it to him. It landed on the ground halfway between them. Then, with one last glance, she tore off running, across the fields towards the shelter of the orchard.

The men held Gregor back several minutes more, straining and laughing until they finally decided to let him go. He stumbled, caught his balance, snatched up the wreath and ran after his bride. The young men coaxed and cheered and laughed until both of them were out of sight, presumably deep in the depths of the orchard, then meandered off to drink to their health and stamina.

Lark and the two others remained by the fireside for another hour at least, until the fire flared brightly and dimmed again. Only then did they cease their chanting and casting and sat back, stoking up the fire with fresh wood and partaking of the food and drink that had been left for them. Guests began actually stopping to talk now, to share a song or two, well wishes and move on again.

Ivan stopped by with one of his sons, beaming proudly to see his sister sitting in her rightful place with the ranie. He had his daughter in his arms, handed her first to the oldest of them. Ruby cooed over the little girl, played with her for a few minutes, little games which, in truth, were testing the child. She seemed pleased with the results, lightly sketched a mark on the child's forehead and handed her to Lyuba. And so the child was passed.

Lark played with the baby when her turn came, began singing to her. Without thinking she sang the song she had been working on for the last week or so, the one that would not seem to leave her alone.

"There is so much on my mind
and thinking was never my religion
My heart beats faster as it flies
and excitement my favourite treasure
Stage has always been platform of my life
Live well, Live long, Be remembered always, my creed
Lately I've gotten in touch with mortality
Gods have shown me there is more than just today

I wander dazed when you leave me
and only near you do I play my soul for song

Lover don't leave me
Lover believe me
This is more than flesh and bone
Love is inside me
Love is what guides me
Now that I see it, I am no more alone

I am violin, harp in your hands
timbrel my heart beats upon
my feet trace their dance as Fate guides their path
and I know in my heart I am never alone
Lately no stage has pleased me
no crowd enough to feed my soul
But knowing you are watching I dance on and on

I sing my world song and dance for you alone
Lover please hold me
Engulf and enfold me
This isn't about sex at all
It's of sharing and caring
Giving and daring
'Til skies open up and stars shall fall."

Silence met the end of Lark's song. Her brother just looked at her, glanced sidelong at their Gruma. Lyuba was sitting with her head cocked to one side, thinking.

"*It is beautiful,*" she said. "*I can hear your soul in it. You have made up your mind on something?*" she asked.

Lark cast a long glance at her brother. "*You might say.*" She shrugged as she passed the child back to her father, "*Is* Sagavis, *sesket?*"

Lyuba laughed. "*Is that not always way with love?*"

She did not answer, but settled back to listen as her grandmother began to sing an old song that only she remembered any more.

Landros tossed and turned in the bed, tired though he was. Lark's scent still clung to the pillow and linens, leaving him in a cloud of her and surrounded by stubborn memories, pleasant and otherwise.

His heart and his mind were at war. His mind was trying to convince his heart to hold ranks, that the Romeri girl it kept trying to run to was not a certainty. The girl might leave at any time without a word or a regret, and her affections were not known as of yet. The heart kept steadfastly insisting she had already given him certainty, that it wanted the risk, that it did not care and that love begets love. Neither side was any closer to winning by the time the rosy tinge of dawn began creeping into the window.

Lark found herself walking through the woods towards a flickering light. She felt airy and bouyant, as she had when she had drifted through the shadow-world and battled with the succubus's serpent. There were no sensations, not the earth beneath her feet or the wind through the trees. She could hear, though, and the night was filled with the keening of a Romer camp in mourning. As she neared the source of the light, she saw that it was a funeral pyre surrounded by bare-headed, wailing Romeri.

Off to the side she saw two figures, and drifted towards them out of curiosity. She recognized Landros quickly, even from behind, and realized that it was her brother, Ivan, standing with him. Ivan was handing him a violin and a gilded rose. "I give you these which were my sister's because she wished them to be yours. Keep them for year of mourning, thereafter do with them as you wish." He then put his hand on the elf's slim shoulder. "You did all that you could, baharen. It is not your fault that priests could do no more for her. There was nothing more any could do. It is simply will of things."

"I should have been there to protect her," Landros countered. There was a harder, pained edge to his voice that Lark had never heard before. "Then I would have been able to keep the giants from taking her from us."

He turned then, looked to the pyre once more and she saw that there were tears on his face. "Her wagon and all she had within are yours, baharen. I have all of her that I will keep." Then he turned and disappeared into the wood.

She noticed another figure at the edge of the clearing, a pale, golden elf dressed all in black come to bid his own farewells. Portholus spoke to the fire, but softly, that none but the dead might hear him.

"Our first meeting was unpleasant and uncalled for. You truly loved my brother, and I am sorry for my callousness. I hope you will find your peace, since my brother and I will not find ours any time soon. I hope only that the goddesses take pity upon us all, and when we finally walk that place with you, we will leave behind a safer world, or, by all that is holy, my brother will not rest."

The wood faded around her. The pyre changed, grew smaller, became confined in a stone fireplace before which sat a chair. Landros sat there, rocking slowly back and forth, staring up at a pair of crossed, elven swords which hung above the mantle, under which lay the violin and the rose. On the small table beside him sat an empty bottle of wine with Elvish markings, and hanging limp in his right hand was a half-filled glass of a clear liquid. His white jug lay on its side some feet away, open and empty and Lark knew then what was in that vessel.

He stared at a small portrait of her on the table beside him, picked it up. His voice was hoarse and strained when he spoke, "First the giants take my family and leave my brother and I orphans, and now they take the only bright light left in my exist-ence. I will have revenge upon them for this or die trying. I swear this on my knighthood, on my honour, and on the love I held for you."

He lifted the glass to his lips then, swallowed the contents in a single gulp and threw it into the fire. The flames jumped as it shattered, then settled again, and Landros leaned forward over the small framed painting and openly wept.

Lark, unable to bear the pain of his sorrow, reached out to him, to comfort him, but he faded beneath her hands and she found her-self in another wood. A cloaked figure passed by her unseeing, headed for a lit clearing just ahead. She followed, recognizing the copse as Colwyn's, and the clearing as the small grove in which she had danced for her elf, then made love their first night here.

There was a gathering in that grove of men, and a few women, with Colwyn presiding overall. They looked up, surprised to see the elf arrive and throw back his hood. To Lark's eyes it seemed that Landros had aged. He said nothing at first, but took off his gloves and removed a bracelet of silver braiding from his wrist and a silver ring from his hand. These he added to a small bag which Lark saw contained some minor odds and ends, a scarf, a pin with a hooded falcon's head among others. This he dropped at Colwyn's feet. His voice was no longer choked with tears, but there was no life or emotion left in it. It was hollow and dead.

"What I do now brings me much sorrow. I return these symbols of my standing in the Order Falconis. From this day forth I can bear that title no more, as my future actions may bring shame to the order, and that is the one thing I will not do: dishonour my king. All of your secrets will go with me to my grave. You have my word on that, but I can be of your fellowship no more."

As he turned his back to the fire to leave, staring straight at and straight through her, Colwyn spoke. "Consider what you do."

Landros did not turn. "I already have." With that he left.

Colwyn stirred the fire sadly, spoke to a small man sitting beside him with paper and quill, "Have the name of Landros the Pathfinder removed from the rolls." He paused, added to the gathered knights, "Let it be know from this day forth that, though Landrosallenthoia has walked away from us, we have not walked away from him. He is to be given all assistance and respect accorded to any knight of the order. He has earned it too many times over."

Lark followed him back to the inn where he lived, where Portholus was waiting for him. Landros did not waste time with banalities, handed his brother a key. "The room is yours and paid for several years to come. In the corner of the bedroom is a chest. You may use anything you wish, but that chest is to be left alone. It contains all that is left of my fallen princess and is never to be opened."

Portholus looked down at the key in his hand. "Brother, what you are contemplating is suicide. We lost our parents and sisters to giants and now you set out to hunt them down? Have you gone *insane*?"

He looked up from packing. "And now they have taken my wife. The time of their taking is over." Shouldering his pack, he headed for the door, paused there, looking back over his shoulder. "I was glad when the two of you made your peace, as I did with her brothers. I wish you well, Portholusallenwyl. Either I will see you again in this life, or I will meet you in the next. And no, I am not in-sane. Just alone."

She followed him from the room into a wood, somewhere far from the city where he made a fire and pulled off his armour and shirt. On his right arm, she saw a tattoo of a falcon in flight. He stirred a long, thick stick in the fire, checking the end from time to time as she watched, uneasy. When the tip was good and glowing, he blew out the flames and pressed the end to the tattoo, ruining the face of it, scarring the arm forever.

She gasped, jumped back covering her mouth as he yelled from the depths of his soul, and collapsed to the ground from the com-bined pain of flesh and heart. After a long moment, he stood shakily. "So it is done," he whispered. "Landros the Pathfinder is dead. Now only Landrosallenthoia the Giant Slayer remains."

He poured some liquid on the wound from a small bottle in his pack, let it dry, then doused the fire and dressed.

There came a great crashing through the wood behind her and Lark turned to see a man some twenty feet tall, head easily tower-ing into the trees, break his way into the camp. Landros drew his swords with a cold expression on his face. "Now it begins," he said in a dead voice. "The beginning of the end, for your kind or me."

The battle enjoined with Lark caught, ghostly, in between. She screamed herself awake. "**Landros, noooooo!**"

The children curled up on the bed with her scrambled out of her way, screaming themselves as she rolled out from under the wagon and leaned, panting, against its side. The twins were there in a moment, Bourne and Randal both trying to calm her and divine what ailed her. Then Ivan was there, demanding to know what was wrong. Seeing the dawn colouring the sky beyond them, she pushed past nephews and brother and went to see her grandmother.

"*Gruma!*" she called as she neared the wagon.

There was a heavy sigh nearby from a figure huddled over a bank of softly glowing coals. "*What is it, Yani,*" she asked.

Lark fell by her side. "*Gruma, I have to go back to city. And must go now.*"

"Why?" she asked in a voice which told Lark she already knew.

"Dreams," she answered. *"Dreams which do not prophesy in whole truths, but with fact and possibility. Was shown something I needed to know, and how things might happen if other things do. I know that what I saw will not come to pass, not as I saw it. Was not that sort of dream. But everything I saw was true course, and I must get back to him."*

"Him," she mused. *"Yes, I rather expected this. Go on. Door is yonder waiting. Be careful, grumahril. Be careful. There is evil yet in that place for you."*

Lark kissed her grandmother and ran back to get her things. She stopped only long enough to bid Ivan goodbye and take the bag he handed her before disappearing into the field where the gate awaited her between two fence posts.

Landros lay asleep, tossing and turning. He was dreaming and he knew it, but had no desire to wake from it. Lark was in his arms, soft and beautiful, passionate and eager. This was not the first of these dreams, nor would it be the last by any means.

Lark opened the door as quietly as she could, slipping into the room soundlessly. She paused at the sofa to remove her scimitar and anything else that might make noise. Nightingale, spying from the cold fireplace, told her that he was sleeping restlessly, but soundly. She smiled, stepped through the half-open bedroom door and crept in. She unlaced her vest and tossed it and her skirts into the chair and crept over to the bed in just her blouse.

She watched him a moment, smiling sadly, then bent and kissed him, lightly at first. Perched on the edge of the mattress, she slid gracefully beneath the covers and kissed him more deeply. Strangely, though he did not seem to wake up, he returned the kiss, brought his hands up her back, under her blouse and wrapped his arms around her with surprising speed and held on fiercely, as if afraid she was going to melt away if he did not.

His dream had taken an odd turn. He felt more warmth and more passion than the moment before, as if the dream were becoming more real. He wrapped his arms around her, desperate to hold onto this phantasm however torturous it was. The longer he could hold onto this vision, the longer it would be before he had to deal with the disillusionment and disappointment that would follow. He buried his face in her hair, ran his cheek along the side of her long dark neck, breathing deeply of her warm spiciness. He nipped, ran his tongue along the indention behind her ear, kissed, nipped again. He could feel her breasts pressed against his bare chest, the gathered silk and the knotted cord all there was between flesh.

He opened his eyes with a start. Lark had never worn clothes in these dreams before. He flipped the woman beneath him, pinning her to the pillow with his weight, half afraid that the succubus had come up to try again, having chosen a more successful form. Lark's laughing eyes stared up at him from a cloud of black hair that had fallen partly across her face like a veil. She purred, "Good morning, my Kestrel. Sleep well?"

"Princess Illyana?" he asked, testing.

She brushed her hair from her face, looked up at him curiously. "Now those are two words you've never used together before. What is wrong, my heart?" she asked.

Convinced, he buried his head against her shoulder, breathing deeply of her. Tentatively, not knowing what was wrong, she reached up and held him, cradling him as she would a child, waiting. He lifted his head, "I thought perhaps you were that damned succubus," he said and kissed her fiercely.

They made love together, slow and deliberate, holding their passion in check to heighten it, not willing to give in to the desperation they both felt. As the tide finally overwhelmed them somewhere around mid-morning, Lark found herself weeping in spite of her ecstasy.

He tried to stop, fearing that he was hurting her, or doing something wrong, but she clung to him desperately, unwilling to let him, made him continue. Lying, exhausted for the moment, beside her, he reached out and wiped away the tears, held her closely to him when they would not stop.

"Please, princess. What is wrong? Is it something I did, or said, something my brother...."

"No," she said quickly, lifting her head to gaze into his eyes. "Is nothing wrong. Only everything right. Is why I weep, for joy. I... I missed you."

He gave an shaky smile, uncertain because he was not convinced nothing was wrong and that she was not just trying to keep him from pursuing the subject. "You are back early," he said lamely. "You said three days."

She chuckled. "Had enough of papa. Showing me off at every opportunity, especially to unwedded men. And, would have asked too many questions today. Besides, is not all right to miss you?"

He pulled her close to him, unwilling to let go. They lay that way for nearly an hour, until the sun streaming through a crack in the shutters made him sit up suddenly, swearing. Lark sat up, startled as he jumped out of bed and began to dress. "What, what is?" she asked, watching him.

"I was supposed to meet with Lord Colwyn this morning! Here it is almost noon and I was supposed to meet him for breakfast!"

Lark rolled over laughing. "Sorry," she chuckled.

He paused long enough to slip his hand beneath her neck and pull her up into a fierce kiss. "No, you're not," he said.

She smiled. "Tell him was my fault. And give my apologies. Had I known, would have sent Nightingale with note."

Landros gave her one last kiss and, grabbing his sword, headed for the door. He popped back in a moment later, "Would you meet me back here tonight after work?"

"Certainly," she smiled.

"Later!" he called, and left without explaining. Her arrival after work would provide him with time to find and speak with his brother before she came.

FOUR

One of Lord Colwyn's maids was just about to bring up the knight's lunch when Landros came in the kitchen door. Seizing the opportunity, he took the tray from her and offered to bring it up himself. The lord did not look up from his desk when he came in, gestured off-handedly for him to set the tray 'over there somewhere'.

Landros set it on the desk anyway, knowing it would cause the knight to look up at him. Colwyn's expression went from annoyance to surprise then back to annoyance again. He scowled at his squire. "Sleep late?" he asked sternly.

He fidgeted sheepishly. "No, sire, I didn't."

"What then?" he asked, taking a large bite from a thin meat pasty on the tray. He was giving his squire no quarter.

"I had a surprise visitor this morning."

One eyebrow went up. "Trouble?" he asked.

"No, not trouble...." Colwyn waited. "Lark... Lark snuck in on me this morning...."

Colwyn sat forward, "Say no more," he grinned. "I dare say you have had no breakfast?" He gestured for him to take the other pasty on the tray and rang for a servant to bring more.

Apparently this order had been anticipated by Landros's arrival, as it was only a moment later when two more arrived.

He sat across the desk, eating his share. "Have any luck with that map I brought you?"

"Yes, actually," Colwyn answered. "Seems the marks all correlate to the 'random' monster attacks we've been having, which have ceased altogether now. For good, we hope. Either it was the site to which they were teleported or released, or it was marked later as where they showed up, we cannot be certain which. Although," he continued, "there are a couple of places marked that have no correlation to anything."

"Perhaps these were places that were supposed to be hit?" Landros suggested as he ate.

Colwyn nodded. "More than likely. I have noticed that they are all places which were not well or heavily patrolled by actual soldiers. Mostly civilian or watchmen where there was any presence at all."

"Easier targets," he muttered.

"Speaking of targets, ...how's your shoulder?"

He shrugged. "Fine, a little sore, but not bad."

"Think you can fight?"

"Yes, sir. Why?" he asked, suddenly suspicious of the grin on his lord's face.

Lark walked back to her caravan with mixed emotions. There was the joy she felt at their reunion and the pleasure of his company, but her joy was well-weighted with the knowledge of what she might very well lose trying to keep that. Her father would most certainly not be supportive of her choice.

She sighed, packed a bag with what she would need that afternoon and evening at Lily's, as well as the bag Ivan had given her. She had been startled to discover this morning that the bag itself had magic of its own, holding easily five times what it seemed to. Ivan had stuffed most of a fully smoked deer into it, along with apples, onions and six pounds of flour. She decided she would give some to Lily, some to her host, some to the warren, and keep the rest for emergencies.

She noted that the grass was starting to object to the lack of light under the wagon. It would be time to move it soon. Tomorrow, she thought as she nibbled on a small hunk of cheese she took from a cabinet. It was not much, but enough to hold her until she got to work. The horses had come down to the river to drink, some of them to play. Lark grabbed her reins and went to catch Dolal. Since he was here, and she didn't have to go hunting him, she thought it would be nice to ride for a change.

He was easy enough to catch with the promise of attention and Lark slapped the reins to his halter and led him back to the wagon. Draping her things over his neck, she swung up and trotted off towards the gate.

Before she reached the bridge to the stable-yard, she heard the sounds of combat. Quietly, she guided the big Pinto towards the sounds, coming from somewhere behind the house and gardens. Rounding a large oak, she saw two fighters, each in chain-mail whaling away at each other, grunting with their efforts. One of the fighters was Colwyn, and the other was Landros. Lark, suddenly furious, kicked Dolal into a gallop towards the pair.

Colwyn looked up from the fight, ignored the blow his squire landed and shoved him back and out of the way of the incoming animal. Landros, startled, looked up to see her charging in on the big paint, her skirts riding up to her thighs and fury on her beautiful, tawny face. She used the animal to separate the two of them, began yelling at Colwyn from the horse's back.

"What is going on here?!" she screamed. "Whatever is problem, is your *squire!*" she pointed. "Are ways other than violence to solve!" Before Colwyn could protest, she whirled on Landros. "And *you!* Fighting with your lord? Is proper this?"

She was thoroughly confused when both of them started laughing. Dolal danced skittishly until Colwyn grabbed his halter to still him, lest he unwittingly step on the elf on the ground who could no longer stand. "Am glad you think is funny!" she snarled at him.

Lord Colwyn tried his best to keep a straight face. "We were not fighting, good lady. Not in earnest. These swords are not even real," he said, holding up the rattan weapon. "We were sparring." He took in her blank look and fished for another word. "I am training him. Teaching him to protect himself better."

As realization dawned on her, a flush began growing. She gave a quick apology and left the pair, trying to cover her embarrassment. No wonder they had laughed. Before she reached the gate, she too was laughing.

Colwyn helped Landros to his feet and stood to watch the Romeri girl ride off. "What a wildcat! I'd hang on to that one if I were you. Not very many women like her!"

"Thank the goddess for that!" he exclaimed.

Colwyn laughed and the two of them went back to their work. "By the way," he added after landing yet another sound blow across his squire's left shoulder. "You are excused for being late."

Blushing, Landros attacked, landing a few blows before having to retreat, rubbing his shoulder yet again.

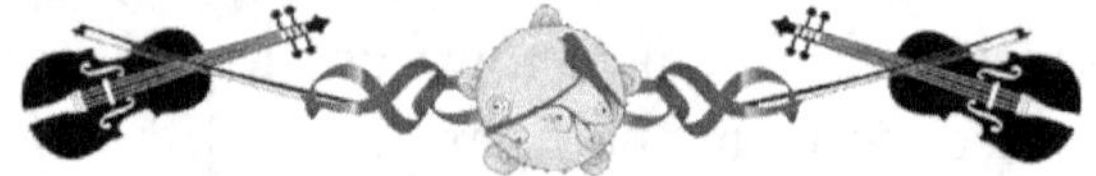

Lily was almost in tears when Lark gave her the food, made sure to lock it all up in the pantry. As the key clicked, Lark caught the faintest scent of magic in the air, and smiled. No doubt that was why the woman still had decent food, though the glimpse she had gotten of the shelves told her that its bounty was being severely tested. She would not hear of Lily paying her for any of it. "Have fed and housed me more than have allowed to pay. Is family. You can't say no."

All Lily could do at that was wipe her eyes and nod, heading back to work before she began crying in earnest.

Dane's lessons went well. It all seemed to boil down to what Lark had already decided. The boy only needed practice. There was really nothing more she could teach him but new songs, maybe a new instrument.

Not having expected her to return until the next evening, Lily had already made arrangements for a musician to come in for the night, so she did not need to stay and work. She sat with Dane in the corner for a while, listened to the minstrel strumming his lute and singing his songs and flirting with the ladies. He even made a few passing attempts at her which she only smiled at, thoroughly amused by his attempts at suavity.

It rankled her a bit that the man would not permit Dane to play with him at all. Any time the boy came near enough, he would snatch up his drink or his instrument case out of the way, as if the child was an idiot as well as blind.

"Ah, my lovely," he cooed in her direction, idly strumming a simple melody. "Can I perhaps convince you to dance for me?" he offered. "I have heard you are a marvellous dancer, and a fair singer as well."

Lark smiled enigmatically. "I do not know your songs to sing, nor, I doubt, do you know mine."

"Dance then," he coaxed. "Why waste such loveliness on the corner?"

"Have yet to play dancing music," she said, sipping at her wine.

Dane, weaving his way in and out of the tables with drinks, grinned at Lark, obviously enjoying the baiting game.

The minstrel began to play a country reel, which she summarily ignored. A couple of people got up and began dancing, but not her. He tried another, and another, each time attempting to coax her from the shadows by the fireplace. She just kept smiling. At last he gave up, begged the dancers for a break. As he went to get himself some refreshments, he paused by her table and bowed. "Ah, as beautiful as a dark damask rose you are, but cold as a snowdrop, and as dispassionate. It, I fear, would take a far better man than I to move your cold heart. Alas for you, my exotic rose, better men are rarer than snowflakes on desert blooms."

Lark refrained from giggling in his face, managed to continue smiling enigmatically until he moved away.

Hearing the music stop, Dane went over to the bar to find Lily.

"Mother, the minstrel is taking a break! Can I play for a little while? You know Lark says I need practice!"

Lily sighed, served the musician a plate of food. "Would it offend you if my son plays while you eat?" she asked.

The man shrugged. "I see no harm in it."

Dane came up to Lark, bowed. "May I borrow your fiddle, my lady?"

As she placed it in his hands, he whispered to her, "He said I could do naught but make him look good. Does that mean he thinks I will play badly?"

"Am afraid so," she mused, hid her anger behind a smile as she nodded to the man in question who raised his glass to toast her.

Dane started by making certain that the instrument was in tune for what he wanted to do, struck a few tentative chords. Lark sat drumming her fingers on the table top, wishing she could think of something to punish the minstrel for his arrogance. Then Dane turned back to her, bowed formally and said in a voice loud enough to carry to the bar, "Oh most beauteous Romer Queen, would you honour me by dancing to my humble tune?"

Lark stared at him for a moment, almost laughed out loud but had the presence of mind not to. She stood, giving him a slight, queenly nod of her head. "*Sesha*," she said regally.

Dane bowed again, perched upon the stool and waited for her to place herself in front of the fire. She stood before him, her back to her audience and whispered, "What will you play?" She noticed that the audience had quieted in expectation of her performance, something they had not done for the minstrel.

Dane just grinned. "The Faery Queen, what else?"

Lark stood stock still as the first chord was struck, waited until the moment was right, and then began with slow, sinuous movements which she directed at the blind fiddler, dancing for him first of all. She moved to the side, dancing for others to see, but still obviously for the boy. When the music spoke up, began to grow faster in tempo and cadence and passion, she moved out to the patrons of the tavern, dancing on the edge of the cleared space like a dandelion puff caught up by a wind devil. The song was one of passion and longing, and those were emotions she was very intimate with right now. It was an easy and welcome outpouring of her soul.

When she finally leapt from the table, returning to the fireside, the crowd was as worked up as she was, quite ready for the return of the queen to her prince's side. She danced slowly again, pleading, seductive, begging to be allowed to return. Then, as the music let her in, she turned, sank slowly until she sat once more at the feet of her 'love'; the story told, the crowd and her own needs appeased. When the last chord faded away, the crowd roared with appreciation. Coins filled the air, merely pennies, to be sure, but more than enough considering.

Lark stood, pressed a kiss to Dane's forehead in thanks. "Right Romeri fiddler I have made of you," she crowed proudly.

Dane shrugged. "The foolish gegenta deserved it."

Lark was pleasantly surprised. The boy had apparently been paying attention to more than just her lessons. She tousled his hair and went back to her corner to collect her things. The dance had provided her with a necessary out-pour, but it had stirred up needs as well. It was time for a serious talk with a certain elf.

She shouldered her belongings and started out the door. As she passed by the Minstrel at the bar, she overheard the man sitting next to him say, "*That* is why a 'filthy Gypsy girl' is the regular here. Any other stupid questions?"

"And they prefer the term *Romeri*," someone else added.

She smiled, deeply satisfied. She was almost to the door when she heard Dane call to her from across the room. "Lark! You forgot your fiddle!"

"You earned it!" she called back, and left without another word.

Landros was in the middle of a heated argument with his brother. He had no clue how things had gotten so hot so fast. His brother had arrived as he had been requested. They exchanged a few pleasantries. Portholus asked why Landros wanted to see him and the next thing he knew they were yelling at each other. Still Portholus refused to tell him what had happened between them.

When Nightingale flew in through the window, alerting them that she was on the way up, the two put the argument on hold. When he opened the door for her, she immediately reached for a kiss. He pulled out of her reach, took her by the wrist and lead her into the room, not bothering to ask why she was earlier than he had expected.

The flush of her success at the Cinnamon Tree was drained away immediately when she sensed the tension in her lover. No, it was not tension, she corrected herself, it was anger. She stopped cold when she saw the other elf standing in the living room.

They exchanged stares.

Landros stopped her about five feet from his brother. He stood between them, speaking to both, and ready for any sudden moves she might make. "Now," he said. "I do not have the time or the patience to deal with this. I have a girlfriend who is not telling me everything and is obviously angry about something. I have a brother that has, after some 'coaxing'," he growled, "admitted that less than pleasant words were traded between the two of you but refuses to tell me the nature of the quarrel. Now," he added, pointing to Portholus, "you've told me I will have to ask the lady. I have asked the lady." He turned to her. "The lady said that things would be sorted out between her and the 'gentleman' in question. I am hereby giving you that opportunity. The two of you are the most important people in my life and it is time to correct this problem. I will not have the two of you feuding! I am also not going to choose between you. You both mean entirely too much to me. So, I am going out. I expect that the two of you will have this worked out by the time I return."

He managed to keep from slamming the door behind him as he stormed out, fervently praying the two of them would use their heads and not try to kill each other instead.

Neither of them moved until well after Landros had left, their eyes locked. Portholus watched her, obviously waiting for her to retaliate in some way. Finally, she took the three short steps to close the distance, kept his eyes locked to hers to keep him distracted. Then, summing up all of her strength, let her fist fly, connecting soundly with his jaw.

Portholus reeled off-balance, half in surprise at the blow and half in surprise at the strength behind it. He managed to save some face by simply sitting down on the couch behind him. Still somewhat stunned, he noticed there was blood on his lip.

Lark stood over him, fists on her hips, dark eyes blazing, her anger, finally vented, beginning to subside. "It is your turn, pup, to listen to me," she snapped. She noticed him beginning to swell up at the 'pup' remark, then hold himself in check, as if he realized he might have deserved it. "If you learn nothing else in your handful of centuries, learn this," she growled, leaning closer. "*Never* accuse someone, or openly question motives, until have sufficient reason and know who are dealing with. Next time could be death of you, and how you think your brother feel then, *sesket*?

"Now," she said, standing straighter as she moved away from him, "with that out of way, all is forgotten." She went to the hearth, seeking some kind of warmth for her soul. All the heat and strength and fire seemed to have bled out of her in that rush of words, replaced by the cold knowledge that she now had to rely upon the help and understanding of a gegenta whose motives she knew all too well. "We have to talk. You, too, have stake in this, and seems you know well enough how to keep mouth shut." She felt her voice tightening.

She turned to face him. "What am going to tell you cannot leave this room. If is to reach brother's ears, must be me who tells him. I will not yet, and cannot or would have done so already. Promise me your silence."

It took Portholus a few minutes of studying her face before he nodded, giving her what she asked.

She sighed, relieved. If he had refused, she did not know what she would have done. "First, let me say that I do love your brother, very much but... fear loving him may not be enough. I still may break his heart.

"Romeri have bad reputation among gegenta, those not Romer. We are not understood and so we are suspect. Because we are not trusted, we do not trust. We most certainly do not 'mingle' our blood with that of outsiders. Romeri who, for whatever reason, wish to marry gegenta become genti, or those who are no longer Romeri but are not quite gegenta. These are people who are trusted more than gegenta, but are still not privy to all aspects of Romer life, are often treated with disdain. Were this all at stake would be no trouble or choice."

When she hesitated to continue, Portholus spoke up. "So what is the additional stake? What haven't you told me?"

Lark looked at him. "Romeri clans are matrilineal. Each clan is ruled by one woman, head of bloodline and solidified by inherited magic. This is ranie, or in your terms 'Gypsy queen', though we hold no court. Each caravan of each clan also has ranie, though not always as powerful. Problem is my mother was clan ranie, as her mother before her was and is now, as I was not ready when mother died. As princess, as your brother is so fond of calling me, I have re-sponsibility to clan. I most certainly cannot marry gegenta."

"I see the problem," he mused.

"No, you don't," she said, stepping closer. "I have made my choice, that night in sewer when I walk shadowlands, before you and I first met face to face. My father will not respect that choice. Father will fume and fury and forbid this. That his daughter would sacrifice her clan for mere gegenta he will not have, and so I will have to choose again. Is Landros and Outcast, or Rushavska and a hollow, bitter heart which will sing no more. To be Outcast is to die to my family. I will be less than nothing, less than genti, less than gegenta. I could just stay with Landros as we have been, and simply never marry. No one will think ill of me for this unless I never go back to my caravan. With our way of life marriage partners are hard met. But I fear is no longer enough for him, or will be soon, and is certainly no longer enough for me. I want to give him family that he has lost and longs so much for and I cannot!"

She gave a strangled cry, pounded her fist on the mantle in frustrated rage. The vibration caused the swords above her head to jump, threatening to fall, but they held in their brackets. She glared up at them, "Oh, I wish *would* fall on me!! Wish *had* been killed in warehouse with Ebastian and Lula! Or never wakened from lightning strike in sewer! At least then my soul would be free and dancing with my mother again, and I would not be here struggling to choose between my heart and my soul! Romeri were never meant to be caged!!"

There were tears streaming down her face as she buried it in the crook of her arms. She sobbed openly, unable to keep her misery inside any longer.

Portholus laid his hands gently on her shoulders, tried to draw her away from the blades. She looked up at him, her eyes wild. "You see now why I cannot tell him any of this? Why I have kept this, my only secret from him, though it kills me to see him suffer from not knowing what I cannot tell him for fear of his suffering? He would not permit me to chose between him and family. He would leave before permitting that sacrifice!"

The look on his face told her she was right. Finally, unable to bear the heat of the fire any more, she allowed him to draw her away, to set her upon the sofa. "Please," she said, getting herself under control. "Tell him we have made our peace, but no more. Not yet. Maybe... if I can solve this...."

Portholus silenced her, gave her a handkerchief from his pocket to dry her eyes, before he began pacing the small area before the hearth. "It has amazed me, your perception. Landros said he had not yet told you what happened to our family, yet somehow you know."

"I am ranie," she sighed. "I know things. I do not know what happened, only that giants left you orphaned and he feels this loss very deeply."

Portholus looked rather impressed. He had apparently far underestimated her. "Our parents were adventurous people, and wandered a great deal before they settled down as protectors of a small human town. A band of giants came down out of the hills and committed a massacre. Both our sisters and our parents were killed that night. Landros took it very hard, and I, well... I was very young at the time. So, yes, you are right that he will not allow you to give up your family for him. It means too much to you, is too much a part of you. He would never permit that no matter what it might cost him. He and I both know all too well the pain of that kind of loss. I can only imagine how much worse it could be to lose that knowing they were still alive."

He sat beside her on the sofa, held her smaller, darker hands in his and stared deep into her eyes. "You have created a puzzle that may take some time to solve and I do not know if we have it. Part of me wished you would walk away, convinced that both hearts would heal given enough time, but I know better now. If you walk away from him now, he will be without a heart in this time of war and, feeling he has nothing left to live for, he may take some foolish action that could guarantee his death.

"Try and think of anything that might help, some way we could convince your father that this is for the best. It is up to him, is it not, to banish you?"

She nodded. "Ranie leads the clan, but each caravan has its own head. And I am not clan ranie. Gruma is."

"Perhaps she would know of some way?"

"Is possible. I will talk to her."

"Find out, if you would, what it takes to be considered a Romer, even a genti. If all it means is a homeless wanderer, then my brother and I have qualified for a long time. Somehow we will find a way to keep your family honour intact as well as my brother's heart."

As he stood, looking down at her, she noticed more kindness in his dark golden eyes than she had believed he could feel. "Before I leave, I need your word of honour that what you have told me is true, and that your love for my brother is genuine. If there is one thing I have learned in my scant eighty-odd years, it is that Love is the strongest of emotions and as such can overcome anything and anyone."

She stood, smiled wryly, brushed the tip of her finger along his nose. "Still doubting? Still seeking irrevocable answers to all questions?"

He sighed, took her hand, pressed a polite, gentlemanly kiss there. "Forgive me, I..."

She interrupted him softly. "Romeri have been known to lie, steal and cheat gegenta. But Romeri *never* lie about love, never speaks of such things with one not involved. Love, like death, is very private thing."

Satisfied, Portholus whisked on his cloak and headed for the door. He paused in the frame to issue a warning to her. "Oh, I would advise you to be very careful going out at night from now on. It is getting dangerous out there, even for the likes of me," he grinned and closed the door behind him.

Lark settled back on the sofa in front of the fire and curled up watching it, brooding. Scraps wandered in from goddess only knows where and crawled into her lap for a long bout of loving, scratching and rubbing. Nightingale, perched on the mantle, decided to take a nap.

FIVE

Landros sat brooding downstairs in the taproom, every noise from above grating on his nerves even though he knew those sounds were not from his own floor. He had deliberately left the poison-proofing pin upstairs, wanting the alcohol to calm him. He had been in here for only a half a bottle when he saw a large Romer enter the room.

The man was easily six feet tall, burly, a deep olive tan complexion and thick, curly black hair and a matching moustache. He wore a simple red vest with gold embroidery and braiding without a shirt, exposing his muscular, hairy arms, and dark, hirsute chest. The dark purple sash around his waist was silk, almost clashing with the green pants he wore tucked into his black riding boots. There was no apparent weapon on him, but Landros was certain he was armed to the teeth. Some of the barmaids and female patrons were eyeing him admiringly. He walked directly to the bartender and engaged him in a short conversation.

Landros did not know why the appearance of this man had set off instinctual alarms, but apparently they were correct. Shortly after going to the bar, the man turned, looked out across the sea of patrons and thanked the bartender. He stopped in front of Landros's table, staring down at him with a discerning eye and less than approving sneer. His accent was heavier than Lark's, but nearly identical. "Are you elf known as Londrus?" he asked.

Landros got the distinct impression the man had mispronounced the name deliberately, as well as having looked him over and found him wanting in some way. He merely nodded assent to the question, not sure yet what level of threat this large man represented. He carefully maintained a casual, unthreatened air.

The man leaned forward over the table, bracing himself with rough, callused hands flat on the surface, on either side of Landros's drink. His pitch black eyes bored into the elf's golden ones. "I understand you have been consorting with Romeri dancing girl by name of Lark."

Landros took a long, deliberate drink from his cup, set the now empty glass back on the table, leaned back with apparent carelessness in the chair. "The name is *Landros*," he corrected softly, "and whom I choose to spend my time and affections on is my affair. But to answer your question, yes, I have. If you have a problem with that, then I suggest you get over it very quickly."

The man took in his posture and tone of voice, then ground, "Problem I have is your dalliance with my sister!" he said firmly. "She can be somewhat blind to certain matters and is very much an innocent. I do not know how you coaxed her into your bed, or tricked her, or beguiled her, or whatever spell you may have cast, but be certain of this, little man, should she fall to heartache, or get herself hurt trying to impress you, or be no more than an occasional night's pleasure to you... you will have me and my brothers to deal with!"

He sat down across from Landros, in a suddenly more genial mood and waved for a drink to be brought to him. "Now, with that unpleasantness out of way, I wish to hear what you have to say about this. My sister has told me nothing, but I have seen way she broods. She is no longer our bright and chipper little Lark. She has been in such mood!"

He drained the half tankard the moment it arrived and waited with almost deceptive friendliness, not even flinching at the taste.

Landros let his rage come to a head before reacting. In the back of his mind, he realized this is probably the precise conversation that had set Lark off in the first place. But none of that was reaching the rest of his brain at the moment. With his usual diplomatic grace, he flipped the table sideways. As the man started to stand, Landros pushed him back down into the chair.

Patrons around them were moving to other tables quickly.

"Now see here, human," he snarled. "My limited patience is at an end. I have no clue why Lark is in such a *mood* as you put it, and will not know until she deigns to tell me. My intentions are between her and myself, and if she thought you needed to be aware of them, you would already know them. If you feel that your sister has been slighted in some way, then challenge me now and we will settle this outside. If you are insinuating that your sister has somehow been soiled by this elf, then I will take that as an insult to her honour, and brother or no, I will reach down your throat and rip out your heart right now!"

With that Landros stood back, beginning to breathe more slowly after having vented some steam. He set the table back on its legs and waited impatiently for the Romer who seemed to be taking his time.

Finally, the man nodded solemnly. "Outside then."

Landros felt a sense of dread well up inside him as he followed the large man out of the taproom. If this was indeed Lark's brother, and all the little signs he had seen so far did not deny this possibility, then he could very well be about to destroy all hopes of any future with her.

The man passed through the courtyard, stopping at the mouth of the alley between the stable and the main building. Landros was aware of another figure standing in the depths of the shadows back there.

"Will that be your second?" he asked snidely, "or is this not to be a fair fight?"

"This is my brother, Raven," he said.

The person in question stepped closer to the courtyard light, turned out to be a boy on the cusp of adulthood dressed similarly to the first man, although he wore an open shirt. "If you will excuse me but moment," the large Romer said generously, then proceeded to have a low conversation with the boy in a rapid, foreign tongue. It was not an unfamiliar sound to Landros. He had heard it before, especially when Lark was in a royal rage.

Speaking of royalty, he thought. If she is a princess, did that make this man a prince? He did not quite think so, vaguely remembering her saying something about a strictly matrilineal line of inheritance, but he may have simply inferred that. Watching the two men arguing, he began to get the impression that the little one was vehemently against him, not to mention winning the argument.

Finally the larger man sighed, waved his hand in Landros's direction and stepped aside. He raised an eyebrow in surprise. Did they think so little of him that they would send a child to duel with him?

The boy swaggered and smirked. "You have been called out for dishonour done to our sister, Mariya Petrovich Rushava, dancer also know as Lark," he sneered.

Landros laughed ironically, "I do not know this woman you speak of as I have never heard that name before."

The boy swelled with rage, "You deny that you have lain with Romeri Lark?"

Landros remained cool. "The Lark I know has another name, and Maria is not it. What that name is remains none of your business. If you choose to continue this conflict, we can, though you will not like the outcome. If so, meet me here tomorrow half-past midnight, and do not be late, for I will not wait long. Though I would get my facts straight, if I were you. It seems that you are soiling the names of two young ladies, both your Maria and my Lark, and, as a genteel elf, I cannot permit that to go unpunished."

The large one said something to Raven, practically dismissing him and faced Landros on more equal footing. "Tomorrow then," he said, and offered his hand.

Landros took it uncertainly, to seal the agreement, then left.

His heart felt heavy as he went back inside. This meeting did not bode very well at all.

On entering the taproom, one of the barmaids came over to him.

"Yes?" he asked, feeling very tired all of a sudden.

"Your brother has left," she said.

"Lark?" he asked.

She shook her head. "I did not see her come down."

He nodded, thanked her with a coin on her tray and headed upstairs. Lark was curled up asleep on the sofa in front of a dying fire. He decided to wait to question her, not wishing to wake her. He picked her up carefully, after removing the raccoon from her lap, and carried her to bed. She only stirred a little as he carefully undressed her. Afraid to wake her, he left her blouse on and set the rest of her clothes aside and crawled into the bed next to her.

Both of them were quiet and moody when they woke, and they lay close in each other's arms long into the morning, though neither of them were really asleep. They spent most of the day not really doing anything, but both reluctant to leave sight of the other. He had a small meal brought up and the two of them ate in near silence. She felt somewhat better, knowing that her burden had been shared, but it had yet to be shared with the one person who mattered to her most.

Landros, on the other hand, had about a dozen questions he wanted to ask about his encounter with the Romeri men, but dared not ask them of her for fear of her reaction. He did not know what to expect, but was in absolute terror of what the outcome might mean. He took several long hours to make love to her that afternoon. The process was slow and savoured, each fearing it might be the last, but neither for the same reason.

Lark left for work just around sunset, though not really in the mood. She danced very little, played less, content to let Dane do most of the work while she told fortunes in her corner. It did not help that there were ill portents everywhere. Few of the fortunes she told were very good, the best of them was a simple standstill. Occasionally she caught genuine glimpses of the future in the faces of the people she foretold for. For some, she had real advice.

One young man in particular struck her, aroused her pity. "Go to offices at hall of justice, tell them you wish to join irregulars."

"Will that win me Maggie's heart?" he asked.

She looked into his hopeful young eyes. "Yes, will win you Maggie's heart, and win you glory. Make you hero."

He went away happy, though she had no heart to keep his silver. She tossed it to Dane when she had the chance. What she had not told him was that he was going to die, one way or another. Magruma was calling him. By doing as she had told him he would indeed win his love's heart ...on his deathbed. He was going to die a hero. She had almost given him different advice, but she had foreseen that path as well, and that one too, ended in death, though with far less valour or sense.

As she was about to fold up her cloth, someone else sat down. She did not even look up as she told them, "No more fortunes tonight. My eyes are tired."

"Not even for a fellow musician?"

She looked up to see the minstrel from the other night. The look on her face told her he was not going to relent. She sighed, held out her hand. He gave her a gold coin. She pushed it back to him. "Silver, if you please."

He stared into her eyes defiantly. "Why not gold? I want a good fortune."

"You will get no true fortune without silver. Coin does not have to be whole, but must be silver."

He did not take his eyes off her, but placed a silver coin in her hand anyway. She sighed again, rearranged the stones. "Ask your question and choose stone."

"Why did you show me up last night?"

"Is not question for runes," she answered.

He grabbed her hand. "I had done nothing to you. Why did you show me up? You deliberately played me for a fool."

She tried to pull her hand away, but he held too tightly. "You played self for fool. You belittle not only popular regular, but owner's son, who, am not afraid to say, is better musician than you. You try to show me up, you showed yourself. Now reap your harvest and let go my hand."

"Listen, you gypsy whore...."

A knife thudded into the table, pinning the minstrel's sleeve close to the wrist. "The next one will pin your hand. Now, I believe the lady asked you to let her go," Portholus threatened.

"Who the devil are you?!" he demanded, still holding on.

She reached under the table with her bare foot and, grabbing a hold of his calf between her toes, pinched him hard. He jumped, but did not release her.

"One of the lady's many protectors. Now let her go."

He snorted. "One of her many gig...."

Before he could finish his sentence, a second blade had flashed into existence at his throat and pressed dangerously close to his Adam's apple. "Don't say it. Now let her hand go." Reluctantly the minstrel released her, and Lark swept her stones into her bag. She practically threw the silver coin back at him. "Now," Portholus continued as soon as she was out of the way. "Apologize to the lady."

The man rattled off a half-hearted apology which prompted Portholus to apply more pressure to the blade. "You have a sweeter tongue than that. Use it. Or I'll cut it out from here," he added in a hissed whisper.

"I very humbly beg your gracious forgiveness, most beautiful and talented lady," he rasped.

Portholus let him go, stood in front of her until the man had left the tavern completely. He turned around. "Are you all right?" he asked.

"Am fine. Hand is sore, but will not keep me from playing. Thank you."

"Are you going home now?" he asked.

She shook her head. "Am going to see your brother."

He held out his arm to her. "May I escort you there?"

"Let me get my things," she said. She disappeared into the kitchen for a few minutes to say goodnight.

It was a clear night as they walked along the narrow boulevard. There had been no sign of enemy activity, which worried her. If it could not be seen it was far more dangerous. The night was too quiet. The only sounds were what drifted out of the taverns. By the time they were within a few blocks of the Cygnet, even that had stopped and there were night-watch everywhere. Portholus must have noticed her nervousness, because he spoke up.

"Curfew," he said.

"Corfew?" she asked. "What is corfew?"

"Eleven o'clock," he said.

She stopped, grabbed his arm. "No. *What* is corfew? I do not know this word."

"Curfew is when everyone is required to be off the streets, at home and all businesses closed. You were not aware of this?"

"No. Have been away. What has happened and why is corfew?"

"The curfew is for the further protection of the people. Anyone caught out and about will be detained and considered potential enemies unless they can provide special papers that permit them to be out and about. It is supposed to keep the people safer."

"If Mayor had not done this before, why do this now?"

He just stared at her for a long moment. "You don't know?" he asked flatly

"If knew would I ask?"

"The Lord Mayor was arrested three nights ago. Landros and some others found proof that he was working against the city. He was arrested and now sits in the city gaol."

"Is make no sense," she muttered, sinking back against a building in shock.

"I agree, it does not."

"Who is... who is ruling, who make this 'corfew'?"

"The magistrate is now acting mayor and in control."

Lark felt her heart sink all the way to her feet.

Portholus put a hand on her shoulder to steady her. "It gets worse. He has instigated something he calls the civilian watch. He has deputized willing citizens to fill in the gaps of the watch so that those men might be freed for the actual fighting. These people have surprising power. If not careful we could find ourselves in the midst of a witch hunt, which is why I warned you to walk more carefully nights."

"Why is mayor still alive? Why is he not executed?" she asked numbly. It was all so hard to believe. The Mayor had not struck her as that kind of man. She found that she could not believe in his guilt, no matter what the weight of evidence; but that he had been left alive shocked her.

Portholus made her start walking again, supporting her gently. "The council would not permit it. There are far too many people who still believe in him in spite of the evidence, the city would be broken if they executed him. It was decided that he will sit in the gaol until the king arrives or we are overrun. Unable to make the choice themselves, they decided to leave it to the crown, whoever holds it."

Lark numbly allowed him to take her to the inn. She assured him at the door that she would be fine, that he did not need to follow her up unless he too planned to stay the night. It was very close to curfew, after all. She went upstairs without looking back, and so was not aware of him curling up by the great fireplace in the common room below.

She entered the apartments without knocking, a Romeri habit when dealing with other Romer. She had unconsciously carried it over to her lover. The room was lit by the fireplace and numerous candles were scattered about. The air was filled with the fragrance of a very aromatic wood. Landros came out of the bedroom, looked up in surprise to see her so early. He crossed the room to her, taking her bag and setting it behind the door, and pulled her into his arms.

"What is all this...?" she began.

He hushed her with a kiss. "For tonight we forget everything outside that door; the war, families, and all the troubles that plague us. Tonight it is just the two of us, and nothing else exists," he said, kissing her again.

As she began to melt in the embrace, she became suddenly aware of her skirt slipping from her hips. Without breaking the kiss or the embrace, he unfastened her vest and, together with her blouse, it joined the skirt on the floor.

Landros let her fall asleep, lay in the bed beside her, head propped up in his hand as he softly stroked her arm and shoulders. He still could not understand why she had chosen him at all, was still uncertain if she would stay, or be able to after tonight, but... he could simply not allow this dishonour to go unaddressed, even by her own kin. It just was not in him. He would prefer not to fight to the death, but he would if they insisted.

The hour approached all too soon and he found it hard to leave her side. He kissed her, gently so not to wake her, and laid a flower that he had secreted away for this purpose on the pillow beside her. He drew on his clothes and his baldric and went quietly into the other room.

Portholus was waiting for him as he had been asked to via a note left for him that afternoon. He looked up as Landros came into the room. "You forgot your armour, brother," he said quietly.

"No, I did not," he answered, going to the hearth and taking down one of the two elven swords. He put it into his scabbard, placing his other blade in its place.

"You really insist on doing this?"

"It is a battle of honour. One I do not wish to partake in for a multitude of reasons, but I have no choice, something you obviously cannot understand."

"I understand this much, brother," he said, leaning forward. "You cannot win this battle. If you lose, you die, you lose everything. If you win, and kill him, you still lose everything. Do you really think that Lark will marry you after you have killed her brother?"

Landros looked at him, startled. He had not mentioned marriage to his brother, though the thought had been drifting in the back of his mind.

Portholus read his brother's face like a proverbial book. "Oh, I thought as much. It's relatively obvious even to the girl. The fact that she is still here should tell you something. But you haven't answered the question. Do you really think that Lark will marry you after you have killed her brother?"

"I don't know," he snapped, irritated that he was so easily read.

"Would you be able to love her if she killed me? Even if in a duel?"

Landros was silent, unable to honestly answer that question. "I have to go," he said. He crossed to the desk, took out a folded letter and gave it to his brother. "See that she gets this when she wakes up." With that he pulled on his cloak and left.

SIX

When Landros entered the courtyard, he saw the large Romeri waiting for him by the stable. He had shed his vest and stood in only his trousers, barefoot, leaning back against the stable with his massive arms folded across his chest. He uncrossed them when he saw Landros emerge from the building.

"Greetings, Landrosallenthyoia," he intoned. "If you would be so kind, is not place for what must be done tonight. Come to camp. Is open and air is clean and is private enough. I promise no harm will come to you on way."

Landros nearly balked when the man said his full name, flawlessly, but with a heavy accent. Not even Lark knew that. This set him on edge, but there was a sense of peace about the man that calmed him. Determined to see this through no matter what happened, he agreed to follow him.

To his surprise, he was led to a shed at the end of the alley. The man looked back, grinned. "Is not going to bite, shed tools," he said and opened the door.

He caught the scent of wildflowers and a sea of grass in the dark portal. The Romer stepped inside readily enough, held the door open. Landros hesitated, not being able to see anything inside and convinced the area could not be big enough for two men.

"Come on, elf," he laughed. "If door closes behind me, when you open will be but horse shed. I gave my word. Even to gegenta, if given, must be honoured."

Goaded, he stepped through. He was shocked to find himself in the very field he had smelled. Not far off, away from the stand of trees where they stood, was a small Romeri camp. There were only three wagons and one huge bonfire under the large, newly waning moon. The roofs of the wagons were red, proving to Landros that these were indeed Lark's people.

The man brought him down to the camp. The few children here scattered out of the way, back to their mother's skirts, watching with wide eyes. Landros felt self-conscious under the scrutiny, but strangely at peace. It was not something he could explain.

They stopped before a figure huddled in front of the fire, throwing strong herbs into the flames. The figure turned, unfolded itself into a tall, thin, ancient human woman in voluminous robes of dark purples, blues, blacks and gold. She wore a great deal of jewellery, and a veritable fortune of coins were strung around her neck and on the red and copper scarf that covered her long grey-white hair.

"Welcome, Pathfinder," she said, her voice gravelly with age, but still strong and commanding. "Come to me. Let me see if you are indeed one my daughter has spoken of."

Landros wondered how in the world this old crone could possibly be Lark's mother before he remembered her saying something about her mother having passed on. This, then, must be Lark's gruma, the clan ranie, the one who spoke to ghosts.

She was nearly a head taller than he, and frightfully thin. Her eyes were white and sightless, but nonetheless seized his own and would not let him look away. She set a bony hand on his shoulder that held more strength than it should have. Her other hand, heavily jewelled, touched his face, as if trying to see it through her fingers as he had known some blind to do. Her fingers tweaked the tips of his ears, but he held his peace, sensing that it would be dangerous and unwise to anger this woman unnecessarily.

"Elven," she mused curiously. "About her height. Yes, with plenty of fire. Sword this one. Already begun, she has, to temper him. Ah, Danine, are you so sure this is one for our Illyana? One she will die for?" she seemed to ask of the air. "One.... Ah, but I waste time. Moon is almost high enough to begin. Then, boy, and only then, will I tell you what I know. When you are permitted such secrets. But by then you will have most of your own answers to present questions." She cackled. "Yes, yes, my daughter. And whole slew of new ones."

Without being given a chance to ask her any questions, the large Romer who had brought him here led him over to a marked off area just beyond the fire. A pretty little girl about eight or nine years old asked Landros for his shirt and his weapons. Seeing that the brother was already stripped to the waist and obviously weaponless, he reluctantly obliged.

A wrestling match, he thought. And badly unbalanced. The man before him could probably wrestle a horse and win. But at least that meant there would be no bloodshed, and for that he was relieved.

The old woman came to stand before them, a black-bladed dagger, possibly obsidian, in her gnarled grasp. The Romer held out his left hand. "Give me your hand, Pathfinder."

There being no menace in the large man's voice, Landros did as he was asked. The man turned his palm up and held it open upon his own, stared deep into Landros's amber orbs with dark eyes so much like Lark's but nowhere near as beautiful.

"Am trusting you, gegenta, to do my sister no harm," he said. This came as a complete surprise to Landros, who now had no idea what was about to happen. "Am placing her upon palm of our hands. When our mother died, she made me swear I would protect her. I am no longer her protector. Am giving you great honour based on what fire I saw last eve displayed, upon your determined defence of her, and upon your willingness to trust her family without reason for her sake alone. Am risking my own honour on that of my sister. If you fail us both, if you prove less than worthy of this singular distinction, *she* will be *goshaska*, outcast. And I, worse, for I brought you into family, and because I will hunt you down and kill you and steal your soul for dark ones. Be warned that I will not do this lightly. For after tonight, killing you is killing my own brother."

Landros spoke up, finally beginning to realize what was going on here. "I do not know this *goshaska* you speak of, but if she is outcast for *my* crimes, you will see fire as you have never seen before. As to hunting me down, if I have forsaken Illyana, you will not get the chance at my soul, for it will already be gone. I would give my life for your sister, and if you have any doubt as to that or my honour, we can settle that here and now."

The old woman nodded, pleased, and laid the blade upon his palm. "We do this," she intoned, "because Romeri who settles with gegenta, married or otherwise, is genti. To keep her, to be with her and keep her happy, you cannot be gegenta. You must become baharen, gegenta who is called brother."

The man still holding his hand open spoke. "I am Ivan Petrovich Rushavska. For sake of my sister, Illyana Petrovna, I will call you brother."

Landros felt the blade slice into his hand then, across the pad at the base of his thumb. The ranie cut Ivan as well, sprinkled a powdered herb on both their wounds. He then seized Landros's bloody hand in his, thumbs locked, wound to wound, and the woman handed the knife to the little girl and bound their hands in a red sash shot with gold.

There was a burning between their palms, as the blood began to slowly drip down their elbows. Landros could smell the herbs through the cloth, could feel them working their odd little magic already. He felt light-headed, planted his feet so that he could hold his balance better in spite of his dizziness.

He heard music, a melancholy but spirited fiddle that began slowly. He became aware of several women dancing in a circle around them with long, filmy scarves trailing from their wrists and hips, creating a hypnotic effect in his peripheral vision. He wanted to look, but could not take his eyes from Ivan's. Suddenly the moon came out from behind a passing cloud and stabbed the pair of them like a falling sword.

Landros found himself in a barren meadow. The now wild music reverberated with abandon throughout, reeling across the field though the musicians and the dancing girls could not be seen. Only one was left, a lone woman just a few yards away in filmy, pale-coloured garments dancing as one with the music. Her long black hair was a sharp contrast to the paleness of her clothes and her dusky belly flashed in and out among the numerous scarves. It was a sight suddenly more beautiful to him that a thousand elven cotillions, and the music more passionate than anything he had ever heard. There was something very Lark-like about her, and he guessed that this was perhaps a vision of her as she would be in a decade or so, perhaps a little more. She was stunning, both in movement and in feature, and her dark blue eyes never seemed to leave his no matter how she twisted and turned. Her body was incredible, under her complete, sensuous control. Surprisingly, his response was not a sexual one, but one of the heart, as if the unseen violinist had stolen it to use for strings and taken his soul for the bow.

As she neared him, she began to fade, and he saw his Lark beyond her. All thoughts of the dancing woman vanished as he tried to walk towards her. She was still young, not even twenty by human years. He stopped when he saw the young Romeri with her. He was dark and handsome and full of passion and delight for her. Lark began to tease him, leading him off towards a small copse of woods. In his impatience, the Romer snatched her up and threw her over his shoulder. Hanging upside down and protesting playfully, she caught sight of Landros. She waved, tauntingly, laughed as they began to disappear into the woods.

He tried to go after her, but found he was rooted to the spot. He felt hot tears running down his face and heard the shriek and pop of a string breaking on the violin. His heart continued to beat, though erratically, in his chest, missing a beat in every four, as if part of his heart had caved in, or vanished altogether.

There was a scream. He had heard that voice too often not to know its source, though he had never heard it raised so, as if it had been torn from her by force. Not caring that he had just seen her betray him with one of her own kind, he turned, tried to at least see her, but found his wrists held in giant fingers. He fought like a demon to no avail as the monster began trying to put his hands together behind his back. The pain meant nothing, though it was excruciating. What hurt worse was a second giant holding Lark in his fist, plucking at her like a boy does a bug he has caught in cruel fascination. He heard his name ripped from her throat one last time before she fell silent.

There was a great tearing sound and he fell to the ground, suddenly free of the giant's grasp, as surprised as it to see that his chest had split and his heart lay on the ground in front of him, in two pieces.

As he staggered to his feet, to run to where the disenchanted giant had flung the doll-like figure, he found himself falling to his knees beside her body in his rooms at the Cygnet. She was alive, merely sleeping in front of the fire. She opened her eyes as he took her in his arms, deathly afraid for her. She looked up at him in puzzlement, smiled weakly. "Have you come to take me home with you, my love? Have you come to take me to my mother and yours? I always knew that in my last breath you would come for me."

He tried to speak, to voice his confusion, but nothing came out, no voice, no breath. She moved her hand in explanation and he saw a silver-hilted dagger fall away to reveal a very self-inflicted wound just under her heart. "I told you to bring this back to me. You should have done what I asked. Now, I disappoint no one, and my honour and my heart are still mine, to take or give. I will be with you soon. Carry me..." she rasped, "carry me one last time to bed. ... in your arms," she added with a smile. "I do not think I could bear your shoulder this night."

He rose, lifted her up as if she weighed nothing. She reached up and touched the tears on his face. "For me?" she whispered. "Oh no, not for me. I go not first into unknown night. You have come back to guide me... to carry me.... Oh..."

As he turned to place her upon the bed, she dissolved into nothingness and drifted away. He turned to see the dagger gleaming evilly on the hearth, and it seemed to tarnish even as he watched, change to the black dagger that had sliced open his hand an eternity ago.

He fell as he reached for it, skittering it into the fire. He did not hesitate to go after it, did not feel the heat or the pain as he seized the hot blade and prepared to use it as she had. As he contemplated for but a second, accusing it with all the hatred he possessed and himself for apparently having left her alone for too long, a slim, dark hand covered his. He looked up, into the face of the woman he had seen dancing in the meadow, so brilliant and vibrant she could have just danced her way from the sun on a golden beam. He found himself sitting on the grass in the meadow again, and all was silent but for the songs of nightingales far away.

"No, Landrosallenthoyia," she said, her voice like silver, her pronunciation of his name perfect in spite of her rich, Romeri accent. "This is not time for that." The dagger squirmed in his grip. He looked down, saw that he was holding a small bird and opened his hand, watched it fly away into the night.

The woman knelt beside him. "Do not fear. None of what you have seen is prophesy. Your greatest fears you have now faced. You have been tested and found worthy. Had you not, you would not awaken from this rite. You must forgive Ivan his methods and concern. He means well and has taken great risk tonight, bringing you here to me. Long ago I foresaw great tragedy in my daughter's life. I saw her die for love denied. I swore Ivan on my deathbed to keep that from happening at all costs. My daughter had better be very old woman when next she comes here, young man, or your soul will be brought to task. You are her protector now. Her family is your family and she is no longer Ivan's responsibility. She is yours, and you are his. For you are her life, and Ivan was sworn to protect that."

She took his hand and opened his palm, showed him a long purple scar there. "This marks you as baharen, Romeri brother. If you are ever in need, show any Romer this and you will afforded what kindness they can, or at least not treated as gegenta. Whole world is your home now, Pathfinder, and you shall find brethren where ever you walk.

"When you see my daughter, do not fear for her. She believes herself in bind, having to chose between you and her father. Do not let this rush you. Take things as you planned, and all will sort out. And, should her father make any objections, show him this, and tell him that Danine has called in her debt."

Slowly she faded, like the ghost she had to have been, and Landros found his hand clasped not in the grasp of the shade, but the grip of the man he must now call brother. Ivan smiled weakly at him, just seconds before collapsing, dragging the elf with him to the ground. Neither man was able to get up on his own, and had to be helped by others. Their hands were unbound and their wounds tended by the women.

Ivan stared drunkenly at him as they fluttered around them. "Ox," he said.

"Ox?" Landros repeated, flinching at something the woman had done to his hand.

"Illyana did not explain?"

It hit him then, "Oh, true names. Ivan is like Illyana? And Ox is Lark?"

Ivan laughed, but nodded. "Scrambled, but yes, Kestrel. Though for you, who use your truth so freely... your Romer name is ours."

"Kestrel? She called me that once." His muzzy mind corrected him. "A few times."

Ox just laughed.

They were still weak, but getting stronger with the help of a tea. Ivan finally got tired of the woman fussing over him and pulled her into his lap, began fishing for affection. She responded with a tirade that was all Romeri but he could see the love underneath it, knew from experience that her resistance was neither genuine nor would last.

Landros was drawn away then, helped into one of the caravans and seated comfortably on pillows in front of a low table. The old woman was there, staring blindly at a spread of cards in front of her. A small ball of crystal hung suspended in the air, shedding a dim light directly upon the table. She smiled kindly.

He felt the need to say something. "I do not know what just happened here, nor do I completely understand what I have seen, but I feel that much has been sacrificed this eve. I promise you that sacrifice will not be in vain."

"Noble words, squire," she said. "Living up to them will not be easy."

"How....!" he began.

She shrugged. "Have many friends in shadowlands. They tell me much. My daughter watches over 'Yani still, and what 'Yani knows, I therefore know, and more. Relax, I keep my own council. By now some of your strength has returned. Go home. 'Yani is waiting for you. Rest, sleep. Will need both soon."

Unsteadily, Landros stood, paused at the door. "Know that you have gained two allies this night," he said. "My brother, Portholus, will be just as loyal. Should I be unreachable, know that he can be approached for aid as easily as I."

As he staggered out of the caravan, the little girl handed him his shirt, which he pulled on. She passed him his baldric and sword with a smile filled with child-like wonder, then darted off into the night. He slung the belt over his shoulder and sauntered over to where Raven stood waiting for him by the trees, holding open the door with an unhappy scowl.

Lark rolled over in her sleep, vainly trying to snuggle back up against Landros for warmth. She felt something odd brush her face and woke suddenly, brushing it away with a start. She looked over the edge of the bed, saw a flower lying on the floor where she had slapped it and sat up. He was not in the room. Getting up, she tried to shake an uncomfortable feeling that suddenly overcame her. She pulled on a blouse and a skirt hastily, picked up the blossom and peered into the living room.

Portholus sat there, staring into the fire. He looked up as she entered the room.

"Where is Landros?" she asked.

He did not answer, but handed her a letter. She opened it:

> My sweetest Illyana,
>
> This evening went far better than I could have hoped and it is my dearest wish that the feelings and emotions that flowed throughout were as strong in you as they were in me. I have gone to meet with a man who calls himself your brother and who has made accusations both to your honour and mine. This is not something that I can tolerate and will correct. Last evening we met and he claimed that his sister's name is Maria and that we are together. I know no Maria and hope to straighten that out this evening. I find no honour in this confrontation, but I can see no honourable path out of it.
>
> I have expected this for some time, however, as I have wondered how your clan would react to an outsider, a gegenta as you call it, seeing one of their own. That you are human and I elven is also a concern. I do not know how this man will react and there may be violence. If such occurs, I will have to defend myself and someone will most surely die. If it is he that falls, I will no doubt be branded by the Romeri as an enemy. This will place any future with you in jeopardy.
>
> We spend so little time in each others arms that we seem to fail to talk. There are still things I need to know and secrets it seems you do not wish to tell. I have shared my greatest secret with you, and it is my

hope that someday you will open up to me as completely. It must be hard since I had to practically threaten my brother's life over the conversation the two of you had, only to find out no more than that you had shared hard words. It is my hope that the two of you will someday make your peace with each other, as you are both the most important people in my life and it pains me greatly to have hatred between you.

No matter what happens tonight, I will love you forever and will do whatever possible to keep us together. If you chose to leave or if I die, you will be in my heart always. Never doubt that, and never forget me.

Landrosallenthyoia

"He really loves you, you know," Portholus said. Lark just stared at him, the letter forgotten in her hand. "Right now he is defending your honour, and his, to the death if necessary. He would not even wear his armour. I gave him my word I would not interfere."

He rose. "They are below, in the courtyard alley, or at least that is where they were to meet. If you truly love him, I hope you will do what is right. Farewell, princess," he said, opening the door.

He hesitated in the portal. "The money was an impressive gesture, by the way. I did not expect anything from you. I most certainly did not expect so much. You may be worthy of him after all, provided he survives the night." With that he closed the door and left.

Lark's mind raged. It *had* to be Ivan. There was no other explanation. She did not really expect to find them below in the courtyard, but she would know where to look from there. She dropped the letter and the flower and snatched up her scimitar. Leaving the scabbard behind, she fled from the room, pushing Portholus out of the way as she charged down the hall and the stairs, taking them three at a time. "I'll *kill* him!" she snarled.

Landros drifted through the front door of the inn. He looked and felt as if he had just been to the ninth plane of hell and back again, fighting the whole way. He looked up to see Lark barrelling down the stairs, hair unbound and flowing wildly behind her, her bare feet thudding on the wooden steps, her blouse loosely tied and falling enchantingly off one shoulder. Portholus was hot on her heels.

She managed to stop before she ran into him. He reached out, dropping his baldric and sword, and took her by the waist. He pulled her close, touched her face gently with his bandaged hand. "You look so much like her," he whispered, kissed her.

There was passion in the kiss, but no strength. He fell back into a nearby chair, nearly pulling her down with him. He winced as she grabbed his wounded hand, laughed at the look of horrified concern on her face. "Do not worry, princess. Everything is all right now."

A large crash was heard from the kitchen. Landros leaped from the chair, reaching for his sword. "Giants!" he cried, pushing her behind him. "They will not take you from me again!"

Portholus was suddenly there and, between the two of them, they managed to disarm him and get him upstairs to the room. He remained fairly delusional as the pair of them prepared him for bed. She looked at his bandaged hand, smelled the linen and wrinkled her nose. She knew those herbs, looked accusingly at him. "I cut myself sharpening my blades earlier," he lied. "I forgot to have it healed.

"I must rest now," he breathed wearily. "Portholus, my brother, we must speak in the morning." Portholus nodded, and, after receiving a nod from Lark, left the two of them alone.

"Promise me that you will return tomorrow eve," he asked her, stroking her hair with his bandaged hand. "I would like to talk with you a while. Please?"

"Am not leaving," she huffed, tucking him in.

He did not take long to drift into a deep sleep. She climbed onto the bed beside him, still dressed, sat braced against the pillows. He rolled in his sleep, rest his head against her shoulder. She sat up for hours, watching him sleep like a child, peacefully for the first time since she had known him.

SEVEN

It was late morning by the time Landros woke. He noticed that Lark had not undressed, and had fallen asleep watching over him. He felt a warm weight on his feet and looked up to see Scraps curled up at the foot of the bed. She stirred. He looked up to find her smiling down at him.

"Good morning, my love," she purred. "And how did your evening with my brother go?"

As Landros started to sit up, she slid off the bed. She propped up some of the pillows so that he could sit up properly, but did not let him get up. In truth, he was not sure he really wanted to. She hung a kettle of water on a hook over the fire for tea and began to dress more properly.

The tea was ready by the time she had dressed. She poured him a cup and sat beside him as he drank it, played absently with his hair as he did. When he was done, she took the cup and placed it on the night-stand.

"Now," she said. "Is my turn to run errands. You are not to get up until you are well enough. If your brother is awake, I will send him in. I know you wanted to talk."

She left the two of them alone for a while, headed back to her wagon and sat down on her own narrow bed. She spoke to the air, hoping her mother, or some other of gruma's watchers were near, but she felt nothing. She waited patiently for several hours, doing some minor chores around the wagon, moving it a few yards away to give the grass time to recover.

It was nearly noon when she tired of waiting. If Gruma was coming, she'd have sent something by now, even if it was just a simulacrum. Sighing, she rode back to Landros's rooms, finally admitting to herself that she had to find her own answers, her own way.

She found him sitting by the fire in the living room with his brother, drinking tea. They stood when she entered, sat again when Lark sank down next to him.

Landros sighed. "I do not know if I am coming or going right now. Everything seems to be going in all directions at once." He looked across at his brother, waved a finger at him. "You have been more preoccupied than usual and the look of worry I see on your face is not a familiar sight." He turned to Lark, tilting her chin up to look at him. "You have become somewhat moody and worrying as well and it definitely does not look good on you. I am glad the two of you have made your peace, and it seems that you are even spending time together. Which has me wondering, since you are both obviously still worried, that there is something else here you are not sharing with me."

He looked deep into Lark's eyes, inclined his head towards his brother, "*He* will not tell me anything. Which means that either he knows nothing, or you have sworn him to silence. Either way, it seems I must turn to you for my answers."

Lark gazed deep into his eyes, read all the pain and anguish there. He looked a bit ragged, as if he and his brother had been yelling at each other for some time before she arrived. She knew he had found no answers there and that he needed them now with an intensity bordering on desperation. His patience was at an end, that was clear. He would not be put off, and indeed, she did not see any point in doing so.

She sighed, glanced furtively from one brother to the other, got up and began pacing before the fire. Landros started to get up, but she pointed back at his seat. "Sit," she said firmly.

Sensing that he was about to get everything he had asked for and more, he obeyed, never once taking his eyes from her.

"I just spent whole morning trying to talk with Gruma. She would not come to me. Yes, I know you and my brother went through something last night. Yes, I know somehow that can stop worrying, but… I cannot help this. Too much is at stake. Last night was ready to risk goshaska for you. If my brother had harmed you, I would have cursed him. Had he killed you, I would have killed him, or been killed by him. And for Romer, there is no greater sin, killing kin. You must understand that I have been often frustrated by my brother in past, with his well-meant interference in my love life. More than one potential suitor has left without word after 'talk' with my brother.

"One in particular, Arturi, I believe was his name, never spoke to me again. And when I saw him at wayside meet some year or so later, he turn very pale, cast about him and crossed his arms. A gesture which to Romeri means I am not here, ignore me," she added for Portholus's benefit. "To do this when someone has seen you and is about to approach is unbelievably rude. I swear he would have made gesture to ward off evil eye had not he noticed Ox watching nearby. Was then I decided I had had enough of papa's caravan and went my own way. Even then he has ever been in shadows, and so no gegenta ever sought my favours for long. Until I came here, until I met you," she added, looking over at her lover through the screen of her hair.

"I somehow managed to escape here," she continued. "With siege, he doubted I would come here or stay, so was some time before he found me." She looked over at Portholus, "That is why I took badly when you decided to have 'warning words' with me. I suddenly realized is just what brother has been doing all these years and I lashed out at him through you. I also did not take kindly to insinuations you made regarding my… motivations."

She felt a rapid movement from Landros and put her hand up, made him sit and hold his peace. "YOU are to say nothing of that to him. What passed between us has passed and my fist closed that subject forever." Behind her, Landros saw his brother absently rub his finger along side his lip with a rueful grin on his face, obviously remembering the incident quite well. "He will not be making same mistake twice, and I will not have you castigating him again for his youth and exuberance, misguided though they may have been."

Landros looked up at her, saw her mother in her. He could easily see her taking up that mantle of power and responsibility. There was a way about her at times that left no room for question.

"Now, what transpired between my brother and you, and why have you bandaged paw what smells of chamomile and elecampane?"

Landros sighed, leaned his head against the back of the sofa, collected his thoughts. "I met with your brother, as I had agreed to do the night before. I fully expected a fight, was prepared to deal with it or whatever challenge they offered."

"What name did he give you, when he asked? Your letter said Maria. What exactly did he say my name was?"

Landros thought a moment. "Maria... Petro...vich, I think. It was close, but not quite right. Then he said you went by the name of Lark. Why?"

Lark gave a small, involuntary chuckle. "Mariya Petrovich Rushava," she corrected. "He was testing you. First to see if I had given you my name. Second, to see if you would betray that. What did he do when you did not give him my real name?"

Landros was slow sometimes to catch on, but he saw that. He found it very significant that she never doubted for a moment that he had not betrayed her, even not knowing why it had to be such a secret. "Ox silenced your brother Raven and told me to meet him the next night." Landros did not miss Lark's reaction to that information either, but she did not say anything, so he continued. "When I did meet him, he led me through a sort of magic gateway to some campsite I am guessing is well away from this city. I met this old, blind woman who spoke to the air as if there was someone there to answer her. She cut our hands and put us through a ritual which I can only describe as some sort of blood-bonding ceremony, or a spirit quest. Maybe both."

He sighed, soul weary from his travels. "I am still not quite sure what happened. I think I met your mother. It seems that a lot of things are different now. Your gruma told me that you would still worry, imagining yourself in a bind you are not in, but not to let that rush me. Your brother and I have a new understanding, to say the least."

He reached out and pulled her to stand before him, held her hands tenderly in his. "There is no way I would allow you to become goshaska, whatever that is. I know what family means, I know what it means to you and I would never let you turn your back on that. Not even for love, and believe me, that I would have felt that pain as much as you. I could not have lived with myself knowing you had made that kind of a sacrifice for me. That you even considered it is something I will remember and cherish always."

Lark knelt in front of him, slowly began unbandaging his hand. There was no blood, the wound was completely healed. All that remained was a dark, purplish scar. She ran her fingers tenderly along its length. "I have seen this once before, on old man who came to our camp. He was very weak and had followed our patterna for days until he found us."

"I'm sorry. Patterna?" Portholus asked.

"Is small signs we leave behind to tell those who follow which way we went. Tells also other things, like good places to camp, no water, hostile gegenta. That sort of thing."

"Ah," he mused.

"This old man was gegenta by look, but that had this scar. He greeted us hand out, showing this mark and papa treated him as would any Romer. Man knew enough of customs not to embarrass us or himself, some little of our tongue. After much feasting, dancing and singing, he told us his story. He had, in his youth, gotten himself caught between two clans of Romeri. I do not remember all of details, but ranie of one had cursed young man of other, or there was some legal dispute and he was put in bad way ...do not remember, was so young and hour so late. What do remember was he helped this man out of his trouble, no thought to his own well being, gave him last of his coin to help him get away. For this, was cursed by opposing ranie. When young Romer later learned of this, he came and, unable to uncurse him, made him baharen, one of our blood who is not born of our blood. Is very powerful and important bond, one no Romeri takes lightly. Even rival ranie could do nothing more to him lest she openly declared war upon his new tribe. If I remember right, he actually went to her clan, asked for shelter for night as is any Romer's right, and explained himself, made his amends and she lifted curse.

"He had come to us that night because was dying. He wanted to die among only people he had left, in hopes of his gods permitting him to be born one of us in another life. If nothing else, that his soul might be free. My father permitted this without question and we gave him bed and lit him candle and camped there until candle sputtered out. We were not able to contact his baharen before he died, so we mourned him as we would any of our own, and told his baharen when we came across him.

"Was first funeral I could remember, and was confused. I knew how papa felt about gegenta, yet here he was treating one as Romeri. Now, I think I understand. This does not make you Romer, but is as close as you can come not being born of our blood. My brother risked much to give me this gift. You see, any dishonour you may incur, dishonours him, any enemy you make, is his enemy. You are now my brother's brother."

Landros stroked her cheek softly, marvelling at her beauty and loyalty and innocence, at his unconscionable luck in coming across her as he had. "One of these days you will have to tell me just what you have told your brother and grandmother about me. Both of them pronounced my full name quite well and that is never easy for humans to do. Not to mention the fact that I never told them, or you for that matter, until that letter tonight."

She smiled, pressed a kiss to the palm of his hand. "I thought was tag to name, meant giant-slayer or something."

He stiffened. "What gave you that idea?" he asked.

She shrugged, "A dream. Is no worry. Besides my mother probably told them."

"I was under the impression your mother was...." Portholus began, confused.

She smiled gently, sank back against Landro's knees, still holding on to his hand, gently massaging it. "She is, but she watches nonetheless. Gruma speaks to her as if she had never passed on, but then, Gruma's ghosts are more real to her sometimes than living folk. She has been blind great many years. As long as I have known her. Has been said she traded her sight for Sight, and sees into shadowlands like we gaze on this world. Is impossible to lie to, which is why she has become ranie again since my mother's candle went out and I was not ready. Is no doubt her ghosts told her name."

Landros gasped in pain suddenly, snatched his hand back.

"What?" Lark exclaimed, startled by his sudden reaction.

His expression stiffened as he tried to control the pain, tried not to laugh with embarrassment. "I still feel my pulse going straight through the scar. Though I am certain your brother is feeling the same. The ordeal was draining on us both." He pulled the raccoon up into his lap, began ruffling his ears. He looked longingly down at Lark. "He would sacrifice much for you, do you know that? I know how he feels," he mused. "Now I just have to find a way to deal with your father."

Lark pulled away, sighed wearily. That was an encounter she was dreading.

Landros moved Scraps and slid onto the floor beside her, tilted her chin up to look at him. "We *will* get through this. I will deal with your father when the time comes. I will not risk losing you, not when I am this close to winning your heart for all time."

She nearly laughed aloud, so astounded was she. "This close?" she scoffed. "I gave this months ago. Just did not know, or want to admit until that night in sewer."

Landros felt a surge inside, as if his heart was trying to leap out of its cage. His joy was nearly complete with that admission. He looked away a moment, took a deep breath before looking back at her. Part of the dream was still bothering him, and he had always been told that the Romeri were very free with their love. "We will have to discuss Romer customs, though. I am afraid that I refuse to share you with another, and do not know how I would handle it if you were to enter another's bed. I am certain there are customs I must get used to, but that is something I don't think I could."

Lark did not know what could have prompted this, but had a sudden mischievous idea hit her. She leaned close, her cheek brushing his and her lips just touching his ear as she whispered in a sultry voice. "I am well aware of my charms, and even you cannot argue their usefulness in accomplishing goals. I will continue to use everything within my means to accomplish those goals, whatever they might be. However, my body, as I told you before, is only thing upon which I place no price and for which I take no coin. I gave you alone that gift. And even when I did not know if that gift would ever be shared again, there was no one else who caught my interest, or inflamed me as you have. My bed is ever empty, save Ivaska and you. That gift is yours alone and I would demonstrate for you right now what great treasure I have given you. But you need your rest," she purred.

Landros felt his body suddenly flush with heat and desire, and the nearness of her was like a firebrand waved too near the face.

She began to pull away. Without any warning, he seized her by the wrist and used her own momentum against her. Before she had time to even squeal, Lark found herself in his lap and breathlessly aware of his intentions. He trapped her eyes in a long, intense stare which seemed to drain the strength to resist from her limbs. Without breaking the contact, he spoke to his brother, still lounging on the sofa. "Portholus," he said. "Leave."

It took a moment for things to sink in and, with a slight raise of eyebrows, Portholus headed for the door.

Lark called after him, without looking away, in a voice gone suddenly husky, "And kindly take furry thief with you."

The sudden absence of the two in question went unnoticed, as the only thing Landros remained aware of was the woman on his lap waiting to see what would happen next.

Lark got up to stir the fire. He watched her closely, admiring the way his shirt clung to her curves, just barely kissing her skin; the way it rode the curve of her hips, leaving everything to a tantalized imagination, but so full of promise in the same breathless moment.

The moment was shattered by a knock on the door. Lark threw the poker onto the hearth and went to answer it. Landros drew the furs up to cover himself, amused by her complete lack of modesty.

Lark threw the door open, irritated to no end to have her evening spoiled. Seeing the young boy in Colwyn's livery standing there shot a deep sense of foreboding through her. "Yes?" she managed.

The boy bowed, obviously embarrassed by her attire, refused to look up as he delivered his message. "I have been sent to fetch Master Landros."

Landros, having been unable to see the visitor, but nonetheless noticed the change in her demeanour, came over to see what was going on. He recognized the boy immediately as one of Colwyn's pages. He ushered the boy inside and closed the door. Lark drifted back to the sofa, picked up her skirt and dropped it over her head, easing some of the boy's discomfort.

The boy relaxed a little and delivered his message. "Lord Colwyn needs you to come with me immediately. You are to pack for war and say nothing to anyone. My lady, my lord requests your presence also."

Landros stiffened. "She is not going into battle," he said sternly, suspecting all kinds of dangerous reasons for the request.

"Lord Colwyn only said he wished her to come with you, that there was a request and something he must say to her. You are to move with all haste, sir, my lady."

Landros sighed. At least he had enjoyed one last caress. Had that been interrupted... he might not have been so kind. "Wait here," he said, and went into the other room to dress and pack.

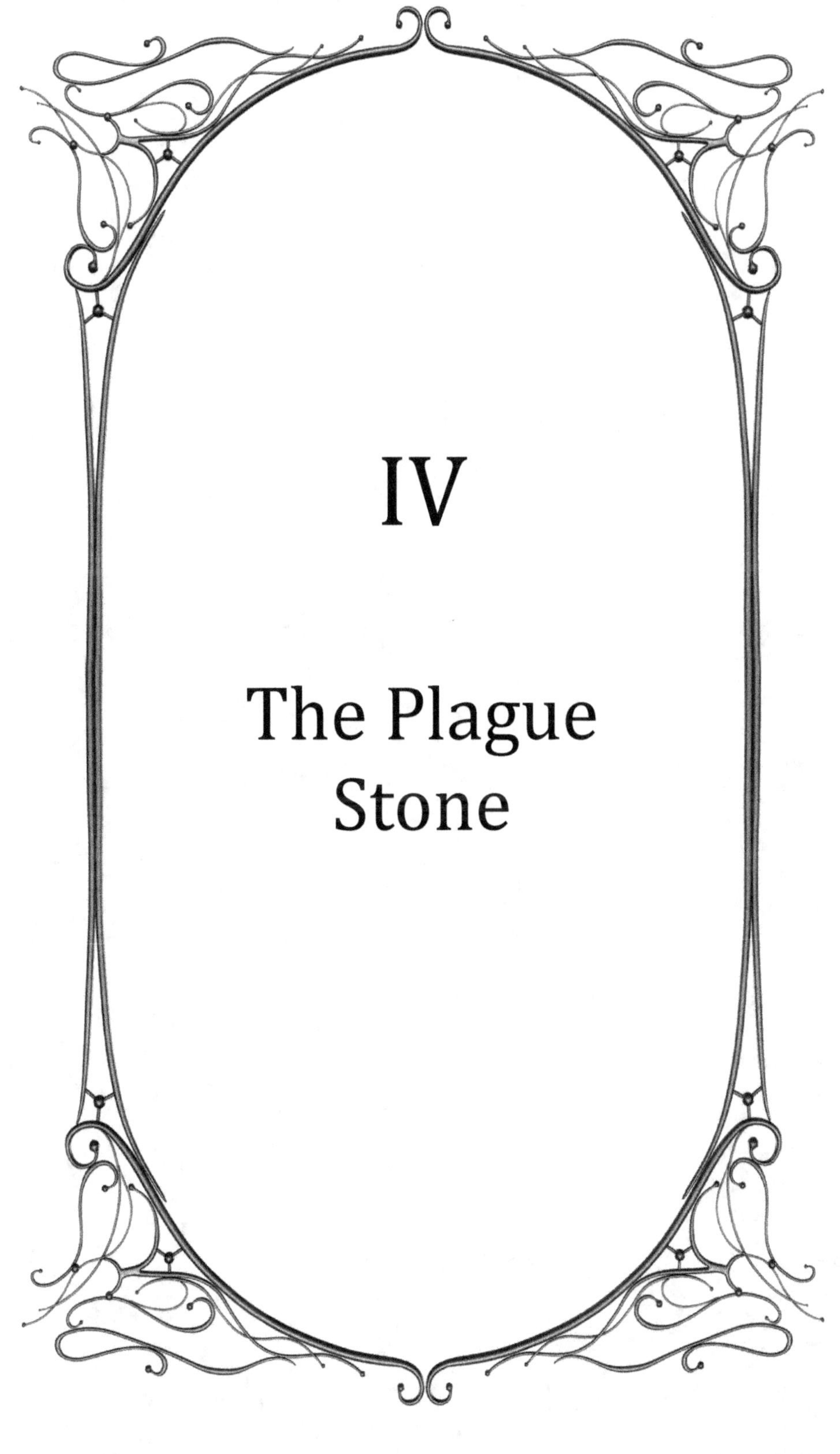

IV

The Plague Stone

ONE

Lark insisted on riding. Dolal's broad back was easily big enough to carry all three of them without breaking a sweat. The page was rather grateful that he would not have to walk home, even if the ride was a little crowded. Landros, sitting behind her, wrapped his arms around her tightly, reluctant for the ride to end when he would have to let go and take his leave.

The stable boy took care of the horse while the page led them immediately into Lord Colwyn's study. The knight was pouring over his endless supply of maps when they entered, a position Landros was coming to expect to always find him in. "Come in, come in," he said, looking up. "My lady, please make yourself comfortable."

"May I ask why she is here?" Landros began boldly. "I have no intentions of allowing her to fight."

Colwyn shook his head, waved him over to the desk. "I would not think of asking such a thing unless it were her desire. You will know why she is here soon enough. Right now, you and I have important business. You remember the idea you came to me with concerning your friends in the outer wood?" Landros nodded cautiously. "Well, the time has come. You are to leave shortly for the temple to meet with Father Orlin, he has your squad assembled and waiting."

Landros held up his hand. "Squad?"

"Yes. I have managed to glean the irregulars for a handful of good archers to send with you. Relax, Squire," he said, with playful sternness. "Every last one of them are elven. I had human volunteers, but I felt that the nature of your situation required elven finesse. Few humans could remain as silent in the wood as an elf, and I need you invisible. Also, there was too much a chance of our wild friends rejecting them." He opened up a map showing the city and the territory just outside. There were enemy forces marked all over the place in several colours, though the places he pointed to were not marked in any way.

"Father Orlin is going to try and get you in here somewhere. Once in, you will have less than thirty-six hours to find your wild friends, collect them and get them into position here," he said, sweeping his finger along a small ridge just behind the enemy lines. "Your orders are to assemble and hold this ridge. It is heavily wooded, so will provide you with plenty of cover. You are to harry the rear of the enemy lines as much as possible, while keeping an eye out for enemy reinforcements. On no uncertain terms are you to engage the enemy directly. You may defend yourselves, but you are not to attack hand to hand. If your lines should be compromised, scatter, vanish, and regroup if possible. Should you be completely overrun, have your wild friends conveniently vanish and you, with your original team, are to activate the artefact Father Orlin will give you to return you to the city."

Landros nodded. Colwyn rolled up the map and handed it to him. "We will be counting on your forces. This map only has the enemy noted. None of our troops are marked in case this should fall into the wrong hands. My lady," he said, turning to Lark and gesturing her to come closer. "I have a great favour to ask of you."

Landros put an arm protectively around her.

"Yes?" she asked.

"Your little friend there," he said, gesturing to the mockingbird on her shoulder, "if he were to teleport in with Landros and his team, would he be able to fly to a designated point and return to him?"

"Provided he does not move too far, or hide too well," she shrugged. "They can work signal."

"Good, good," he said. "In that case I would like very much if he could be persuaded to help us. Landros's mission is very important to our overall strategy. It is imperative that we know whether or not he can get into position." He pointed out an area on a second map, this one marked with both forces. "I will more than likely be found around here somewhere. Just have him look for a blue and white striped pavilion. From there he will be brought to me or I to him. He does not look like a typical messenger bird, so I seriously doubt they'll give him a second thought.

"Landros, I want you to send him as soon as you are in position with some indication that you've got your wild army without giving any numbers. Never give any specifics in your reports except for the enemy's numbers and positions. I want no one compromised. If your lines are broken, give three draws on a hunting horn for signal and scatter. Here," he added, getting something from the corner of the room. He handed Landros a bow.

"I have...." Landros began.

"I know, but this one has been charmed. It shoots with a good forty or so pounds more than it draws, so the arrows go farther and enter deeper, and it is very accurate."

"Thank you," he said taking the bow.

"Now go, you only have thirty-six hours."

Landros shouldered the bow and started for the door. He stopped, turned and pulled Lark to him in a passionate kiss. The release was reluctant. She pulled something from her belt, pressed a silver-hilted dagger into his hand. "I must have back," she said. "Bring this back to me, yourself."

He took the knife, stunned for a moment. This was the knife she had killed herself with in the ritual dream, the one she had told him to bring back to her. The thought shook him to his very spirit, but he fastened the sheath to his belt and with one final, all too short kiss, made himself leave, the bird right behind him.

Lark sank into a chair, feeling somewhat deflated and hopeless. She felt a hand on her shoulder, looked up to see Colwyn standing there, trying to be comforting. "The bird will keep you informed," he said.

She covered his hand with hers, nodded. "I... need to go," she said. "Working will help my mind."

"Just do not wear out your body in the process. He needs you in good health."

She nodded mutely and got up to leave.

"Don't worry," he added. "He is very good at this sort of thing. He will come back. He has too much too lose if he doesn't."

She quietly closed the door behind her, not entirely convinced.

Rue met Landros when he arrived at the temple. Her presence in the Matron's halls was a surprise enough, but the look on her face made him stop, suddenly very concerned. "What? What is it?" he asked.

"Come with me. I know you are in a hurry, but..." She shook her head, grabbed his arm and led him into the priest's quarters.

No one stopped her. She halted before a narrow cell door on which was hung a black and purple cloth. She lifted the fabric and opened the door for him then stepped aside.

He entered the room, a barren, guest cell with nothing personal in it to mark it anyone's home. All he saw was the man upon the bed in the midst of it. Father Mullen lay in his priestly robes, neatly arranged and hair combed in a way he had never seen him ever wear it. He was wasted and thin, worse than the last time he had seen him, just weeks ago. He looked peaceful, at least; free of the wracking cough that had been plaguing him.

Shaken deeply, he crossed to the bed, intending to kneel beside the body of his old friend, to touch him, and bid his good-byes. A gloved hand grabbed his arm, pulled him back. He turned to see Mother Zedia standing there with a long veil over her and the corner of it pressed to her mouth. She shook her head, moved him back.

He turned, tried to move towards her, but she held him at arm's length. "Mother, what is going on? When...."

She shook her head again, more vigorously. "You were brought here to know, because you asked to be," she said, never once uncovering her face. There was a hoarseness to her voice he was not used to. He assumed it was from crying. "I cannot allow you to touch either of us, even in farewell. The new watchers of the Lambs are even now keeping an eye on the children for the signs."

"Signs of what?" he demanded, beginning to get a bad feeling in his gut. He knew nothing of omens or portents, but none of this struck him as an auspicious way to begin a mission of his importance.

"Plague," she whispered. She turned her back to him, coughed into her veil. After a moment, when she was confident the fit was over, she turned back. "I began to get his symptoms just five days ago. They were noticed when I sent for help from the temple to get him here last night. He died several hours ago. I am truly sorry. I wish... you could have been here. He asked for you, but... the Mother would not permit you to be sent for. It was too dangerous. It is still too dangerous. You must leave now. Only time will tell if we truly have a plague on our hands. Go, may the Goddess be with you and the children. Only She knows if I shall see you again."

He staggered out of the death chamber, reeling. He owed the late priest a great deal, hated to see him like that. Rue was there, set a hand on his shoulder, trying to be considerate.

"I have to get you back," she said. "I... I'm sorry. I wasn't supposed to...."

He nodded, gestured for her to lead him to Father Orlin. He spoke quietly as he walked beside her. "Make sure Lark knows.

Have her check up on Billy. Oh, and tell her to keep an eye on the army, they're going to need guidance. ...And for signs of this...."

She paused just outside the inner courtyard from which the last teleport had been managed, stared at him confused. Before she could ask what he had meant, he surprised her again by pulling her into a tight hug.

She returned the embrace, still in shock.

"Take care of yourself, Ruellanalen Kaul," he said. "You're better at the people stuff than Adrick," he grinned, and left her stunned, stepping out to meet the five elves that had been assigned to the mission. She saw a mockingbird drop out of the sky to land on his shoulder.

Rue watched for a few moments, while Landros explained the mission to them, before she turned and wandered back towards her own temple wing. There was still a lot she needed to do, and the first of that was to find her friend.

Lark was sitting with Dane by the hearth in a nearly empty tavern when Rue finally found her. She was placing his fingers on the frets of a mandolin.

Rue sat at the nearby table, bought an onion pie from Lilly, ate whilst she waited. The boy was having some minor difficulties with hand positions. He kept wanting to raise the instrument higher.

"Hardest part isn't frets," she was telling him. "It's here, where music comes from. Your fingers are softer on this hand, because are used to holding bow. Now you must use thumb and other fingers to strum instead of saw. Is like picking single notes, like you pluck fiddle, but this is whole song, not just handful of notes for accent."

"Are my fingers going to get sore? Like when I was learning the fiddle?"

Lark smiled. "Yes. Will get sore before they toughen up. Can use pick if like, but I find gives less versatile control."

She took the instrument from him and demonstrated, pulling a pick from her pocket. She strummed and picked out a few single notes, then put the pick between her teeth and let her fingers dance across the strings like a frantic spider.

Dane laughed.

"Hear difference?"

"Yes. I like it. It has a different soul than the violin."

Lark's eyes sparkled at that, and she set the instrument back in his hands. "That it does. Remember how we began fiddle? Same principal. Find your chords and practice them one by one. You get basics down, and next time will bring *my* mandolin and we'll play at echoes."

"I like that game," he grinned, bending his tow-head over the strings and felt for his fingering.

Lark joined Rue at the table, accepted a small pie. "So," she began, "is social call? Or other? Need we pay visit to Keltree?"

Rue shook her head. "Sadly, none of the above. We have been warned that there will not be much rest soon. We're as ready as we can be, but when the casualties start flooding in.... I'm taking what private time I can. Even the priests who live with family outside of the temple are being called to either the main or the outlying shrines and chapels. No one will have free time soon."

"Am sorry to hear," Lark said. "Should rest while can."

She nodded. "I will, but... I saw Landros a little while ago."

"Oh?"

"He had a mockingbird with him...."

Lark gave her a sad little smile. "Nightingale went with. To help."

"Keeping tabs on him?" she grinned. Lark merely gave her a half-dismissive gesture at that, but there was light in her eyes. "Glad you two are getting closer. But I brought it up because he asked me to tell you something."

"What?"

"Do you know about the House of Lambs?"

Lark nodded, she had already been told of the orphanage Landros used his magic tablecloth to provide food for. "I think he knew people there. Is where Billy's sister lives."

Rue's expression tightened and that caught her attention.

"What? Is something wrong with Billy?" she asked, trying not to panic.

Rue shook her head, set her hand on Lark's to calm her. "Nothing like that. The Father who ran the House died a few hours ago." Lark's free hand covered her mouth. "He died of the plague. And the Mother who ran it with him has the same symptoms."

There was a sour note from Dane's corner. Glancing over, he was frowning over his positioning, trying the chord again. Lark looked back at Rue. "And children?"

"I don't know. The new wardens are keeping an eye on them, but I don't know anything. Though he asked that you check on Billy, probably for that reason. He also said something strange," she frowned.

"What?" Lark pressed, worried what else might be amiss. Her mind was raging from the House of Lambs to the Warren.

"He said to ask you to keep an eye on the army, whatever that means. Does he want you to use a crystal ball or something?" she asked. She cocked her head at the sudden smile on her friend's face. "Care to explain?"

Lark shook her head. "I shouldn't. Is... his secret. Is not real army like you think. But does mean I have to start looking after my caravan. You should go, Rue. Rest while you can. If you see Keltree..."

"Not likely," Rue interrupted. "He's likely getting his own little band prepared for the main ruckus. He's been 'cleared for dragon-slaying'."

Lark sighed. Just one more soul she had to worry about.

Rue gave her hand a pat. "Don't fret, I heard he's got Rog, Barak and Lith with him. Maybe even Adrick, but I'm not sure about that."

"Still. If you see Vanessa or Navarie, tell them I say hello?"

Rue rose, hugged her. "I will. You be careful."

"Same to you."

Lark stood behind Dane, listening to him play but watching her friend leave the empty bar. "All right, my little Bat," she said softly. "How do I find South?"

He plucked three short notes on the strings, repeated them. "Just step out into the stable-yard and whistle that." There was something different in his tone now, something more mature. "Corporal Cat's-Eye is usually about this hour. Either she or one of Felise's quarter will find you."

She set her hand on his shoulder, squeezed gently. "Thank you."

"Is it true then, there's a plague?" he asked.

She shook her head. "Just because few folks have died of sickness, does not mean epidemic. Should be cautious, though. Will be back."

Lark stepped through the kitchen to the stable-yard, let loose a short, sharp whistle of the three notes he had played for her, and sat back to wait. She spent time with Ivaska by the chicken coop, watching the few thin hens scratching in the dirt. She called up one of her little winds, used it to gather up bugs over by the midden heap, scattering them in the small henyard. Ivaska danced and woofed as he watched the hens go after the insects in a flurry.

"She had to pen 'em up, cause someone was luring them away," came a small voice.

Lark turned, saw a scruffy little girl about seven, in tattered pants and a shirt that was too big for her, standing at the corner of the barn. She nodded her head to the child. "Would you be Cat?" she asked softly.

Ivaska happily trotted over to the girl for scratches, allowing Lark an excuse to come nearer.

"I am Corporal Cat's-eye, yes, yore highness. An' you be th' Standard." Lark ruefully nodded. "What can th' West do ya for?"

"Need to see South...." She stopped, shook her head. "No, need to see Queen."

There was genuine fear in the girl's eyes at that. It meant the matter was serious. "Ya need a round up?"

Lark thought about that, then shook her head. "No, but everyone must be accounted."

"Gimme an hour."

"Will be inside."

With that, the girl vanished around the side of the barn and Ivaska followed Lark inside. As she crossed the kitchen, Heleda passed her, headed out the back door and bellowed for Norwin the stable-boy. When she stepped into the taproom, the whole atmosphere had changed.

Lily was standing at the bar, her brother-in-law behind it, with the two maids who helped out around the inn sitting at a table looking worried. Dane was seated on a bar stool next to his mother, his grandfather's mandolin clutched in his arms. Heleda came back in, ushering Lark and Norwin over to the others. "You might as well," Heleda said. "She wants us all."

Lily was holding a piece of paper, waited until everyone was gathered before she spoke. "This is an official decree from the Magistrate." Lark had a sinking feeling about this.

She cleared her throat, continued. "From now until further notice, all public houses are hereby closed. Inns, such as myself, are able to remain open on a provisory basis. The provision being that they have guests, or that they are serving as temporary lodgings for the war dispossessed."

There were several groans and verbal protests, and a grunt from Neneis, but Lily held up her hand for silence. "Furthermore, if we agree to serve as a public shelter or as a shelter for the private militias, we will be compensated at the end of the conflict." This caused even more protest.

It was Neneis who called for peace and spoke this time. "And if we feed and house any of these, the dispossessed or the militant, can we charge them?" He held up his hand, shook his head. "I don't mean the refugees. Those who shelter here I would not charge. But the military? If Coolie and his bunch of goons decide to come here to take a load off, will they drink us dry and not pay a copper royal?"

"It does not say," Lily answered. "I can ask. I am sure the guilds will be up in arms about this. Come nightfall, a new curfew goes into effect and will remain so until further notice. What I need to know is... which, if any of you, will remain here for the duration and who will go home?"

"But what if there are people? The militias?" asked one of the barmaids. "You can't handle that on your own."

"That's part of the options," Heleda explained. "If she wants to stay open or not."

"We have no official guests right now. I have no reason, according to this, to stay open unless I house militiamen," Lily sighed.

A small voice came from Dane's hearth corner. "Would you like to?"

They all looked to see Cat's-eye leaning against the shadowy wall behind the minstrel's perch. She obeyed Lily's beckoning hand and stepped further into the room.

"Would I like to what?" Lily asked.

"Have official guests?"

"And where would these guests come from?" asked Neneis, ever suspicious.

The girl grinned. "Oh, th' neighbours," she shrugged. "Not *yore* neighbours o' course. But there's folks near th' breaches that are vulnerable, like th' North Wall. People who'd jump at a chance t' get farther from th' fightin'. Some folk what'll end up in Tent Town if no one takes 'em in. Folk with skills."

Lily thought fast. "I have eight beds upstairs. Most of which will sleep two comfortable, three cozy and four tight, plus floor space. If they help, divide labours, I'll house them."

Neneis had his doubts. "Lily, are you sure?"

She turned to him, took his hand across the bar. "When the fighting gets heavy, we can turn the taproom into a refuge. Put people in the barn."

He sighed, "Ought to put the chickens in there anyway."

Heleda spoke up. "You know that might still require us to serve the civilian watch," she began. Her eyes flicked towards Lark, worried.

Lily nodded. "You may be right. But so long as I'm not providing entertainment, they can't demand more than they can of any householder. Neneis, you keep a record of everything the watch consumes, especially if it's beyond the reasonable. If we do this, food will get slim quick." She turned to Heleda, "We'll do a basic breakfast: porridge, biscuits, things that will go farther with less."

The large woman nodded, "Forget lunch, we'll have stews, soups and the like that will stretch even that. Save the eggs fer the wee. Mind I take that corner room? Me an' my Bartholomew? The one by the kitchen stair?"

Lily frowned, "Will that be enough for you two?"

Heleda flapped her apron dismissively. "He ain't but a scrawny thing."

"Can he sleep with me then, mom?" asked Dane. "I don't take up much room either."

Lily laughed in order to fight off tears. She turned to Lark, "That is if you won't be needing the room?"

Lark shook her head. "Have too many choices of places to lay head, will be fine. But if are having no entertainment, I should not put in appearances. Coolie is civilian watch, yes?"

Neneis grunted his affirmation, began wiping down mugs with a sour face.

"Then best I am not seen here." She took Lily's hands in hers. "Will be fine. Will keep tabs on you, words can be traded. Dane knows how." She turned to the boy in question. "And you, you should practice early day, at times no one think means are entertaining."

He laughed. "Until I get the hang of this thing, no one's going to mistake this noise for entertainment."

She ruffled his hair. "Don't underestimate self."

Lily turned to the barmaids to ask them if they were staying. One opted to go home to help her mother if there wasn't paying work. The other decided to bunk with Heleda.

Finally, the proprietress turned to 'Cat'. "Young lady, would you be one of these guests?"

She shook her head. "No need, ma'am. But I kin have you eight families in need before curfew. One of 'em's a baker!" she grinned.

Lark frowned. "Lady baker and daughter she calls Boodle? Bakery burned not long ago?"

"That'd be th' one, Miss," she said, her grin growing wider. "Nice bit o' fire-fightin' that!" she winked.

Lily held out her hand to the girl. "You have a deal. You can stop in any time you need. If you'll come with me to the kitchen before you leave, I'll give you an onion pie."

"That'd be toppers, Ma'am. But I needs a word with th' Romer miss."

She nodded. "Don't we all." Lily paused long enough to give Lark a hug, then shooed everyone off to whatever they needed to do, leaving Lark and the girl alone in the tap room but for Neneis and Dane.

'Cat' drew Lark back to the hearth corner.

"Thought you said would take hour?" Lark asked quietly.

The girl shrugged, "Got lucky. Terri said to take ya to th' Warren. I'll leave ya there and go round up some 'guests'."

"That was very nice of you," Lark began.

She shook her head at that. "Nope. Totally self-serving," she grinned. "I gots to look after my quarter, you know? John's got tall grass and Billy's got hungry goats. Two problems, one solution. But whenever yore ready, Standard."

"One moment, Corporal," Lark laughed as she gathered her things.

Lily met them at the kitchen door as they were heading out the back way, handed both of them a pie. "Be careful, both of you. It's about to get very dangerous out there."

Lark found the Warren much as she had left it, though there was evidence of more inhabitants than the last time. Cat's-eye was true to her word, and no sooner had she slithered out of the tunnel, she was darting across to a different one and shimmying her way out in a flash.

Terrisera was waiting, pouring over several flyers the children had brought her. She glanced up as the corporal crossed the warren, saw Lark and waved her over. "What news, Standard?"

Lark smiled. "You sound like little general, or war queen."

Terri gave her a rueful smile, still sorting through the papers. "Is that not what I am? Or trying anyway. Have you news from the General? I've had word he was called to the Temple and hasn't come out again."

"He... he has left city." Lark suddenly had the girl's full attention. "He has been set to important task. Asked me to do what can in his stead."

Terri sat down on the nearest crate. "What... what are your orders, then, general?" she asked.

Lark shook her head. "No, I have said this I will not do. You are doing good as are. Corporal Cat's-eye is even now finding temporary shelter for people with no safe place, to help friend of mine who needs people to house or will lose to civilian watch. Just report to...." Lark sat down herself then.

"What?"

"Just realized, Lord Colwyn will be leaving himself. There will be direct conflict in matter of days. Tomorrow and then...."

"Open war?" Terri whispered.

Lark nodded.

"Oh. So... one way or another this ends soon?" she swallowed.

"Sadly, yes." Lark shook her head. "Is not why I come. Have concern. Need to see South. House where sister lives... Father there... has died, sickness. I have to know if Billy is like-wise ill, or if any of children are. You need to make accounting."

She nodded. "I'll have heads counted. Where will we find you?" She waved one of the papers, "I doubt you will be entertaining at Bat's for a while."

Lark nodded, sighing. "Sadly. Will likely be either at Cygnet or on Lord Colwyn's property, in my caravan."

Terri thought for a long moment. "Will have to send West to you then, if need."

"Tell you what, if I am at caravan, will leave red ribbon on hinge of gate. Will talk to stable-boy, he will leave alone, and if ask for me, will carry any message. If not there, will be at Cygnet or 'running errands'."

Terri laughed at that. "That what they're calling adventuring these days?"

"When need to be circumspect," Lark smiled.

"You need to learn the tunnels, though," the girl commented. "You can get anywhere in town unseen using the loways. Let the big'uns have their highways, full of soldiers and tollmen." She grinned broadly, "But we'll rule the roost from down here below."

Lark laughed with her. "It is always ones they underestimate what topple kingdoms."

"Or keeps them afloat."

"Right." Lark moved a little ways off as she looked around. "Do you have everything you need? I see more pallets than before."

Terri shrugged. "We're good. We still have some of the food you brought us. I've been rationing it. We're collecting scraps, making our own blankets from them. A couple of South's kids have been making rat traps, so there's meat."

Lark nodded, hearing her but at the same time not. She could feel a latent power down here, but not pinpoint its source. The runes she had refreshed were still clear and strong, she felt their strength as they pulsed. Closing her eyes, she saw the lines of power glowing all around her, could feel the ebb and flow, the protection. Sometimes, one of the lines would grow brighter, and she began to realize this was because a child was using it. It was like a great, benevolent web.

Every now and again, she felt a sharp tapping at the lines, and one would glow red for a heartbeat. Then it would flare and die down and go back to normal. A little while later another line would be tested. She was beginning to see a pattern when she felt something at her elbow.

She jumped, reached blindly for whoever was standing there as the room started spinning and the light web faded. Billy grabbed hold of her, "Princess!" he exclaimed.

"Is all right. Just... shifted sights too quickly."

"She was looking at the magic," Terri explained.

Lark turned to the half-elven girl. "You can see?"

She shrugged. "Sometimes. It's not as easy as it was for my mother, but I know there's something here. Something you woke up, and I know it protects us."

"Seeing magic is usually first step to wielding," said Lark.

Terri shrugged. "Maybe. Not much for religion though."

Lark shook her head and smiled. "There are other paths to magic than priesthood. All roads are equally valid, though not all roads are as easy to walk. We can explore this later. You have time."

Nodding, Terri turned away, going to talk to another of the young ones sliding out of the tunnels, leaving her alone with Billy.

"You wanted to see me, yore 'ighness?" he asked.

"Yes, how is your sister?"

"Not sick yet," he said, sobering quickly. "I 'eard they'd taken Father Mullen to th' Temple."

"His candle has gone out," she said gently. She watched him try to control his grief, digging at his eyes with a sleeved fist, breathing in short huffs. Setting a gentle arm on his shoulders, she gathered him in, let him deal with the news. None of the other children now milling about the Warren did more than glance in their direction.

It took a few minutes, then he wiped his face and pulled back. "Fank you," he mumbled. "Any news o' Mother Zedia?"

She shook her head. "All Rue told me was that she is also sick. Have you been to House since?"

"Yeah, last night. New wardens tried t' run me off. Fankfully one o' 'em 'as an' 'eart. She caught me inna kitchens bringin' in som dannylions I found. Thera's partial. When I aksed, she tole me I shouldn' come back if I gots anywhere else t' go. One's what are sick theys got onna top floor, an're keepin' th' others separated. But somehow, ever' mornin' there's a new one gots th' cough. They's at a loss. It be loik that in lotsa places. Ye hear coughin' behind closed doors, people inna taverns."

"I do not know what else can be done," Lark mused.

Billy noticed she'd gone pale. "Princess? Are yous all roight?"

"Am fine, Billy."

"No use lying, yore highness, beggin' yer pardon. But Is can see yer not."

Lark took a deep breath. "Honestly, plague terrifies me. Is how... I lost my mother."

He set his hand on hers, proud that it was his turn to comfort her. "We'll find th' cause, don't yous worry. We gots rat-catchers at it, we's boilin' th' water 'fore we uses it. I remember what Mother Zed tole me. I's made sure they all knows."

"It may not be simple as that. Or surely priests would have cured Father. But will help. That and staying away from anyone sick." She shook off the terror and melancholy that threatened to follow it. "Now, thought had talked about calling me princess."

He flushed. "Well, we's among friends here, ain't we?"

"Am beginning to see how is you stay out of trouble," she grinned. "Now, I should head back to Golden Cygnet. Need to see someone."

He stood, offered his hand to help her up. "I knows just th' tunnel, my lady."

TWO

Lark was sitting in the taproom of the Golden Cygnet, at a corner table with her rune stones scattered before her. Being a rooming establishment, it was exempt from the strict closures, but it was accepted that it would only be serving the residents, guests and whatever watchmen or militia were in the area. There weren't many. Billy had led her up into a laundry yard behind the place sometime after noon and had left her there, promising to check back.

Having made certain that no one was upstairs in the room but for a certain racoon, Lark had decided to wait for Portholus in the taproom. She had been nursing the same watered goblet of wine when someone noticed her trying to make sense of the stones and asked if she told fortunes. She smiled, sweeping them up as she offered for them to sit. The Eoh rune seated atop the Wyrd did not escape her notice, however. But how to interpret a rune of death on top of the blank stone eluded her.

It did not make her happy that Eoh made an immediate appearance in the person's reading. She had to explain that it could also mean great change, an end to the old way of life or of doing things.

They laughed at that. What was this war, but an end to a great many things?

She read the rest of the stones, giving them clearer guidance in the matter at hand, and they went away satisfied.

Lark read a few more fortunes as she sat there. The taproom wasn't as busy as it could get, but it was bustling. As night fell outside, she noticed there were more men in the room than before, and all of them armed or wearing a badge of some sort, likely proclaiming them members of the Civilian Watch.

She was beginning to think she should just go upstairs, when someone set a small chunk of polished quartz on the table in front of her. Looking up in surprise, she saw a rather gruff and disgruntled Rog. His face looked as if he was warring with several conflicting emotions. She realized then that someone must have told him that the stone was not magical.

Finally, he said a very gruff, "Thank ya," and started to walk off.

"Wait," she called. He turned and she held the stone out to him. "Keep."

He shook his head. "Don't need it. It done what it supposed to."

She smiled shyly. "Keep to remember you have nothing to fear. And to think of me, ...with fondness, I hope."

He stared at the rock fiercely. Then his expression softened and he accepted it, though he held it in his hand for a long time.

Before she could say anything or he could walk away, he saw something behind and to the left of her and his expression changed. She looked, saw a small elven boy, about six or so. The child was dark-haired and waif-like, large-eyed and was studying the dwarf warily, though he stood just behind and to the side of Lark's chair as if waiting to be noticed.

"Would you be Mouse?" she asked softly.

He looked at her with a brightness in his eyes, flashed a brief smile as he whispered, "Squeak."

She turned, gestured for him to come closer. "What is, my wee Cardinal?" she also whispered.

He flicked his eyes to the waiting dwarf. Lark looked up. "Rog is friend of mine and *General*," she added lowering her voice at Landros' title. "If is trouble, is good person to ask for help."

The dwarf's cheeks went a little pink at that, she noticed but did not acknowledge. There was a lot she was learning about dwarven ways that synced nicely with Romeri customs.

"Good. Is too big for one," the boy said softly. "Where can we talk? There are cats in the room."

Lark's eyes flicked across the crowd. There were more here than before, more badges. Some of which were eyeing her and her table. She nodded. "Have room upstairs. Will join?" she asked him, making sure that Rog knew the invitation extended to him as well. "If you have time?"

Rog nodded. "Gimme a minute," disappearing towards the bar.

Lark led the child to the stairway reserved for residents, waiting on the third step so that Rog could find her easily. She noticed that there was a man who worked at the inn seated on a stool beside the staircase. He nodded to her, recognizing her as an authorised guest. Either Landros had made some arrangement before he left, or being so often seen in his company had its advantages. The man took careful note of Rog as he joined her, nodded once to Lark and went back to surveying the room.

When they had reached the second floor, headed for the third, Lark heard something from below that made her stop and hold up her hand for silence. They listened.

At the bottom of the stairwell, they heard the guard arguing with someone. If they didn't have a key or an invite, they weren't going up. The upper floors were for residents only.

She smiled, but it was a worried expression. Pressure from the child's hand made her look down. "Cats," he whispered.

That one word sent a chill down her spine. She hurried them up to Landros's rooms on the third floor, showing them into the sitting room.

She summoned a were-light instead of lighting the lamp, and did not bother to light the fire. She did not think they would be here long enough to enjoy it.

Bidding them to sit, she poured the child a cup of water, which he drank readily after smelling it. Before she could offer Rog anything, he held up his hand, cocking his ear towards the bedroom door. "Anyone else here?" he whispered.

She shook her head. "Portholus would have lit lamp." Then she smiled, realizing what she was hearing. "Relax." She then opened the bedroom door and called inside. "Scraps, out!"

The raccoon waddled swiftly into the room, excited to see her, but stopped when he noticed there were people here he did not know.

She scooped him off the floor and carried him over to the couches, set him down next to the boy who was absolutely delighted with the animal. She looked over at Rog and softly laughed. "Friend of Landros. He comes and goes."

She turned back to the boy who had the animal on his back and in throws of the ecstasy that was belly rubs. "Mouse, you come to tell me something?"

Nodding, the child pulled the raccoon onto his lap and cuddled him, petting him for his own comfort. "Terri said to look for odd things, involving the sickness. I think I've found something."

This caught Rog's attention.

"We been making a map since you told us about it, marking where we know folk are sick. I saw a contention of it..."

"Contention?" Rog asked.

"You mean concentration?" she offered.

"Yes," he nodded. "It's in my quarter, near the borders of the Piper's patch. I've been nosing, asking the critters. There's a place even the mice won't go now. Smells wrong they say. There were huge rats that came out of there before the place went bad, rats that weren't before. The crows avoid it, say those that go there, die. Even the ants won't touch the shells."

The chill ran down her back again, circled around to settle in her soul. "Did not know you could speak to animals," she said, trying to get her fears under control.

He nodded. "Mum said I was Grove-marked. Told me the woods was where I belonged. She was sorry she couldn't get me there before...."

Lark set her arm around his shoulders, pressed a kiss to the top of his head. "Have you anyone left?"

He shook his head.

"Well, when war is over, I know tribe of elves who live wild in woods. They would love chance to take care of one such as you. General knows them. He can take you if you wish."

The child's eye lit up, then saddened. "But my friends?"

She smiled. "They will only be heart-beat away. Is not far. Day at most. And they will be happy for you if you are happy. But that is for later. For now, let us save friends, *sesket*?"

"*Sesket*," he nodded. "I know the place."

Rog immediately begin digging in his bag, pulled out a map which he spread out on the floor.

Mouse set the raccoon down and slid to the floor with him, looking the map over and trying to make sense of it. "Where is Tent Town?" he asked softly.

Scraps parked himself on a corner of the map, holding it down and mimicking the people, pouring over the map like he knew what he was seeing. Lark pointed out the area.

"Here is great tree in middle," she said. "Used to have my caravan there. Here is North gate and here, subwall which divide from warehouses above guild street."

This seemed to clear things up for the boy and he immediately traced a circle around an area south east of Lark's tree. "It's in here somewhere."

Lark shivered. She had been living near the epicentre of it. It occurred to her that she might have accidentally cursed those who had stolen from her after the hurricane. She realized in retrospect that they had only been trying to survive.

The map labelled the area known as Tent Town only as the Fairgrounds, even though there had not been a fair in the area for at least a decade. Lark knew of an old man who had dug himself a semi-permanent shelter in the northern part of it, and had been there at least a dozen years or more, or so she had been told. Because of this error, the map only showed significant landmarks, such as her oak, something that used to be a grandstand, and a well.

"Too bad they don't care enough about Tent Town to make accurate maps," Rog grumbled.

She smiled. "Would do no good. Changes too quickly. In two months I live there, way in and out change four times. People pitch where find space."

They noticed the grandstand was near the edge of the area Mouse had pointed out, but the well was smack in the middle.

"Convenient," the dwarf groused. "Are the chances good it's not a decoy?"

Lark shrugged, "Is where I would put. Is only water source for area, beyond rain-catching."

Scraps' head went up seconds before they heard the key in the lock. They all looked up as the door swung open, and a black-hooded figure stepped in, sword at the ready. Rog's hand was on his axe when Scraps shrieked and leapfrogged to the couch and into the figure's arms.

Portholus had no choice but to catch the animal, but still tried to keep the sword levelled. Lark's laughter did not help his mood, though it did ease his fears. "I see fey light beneath the door, hear whispering beyond it, how do you expect me to react in this climate?" he growled.

Lark made introductions, told him to close the door.

"I didn' know Landros had a brother," Rog mused, setting his axe down.

Portholus shrugged. "We don't talk about each other much. We just are. So," he said, sheathing his sword and sitting on the couch with the raccoon searching his pockets, "what mischief are we plotting?"

Lark explained.

"Wait, Father Mullen is dead?" he asked, going pale.

"You knew him?"

He rubbed his face, trying to come to grips with the news. "A little. Helped me out of a jam a long time ago. I was pretty sure Landros kept in touch. Damn... Does Landros know?"

Lark nodded. "Found out just before left. Had Sister Rue tell me. But Mouse here thinks may have found source. Am thinking someone put diseased something in well here in Tent Town. If can find, remove and purify well, might go long way to help stopping plague, if not cure already sick."

Portholus poured over the map. "Doesn't explain how the House of Lambs was affected, if that's the source."

"There were rats that ran out of there, before people got sick," Mouse said in his tiny voice. He seemed to be in awe of the tall, debonair elf.

Portholus nodded, ruffled his dark hair. "That would do it. So, let's get us a priest and go check it out," he said.

Lark sat back on her heels, looked at him. "Is no money in this," she said.

He almost looked offended. "There is no money or fun in a plague town. Bout time I pulled my weight, or so my brother would say. Besides, it's well after curfew and it's going to be tricky getting there. Which happens to be my speciality." He eyed the dwarf. "Not sure how to work around you, though. Never worked with a dwarf before. Hells, don't usually work *with* anyone," he chuckled. "Welp, first time for everything!"

"Don't have to..." Lark began.

He stopped her with a look. "So my brother gets back and finds out I *knew* you were going out to stop a plague and *didn't* go with you. How you think that's going to play out?"

"Two of you will be death of me," she playfully groaned.

"I hope not. He'd kill me."

Mouse and Rog were watching the exchange wide-eyed, before Rog shook his head and interrupted. "Well, I can get us on the streets legally."

Everyone looked at him, even the raccoon, even though he didn't know why. The dwarf shrugged. "I'm one of th' civilian militia. I got papers to be out and about," he grinned. "Might even have enough clout to snag us a priest."

"Rue maybe?" she asked.

"Can't hurt to ask, but won't be no guarantees. Adrick I could get ya. He's already assigned to my unit."

"Can Adrick purify?" she asked.

He expelled a grumbling breath. "Yeah, no. Rue it is, or someone who can purify. Grab whatcha need an' we can be off."

Mouse tugged on Lark's sleeve. "Bad idea. Front door."

They looked at him. He clarified, "Rog-sir can use, no problem. But... you, me?" he said, looking into Lark's eyes. "Cats."

She turned to face him fully, took his small hands in hers. "Mouse, you have said cats several times now. What means?"

He closed his eyes, took a deep breath. When he spoke, he looked up at her with his bright green eyes, full of fear and foreboding. "Means some have been watching you. Badges. Cats. Get feeling they're hunting."

She paled. "Why would be hunting me?"

Rog shrugged, "Kin ya think'a of anyone you've pissed off who might have enough power to be a problem?"

She groaned. "Knew Magistrate being in charge was no good for me."

"Best to avoid it altogether," Portholus announced. "Master Dwarf, if you would fetch us a priest we can use, the lady and myself will meet you here," he said, pointing to a small warehouse near one of the gates in the sub-wall. "I believe that one is abandoned at the moment."

Mouse shook his head. "Nope. Best meet us behind the Butcher's Block. There's an alley there that's easy to get into and leads right into Tent Town."

"Why there?" Rog asked.

The boy just grinned. Lark smiled. "You take high road to Temple. We shall take low road and meet in alley. You remember low roads, *sesha*?"

Suddenly he got it. "Oh! Right! Right! Good luck then. Might want yer boots though," he commented, glancing at the slippers on her feet as he stood.

Portholus looked from one to the other as Rog put away his map. She just laughed and went into the small bathing room. It would not do to need to go in the middle of things. When she came out again, Rog had left and Portholus was engaging the boy in an Elvish conversation.

Smiling, she went into the bedroom to change into her 'mucking about' clothes and boots. She thought she had seen traces of hero-worship in the boy's eyes. It wasn't much of a surprise. The two brothers were probably the first full elves he had seen in a while. Lithgorin aside, there were not many in town. And those there were, mostly kept to themselves.

With Mouse's help, she convinced Scraps to stay here and not follow them. When she was ready, they followed Portholus out the back way, into the laundry yard behind the building. She remembered where the sewer entrance was, having come out of it not that long ago, and they slipped out of sight without anyone the wiser.

THREE

Portholus was thoroughly impressed with the underground 'roads', even though many of the pathways made him hunch over to get through. Mouse popped his head out of the grating at the back of the now empty butcher's hall, making certain the way was clear before bringing the others up.

Nervous about the patrols she could hear in the area, and not convinced the sheltered back alley was hidden enough, Lark threw up an illusion of a wall of debris between them and the southern opening before they settled back to wait.

"Where do you know the dwarf from?" Portholus asked, almost too casually, keeping his voice low.

She smiled. "Met him after met brother. Have several adventures together. Is good friend."

They were only waiting about twenty minutes when they heard the sound of people approaching. Lark listened, thought she recognized the voices. She made a low, mournful whistle of the quail, waited. The voices went quiet. Then the whistle was echoed back.

There came a low, gruff voice, "Did I do th' damn thing right?"

She gave a soft laugh and dropped the illusionary wall. A few seconds later, Rog and the priestess walked past the opening. She called out to them, keeping her voice hushed, drew them into the alley with her.

Sister Rue's eyes glittered as she looked Lark over. "By the goddess but you work quick!" she exclaimed quietly.

Lark hugged her, smiling. "Serendipity, really. Luck Rog find me when Mouse found me, and Landros's brother here..." she waved him over. "Portholus, Sister Rue."

Rue went quiet as the tall, handsome elf bowed over her hand and kissed it. "My lady," he said.

Lark elbowed him. "Sister, not 'my lady'," she corrected. "With that one you play for keeps, or you don't play at all, sesket?" she warned, glaring at him.

He cautiously pulled back, held up his hands in surrender. "Habit," he grinned, moving away. Though he did cast a sideways glance or two her way.

Rue pulled herself together quickly, got down to business. "What exactly are we looking for?" she asked as they followed the elven child down the other end of the alleyway.

"Don't know. Source of sickness. Think has to be in or near Tent Town well."

Rue pulled her to a stop, called the child back. She turned to take Lark by the shoulders, pressed her forehead to hers. "You don't have to tell me that this terrifies the hells out of you. I can see it in your eyes, feel it surrounding you. ...Your mother?" she asked.

Lark tipped her head in surprise. "Don't remember telling you...."

She smiled sagely. "Adrick is not the only one of us to have entered a higher circle. Your fear is a physical thing right now. And that isn't good." She gestured for all of them to gather around her. "Take hands. I am going to do what I can to protect us. It will only last a little while, a few hours at most, and it isn't a guarantee. If you come in direct contact with the source, it might not be enough. But it is better than nothing."

They circled her with the child in the middle. Rue held up her medallion, raising her crossed fingers and began to pray, casting a spell that fell over them like a caul. It felt warm, and tingled a little before settling into them. Lark thought she saw the briefest outline of plague masks over their faces. Ignoring it, she did what she could to fortify the spell, bolstering it from without.

Rue's eyes flashed open as she felt the insertion of Lark's magic. But it blended so well it did not feel like an intrusion. Finishing her prayer, she looked over her friend in a new light.

"Something is different about you," she smiled. "I like it."

Lark smiled. "Power settles in."

With that, they slipped through a gap in the sub-wall and into the sprawling disaster that was Tent Town.

Lark turned here, knelt in front of Mouse. "Cardinal, I know this is your quarter, your ward. You know this place as I once knew it. But this is dangerous. Even with protections, I will worry for you. There may be physical threats. Please do not come with us."

He swallowed, looked like he might protest with anger. "I am a mouse," he said. "I can go nearly anywhere and not be seen. But I know where I should not go, even though I have been before. I will watch from the walls. I will warn you if the cats come."

She took a deep breath, let it out slowly, thankful he would not fight the matter. "Do you know whistle men make to pretty lady?"

He blushed. "Rude whistle?"

She nodded, smiling. "Yes. Rude whistle. Can you whistle?"

He bobbed his dark head.

"If cats come, make rude whistle. Is how Nightingale warns me of cats."

He looked around at that. "Where is Nightingale?" he asked, suddenly realizing he hadn't seen the familiar about.

She gave him a sad smile. "Is with General. Keeping safe. Now, North, you stay safe."

He nodded and vanished behind a lean-to.

She stood, headed back to the others.

"Where's the boy going?" Portholus asked.

"To watch backs from crack in walls."

He frowned, but asked no further questions. They began to

make their way through the ramshackle array of dwellings with only a thin were-light to guide them.

Lark fell in beside Rog as they wound between and around various shelters. She kept her voice down. "So, how find out stone was... not really magic?"

He snorted. "Some stuffed shirt minstrel I had the misfortune of being paired with on a mission. There were rivers..." he shuddered.

"Are angry?"

"I was..." he admitted. "At first. Pompous jackass had a field day with it. I understand now, though. Mostly needed to see yer face when I confronted ya. Yer heart was in th' right place," he paused. "And it did help. I don't handle embarrassment well."

She gave a soft laugh. "Who does?" she shrugged. "Was intended to help avoid this. Was bit worried would try to swim, though," she confessed.

He shook his head. "Even I know not to test th' limits of magic. It helped enough. And I can appreciate the gesture. Now that I know you weren't being mean about it. Still feels a little... I dunno know... deceitful, though."

She bumped companionably into his solid shoulder. "No. Merely trick you into understanding strength of own mind. You are no Rube."

"Lark," Rue called.

She turned back to the sister who was looking around worriedly. "*Sesha*?"

"What is wrong with this picture?"

Lark stopped, cast not just her eyes, but her senses around them. She remembered what it was like coming home late at night through here, feeling life all around her, even if she couldn't see it. There would be shuffling, sniffling, breathing, sounds of intimacy. Now there was nothing. It sounded more like a graveyard than a camp. In the far distance, she could hear deep, hacking coughs, but where they were... was silence.

She sent her light up, flew it about until she found her tree. Its crown looked damaged, as if it, too, were dying. From there, she triangulated the location of the well, and redirected them.

The tattered tents around her flapped dully in the thin wind. No signs of life anywhere. She was afraid to peek, to check. She did not hear the buzzing of flies or other signs of death and carrion. The area did smell faintly of sickness and putrefaction now that she thought about it, but not enough to make her think she was walking through a carnal field.

The well was in the only cleared space in the whole fairgrounds. It was the only place that was paved and thus harder for folks to pitch tents on. The only reason the lean-to sheds and other dwellings had not crept up onto the pavers was that everyone needed access. It was the unspoken, unbreakable law of Tent Town.

The headwall of the well had been repaired over the years by residents with fragments of stone they had found. It made for a less than perfectly stable surface in places. The roof over the rusty winch was as bad as Lark remembered it, leaning and leaking, full of wet-rot now, after the hurricane. Someone had splinted one of the supports, and it seemed to be holding.

Carefully, she leaned over the still mortared edge, split her light in two and sent one of them down the shaft. The water was nearly twenty feet down, and the light reflected blackly off the oily surface.

"Looks kind of nasty," Portholus commented.

Lark shrugged. "Fall-out from blasts, ash, all kind debris get in. Was filtering even when lived here month or so back. Seems longer," she added, shaking her head.

She plunged the light below the surface, watched it shine dimly through what turned out to be a thin layer of oily dust. It sank maybe six feet and then began to fade away.

"Is it going too deep or is that silt on the bottom?" Rue asked.

"Don't know. Never looked in like this." That made her think. She closed her eyes, taking deep, calming breaths, and opened them again, using her other sight. Her sense of smell was completely out of commission right now, so if there was magic, she could not use that sense to find it. Her eyes, however.... Deep below the surface of the water, she saw something that shimmered a putrid, malevolent green.

"Rue, do you see..." she pointed.

Rue shifted her own sight and gasped. She suddenly covered her mouth and rushed over to the edge of the pavement and retched.

"That bad?" Rog commented dryly.

Portholus glanced into the well, then over at the priestess. "I feel like I should be able to smell something."

Rog frowned. "Yeah," he agreed, sniffing the air.

Rue waved her fingers above her head, trying to sign something, but it made no sense. Finally she choked out, "Spell."

She got her nausea under control, straightened her robes and came back over. "It's my spell. If you could smell anything right now, you'd be over there with me," she groaned. "It filters the air of miasmas."

Lark looked at her over the well-head, "So what is?"

"Do you know what a bezoar is?" she asked.

Portholus made a face at that.

"*Sesha*," Lark said slowly. "Is bezoar?" she asked, pointing, confused.

Rue shook her head. "That is the opposite of a bezoar."

Lark paled.

Rog frowned. "What in th' nine hells is a bayzor?"

Rue turned to him. "You can find them in the intestines of goats most often. They are rock-like things that develop from undigestibles. They are supposed to protect one from poison."

"Do they work?"

Lark gave a sharp laugh at that, and Rue went on.

"In my experience? Only with arsenic."

That surprised Lark. She had always thought it an old wives' tale, a charlatan's remedy.

Rue continued. "You're better off with charcoal. That," she pointed at the well, "is a nosoi."

"What is a nosoi?" Portholus asked.

"Plague stone," Lark answered. "Is said to be made from calcified remains of victims of seven incurable pestilence."

Rue nodded. "The seven incurable plagues. The first seven diseases to afflict the world. I do not know the truth of their origins, but... I have no doubt that is one of them."

"S'how do we destroy it?" Rog asked, beginning to sweat.

"First have to bring up," Lark commented.

"Then we have to counter it... somehow," Rue finished. "Without touching it."

"How in the nine hells are we supposed to do that?" Portholus snapped.

"Poltergeist," Lark answered.

They all looked at her. "My little winds. Remember how I got Ivaska into boat?"

Rog let his head fall back on his shoulders, stared up at the dark, cloudy sky. "Of course. Do ya know what to do with it after?"

Rue nodded. "I think so. Ideally, I would take it to the Temple and let the triumvirate deal with it, but... I don't want to carry this thing through town. It's too risky. The longer we are near it the higher the chances of it breaking through my protections. We'll just have to deal with it here, as quickly as possible."

From somewhere near the wall, there came the shrill sound of a wolf-whistle. They looked up and around. Lark saw a small form standing on the sub-wall several hundred yards away. Portholus and Rog turned, weapons at the ready, hearing a shuffling movement amid the shelters around them. Rue could feel something cold and slimy slithering down her backbone.

"Undead," she breathed.

"What?" Portholus snapped.

She turned, held up her medallion and her crossed fingers, began praying fervently. They all could see the shimmering of a shield rising around them; could see the fluttering movement of corpses walking, crawling towards them with unnatural fluidity.

Rog spun his axe in his hand. "I *hate* undead!" he growled.

The first to come into full view was a lank-haired woman who had clearly died of the plague, crawling spider-like across the stone. She crept up to the shield, tried to push through and was propelled into a nearby shack with extreme violence.

"I think I should warn you that the nosoi being inside the shield is very likely going to weaken it," Rue called. "You need to work fast, Lark!"

She did not need the extra urging. "Portholus," she called as she began to whip up the strongest poltergeist she could manage, "my old neighbour is behind us with wagon wheel. Maybe you can do something?"

Portholus turned, eyes wide as the man swung a broken wagon wheel as if it was a razor-edged shield. He repositioned himself to that side of the well, as the wheel impacted the shield, testing.

"Feel free to stab or swing through!" Rue called out in between reinforcing the magic. "Just don't put your hands into the barrier!"

That said, the two men began to slice and stab anything that got close enough. Most of the undead that touched the barrier were shocked backwards, though each time with less and less force.

Lark tuned it all out, concentrating on filtering out the nosoi from the muck at the bottom of the well. It was not easy. Several times she brought other things to the surface, including bones, old cups and coins. Even a broken bucket. She was about to let the bucket go, when she realized the sickly green glow was in the muck inside the vessel. Bringing the light up with it, she lifted it out of the well. She spared a look below, making certain there was nothing else down there, before she had the poltergeist tip the contents out onto the pavement.

There was an unbelievable amount of sludge, finally unearthing what looked like the corpse of a raven. Clutched in the bird's grasp was a twisted, white lump of calcified stone. With her sight still up, there was no doubt it was the source of the now pulsing green light. She felt ill, like she wanted to repeat Rue's performance of earlier, but she swallowed it back. She had no idea what to do with this, but knew as long as the undead were swarming them, that Rue would not be able to do anything.

Overturning the bucket on the carcass and its stone, Lark sent her poltergeist outside of the shield, began bowling over the scrabbling dead. She grabbed chunks of shack debris, sending it raining down on their heads.

Anything that got close enough to the edges was dealt with by the swift sword and axe-work of the two men. She did a quick count, and as far as she could tell, there were little over a dozen of them of one sort or another. She wracked her brain trying to figure out how to make it manageable.

"Rue, how long would take to break nosoi?"

"Just a few minutes, I hope!" she cried, struggling to hold on to the shield. "If I even can," she added in a mutter.

Lark closed her eyes, looking inward, begging for inspiration. She focused on her new-found powers, casting for solutions. A flash of insight struck her. They did not have the power of three, but what they had could still be enough if used wisely.

She yelled at the men, "When shield breaks, head for wall! Follow light!" She then stood in front of Rue.

The priestess looked frantic, trying to maintain her weakening hold and not be distracted. "What are you doing?" she cried.

"Flow with me. When gathered, push out!" and then Lark locked her hand over the one holding the medallion. She pressed her own crossed fingers to Rue's, the folded fingers interlacing.

Rue felt a sudden surge of power, a veritable storm running through her shield. Lark began to spin everything, swirling her power and the shield into a vortex that made the men take a step back. It was dizzying to watch, so neither woman did. They locked eyes and wills, until it reached a screaming, fever pitch, then blew it all outward, levelling everything around the well for a hundred yards.

It was painfully silent for about three seconds before they heard the shuffling of the dead trying to untangle themselves.

"*Run!*" Lark yelled, letting go of Rue and turning. She paused only to scoop up the bucket with the bird and the stone and led the way with her light, taking the straightest path to the nearest wall.

"Now what?" Portholus cried when they reached it, seeing nowhere else to go. The breach they had slipped through was far away, behind twists and turns of still-standing shacks and tents.

She dumped her bucket again, kicking the bird over so that the stone was facing them. "Now you guard. Now we work."

Rog understood immediately what she had done. They had a wall to their backs, and the enemy was scattered. When they came again ...and they were coming... they would be in more manageable numbers. He took two long steps away from the women and gave himself room to work.

Portholus looked back at Lark, kneeling on the ground with the priestess, locking hands again over the dead bird. He thought she was crazy, sure. But if anything had a chance of working, this would be it. Well, he thought, as he turned to face the on-coming dead, if he didn't walk out of this, at least he wouldn't have to face his brother for getting the girl killed.

They locked their hands the way they had before, forming a circle around the nosoi. Rue looked fearfully at her. "I... I don't know what I'm doing," she confessed.

"Neither I," Lark grinned madly. "Instinct. How you heal disease?"

"With herbs and ...."

Lark shook her head. "No. With magic! How you heal simple disease?"

"That's it?!"

Lark shrugged. "Will see. Can only try. Heal small and make bigger. You focus, I will amplify, like on Evandair."

They closed their eyes, blocking out the sounds coming towards them. Rue prayed, pouring her soul into her pleas to not just her own aspect, but the whole triumvirate, begging to break this nightmare thing, to eradicate the anathema.

Lark called forth everything she had within, drew on generations of her family, drew on what lay below, sleeping, calling to her. This she did for the protection of her caravan, of the ones she cared for, and yes, even for the ones she did not.

The rest of the world fell silent, trapping them in a tornado cycle of power. Rue drew from above, channelling warmth and love and healing, while Lark pulled from below, from the earth and its foundations, amplifying everything and helping to focus it until something had to give.

There was a sudden crack, a shifting of the ground, and a small fissure opened beneath the bird. The two women jumped, looked into the circle of their arms and watched the sodden raven's corpse decompose at an alarming rate. It withered to bone and then dust in the space of five heartbeats. The stone likewise melted away as if it had been no more than salt in the rain.

Lark glanced around, saw the dead that had not already fallen to the blades of the two men slump to the ground, wearing somewhat startled expressions. On the wall above them, Rue noticed five children with slings. And then neither woman remained aware of anything at all as the circuit between them broke, and both collapsed.

It was Lark who woke first, being somewhat roughly handled by a panicked Portholus. She slapped away his hand in annoyance, snapping, "Away with you, *pashaska*! Am awake!"

He exhaled explosively, left off and helped her to sit up. "Damn it, woman! You nearly gave me a heart attack!"

She blinked. Above her, on the wall, she saw the crouched form of Mouse and a handful of children with slings, some of whom were, even now, disappearing over the wall. She waved in thanks. "Well done, North," she called. He merely nodded and slid down their side of the wall.

Rue was sitting up, helped by Rog. The heel of her hand was pressed to her temple. She looked over at Lark and started laughing. "Is your head still buzzing?" she asked.

Lark shook her head. "No." She frowned, shifted her sight and smiled, letting it go. "Still have work to do, Sister. Go, purify well. Think will end buzzing."

Frowning, Rue got up, walked unsteadily back to the well with Rog keeping guard. The poor dwarf wasn't ready to trust anything just yet.

"Is it always like this?" Portholus asked.

She shrugged. "Sometime is less passing out."

Mouse giggled at the elf's reaction to that. "Sometimes she lights up the whole Warren," he added, winking at her.

She waggled her finger at him. "You.... Oh!"

Portholus looked up at the boy. "Thank your friends for us."

Mouse shrugged. "It's our job. Can my lady travel?" he asked, ignoring the questioning look Portholus gave him at that.

"Maybe. Should wait for Rue and Rog."

He shook his head. "Cats are coming. They'll be fine. You won't."

Lark frowned, still not sure why the boy was so insistent she not be anywhere there were watchmen. Still she hesitated.

"I'll tell them, if you go now." He pointed away from where they had come in. "Follow the wall to a vine growing into it. I'll meet you there." Without waiting to see if they would obey, he trotted off towards the well.

"Best do as says," Lark said, getting to her feet.

Portholus just looked at her. "And why is that? He's just a child. He's barely twelve."

Lark stopped. "Twelve? Looks more seven!"

"Elves mature slower," he grumbled.

She shook her head, started walking. There was a great deal about elves she did not know, apparently. "We do because he is Cardinal of North. Is his quarter, and he knows it better than anyone. Has little ears and little eyes everywhere, him more than others," she added with a grin. "Has furry ears, too. Best to do, ask after."

They had just found the vine that was trying to be a tree, wedging its way into a crack in the wall, when Mouse turned back up. He ran past them and monkey climbed up the vine, gesturing for them to be quick and quiet. Lark kilted her skirts and shimmied up after him, with Portholus not far behind.

Before she could ask about the others, Mouse gestured for silence and stepped off the wall onto the ledge of a building built right up against it. He led them to a corner and from there up to the roof. They crept low across the warehouse shingles, noting gaps where they could see all the way to the storage floor.

They had a fair view from up here, and could see a growing amount of light pouring into Tent Town. When they were far enough away from it all, Mouse huddled them up by a chimney to rest a moment.

"I told them," he said. "Dwarf agreed."

"Why the hell are they safe and we're not?" Portholus asked. "I mean, I get why *we'd* not want to deal with the watch," he added, fidgeting a little under Lark's sudden scrutiny.

Mouse grinned. "They're legal tonight. He's got mission paper. And a priest."

"Wouldn't all with be covered by paper?" Lark asked.

Mouse shook his head. "Not no more. And there's a whisper about Romers."

That made her blood run cold. "What whisper?"

He shook his head. "Dunno. Might ask the General's Lord. Be safest there or the Warren. So where'll it be, Standard?"

There was an unnatural maturity in the boy when he said that. He ignored Portholus completely, all his focus was on her.

"Need answers. Take to manor."

The boy nodded, bade them wait and disappeared.

"What the hell are you two talking about?" Portholus growled, grabbing her arm, though nowhere nearly as roughly as he might have once. "Keeping secrets again, girl? I thought we were past that?"

She grinned at him. "Is brother's secret, not mine. Am merely keeping.

FOUR

Lark had left Portholus in the tender care of Mouse. She had talked him into heading back to the Cygnet by convincing him it was where Rog would look for him. She tied the red ribbon on the hinge as she said she would, and the stable-boy did not ask. She did not have to wonder if the master of the house was up or not. The yard was lit and busy, as everything he'd need to fight was gathered and packed. Lark even noticed a large blood bay warhorse being led in from the fields.

She slipped into the house without an issue, asked the least harried maid she saw where she might find the lord. Told his study, Lark waved the girl off with a smile. "I'll find," she said and wandered up the stairs, remembering where it was.

The lights were on and there was a great deal of activity. Servants were gathering maps and putting them in portable cases, several armoured men were coming and going, getting their orders and making their reports. Lark slipped into the chaos easily, found her way to the chair she had occupied... was it just that morning? Folding herself into it, she waited until the Lord chanced to notice her. Without a word, she conveyed that she could wait, and with a nod, he finished with his men, issuing last minute preparations and orders to those who would not be on the field with him, but nonetheless answered to him.

Finally, the room got quieter. She barely noticed when he closed the door and leaned against the desk until he made a small, deliberate noise to call her attention. "I really don't have a lot of time, my lady," he said gently.

She apologized, unfolding herself and turning to him. "Am... drained. Plague is over," she said bluntly.

"Just like that?" he asked, incredulous.

"Maybe. Cannot be sure, but think so. At least, no more get sick. Mayhap sick get better? Cause is gone." And she explained what had transpired in the last few hours.

Colwyn poured her a drink, handed her the brandy glass. She sipped, was surprised to find it pure. She glanced up at him as he sipped his own. "Last of it, really. After tonight, it's do or die, so why bother saving it?" he chuckled. "Well done, my lady."

She gave him the barest nod, accepting the praise and he studied her as she sipped.

"What else ails you, my lady?" he asked.

She glanced up, figured the best way was to just come out and ask. "North was very adamant tonight about keeping me away from cats. By this he meant officials. Would not say beyond 'whispers about Romers'. I wondered if you knew anything?"

He threw back the last of his brandy, set the glass down. He walked around the desk, putting in order the few papers remaining, anything to avoid meeting her eyes. "The Magistrate... is trying to crack down on what he calls 'unsavoury types'. He has put into place regulations that amount to little more than anti-Romeri legislation. They aren't laws yet, but... with martial law in place all he really needs right now is an excuse. Those who are suspected of mischief or collusion can be incarcerated until the end of the siege without being seen by the courts or having any real proof. Swears the cases will be seen as soon as the war is over, but until then..." He slammed the now neatened stack of papers onto his desk.

"It smells like a cess-pit, and there isn't a damned thing the council will do about it. With the knowledge that people all over town have been subverted or just convinced to stay out of the way, the council is unwilling to take any chances. Anyone can be accused of collusion and locked up until they have the time to get around to dealing with formal charges. Which makes it easy for the guilty to get their problems out of the way."

She watched him carefully. "Why won't you look at me? What not are telling me?"

He planted his fists on the desk, stared hard at the surface as if he wanted to bore a hole through it. He took several, deep, angry breaths. "There has been word of other Romeri in town. Men. Men no one can now find and were not known to have entered the city before the gates closed. There have been whispers that they have been coming and going, via magic or stealth, and since no one can do that, they must be in league with the enemy. Since you are the only Romeri known to be in town, you are likely being watched, as they will assume the men will find you."

Finally he looked up at her. "Is any of this true?"

"My family. ...My family have ways of going where we wish, and my brothers have come, and gone. But never in service of enemy. All for me, to convince me to leave, which I wouldn't, then to fetch me for my father's daughter's wedding. Once to test my Kestrel's intentions," she added with a brief grin. "Twice has brought food, which have shared."

He nodded. "I had wondered where the apples came from."

She met his eyes finally, "How... how much trouble do I bring?"

"How do you mean?"

"To you, to self? Is presence in your wood danger to you?"

He shook his head. "Even he would not dare to enter my home without proof. As for how much danger you are in outside of these walls? I think your Cardinal has the right idea about cats. The Magistrate already does not like you."

She sighed, curled into herself again and sipped. "This have noticed. Do not think likes women."

"You would be right. If you have to leave here, stick to the shadows or in disguise, or with others who are above reproach if you can. Failing that, if you are chased, you can claim sanctuary at the Temple. Not the shrines," he added, "the main temple."

She nodded. "Will remember. Will stick to under-roads if must. When do you leave?"

"Before dawn. I might catch an hour or two of sleep before my people and I head for the gates."

"Are not gates watched by enemy? Will they not bombard when open?"

His grin was feral, "Only if they notice."

She rose and set the glass on the desk. She came around to his side of it, bade him sit down. Curious, he obeyed, sensing something of significance in her.

Dipping her finger in the dregs of the brandy, she drew the rune Thorn upon his brow. "Mahril give you endurance to keep you going and keep you safe. Mahren expand your shield to protect those in your care. Magruma to walk before you and not look behind to you. This blessing I give: strength of arms and strength of shield, as friends such as you are rare and to be treasured."

Colwyn shivered suddenly, unable to explain why. He had felt something settle over him. He bowed his head to her, "You have my gratitude, Rana."

She smiled. He had some knowledge, but it was clearly imperfect. "Ranie," she corrected. "And I am, and this is my clan, my caravan. And I will use every tool I have to protect this."

She took a step back before turning and walking out of the room, sweeping up her bag as she went. She left him sitting at the desk lost in wonder and slipped out into the back garden. She paused at the roses, cupped one full bloom in her hand and drank deep of their soft perfume. A few of the petals fell away in her palm, despite the gentleness of her touch. She collected them, slipped them into her rune-bag and walked back to her caravan.

The night was cool, and full of distant sounds that told her both sides were preparing for open conflict. Still, she opted to sleep under the wagon, where she could keep half an eye on the sky and smell any changes in the air. Eventually, she slept.

Days had passed. Her sleep stayed fitful, plagued with dreams of something hunting her. It was not like previous dreams, where she was actually pursued, not like the nightmares while the vampire had held sway, trapped within the soul ring on her hand. Or any normal dream playing out active fears. Neither was this like the visions she had experienced on the brink of death, showing her possibilities and the truth of now.

This was as if she was someone else, something else; like an animal hiding in its burrow listening to a terrier rooting about above, seeking and hungry and implacable. It wanted to eat her heart. Slowly, she came to the realization of what was happening. Something terrified, to which she already had a tenuous connection, had reached out to her, slipped in to plead. Her caravan was calling.

Aware now, she settled, closing even her dream's eyes and taking long, deep breaths. She thought calm thoughts, protective ones, and slowly she felt the presence ease, the fear slip away. Anger threatened, but it was aimed outward. Lark felt the heartbeat, and the weight of something coiling around her, felt the breath of some great thing fall on her from above. It smelled of amethyst and amber, earth and musk. With it came visions.

The hooded one, the mage Lark was certain had died several times in the last few months, was near the square, searching an old building. They were near a damaged and abandoned guild hall whose windows looked familiar to her. They were skulking in the alleys a block from the Cinnamon Tree. They were sniffing about in the sewers not far from Edis's hole in the ground. This was not a layering of time, the same person seen at different moments in different places. This was several people at the same instant. There was a flickering about them, though. As if something were inhabiting each of them, driving them, more aware in one than the other in turn, but always present in all. This presence made her skin crawl.

The other spirit tightened about her, and she heard the crying of children, young things that were not human, witnessed the screaming death they suffered the last time this evil thing had found the den.

Outside the walls, three armies engaged. Mass charges spilled from the open gates, hammering into the mess of men and monsters that surrounded it, hidden in the thin forests, thinner now for the trees taken to fuel the siege. Just as it seemed those small forces would be overwhelmed, the enemy were hit from the sides by even smaller groups that had snuck out and hidden by magic. Siege forces were driven back, seeking more secure ground, only to be brought down by silent arrows flung by the very trees.

This last she saw, not through the entity simultaneously trying to protect her and begging for her aid, but through Nightingale. He hovering on the wind above it all, feeling like a mighty roc as he watched. Occasionally, he would spot a danger to his side, and would swoop through the trees above the fray, screaming his wolf whistle in warning, then soar back up to over-watch, to enjoy the chaos wrought by the reactions of those who had no idea what that sound had meant. More than once he had forced enemy bands to give themselves away when sneaking up on the city's forces. Always, though, he flew back to the elf he was supposed to be watching, while keeping a weather eye out for eagles.

What struck Lark in all of that, was that the hooded mage and the possessing entity, while part of the fiasco in the woods, couldn't care less which way it fell out. Trying not to shudder, she focused on one of them, trying to fathom why. It all tied to why the city was under siege, and that all-important, unanswered question posed that afternoon in the Square: Why had they not just rolled over the city and taken it, when it was painfully obvious they could have.

It was the dragon who provided the answer. Every pained movement she made, suffering under the anguish of the city above her, caught the mages' attention, brought them that much closer to finding her. All the while the monsters were being created in the tunnels, she had held her breath, tried not to writhe in agony, to lie still and not give away her position as the mage spent the aftermath hunting. That Lark had reactivated the faded runes scratched in the warren nearly a millennia ago had helped immensely.

Something large and violent thudded and vibrated through the world, followed by a dozen, tiny stabbing needles and a painful screech in her ears. The dragon moved against her, pushing her away and fled as if in fear. But fear of what Lark never had the chance to figure out before all hell broke loose.

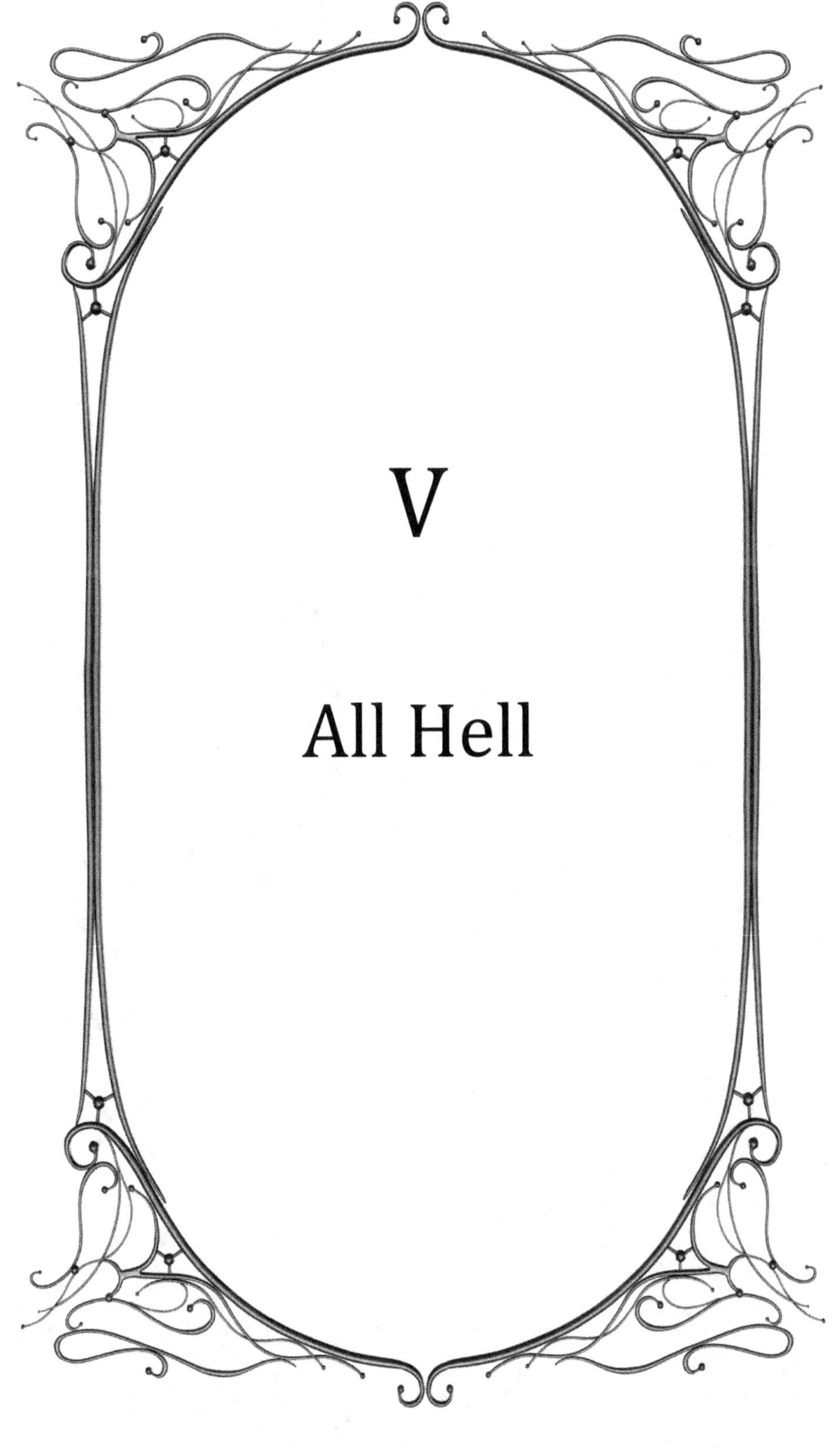

V

All Hell

ONE

It was just before dawn and the bombardment had begun. Boulders and enormous balls of flaming tar were catapulted over the walls before the sun had fully breached the horizon. Lark opened her eyes with a gasp, looked up at the terrified racoon trying to hide between her axle and the underbelly of the caravan. Her neck and shoulder were cold, and she felt the mark his nails had left when he had been startled awake.

She reached up, calling soothingly to him. Eventually, he came down, crawling under the quilts in terror. Heaving a sigh, she rolled out from under the wagon and gathered her bedding. Scraps complained as she uncovered him. "You want go inside?" she asked. "Safer there."

She laughed softly as he scrambled onto the rear steps like lightning, began scratching at the door as he tried to open it.

She shooed him aside. "Ah! Scratch paint!" she fussed. "Lord Colwyn work so hard on it. Is bell," she added, pointing out a small bell on a coiled ribbon of polished brass that had been added to the side of the back ledge.

Keeping his eyes on her, he waddled over, reached up, grabbed the clapper, pulled down on the springy metal, and let go. The bell bounced back up, jangling like a mad-thing. All the while, the animal glared at her.

She refused to be baited. "Thank you," she said pertly, and opened the caravan door.

Scraps was inside like a shot, rooting about for a place to hide. Lark scooped him up and tossed him onto the bed, dropped her quilts on top of him. The pile writhed and flopped for several minutes before his face popped out, sneezed at her, then wiggled back into the den he'd made.

"Are welcome," she retorted.

She changed, putting on her new motley skirt and the red velvet vest. She kept his shirt on, though, desperate to keep some part of him close to her. She ran her hand down the front of the velvet, wondered the wisdom of wearing it when she knew damned well things might get 'mucky'. But she felt like she needed her clan trademark about her as much as she needed his shirt. It was like being wrapped in her family. Like Landros's armour.

The only compromise she made to the potential hazards of the day, was to remove most of her jewellery, even her earrings. The soul ring, she obviously could not remove, but she also left on her grandmother's emerald. It felt wrong though, wearing only that little embellishment and nothing else; obvious. She worried that it might attract the wrong attentions, so she wove a little illusion over them, blending them in to her fingers. Someone of power who was looking might see through the simple misdirection, but no one else would think twice. She even chose a plain black kerchief to hold back her curls instead of her usual yellow scarf.

She opened a cabinet and took out the last of the Alphasian apples Ivan had given her, putting it into her skirt pocket. It would have to suffice for breakfast and lunch. She had no idea if there would be a chance for supper, as she expected there to be a great deal of work ahead. Taking a handful of hickory nuts from a jar in the back, she set them in a bowl for Scraps. She also opened the window a little, so he could get out if he needed to. Before she left, she marked the door with runes for the first time since she had moved, placing runes of protection upon it, rather than locking.

As ready for the day as she could make herself, she headed towards the manor to see what help she could be. Besides the apple, there were two silver harps in her pocket, and she did not even bothered to bring her bag. Nothing would be needed today but Quicksilver.

She had just reached the footbridge when a boulder, covered in pitch and blazing like a small sun, struck the eastern wall. She heard the screaming of what few horses were still in the pastures and the thunder of hooves as they ran from the stink and the noise.

The head stableman poked his head out of one of the out-buildings, started to panic. She waved for his attention. **"Get horses safe,"** she bellowed when she had it. **"I will get fire!"**

The man did not know what his master's guest could do that he could not, but he did realize where the priorities lay. He began ringing a large bell by the stable, calling all the servants who had remained behind to come and help. He began giving orders to prepare to put out fires, in case another fireball descended upon them.

Lark ran towards the burning rubble of the wall as fast as she could. By the time she reached it, the fire had begun to spread, catching a patch of mulberry trees nearby and the tall grasses the horses had not yet gotten to. Fortunately, the river was close enough to be useful, and she was able to magically gather a great deal of the water and rain it down on the fire. This, however, was a mistake, causing the fire to spit and hiss and spread faster, filling the air with a choking black smoke. Pulling the water back, she settled for wetting down everything not already in flames, hoping to slow the progress.

She thought quickly, remembering what her mother had taught her to do with a stove fire if fat or grease were spilled, to deal with fire that water wouldn't douse. She didn't have something large enough to smother it. The sensation of moving through the earth slithered over her, causing a momentary shudder until it gave her an idea.

Taking the magic that had gathered the water, she reached into the earth instead, pulling up as large a chunk of the ground as she could and sifting it over the flames. She shook the grasses until the roots lay bare and then dropped them out of reach of the fire. Then began to dig a large hole, once the ground-cover was out of the way, and dropped blankets of the rich loam onto the remaining flames.

By the time she had it out, she was as winded as if she had dug it. Through the new gap in the wall, she could see others trying to figure out how to deal with the splashes of still-burning tar which were smoking fiercely as they threw water on them. She grabbed one last, large pile of dirt, dropping it on the largest puddle she could see and yelled across the gap, "**Shovels! Use earth!**"

Finally someone understood and began using the water bucket to grab dirt from the pile and toss it onto the smaller patches of fire.

At that point, Lark had no choice but to sit down.

Someone popped their head around the rubble when she disappeared, frowned to see her sitting. Then they saw the amount of raw earth and how far it was spread, compared it to the size of the hole and seemed to change the question they had come to ask.

"Are you all right?"

She nodded weakly, aiming her thumb at her work. "Yes. Used magic but... exhausts only bit less than digging."

Their eyes grew. "Only faster." They glanced back to their side of the wall, turned back to her. "Was gonna ask if you'd help over here, but... I think we can get it with the pile you dropped. ...Thank you... for telling us how."

She laughed, which devolved into a wheezing cough. "Learned hard way! Tried water first. Smoked like grease fire, so... Mama always said, 'No water for fat. Smother fat fire'."

The man chuckled, "My mama said that, too. Rest." He started to leave, then peered back, "If we need more... dirt... can we?" he asked sheepishly, pointing to the hole.

She heard the breathless voice of someone coming up behind her. "Yes," they huffed. She turned to see the head stableman pausing to catch his breath. "Just... aim for the edges of the hole," he panted, raising an eyebrow at the depth and breadth of the one she had made. "I'll get a bucket brigade prepped, in case of others."

The man gave him a nod of thanks, added ruefully, "There already have been. I've seen at least three other columns of the black smoke in our sector alone."

The stableman turned to a young man who was running to join him, a servant from the look of him. "Kane, grab a bucket of dirt and go out the breach. Find where else the projectiles hit. You'll find them by the columns of black smoke. Tell them, show them if you have to, to use dirt or sand to put out the fires. They have to be smothered. Water makes it worse!"

Kane nodded, dumped out the water in his bucket and scooped it full of dirt, ran to do as he was bade.

"Come back when you're done! And **be careful!**"

A hand went up in acknowledgement as he was picking his way over the broken stone.

The stableman turned to Lark, offered her water from the bucket he was carrying, which she took eagerly. "Are you all right, my lady?"

She nodded. "Just need few minutes. Was lot of work!" she grinned. "No concern."

He frowned down at her. "Oh, I am sorry to tell you, my lady. There is very much concern."

She looked up at him, worried.

"The master had very strict instructions regarding you and your safety. We are to look after you as best we can."

Lark's eyes drifted to the gap in the wall, wondering if it was going to be her only escape if she needed to leave. The man caught her worried look and shook his head.

"Oh, forgive me. If my lady wishes to leave, she is allowed to do so, though advised extreme caution. There is a very short list of whom may be told if my lady is in residence. And folk have come asking."

Her eyes widened, and the man grinned, straightened himself proudly. "Oh, I truthfully told the watchman that I had no idea where you were. Of course at the time, I hadn't. It really is a very short list. Oh, and of course any child."

She nodded, remembering that Colwyn knew about the 'army'. Of course, he would have made allowances for them. That brought her back around to the dream that woke her. The hooded mages were hunting for the Warren, were getting closer to finding it. There was no question in her mind that, if they found it, the children would be slaughtered.

Getting to her feet, she gave the man a long look. "Sorry, what is called?" she asked, feeling bad that she did not know. She normally only saw the stable boy.

"Henry, my lady," he answered.

"Thank you, Henry. Have any children come to call this morning?"

"No, my lady. Not as of yet."

"I must go to them. This," she gestured to the broken stone and scorched trees and the scattering of raw, black earth, "is like to frighten them, and are alone. If any come, tell I have gone to them. If friend asks after, tell to ask street children."

He nodded, though he looked concerned. "As my lady wishes. I would advise that she goes afoot and out the breach."

"Again, Henry, thank you."

"Is my lady recovered enough?" he asked, concerned, walking with her to the edge of the rubble.

"Enough," she admitted. "Must suffice. Am needed. Be well, and keep safe."

"And you, my lady."

Lark climbed carefully through the breach, discovered some of the stones were still hot. She avoided the areas where the neighbours were utilizing the dirt pile she'd dropped, paused to manually toss a handful of soil on a small blob of tar near someone's garden shed. After that, she made an effort to avoid people altogether.

There weren't many folks out unless they or their neighbours had been hit. Most were hiding in their homes, praying they'd be overlooked, or that their loved ones would return if they were out fighting. This was a terrifying time for everyone.

Calmly eating her apple, she kept her eyes open for any entrances to the sewer systems or signs of Landros's wee army. She thought about whistling for them, but hesitated for no reason she could explain. She was worried, yes, but not yet in a hurry. If the children were smart, they were huddled below anyway.

She realized that she had never been in this part of town before. The homes were better, though not all were massive manors with acreage like Lord Colwyn's. There were a few of those, but not many, and she slipped through the alleyways between garden walls like a carefree shadow, seeing no one, though she did hear the occasional dog noticing her presence.

That made her think. So far, except in places where the poorest were desperate, they had not yet been forced to eating pets. It might not be long, though. Already folks had been relying on rooftop, kitchen and balcony gardens for food. She was extremely fortunate that the chicken thieves had been run off by Ivaska, instead of desperate enough to turn on him.

She noticed a blackberry vine growing up the wall of one manor, well past the flowering stage. Pausing, she inspected under the leaves to see if she could find any black ones, or even still partly red. She did like them a little bit tart as well as sweet. Though she did not hold out much hope, for either there being any berries left or their being sweet. There had been too much in the air and the water of late for the harvest to be beyond edible.

What she found was not berries, but an array of shiny, little black spiders that uncoiled as the leaves moved. She jumped back, watching warily. But the spiders only crawled around to the top of the leaves and watched her. They did not attack. It might be an illusion, but she didn't care. There was magic involved, she could smell that much. She gave them a small bow and continued down the alley.

By the time she reached the less manored lanes, she was still wandering quasi-aimlessly. Down street was a fire brigade dealing with one of the projectiles. She shaded her eyes and studied their movements, saw that they were using dirt and rugs instead of water and nodded, turned the other way. She did not want to encounter anyone she did not have to.

She had turned down three lanes, seemingly at random, before she realized it wasn't random at all. She was following an unconscious sensation, much like a pigeon going home to roost. This made her feel a great deal better about things. She still had no idea where she was going, but at least she had a guide.

She was passing a tiny alley between a cluster of town houses when something caught her attention. It was a smell and a sensation. She turned down it, walking cautiously, sorely missing her feathered lookout. At the end of the narrow lane, she found a private courtyard with its own well, a small, neat centre garden shared by the eight or so town homes that stood around it. It was quite pretty.

There were a few children playing near the garden under the watchful eye of a servant setting out laundry in one of the tiny yards. A couple of boys tossed a ball back and forth over a hedge and tried to catch it in cups. There was a little girl skipping rope by the well.

Lark looked them over even as they warily studied her. None of them looked like members of the army. In fact, one of the boys watched her with his nose in the air. She decided to keep half an eye on them, but to follow her own nose to see what had drawn her here.

It was the well. There were signs of magical probing here. She looked in, cast a little spell, looking with her other eyes to see if this well had been contaminated too. Aside from some minor debris: a few leaves, a fragment of charred wood and a fine layer of what might be ashes; it was clean and pure.

The second her body relaxed, she heard a shrill wolf-whistle from one of the buildings.

The servant looked around, angry at whoever would dare to whistle at her, but saw no one. The children stopped playing.

Lark felt a chill run up her spine. She raised her voice. "Children! Run inside, now!"

She put her hand on her sword, looking around for the source of the trouble, watching the skies for more bombardments, but nothing came but the whistle, repeated. The sky was clouded over, but nothing that screamed abnormality.

The children just stood there, staring at her like she was mad.

The tingling began again, creeping up the back of her neck, raising the little hairs there. She caught the hint of ozone. Without thinking about it, she lunged for the little girl nearest her, snatching her up a full second before a bolt of lightning struck where they had both just been. She yelled again for the kids to run, swung the girl over the hedge where the servant was and screamed at her to get inside.

A second bolt struck, close enough to feel the ground absorb the shock. She ran herself, though not in a straight line, staying closer to the paving stones and avoiding things that might catch fire if struck. Three more bolts followed her, missing by just a few yards, though each one got a little closer. Then the hairs on her arms and the back of her neck stopped standing on end and she allowed herself a moment to catch her breath.

The children were gone, as was the servant. The wooden ball the boys had been tossing was a charred wreck and smouldering as it rolled slowly through the grass. Lark gathered water from the well and dowsed it, wetting down the grass behind it as a precaution. The lightning, and whatever had summoned it, was done. That it had struck the stones near the well and not the taller buildings around her was suspicious.

Again, the wolf whistle came, though this time she had a direction and moved that way, looking for who could be sending the signal. She knew it was not her familiar, because she could sense him miles away, and it didn't sound quite the same.

As she paused at the mouth of a narrow passage between buildings, this one blocked off by fencing near the main lane, she began to hear voices from the far side of the courtyard. The heavy, authoritative voices echoed off the walls of the alley she had entered to get into the courtyard.

"Back here!"

"Do you smell that?"

She heard a voice whose timbre sent a runnel of cold fear into her belly at the same second his visage darkened the courtyard and saw her. "Gypsy bitch!" There was a grin on his face as he said that.

Without even thinking about it, she bolted down the passage.

Her heart pounded as she heard their pelting footsteps trying to negotiate the courtyard, and she turned to find herself trapped against a tall fence with no gate. There was a stack of old, empty shipping crates in a corner, but nothing that would have held her weight. She whirled, planting her back against the offending wood, ready to pull her scimitar when something grabbed her arm and pulled her aside. She jumped, knocking over the crates.

Whatever had a hold of her let go and the stone she had been standing on shifted, sliding aside to reveal a gaping hole.

"In ya go, Standard. Quickly!" a female voice hissed.

She obeyed that voice instantly, slithering into the darkness feet first, and catching the slight, invisible weight of whatever had followed her down. The stone was put back into place and they waited in the darkness, holding their breaths and listening with all their might.

They could hear the patrol reach the fence, the grunts of the men as they kicked the crates about. "What'd she do? Fly?"

Coolie's voice growled. "Bitch probably scaled these and went over. Fan out over the next street."

"Can't have, Coolie! They'd have shattered under her!"

There was the sound of flesh meeting flesh. "That's Sargent Coolie, Constable Rowber!"

"Ow, sorry, *Sargent*. But ain't no way. My-five-year-old nephew'd fall through these!"

"Don't underestimate that female!" he snarled. "I've seen her leap from a chair to a barmaid's full tray to the stair rails without tipping the drinks! Now go around, fan out and **find her**!"

Lark waited until she was certain they had all left before activating her pendant and shedding a little light in the tunnel. She was in what looked to be an unused side-cellar. There were more of the crates down here, but these were older and far more rotten. She saw something break off a piece of one, scrape something across the pulpy surface.

"Make good kindling, this," came the voice again. "Will have to send a squad to come get some. Will ya help me carry what we can?"

Lark frowned at the talking air. "Yes, but only after see who is rescue me."

"Oh! Sorry," came the voice, dropping the board. A girl of maybe eleven faded into view as she turned a small horn ring on her finger. She was neither plain nor pretty, but with a pleasant face dappled with freckles. Her frizzled curls were held out of her face by a grey servant's kerchief, and her dress was a soft blue with a dove grey pinafore. She did not even look the slightest bit dishevelled. She laughed quietly as Lark frowned at her, not being able to reconcile the young maid before her with the tomboy child she knew as Cardinal West.

"Again, sorry, Standard. Yeh caught me workin'."

"Is war on. Why is working?"

She shrugged. "Th' high an' mighty can't very well greet th' victors in soiled undies," she chuckled. "'Sides, if mother hadn't sent 'em today, likely they wouldn't use her when th war's over. Th' rich can be bitchy that way. Shall we?" she asked, gesturing deeper into the cellar. "Yeh are wantin' th' Warren, yeah?"

Lark nodded, followed her dutifully to what looked like an old coal chute gate, but which opened into the underground. "Am glad you were working. Saved me twice."

She shrugged, grinning. "I saw something on one of the roofs from the windows of the house, saw it watching you. I know a spell when I see one. It set off the lightning and vanished. Then the patrol..."

"How did know patrol was coming? Was in courtyard outside and you in alley?"

The grin faded. "One of the house servants ran out to find someone. I saw them coming and ran to get you to the cellar."

"Which brings other question," Lark said, giving her a sidelong look. "Where get ring? And why so clean?"

West's laughter rang out through the tunnel, pure and free. "My mother... she cheats?"

Lark tipped her head in askance, a very birdlike gesture.

"So, she has a little inner magic. Never really wanted to study th' grand stuff. She's a simple soul. So, she knows a lot of charms, ya see. Mostly housecleanin' stuff. She does a lot of laundry th' normal way, but anything special or ...after th' help goes home... she cheats," she shrugged. "She also makes this laundry soap that repels all dirt for like a day. She likes me to look immaculate when I make deliveries, and she despairs of my preferred clothin' choices... So, I get soaped too.

"The ring," she continued when Lark tapped her finger, "I found. There was a scuffle near th' warehouse district where I was deliverin' aprons. Big fight. I hid, of course. This guy pops off a small fireball, way too close to my hidin' place for my comfort, and misses th' guy he was aiming for completely cause there was an invisible someone in the way. He couldn't see it, but I was at just th' right angle to note that th' force that stopped th' fire was kinda people-shaped? When everythin' died down and all th' other bodies were whisked away, I crept out and tripped over it. Waste not, want not, right? So I rolled th' corpse," she shrugged. "Th' moment I felt th' ring and pulled it off, he became visible," she shuddered, "and I would much preferred him to have stayed *in*visible. It was bad enough I had to smell him."

Lark grinned. "So you kept."

"I've found it useful as Cardinal," she shrugged.

"Is damned useful," Lark agreed. "When all is over, take me to mother's laundry. Wish to buy some soap," she winked. "Maybe extra for family."

The girl smiled and led her to a small side tunnel where she asked Lark to douse her light. She did, though wishing she could see these tunnels. Closing her eyes as she entered the narrow passage, Lark let her ears guide her, following Felise by her warmth and what little noise she made. She let her other senses wander a little.

She began to feel the tunnel around her, even where the walls were not touching her. They were smooth, almost as if bored or burned, the earth turned to stone like sand to glass. And, she realized, she could sense them all like fine threads stretching away in the dark. Most of them led to the warren, but some of them led nowhere at all, or butted up against sewer walls. Many had collapsed or just ended. Some led to little pockets, small chambers, places to hide or hide things. She realized that Terri was living in one of these and had been for some time.

Before she could come to any other realizations, she was crawling out into the warren itself.

There were more children here than Lark remembered being in the army. They wore clothing from all walks of life, and huddled in a frightened mass in the middle of the cavern listening to Terrisera who was trying to calm them down by explaining the rules of the warren.

There came a terrible noise as something hit the ground above them, shaking dust and debris from the roof to drift over their heads like snow. There were shrieks and the sound of sobbing from the small mob. Lark's heart surged in her chest, felt their pain and fear almost physically.

She marched up to them, wading into the very centre of the pack before she stopped, hands on her hips and scowling down at all of them. "What is meaning of this?" she demanded, feigning disapproval. The children immediately silenced, staring at this brightly-coloured woman in their midst. She felt so much bigger than she was, though she was only head and shoulders above the tallest of them.

She glanced over at Terri who stood on the outskirts with a look of relief on her face. "Is all this army? I see civies here. I hear snivelling little mice. Where are General's smart, strong, brave little soldiers?"

"The soldiers brought them, Standard," she answered, taking her cue from Lark's tone, and using an authoritative voice. Children in fear need a strong authority to assure them that they are safe. They responded immediately, eyes bouncing between the two females.

"From where? Stole from parents? Is foul lie that Romeri take wanted children." If they had stolen these little ones, Lark was going to rage.

One of the soldiers spoke before even the cardinals could answer. "We asked first."

She turned to the one who had spoken, a ten-year-old boy who had the look of an acolyte about him. "Who is you?"

He stood up straighter. "Captain Jeris of the Temple district under Cardinal East!"

"Explain, Captain," she said with a nod.

"There are places where the buildings aren't safe. Where catapults and fireballs have hit," he explained. She nodded again for him to go on. "The adults have enough to worry about. When I tell them I got a place their kids will be safe and hidden no matter what happens, most of them hand 'em over. They all know when the dust settles to go to the temple to find each other. Just never told 'em that the young'uns aren't staying in the temple itself," he added with a grin.

"Admirable. **But**, what if parents go to temple to seek before 'dust settles' and no one knows where?"

He started to deflate, then shook his head. "But someone knows. Sister Rue in the Maiden's hall. She knows I have them somewhere, just not where. She has ways to get messages to me. Oh, and Mother Mylenai knows."

This brought Lark up short. "Matron knows?"

He shrugged, grinning. "Don't ask me how, Standard. I have no answer. But she thrust about six of them on me and told me to hightail."

She gave him a regal nod, which he accepted with a bow, his right hand, with crossed fingers, placed on his chest. In all, she was pleased.

Then the cavern shook again, another flurry of dust and not a few beetles. The children shrieked and cried. Even Lark flinched, throwing her arms over those nearest to her. As soon as the shuddering ended, she stood again, raised her voice to those still crying, making the inarticulate noise Gruma used to make to get her and her siblings' attention when they were loud or rambunctious. All eyes were on hers in an instant, breaths held.

"Not all of you are part of army. Is understanding you have not same training and discipline of those who bring you here. But are rules for being here. May not think have strong hearts and braveness like South, or West, or Captain Jeris," she said indicating them, "but you do. It is hidden inside, even if cannot see it right now. But even if are not feeling very brave, if are missing mother, father, family, friends, is alright to feel these things. Is not alright in this moment to show them."

She turned slowly as she spoke, addressing all of them. She spotted a few of the children they had brought back from the island, made sure to meet their eyes as she spoke of shared things. "You are all little mice hiding in dragon's nest!"

There was a small outburst of fear at that, and she chided herself for saying it, even though as she did, she realized she could not have said anything else. "Is all right. Is mama dragon, good heart. Keep safe. But cats and foxes, they dig, they sniff, they listen up there," she continued, pointing to the ceiling, knowing, even as the words poured forth, that everything she was saying was absolute and literal truth. "They hunt for here. If they find... they hurt mama. Maybe eat few mice."

She heard the faint whispers of the children who had played the mice game with her explaining to those nearest them. Lowering her tone, she smiled. "So, even if scared, is better to be quiet scared." She ran three fingers from her eyes to her jaw, tracing nonexistent tears, "Weep if must, but no sobbing. Breathe, slow and even. Scream only if grabbed, to let us know cats got you. But if not have you, don't tell them where to find! Is mice who squeak whom foxes eat!" She said that last as she mock pounced a child who had been grabbed by the boy behind her as a joke and yelped.

The cavern was filled with a soft, nervous laughter. She lowered her voice. "Second rule, go no where alone. Always someone to watch back, someone to report if something happen. Rule three, if adult or one of army gives you orders: Do. Can save life. If something get in... scatter, hide.

"If I can, and am near enough... if you hear me yell '*da peshi*' you must make like rock and don't move, like them," she said, delightedly pointing out nine children who had immediately dropped and curled up.

Obliging, she made them look like rocks, which caused a ripple of awe and surprise. One kid actually reached out and poked one, jumped back exclaiming, "She perified her!"

The stone in question, just laughed, unrolling and sitting up, shattering the illusion. It was Analie.

The boy poked her again. "But... I swears she were hard as rock!"

This startled Lark, though she didn't show it. Perhaps it had to do with her recent power surge.

"No, siwwy!" Analie laughed. "Was just a i'woozhun!"

"Bloody good one!" He was elbowed by someone for his language and he cast his eye on the only apparent adult in the cavern. Some of the other kids just giggled at him.

"Now, we know rules, *sesket*?" Lark said, only raising her voice a little, but recapturing everyone's attentions. Well over a hundred small heads nodded. "Good, now, huddle close. Maybe I will sing for you."

She spent the next hour singing soft melodies, Romeri lullabies, anything she could remember to take their minds off the bombardment above. She crooned almost without thinking. Once she had stayed up with one of Jena's boys when he was a babe. His twin Bourne was ill and Ivan and Jena had taken him to a shrine hoping for a healer, leaving Lark to watch Randal who could sense his brother's pain. She had sung to him to lull him, to pacify him, hours of mind-numbing, soothing sounds until she had hypnotised both of them into slumber. Ivan told her she had never once stopped singing, though when they had come to check on her, she was clearly asleep.

This was just like that. Only this time, something was different. She was coming into tune with something rather than losing all awareness. The children around her were mostly at ease, some were hungry, some still scared but being quiet, some were just sleeping. She could feel their breathing all around her, feel the weight of their fears and dreams.

At the edges of herself, she felt itching, like fleas, but she knew they were not. It was not her own body feeling any of this. She felt an urgency, a growing panic, saw again the visions that had brought her here in the first place. So, she focused. The attacks above were growing more violent, wresting movements and out-cries of pain from the life-force surrounding her. With a little effort, she could see the tunnels again, could find every side-pocket, col-lapsed and otherwise, feel every attempt above them to poke and prod and scratch a way down.

Sending a tendril of power through the web of tunnels, she closed them off, hid them; an act which seemed to enrage the sex-less things trying to find them. And they were things, she realized suddenly. The dragon afforded her a peek beneath the hoods, be-hind the masks which were not exactly masks. What lay beneath was humanoid only in form, wooden poppets the size of a man. The mask was an illusion meant to obfuscate and confuse.

What they wanted was far clearer. Many centuries ago, when the great dragon and her brood was killed, the dying mother had embedded herself into the very stones of her warren with the last ounce of her magic, protected by the one who had come to drive out the faceless evil seeking her power. The heart was gifted to someone, guarded them, was guarded by them, taking it out of the reach of evil.

But the keeper was mortal, bore no heirs and, a year ago, died.

This shocked Lark to the core. She had already guessed that the heart was the purpose of the siege, and that the slow prodding had been designed to wake it enough to give away its position. But this kind of confirmation hit hard. They had probably tried to find it in other ways, failed, but used the knowledge gained by studying the city and the people in it, learning just how to 'poke the bear' without getting mauled.

In that moment, she also knew that the only way to protect the heart and its power from those that would abuse it, was to accept the gift she was being offered.

She sat, frozen, for several minutes; even stopped singing. It took a couple of those moments for some of the children to notice. Analie, who had been curled up, half in her lap, sat up and looked at her, concerned.

"Pwincess?" She squinted up into her eyes, tapped her shoulder. "Biwwy!" she called. "Pwincess not hewe!"

Billy jumped up, handed off the little ones he had in his own arms and waded carefully through the pile of children. When he saw Lark sitting cross-legged on the floor, he frowned. "She's roight..." and then he understood what she meant. Her eyes were glazed, seeing a different world entirely. He had seen her do this, when she was studying something for magic, or caught up in something that was about to be both bizarre and spectacular. He picked Analie up, gesturing for the others to move away, to give her room. "She's all roight," he called softly, soothing those prone to panic. "She just needs room. Be ready to get outta th' way."

Lark was aware of the children moving, heard and saw everything as if she were not herself. Those who had been in the warren when she had reactivated the runes had an inkling of what was about to happen, and were swift to motivate the others.

When she was in an eight-foot clear space, she rocked up onto her knees, let her arms drift up and out to shoulder height. Her fingers rolled up and outward, calling up tendrils of power and began weaving a web that touched every rune, connecting them to her and through other threads, each other. The lines shimmered into visibility, circling, arching over and avoiding the children while still making them part of the pattern. The Cardinals, however... she bound threads to them, creating secondary webs to other, specific children. Though why she had chosen the ones she had, she could not have said.

That done, she bent over, placing her hands on the stone and slowly crawling forward, turning, circling. Like a hound trying to find the scent. The pack moved out of her way, but remained circling her. And her movements did not disturb the glowing threads, but twisted them into a perfect, funnelling spiral.

She stopped, hovering over a single square foot of floor. Placing her hands on the perfectly smooth stone, she could feel heat, perhaps the reason this chamber did not hold the chill of normal caverns. She could feel the slow, agonizing beat of the heart below her, the pulse of its magic, breathed in that fragrant breath of amber and amethyst, earth and musk. Her own physical rhythms joined with it, the two finding a middle ground they could both live through.

There was a sound from the children, gasps of awe and fear. Lark looked up, saw the shadow of the amber-scaled dragon bending a swan-graceful neck to bring her angled nose inches from Lark's hair. She stood, hearing the being's voice with her whole body.

My daughter, my heir. I give you all I am.

Lark shook her head. "No. I am not... this is not ... am not worthy. I found by happenstance. Was with one who organized all this, all them. Merely observer. This gift belongs to one who has been near all this time, who found this place and made it home, for herself, for those likewise lost."

She started to reach out for Terrisera, but the dragon's voice was as gentle as it was regretful. **No, child. As long as she has been here, she has never heard me. You were not even here, and yet you heard me. Would not leave me, even though you should have. You died for me.**

Lark drew in a sharp breath, half-sob, half-gasp. She felt the dragon's touch along her cheek as if it were her own mother's hand, or that of Mahren. She had not felt such power and love since the ritual to purge the ring.

"I... I died for city, for children."

And you came back for...? she prompted.

Lark was silent. Then, "For love. I chose this place my caravan, so I could keep man I loved. For Romeri ranie cannot marry ge-genta. It would weaken clan in eyes of others. Even more since is not human."

This city is mine. For all it grew over my grave, I have protected, guided it. Took it over centuries, with subtlety and influence, from the monster who built it over the bones of my children, hoping to find me, and take my power for itself. If this is your caravan, little ranie, the only way to protect it, *truly* protect it ...is through me.

There it was, the fateful choice. There was no evil in the offer, and it *was* an offer, not a negotiation or an ultimatum, for all it sounded like one. She knew she alone did not have what it truly took to fulfil the responsibility she had undertaken. It was greater than she was. Without a word, she agreed, still not feeling worthy. Her last thought was that such power was too much for a single mortal to hold uncorrupted, and that, truthfully, no one was worthy.

As she inhaled, the dragon exhaled, their perfect syncopation of a moment ago now in perfect opposition, feeding each other. She smelled the magic, realizing that the pure scent of it was that musky amber she now associated with the dragon. The faint, musty odour she had always scented around spent magic was just that, impure. Even goddess magic was filtered through the priest, and she realized in retrospect that Maiden, Mother and Cronely magic each had their own subtle flavours.

She felt herself inflating, stretching to accommodate this in-coming surge that was changing, merging with every part of her. It wasn't subsuming her, though, making her someone she was not. It was refining her. Making her a more sturdy vessel for that which would amplify everything she was. For a moment, she thought it would tear her apart.

Slowly, she became aware of it easing off, of something else happening around her. She focused, heard even as the dragon spoke and heard, the responses to the questions she was asking. The Cardinals had been offered fractions, even Terrisera. In essence, the dragon's children. Lark could even see the ghostly forms rising, crawling out of the tunnels from the chambers that had been theirs, slipping into the bodies of each of them as they agreed. It was beautiful to watch, and Lark felt a mother's pride and joy to see the souls finding flesh again, that once had been so lost.

You were right. All that I am, and they were, is too much for one tiny mortal form. But shared... these are pure, and my children already love them.

A laugh got stuck in her throat at that thought. The very idea that Billy was 'pure', was laughable.

The dragon corrected her gently. **Consider his motivations,** she purred. **And no one is without a single selfish thought. Not even my children. Not even myself. I could have scattered my power to the winds and the wilds when I died, as most dragons do. But I was too angry, too afraid, and so I stayed and put everything I came to treasure at risk, time and again, because I was selfish. But you have managed to have your selfish desires, and still act with altruism. Together, perhaps I, too, can come to that perfect state.**

"Will you always be here, in my mind, talking to me?"

The voice felt sad. **No. Once the transfer is complete, we shall be complete. I can help you know things, by remembering things you never experienced. But my voice? You might hear it in dreams, you might hear it in my love, but you will not hear it again as you do now. And so my last words to you are to protect them. Use what I have given you, to keep them safe. And remember that I love you.**

That last choked her, brought her to her knees as the voice was at once the dragon's and her mother's. Her tears moved freely, splashing to the smooth, cool stone between her fingers.

She felt tiny hands touching her, tentative at first, then openly comforting. Soon she was at the heart of a pile of children, those who could not reach her touching those who could, sharing her pain, returning to her the comfort she had given them just hours ago.

Someone, Cpt. Jeris she thought, began singing. It was a lullaby-like hymn that she remembered hearing snippets of at the temple. It was the soothing of grief and fear and the promise of the healing gift of time. Soon the others were singing, the song spreading like a flame to everyone it touched. The cavern hummed and echoed with the sound of it.

Lark sat up, sang a counterpoint to the song, a mother's promise to protect, shelter and teach. As she did so, she stretched the magic that held all of them together, reached through the five newly merged, combining with them and showing them what she was doing even as she guided them to help her. The runes lit up, making the chamber almost too bright to see, hardening the magic into a barrier of security through which nothing unwanted was getting.

She stood, looked to each of the five of them. They understood implicitly what had happened, what needed to happen, each accepting their place in all of this. She could almost feel them in the back of her mind, like a faint whispering. Pressing on that sensation, she tried to send a thought, was delighted to see them jump, their eyes lighting up as they realized speech without voice was capable.

I wonders 'ow far this goes? Billy thought.

Far enough, I think, Terri responded.

At very least, to edges of dragon's territory, Lark guessed. **Will have to explore that when it is safe to go out, to experiment. For now, is there any food down here? Think children are hungry.**

I know I am, replied Mouse, blushing as his stomach echoed the sentiment, loudly.

Terri's eyes lit up. "Lieutenants Michael, Gwen, Georgie!" she called out, no longer feeling the pressing need for quiet.

Three children stood up at attention. "Aye, my Queen!" one of them snapped sharply, standing stiffly.

"Fetch the cauldron. Centre of the cavern. No firewood."

That last caught them off guard, but they still immediately jumped to.

Terri continued giving orders as the rest of the children were ushered off and out of the way to make them more comfortable.

When everything was done as she had ordered, Terri stepped up to the cauldron and began to sing a little tune as she chopped, ripped, and divided ingredients and dropped them in. Water appeared in the bottom to meet the level of the food, and the cauldron itself began to heat up gently.

Lark peered in, realized that what little she was putting in was multiplying just a bit. Mushrooms which were withered and dry plumped up, limp vegetables that might have ended up pig feed in better times seemed to perk up and freshen. Even the bits of dried meat she added took on the appearance of stew chunks. She could see the magic involved, and it was wonderful to watch. Even though she realized what the multiplication was taking from the girl.

She frowned, set her hands on the edge of the pot to feed it power, so that it wouldn't draw so much on her.

Terri glanced up, shocked, but kept singing until all that was left was to wait.

"Where learn this?" Lark asked. "Dragon teach?"

Terri blushed. "My mother, actually. I've never been able to do it quite so ...well? I've been able to stretch things a little, the way you do with soup but... the..." she pointed to the floating vegetables in the slowly bubbled fluid that looked as if it had come out of the garden a few hours ago. "That. That I've never been able to do, or to double... triple the output. I think the boost... awakened something inside."

Lark smiled at her. "Yes, well, be careful. Making more... comes from somewhere. If is no where to come, will come from inside. You can feed your family of yourself if not careful. Like making milk for baby."

Terri frowned. "But the body just does that. ...Right?"

Lark smiled. "If mother does not eat enough of right things, there is no milk. Some can make milk at expense of body. Same with making baby. It come from somewhere. Either you eat it, or it eat you."

She nodded solemnly. "I will try to be careful. Husband it. Hopefully it won't be needed as badly much longer."

"One way or another. This ends soon," Lark agreed.

TWO

Landros watched the sky beginning to darken, scanning for signs of the mockingbird. He sent him to Lord Colwyn with a scouting report hours ago and worried that he wouldn't get back before it was too dark to fly. He desperately needed the information he should be bringing back. He also needed to move the moment it got dark and was afraid that if he did, it would take far too long for the bird to find him again without putting himself at risk.

Earlier, when the band of orcish troops they were observing moved, he had sent the rest of his men to follow, but not engage. He could find them easily enough, knowing one of them would leave a trail only another Elven pathfinder could follow. But he wanted to slip in whilst the camp was sleeping and eliminate the lot of them, take what supplies he could and vanish again well before dawn, and the time it would take could mean the difference between success and failure.

Finally, he heard the flutter of the bird coming in fast. Nightingale started screeching at the last second, performing a panicked slalom in between branches before dive bombing into his hood. Landros barely had time to register the feathered missile before he had a hawk in his face, shrilling in surprise at finding its prey escaped in such an unusual way. Instead, it landed on a branch a few feet away from the elf and tipped it head, studying the situation.

It was a lovely red-shouldered hawk, though its feathers had seen significant roughing up. Hanging from its ankles were stained, oily jesses that were knotted and frayed.

Landros pulled on his gauntlet, drew a scrap of jerky from his hip pouch and offered the meat. In his hood, Nightingale hissed and pecked his ear, offended that the elf would befriend his assailant. He made a tiny movement of his shoulder to silence the songbird and kept his eyes on the lost hawk.

"Decided you'd had enough of hunting for others, skybrother?" he asked in Elvish, keeping his voice low and even. *"Come on. The meat is free."*

After a bit of coaxing, the bird realized the humanoid was no threat, that it wasn't going to get the little grey bird and hopped closer. Finally, he stepped onto the gauntlet, attacking the meat. Landros ran his hands down the back feathers, smoothing out a few, checking the bird's condition, all the while, speaking in soothing tones.

The bird had likely fled its captivity. Many birds of prey did. If you were doing falconry correctly, you raised your birds right and released them after a few years anyway, to let them breed again in the wild. Oddly, released hawks were more successful hunters than wild ones. This one... did not look like there were any plans to let him go. He handed the bird another piece of meat, to distract him whilst he pulled off the greasy jesses.

The skin under the leather was irritated, but it would heal. The hawk nibbled at his fingers when he felt the skin where the binds had lain, but not hard enough to hurt him. He chuckled, letting the leg go. *"Go on, brother. You are free. And my little grey friend is off the menu."* With that, he tossed the bird back into the sky and watched him fly off in the failing light.

Only then did Nightingale come out of his hood and land on his knee.

Landros lifted the jesses to his nose, sniffed. He cursed. They stank of humans living in close proximity of orcs. The bird had belonged to an enemy noble. Sighing, he turned to removed the message around Nightingale's tiny leg.

"*So what does his Lordship have to say?*" came the voice of Kerolanda, his second in command. She was perched higher in the tree behind him.

She had not startled him. While he had not heard her arrival, he had eventually noticed her presence. He translated the message from the partial code he knew specific only to the king's falcons. "*It says we should cripple what we can tonight. Run off horses, kill sentries, damage catapults if possible, etc. Burn what we cannot steal. There is rumour of an army coming.*"

She perked up at that. "*Who's?*"

"*The King's they think,*" he answered in a hollow voice. Hope was choking him. "*We're to do what we can tonight and prepare to rally with the army. We're to make certain they don't get surrounded or cut off.*"

She gave him a feral grin. "*Sounds like a busy night.*"

"*Speaking of busy, where are the others?*"

"*The orcs have met up with a small merc group led by a half-ogre and set up camp just over a mile south-south-west of here. Nalenil took six wild ones to cover the northeastern side, and the rest of us and two of the wild ones are just south of a boulder ridge waiting for you.*"

He nodded as he gathered what little he had with him. "*Good, we'll slip back and send the two wild ones to spread this message to their kin.*"

Kerola scampered down the tree to wait for him below.

As he slid Lark's dagger into his belt, Nightingale made a sad little noise. He had felt his mistress's surge of power, known when she had merged with the thing below the city. He had been temporarily incapacitated when it had happened, but felt incredibly invigorated after. It was how the hawk had almost caught him. But he had no way of telling Landros, and the elf who *could* speak with him had not been near him all day.

Nightingale was pulled from his sad little thoughts by a finger stroking his chest. *"Yes, I miss her too, little one."*

Feeling her absence sorely, Landros dropped to the spongy turf below, waited until the bird returned to his hood, and followed Kerola to the enemy camp.

It was somewhere around midnight that Lark realized the bombardment had stopped. She had awakened briefly, aware that some change had taken place. The bodies around her shifted a little as she raised her head, listening with more than just her ears. She lay her head back down, focusing on Nightingale.

Her familiar was sitting on a tent pole, watching movement in the camp around him. The campfire showed only a flickering of something at the edges of his vision, but the bird was not worried. He sensed her watching through him, chirped a sleepy hello and turned to look at something he wanted her to see: a familiar, hooded figure standing up at the corner of a tent, loosing a single arrow into the back of the man sitting at the fire. She would know that body anywhere, in any garment.

For a half second, she could even smell him. Then was interrupted by a female elf walking out of the tent below their perch cleaning her blade, and the faint stink of orcish soldier rose up to them.

He was working and well, she decided. Perhaps it was something he and his wild friends had done that stopped the catapults. It would not do to look a gift horse in the mouth, so she bade her familiar a fond 'miss-you/farewell' and faded back to the present.

Satisfied, she curled up around Analie and went back to sleep.

To her surprise, Lark remained asleep long after most of the children had gotten up. She woke to find herself alone save for the three smallest, and covered with someone's threadbare blanket. She felt sluggish, but someone was trying to get her attention. Blinking, she looked up into the concerned face of Felise.

"What?" she asked, worried. "Am sleeping too long? Am all right," she assured the girl.

West shook her head. "No. It's Bat. Something's happ'nin' at th' tree. Yeh have to hurry."

Adrenaline cleared her fuzzy head instantly and Lark was up like a shot, sprinting bare-footed across the warren for the tunnel she knew ended near the inn. Felise was right behind her but had a hard time keeping up. She was crawling full speed through the tunnel, tumbling out and rolling to her feet in one smooth motion. She never once activated her light, pelting down the dark sewer tunnels unerringly. In short order, she was flying up the ladder to the alley and running the two blocks to the stable-yard.

Ivaska started barking the moment he heard her, but she was surprised he did not run out to her. Rounding the corner of the barn, she saw that he was tied up on a very short rope to a hitching post that he was slowly working loose in his frenzy. The yard was eerily silent, not even the chickens made much sound.

She had almost reached the kitchen door when she heard Dane's voice from inside yell, "**Hey, Rube!**"

She skidded to a halt, but it was too late. There was movement from the barn and the opening of an upstairs window. Her hand was on the hilt of her scimitar and her other fingers already weaving the runes of a barrier when something terrible and cold struck her from behind. It sank into her bones, running up and down her skeleton, locking up muscles. Inside her, the dragon roared in agony. The pain was excruciating, worse than the poisoning she had suffered from the warehouse and the nails and the hooded mage's tainted dagger. Everything contracted, curling her up like a dead spider, stealing even her ability to scream. The blackness that swarmed up to engulf her was a blessing.

THREE

Lark woke, shivering in the dark. She was lying on hard, damp stone that did not feel natural. Everything about it screamed at her, made her want to flail in terror like a wild bird suddenly put in a tiny cage. Her whole body trembled, weak.

She sat up, felt around her. Even the dragon, lying dormant within her, knew this was not a safe place. This was a place of forgetting. It did not take her long to find the edges of the chamber: maybe seven feet one way and five another of rough hewn but tightly fitting stone. There was a slop bucket, a pan and a smaller bucket holding what seemed to be clean water. The door was petrified wood.

Panic began to set in, was interrupted by a soft, vaguely familiar cackle. Someone stood outside the door. She looked up to where the sound came from, and about two-thirds of the way up saw the glittering of dark eyes grinning at her. With what light she saw them by she had no clue, she could only assume another gift from the dragon.

"*You were warned Rushavska,*" came the dreaded, withered voice from that day so long ago in Tent Town. "*But you could not stay away. Had to steal what was not yours to take!*"

Suddenly, disparate fragments and images began to look like a cohesive whole, bits of a puzzle making sense. Like casting magic to read a foreign tongue. The hooded mages had been poppets, she had gathered that earlier, wooden homunculi to be possessed by their master at will. That was a very Romeri kind of magic. She began to recall details of that old woman, how she had known not only Lark's clan but her patronymic, which meant she knew her name.

She thought back on the details of the old bat, her mind working lightning fast. Two hoops in one ear, the left if she remembered correctly. Strand of gold beads. She wore black and purple, not unusual for an elder ranie, but she wore green, too, also not that unusual. Lark herself occasionally wore greens. Her father wore dark-green pants very often, a hold over from his mother's clan. But this... this was a particularly vivid shade of pure green.

There was a clan, a horror story really, a cautionary tale among the Romeri. They were extinct now, the women rendered barren by some curse, it was thought, and by their penchant for necromancy and poison. They were the only clan to wear that particular shade of green, as other clans automatically associate it with evil and bad luck. She did not remember how that green was supposed to mark their wagons, like the red roofs of the Rushavska or the yellow doors of the Bravida, but the women, and only the women, wore two gold hoops in their left ears.

"*Mushyan*," Lark hissed, making a fist and passing it in a tight circle before her face, a warding sign to keep away evil.

The crone cackled. "*Not so stupid as I thought, thief.*"

Her mind raced. If this woman was indeed Mushyan, she was centuries old. But then, they had been known to dabble in necromancy. Who knows what foul magics had been used to keep her alive.

"*I am not thief, witch,*" Lark growled. "*I merely answered plea for help and accepted gift then offered. Whereas you murdered for it.*" It did not surprise Lark to realize, even as the words left her mouth, that they were true. This witch had been the evil power that killed the dragon and her children. She had been stopped by an elven woman who's name meant Star. Lark knew this as the dragon had known it. *"You have no right to this power. It would sour in your hands. Death cannot wield Life."*

"How little you know, brat. To wield life and death at the same time is to hold ultimate power over everything! With it I can bring back my people, be strong enough to lead all the clans, and bring the gegenta to their knees before us!"

Lark felt pity for a brief moment. *"Foolish dreams, old woman. Their way of life destroyed them. Even now we live in the shadow of their wickedness. They are best gone, and remembered only as warning to others. Whatever guilt you feel for their fall, let it go and live while you can. Eshanai cannot save you."* It did not even occur to her to question how she knew the dragon's name.

The old woman snorted. *"That is was that elven bitch, Ilanil, told me. I did not believe her, either. But is no matter, Petrovna. Whole sordid saga ends soon. Siege will be over in matter of days, and then I will fulfil my end of things by ending your lover's king. And then you will be mine to torment while I figure out how to get that dragon out of you!"*

She smelled something foul and acrid and knew the witch was gone. Only then did she sink down against the wall, wrapped her arms around her knees and sobbed.

Wrung out, terrified and utterly defeated, it was several minutes before she realized that someone was speaking to her. It was a deep voice, faint through the wall, but it was the depth of it that allowed it to carry enough to be heard. She took a deep breath, held it as she listened. It came again, somehow familiar. Eshanai was still weak, but was able to impart remembrances and tiny hints. Lark leaned her head against the stone wall and immediately could hear more clearly.

The voice was deep, a little hoarse from disuse and the cold damp. "Are you all right, girl? Physically?"

She had heard that voice before, but could not yet place it. "Who is?"

The voice cracked as he answered. He coughed, spat and tried again. "William FitzWaller, former Lord Mayor of Portswain," he answered. There was a rueful tone in his voice. "And you are? I've heard that accent before, but I cannot remember where or what language you were speaking."

Lark laughed at the irony. "I once fainted in your arms."

"The Gypsy girl? The one who helped bring back the stolen children? Oh, this city is going to hell swiftly if they've thrown you in here," he growled.

"Oh, magistrate has been trying to get me in here for one reason or other since we first met."

The mayor chuckled. "You're competent, female and attractive. Not to mention independent. Of course he hates you. What charge did he trump up for you?"

"Do not know. Was ambushed. Woke up here."

"That's not legal," he snarled. She heard the sound of him striking something.

"Yes, well, city is under militant law. Magistrate says if cause trouble or is suspect, put in cell, sort out after war. ...If they remember you," she added with a shiver.

"Well, welcome to the oubliette, my lady," he said. "This is the place they throw you to forget you. You're lucky if they remember to feed you or swap the slops. Goddess, but I believe I've lost fifty pounds in here!"

Lark hugged her knees. Her terror had begun to rise again. Flickers of close calls and chains flittered through her memory, which prompted her to look at her hands, remembering her most recent flirtation with captivity: the vampire. The opal was still on her hand, of course, but everything else was gone. Including, heartbreakingly, her gruma's emerald. The scimitar was expected, but anyone who was foolish enough to try to use it would no doubt come to a bad end.

She sighed, trying to calm down. The dragon was weak, still reeling from the necromancy that had been used on her. Lark rose. She was not without power of her own, though. Crossing to the door, she drew the rune of opening upon it only to get shocked for her trouble. She swore in Romeri, felt the zap all the way up her elbow.

"The place is warded against teleportation and gates," came the Mayor's voice. "In case that was you trying something."

"Gates?" Lark asked, her attention caught quickly by that one word. That was the difference between what the mages and the priests at the temple used, what was blocked from getting in and out of the city, and what her people used. Her clan specifically, or at least her caravan. Gruma was very good with gates.

"Yes," he said. "I know because …I made sure of it. We had a prisoner about a decade back, when I first became mayor, who was known to be really hard to hold on to. I had these lower cells warded against all travel magic. Gates *and* teleport."

"Am surprised you know difference. Not many do, even some mages," she commented, began pacing.

"I used to be an adventurer, remember? I've seen a great deal. When we discovered we couldn't teleport out, I'm embarrassed to say that I either did not remember about gates or assumed both were blocked. It wasn't until I heard the magistrate talking about how gates were now also blocked that I even thought about it."

"Did he seem upset by this?" she asked suddenly.

"Maybe." He thought about it for a moment. "Yes, but I don't think it was quite the way you'd expect. It was almost like he was upset they hadn't been before. I don't know who he was talking with, but… you don't think the bastard is in cahoots, do you?"

She sighed. "Fairly sure now. Much of recent happening make more sense if is. Tell me, were you guilty of what accused?"

She heard the deep, soul-shaking sigh. "To a point," he answered. "All to a single point. Which is what made the frame-up perfect."

"Tell me," she asked, wanting to know as much as she could, but also needing something to keep her mind calm enough to think.

"It's a little… complex, but.… I had granted an Irregular's Permit to a woman and her band, even sent her a letter thanking her for her service and informing her that I had a special request of her group. And I did. I had some intel that there would be a feint at one of the weaker spots of the walls, but that there would be a force at the East Gate to take advantage of the reaction to the feint tactic. I wanted DeLaSkintz to fortify the sixty-third just before midnight, knowing that some of that unit would be making certain that the feint didn't result in an actual breach. All the evidence they brought forth was factual and true except for the single, most damning piece: the letter stating that they were to open the gates just after midnight, allow the enemy in and assist in the takeover. Well, also the orders for the sixty-third to hand the post completely to DeLaSkintz and for the whole unit to fortify the feint point. It was cleverly done."

"If this Mushyan woman is behind any of this, all will be clever."

"That they got my own aide to lie is what hurts the most," he grumbled, on the edge of yielding to depression himself.

"If even was your aide," she said dismissively. "There has been much of imposters lately. This hooded mage we have been fight-ing?"

"Yes?" he asked.

"Nothing more than wooden homunculi."

"A Goddess-damned doll?!" he roared in disbelief.

She chuckled. "Yes. Possessed from time to time as needed."

He swore a little less than softly. "No wonder we couldn't figure out who it was!" There were several minutes of verbal fuming. "What did the old bat want? I didn't understand it, but I know gloating when I hear it."

Lark waved her hand dismissively as she began pacing, forget-ting he could not see it. "Just this, gloating. Telling me what will do with me when all over. Bragging of purpose, how siege will end in days and, with it, king."

"Wait, the king will end? What did she say about that!?"

She groaned, as irritated as he at having no useful answers. "Nothing helpful, just is part of her bargain. When siege is done, she will deal with king."

She heard him kick something in frustration. "I know is seem helpless, but are not, in fact, helpless," she said, taking her turn to soothe him. "Romeri have ways even that witch has forgotten."

There was a soft, feminine chuckle from the door, "I sincerely hope yer not referring to me, Standard. Even I don't have th' skill to pick this lock, an' th' key... well, that's out of my reach."

She flew to the door even as the mayor was demanding to know who was out there. "West!"

"Yes, ma'am. Are yeh well?"

"Physically. Weak, but... unharmed. Also unarmed," she growled.

"Oh, not fer long, Standard," the girl laughed. She rattled something on the other side of the door and Lark recognized the sound of her scimitar in its wooden sheath.

"How?"

A small pouch found its way between the bars of the little window. Lark dimly saw it in the darkness. She was beginning to realize that the dragon's gifts were numerous and included vision like the dwarves, to see where there was no light. She took the pouch, felt it. There was a least one ring inside.

Opening it, she found Gruma's emerald, which went immediately onto her finger, and her light pendant slithered into her palm on its chain. She started to put it on, then thought better of it, held it back out to Felise.

"Give to mayor," she said.

"Yeh want me to give this to th' magistrate?" she squeaked, though she accepted the chain from her fingers.

Lark gave a soft laugh. "No, *real mayor*. Is next cell on left. Is framed, good man. He can't see in dark."

"Might I ask what is going on?" came the man's patient, bear-like voice. He was also near the door, listening. Lark heard Felise move to his cell and open the mini door. "Who is West and why is she calling you Standard? And how the hell did she get down here with a weapon?" There was a hesitation. "She did mean she was bringing you arms, yes?"

"Put hand out little door," Lark told him. Sounds told her he had reluctantly obeyed.

"A necklace?" he asked.

"Put on and think *Ilyen*."

"Think it?"

She smiled. "Or say. But think is enough."

"Eel-yen," he said. Then "**Ahhh**!"

Both the women laughed.

"**Ow**! Some warning would have been nice!" he growled.

"Sorry," she smiled. "Did not think about you having been in dark for weeks."

"Can you dim this thing?"

"*Ahmi*," she told him.

"Oh, thank the Mother!" he said.

"He turned it off?" Felise asked.

"No. *Ahmi* means 'only me'. Is give only light *you* need. No one else can see. Is useful for sneaking."

"And to turn it off?"

She taught him how to control the thing.

Then something occurred to him. "Wait. Is this yours? I can't leave you in the dark. I was going crazy myself, I can't do that to you. ...Or are you leaving now that West is here and leaving me behind?"

"Oh, I ain't got th' ability to get her out, yer lordship. Fer all I wish to," Felise answered.

"Then why?"

Lark smiled, pushing away the thought of being here for even a moment longer. "Let us just say that I no longer have need of it. Felise, you same?"

"Aye, Standard. I think all th' Cardinals can. Let me tell you, th' tunnels... they're kinda pretty."

"Again, she calls you Standard."

"Do you remember Landros's little idea about militias?" she asked, testing the man's integrity.

"I do. Damned brilliant that."

"Well, orphans and children of streets decide they are army and Landros their general. They are 'invisible'."

"Literally," he muttered. Apparently he had peered out of his little window and not seen Felise though he could tell in other ways that she was there. The girl laughed at that.

"West here, is in charge of west quarter."

"And they call you standard because...?"

Felise answered this one herself. "Because she refused a rank in th' army, so our queen decided she was our standard."

"You know a standard is a flag, right?" he asked.

"A standard," Felise corrected patiently, "is anything around which troops may rally which symbolizes what they fight fer."

That made Lark blush. She had never thought of it that way. That the children viewed her thus nearly brought her to tears.

"West," she said, distracting herself so that her tears would not fall, "was behind me when was captured. Please tell me that Lily and Dane are safe. Did you see what happen?"

Any chipperness Felise had displayed vanished at that. "Yeah... I saw yeh go down. Th' hooded one came outta th' barn and flung a spell at yeh. I was twenty feet away and it still felt cold. I don't know what yeh were hit with."

"Necromancy of some sort," she answered. "But then..."

The girl sighed, gathered herself. "Then they gathered yeh up an' arrested you and Lily. They were goin' t' arrest Neneis, but she insisted he worked fer her an' had nothin' to do with how she ran th' business."

"What for they arrest her?" Lark asked, furious and heartbroken that she had brought trouble to her friend's doorstep.

"Th' charges against you say that yer colludin' with th' enemy, and because she was harbourin' yeh..."

"But was not!"

"We all know that, and so does everyone who was there. But she has in th' past. Also... that pantry a' hers... She swears her late husband built it fer her, but they don't care. She was 'hoardin' necessary foodstuffs an' valuable resources fer her own profit'. And yes, they don't care that she wasn't gougin' her customers like a lot of places ha' been, or that th' rich aren't doing exactly that just without magical pantries. It's an excuse, no more."

"Where...?"

"Not here," West said quickly. "She's on th' upper levels. No where near as bad as down here. She's all right and makin' friends. There's a number of people in her cell that been falsely accused. If it comes down to it,... her I can get out. Hell, I can probably let out th' whole damned cell block and overwhelm th' guards, but you... I don't know if I can break yeh out of here."

"Dane? Neneis?"

"Dane is with us," she said. "His uncle knows it. He's taking care of th' Tree. Th' dog is with Dane."

"Does Lily know son is safe?"

"She does," Felise answered. "I spoke to her afore I came to find yeh. But there's something else yeh need to know."

Lark waited, but it seemed the girl was reluctant. "What is so terrible?"

"I... folla'ed th' witch down here to yeh. Well, I followed one of th' Magistrate's aides, some smarmy guy called Cullis."

"That's MY aide," the mayor roared. "That's the little worm who lied about me in court!"

"I'm sorry, then, yer lordship," Felise said matter-of-factly. "But yer aide is dead and th' man who testified ain't him. I saw his face flicker."

"Illusion failing?" Lark asked.

"No, I don't think so. I've sorta started seein' magic... and it's been ...winkin' at me? Whatever it's on kinda flickers, like a blink. I can see more about it if I concentrate, but I don't really know what what I'm seein' means. Was hoping yeh might help me figure it out later."

"We can try. But did you hear anything, between man and witch? There is reason you mention," Lark said, gently leading her back to the point.

"Yeah, well.... There's an army coming, from th' Capitol."

"Excellent! We're saved," began the Mayor.

"But we ain't, yer lordship. Th' king doesn't know about that army. Th' witch made an agreement with an advisor, some lord who thinks th' king is a poor heir to his father and don't like how he runs things. He's been keepin' th' king from findin' out that Portswain's been under siege."

"Why?" the Mayor choked. He was becoming overwhelmed by betrayals.

"It has to do with th' gypsy witch," Felise snarled, turned her head and spat, meaning the word as a slur with every fibre of her being. She turned her ring off for a few moments, bowing her head to Lark. "I don't hold yer race in contempt, my lady," she said to her. "Yers is a noble people for th' most part. Kind and generous to those who are so to them. This woman, however, is every bad thing ever said about yer people, and don't deserve th' name of Romer."

Lark took a deep breath, realising the woman must have said something truly terrible to have brought this sweet, buoyant girl to such venom. "There is other name for her, which holds for our people every ounce of fear and loathing and ...foulness you mean. She is Mushyan. Clan long ago destroyed by weight of own evil; clan who once stole children and sold them or used them in rituals, who engaged in truly mad and evil things. She is our bogeyman, this last ranie of worst of us. Use this word instead and even Romeri will spit and ward."

Felise bowed her head, cheeks pink with her embarrassment and the strength of her anger. "*Nekka, Daskvi.*"

Lark was caught off-guard by the draconic words. Not just that the girl had used them, but that she herself had known their meaning. 'Forgive me, mother.' The words themselves warmed her heart, and it was then that she realized what was happening. There were still lingering influences from the dragons.

"It is all right, West. For little while still, we will speak their minds and feel their emotions. We must learn to know them for what they are, accept them, but make our own choice whether to speak or act."

The girl nodded, took a moment to get herself under control. *"Should he know all?"* she asked in the dragon's tongue.

"I see no harm in it. There is nothing that can be done about it now, and if things go back to any nearness of what was before, his knowing importance of our place in things will only help us."

She nodded, flashed a grin. *"Think we'll keep th' language? I kinda like havin' a secret tongue."*

Lark smiled. *"I will teach you Romeri then, just in case."*

"Fair enough, Standard." She then stepped back so that she could face both of them at the same time, shifting back to Tembian. "Please understand that not all of this was spoken, or all from th' aide. They spoke until they came to th' entrance of this place, and when th' witch left, I followed her to a place where she communicated with someone I couldn't hear. But this is what I understand of what's goin' on."

She began with the dragon, and the power that had been hidden below the city for so long. How the witch had desired the power for herself and slain the dragons for it, but lost it to someone else who kept it safe until they, too, died.

"When th' power became available again, th' Mushyan began tryin' to find it. It was still well-hidden, so she sought to wake th' dragon, force it to give itself away. To that end, she made a bargain with a lord close to the king. Th' agreement seems to be that he would keep th' king ignorant of th' siege as long as he could or until she got what she wanted, then he would swoop in at th' head of an army, defeat th' invaders and come in as th' city's saviour. After which, she disposes of th' king, making him th' new ruler, and everyone gets what they want."

"How is she going to dispose of the king?" asked the Mayor

Felise shook her head. "I don't know. They spoke only of a plan already in place. They didn't discuss details. And no, I don't know who the traitor is. I know she practically hired th' army, promising them that she could keep th' king from stopping their invasion. When th' noble comes sweeping in, she'll have 'done all she could' and don't really care after that. Nevermind that she's been double-crossing them th' whole time.

"Oh, and none of th' parties know she's just a Mushyan witch. Every time she deals with them, she appears as th' hooded mage. What she and that aide were discussing was that it was time for th' noble to swoop in and 'save th' day'. And to make certain th' magistrate holds up his end of th' bargain."

She paused to wait for the explosion. The Mayor did not quite oblige her. At least, not the way West expected. When he asked the question, it was cold and terrifying.

"And what, exactly, *is* his end of the bargain?"

Felise's grin was wicked. "Oh, just that she gets Lark here. He gets all th' glory for holdin' th' city together durin' tryin' times, savin' them from treachery and so on. All he had to do was let some things in, not enough to get th' city actually sacked, but enough. He's been orderin' men to other positions, creatin' weak spots, blamin' them on you, and just happenin' to have his own people on hand to prevent disaster."

"So he's going to get away with this," he growled.

Something Felise had said made Lark smile. "No. Is not."

"How do you propose to stop it? You're slated to be given to a necromancer as a toy and a sacrifice in a matter of days, and by then the king could be dead. According to ...West... here, there is no way of getting you out to stop it. And without concrete proof no one is going to take our word for it. If we even get to have a word." The Mayor sounded frustrated, angry and despondent. "For all I know they plan to take me to the Capitol to face the 'king's justice' and I'll end up blamed for killing the king."

"Felise," she said, leaning on the door, "Where did witch go to communicate with noble? How do?"

The cardinal shrugged. "She went into an empty cell on th' next corridor over. Eyes went kind of blank and she talked to the air as if it were a person."

Lark rubbed her hands together with glee. "Can you get back to me? Get me message?"

Felise's thoughts drifted through Lark's mind. **Of course. I think you can reach each of the cardinals this way. Distance has yet to be tested, but we'll figure it out.**

Excellent. These are orders.

The mayor peered out of his window at the silent exchange, watched the child's face go from blank reception to wicked grin and tuck the scimitar into her own belt. He could not see Lark even if he wanted to. He was startled when the girl saluted her, then turned to give him a saucy grin, and faded from sight.

"My lady, would you care to explain what's going on?"

She just smiled, moving away from the door. "Best I do not. Is chance of being overheard here. Besides, is best as surprise."

After that, she seated herself in the middle of her cell and began to concentrate. "*Mother, I know you are here.*"

FOUR

Landros was standing in the command tent with Kerolanda and Nalenil at his side. Lord Colwyn was there with two other lords listening to what Kerola was telling them and marking the map. Nightingale was sitting on Landros's shoulder, listening to something else entirely.

Suddenly, the bird hopped to Nalenil's ear and bent to chirp at him. He nudged Landros, whispered in Elvish, *"You best step out of the tent, Commander."*

"Why?"

"There's like to be violence otherwise?" He said it like a question, as if he himself was unsure of the reason.

Nightingale looked expectantly up at him, gave him a 'go on' tweet.

Sighing, Landros gave a discreet sign to his lord and slipped out of the pavilion. He saw immediately what the trouble was, and crossed to the where the guards had circled a very tall Romeri man who was waiting less than patiently. "Ox!" he hailed, causing the guards to flash through a mixture of emotions from confusion to chagrin to relief.

They stepped back and allowed Landros to approach, watching the two men embrace like brothers. When the elf allowed the larger man to set an arm around his shoulders and began to lead him off, none of them tried to stop them.

Landros drew him over to the camp's epicentre, began to adjust the cooking fire. It was central enough that there was just too much noise to be overheard, and no one near enough to decipher or care what was said.

"Ox, my brother, do tell me why you are here. I will not ask how or how you knew where to find me because I know your sister and I have the feather tattle-tale."

As if summoned by his name, the mockingbird landed on the top of the tripod, chirping a cheery hello to Ivan.

"Astute as ever, Kestrel. But matters are dire and we need you and lord we can trust."

Landros glanced up, not fooled by the casual tone of the Romer poking his nose into the nearly empty stewpot. "What level of trust are we talking?" he asked.

Ivan shrugged, "True names."

The wedge of wood slipped out of his fingers and Nightingale gave a taunting whistle. He aimed a twig at the bird. "Did you have any inkling about this?"

The bird just shrugged and began to sharpen his beak on the tripod end.

He sighed and went back to adjusting the fire. "Only one lord out here I trust that much. Little one, go tell Nalenil that we need a private audience with Lord Colwyn. Tell him it is urgent," he said, glancing across to Ivan for confirmation. When he nodded, Nightingale sailed off and the elf looked more fully at the burly human. "Do you really want to exchange true names or were you just wanting someone we can trust that much?"

"Ox is fine. But need to know it would be safe if it came to that."

Landros nodded. By the time he had the fire reset for maximum efficiency, the other nobles were leaving the pavilion. They waited until those lords had gone to their own men before making their way into the blue and white striped tent. He made it look as if going in was a spur of the moment choice, a 'hey, while you're here let me introduce you'.

Nalenil was still inside, helping to put away maps and papers. He didn't even glance up at the pair of them when he spoke. "I didn't know if you wanted me included or not."

Landros nodded. "Stay. You may be needed. If Kerola needs to be told, you can fill her in later. I trust their silence," he told Ivan.

Nalenil nodded and continued what he was doing. "Master's in there," he said, indicating a partition of the pavilion.

Landros brought Ivan into what amounted to an interior room of the tent, surrounded on all sides by thick fabric and 'chambers' containing armour, weapons, supply crates and his horse. The interior room had a cot just big enough to sleep a large man comfortably, and a couple of folding chairs.

Lord Colwyn was sitting on the bed with a lap secretary, penning a letter which he immediately set aside in a locking box and placed the secretary under the cot.

"My Lord," Landros began, "this is Lark's brother, Ox."

He stood, offered to shake hands as if this was purely a social call. "*Droshvi*! Colwyn Abberwood. Come, sit, be welcome," he said taking Ivan's hand in the Romeri manner.

This pleased him to no end, and he pulled the lord closer, meeting his eyes and asked. "Have you our tongue?"

Colwyn laughed, shaking his head. "Would that I did, my friend. I know enough to get me out of trouble and... likely into it again. But my tongue knows the dance."

Landros watched the two men, fully aware that there were two, maybe even three conversations going on here at once. He took the time to fetch a pitcher and offered both of them cups before taking one for himself.

"Please forgive that I have no wine or spirits to offer," Colwyn said before drinking. "Best I have right now is purified water."

Ivan accepted and drank deeply. "You have knowledge of us?" he asked politely. "I know my sister did not teach you this, and my brother," he jerked his thumb at Landros with a grin, "barely knows anything."

"I've met a few. I rode under roofs the colour of the sky for little over a month when I was young and stupid. Fractured peg and stranded on foreign soil. They were kind enough to offer me a bed and a bandage. Interesting custom, I noticed, painting a perfect, purple spiral on the ceiling just over the pillow. Fell asleep many a night following that line inward. Helped with the pain. Did *not* help with the fever!" he laughed.

Ivan had cocked his head for a second, then laughed, nodding. "Myrtle," he commented. "Good woman. Though, no, that isn't Gavori custom, that's just Myrtle!"

"Amazing that we know the same woman, in all the wide, wild world," Colwyn laughed, genuinely surprised.

Ivan shook his head. "Not really. She is momma hen, that one. Anyone who's crossed a Gavori path, knows Myrtle! When our own healers fall short, it is to her we go if we can."

"Well, Ox, I am glad we have found common ground. What might I do to sweeten the earth between us?"

"Ivan," he replied but left it at that. He noticed the change in Colwyn's eyes at the trust shown and nodded. "I need to steal my brother here."

"Well, Ivan, I am sure I can spare him his current task. Though we are so close to completion," he said, glancing at Landros. But the elf knew as much as the lord did about what was going on and was no help.

"Whatever is left, Nalenil and Kerola can handle," Landros answered. "My brother does not come here lightly. The family is in Alphasia at the moment, so it is a long trip."

Ivan shook his head, spoke into his cup "Tembia. Or will be by dusk. Taking bridge from Giant's Gates."

Landros shuddered at that name. He knew the stone archway he spoke of, though he had never known it to be a Romer gate. It was only a day away from where he had grown up. Where he and his brother had lost everything. "Why the return?" he asked casually. "Surely the apples hang fat on the trees in Alphasia."

There was a twinkle in Ivan's eye as Landros began picking up on the pattern of under-talk. "Different fruit is in season, brother."

Colwyn was interested in this. "What fruit would that be?"

"Ah, we need antlers of emperor stag...." Colwyn froze. "Without this ingredient, great plague comes."

Landros was confused but his lord seemed to know what that meant.

"Nothing but the stag will do?"

Ivan shrugged. "So the ranie say; Gruma, mother *and* sister."

Landros perked up. "You've spoken with your sister?"

Ivan's grin vanished. "No. But mother has, and she has spoken to Gruma and no one is liking conversation. Hence need for antlers. Apparently hunting birds are better than hunting hounds, Kestrel."

Colwyn started to frown at that, misinterpreting some of what he had heard, then the rest sank in. He grinned. "Appropriate."

Ivan shrugged again. "Is was sister calls him. Mother, too. Only women know why."

Nalenil entered the small chamber and bowed to all. "Your pardon, my lord, but the pavilion is empty and none linger near. Do you wish me to stay or vanish?" His Elvish accent was strong, but he spoke with deliberance, to make sure his meaning was clear.

Colwyn shook his head, waved him nearer. "You heard that your commander may have another assignment?"

"An important one," he answered, nodding.

"When we are done here, I will need you to get with him and confirm everything you already have going. Leadership will be transferring to..." he hesitated, glanced at Landros.

"Kerola," he answered. "Nalenil is a liaison and scout, his skill is not in giving orders." He turned to the elf, shifting down to Elvish for speed and ease of comprehension. *"You and Kerola know the next phase as well as I, and what you do not know you can figure out. Work with Colwyn and keep your eyes and ears open, especially for this incoming army the wild ones have seen."*

He clasped the smaller elf's arm and shoulder, pulling him close in an embrace. *"Be careful, brother. If we do not see one another again, live well and remember me."*

"And you me, brother. Tread carefully, though. Emperor stags are deadly if surprised and cornered, and they have great herds to guard them."

He grinned, let go. Nalenil slipped out of the chamber and the pavilion and flitted off to find Kerola. Turning back to the other two, "So, there are no eavesdroppers now. Is it time for plain-speaking?"

Ivan roared his laughter.

When he could breathe again, he sobered, began laying out what he had been told. "This army that is coming will indeed help to end siege," he said. "But sister is certain that leader's motives are impure. That he is reason no one else has come, is playing at hero. Will bear watching."

"How does your sister know all this?" Colwyn asked, refilling Ivan's cup.

It was clear that the large Romer needed a moment to calm himself before he could answer that question. Finally, he decided to hold off on the part about his sister being in prison. "One of cardinals spied on real hooded mage."

"Real?" Landros interrupted. "You mean the others were..."

"Possessed poppets. Cardinal heard mage talking to man leading rescuing army. None of this bodes well for king or kingdom. Only way to disprove any of what will say, is for only man in country who's word weighs more to call him liar. For this, we need you," he gestures to Colwyn, "lord we can trust to gain us access to king. Then, using gates, we bring back in caravan, follow army into city and simply be in right place at right time."

"What do you need me for, exactly?" Colwyn asked, a little too causally Landros thought.

"Way to get king to agree and come. Means for him to trust. Certainly will not go with Romeri man simply because says is needed and will be safe. Provided Romeri can even get in to see him."

The knight leaned back, grinning like a bobcat. "Ah, but you already have what you need to catch a king." He gestured magnanimously at Landros who frowned at him, tipping his head in confusion. "On your hand, boy. Show that to any guard in a white tabard and you will be granted immediate access to his majesty. ...Well, as close to immediate as is feasible. He will be informed immediately, at any rate. Getting you to the palace will be trickier."

It was Ivan's turn to grin and gloat. "Oh, about as tricky as stealing apples in crowded market," he chuckled. "New brother-in-law has been in palace before. His old caravan has performed for king's birthday. He knows of perfect archway for gate. Getting into palace will be cake. Finding and getting to king... more like teaching deaf man to whistle tune. Not impossible, but damn difficult."

Colwyn sat up, getting out his secretary again. "Where is the archway?"

Ivan described the location as best he could, as it had been told to him by Gregor.

The lord nodded and began drawing a rough floor plan on a piece of paper. "Depends on the time of day," he began. "But during supper is the best time to get in from here. There will be a lot of people milling about, and if you go in dressed as servants or minor nobles, no one will think twice about you. I would go this way and up this staircase. This room here is his private drawing room, where he withdraws after meals to unwind and escape his guests. He'll be in here for at least an hour, sometimes more. Best if you slip in *before* he arrives. The guards will step in and clear the room, but Landros can show them his ring and they should allow the king entry and privacy. Like I said, white tabards know what to do when they see that ring."

Landros looked the map over for several minutes before handing it back. "Ivan, my brother, are we ready to go?"

"Have you everything?"

"I just have to grab my pack."

"And Nightingale?" Ivan asked.

Landros looked to his lord, "I do not think it right that I leave him here, for all Nalenil can communicate with him. But, bringing him with us might be... risky."

Ivan shrugged. "Not to mention familiar going through gates without mistress might make her head spin. Bad enough he is miles from her."

Landros nodded. "I'll send him back to her."

There was a look in Ivan's eye at that, even as he nodded agreement. Landros caught it, but resolved to ask later, in private.

He stood, bowed to his lord and was surprised when the man offered his hand. When he accepted it, he found himself enveloped in a hug.

"I'm no priest to speak for the three, but go with blessings and be careful. We will be prepared on our end. At least those I can trust," Colwyn added as he pulled away. He then turned and offered his arm to Ivan. "I understand why, but nonetheless thank you and your clan for the services you are about to render. It will not be forgotten."

Ivan accepted, clapping him on the back. "Blame my sister," he grinned. "Though... it is kinda fun."

With that, the two men left the inner room, walked around to where the great blood bay was kept. The horse snuffled his hair as the elf bent to the straw near his head and picked up the pack he had stowed there on his arrival. He gave him a fond pat as he and Ivan slipped out the side flap and walked into the woods.

They had gotten maybe thirty feet past the guarded perimeter when Nightingale landed on his shoulder, fussing at having been left behind. Landros stopped, took the bird on his fingers. "Go back to her," he said.

The mockingbird just cocked his head, confused.

A little frustrated, he fished a smallish gold ring out of a side pocket of his pack and held it up. "This. Take to Lark?"

The bird chirped excitedly.

"Yes, you can go back to her. But be careful."

The bird took the ring in his beak and fluttered off.

"Excuse?" Ivan asked, meaning the ring.

He readjusted the pack, "I was going to give it to her anyway. I got it off an enemy soldier. Supposedly, it provides some protection."

Ivan snorted, "Didn't work for soldier."

"Yeah," he chuckled, then turned serious. "Now what are you not telling me?"

Landros was in a foul mood when he and Ivan gated to the Romeri camp. He found himself walking out of a wagon and nearly lost his footing on the unexpected step. Ivan only chuckled and nodded deeply to the old woman Landros remembered from the ceremony. He followed suit, winking at the little girl from that night who was peeking at him from behind the skirts of the buxom young woman who had bandaged Ivan. The girl giggled. The woman had an infant in her arms which she handed to Ox.

"Here, Anji will keep him calm," she said as he took the babe.

Old Ruby snorted, "Or at least mind his temper."

Ivan led him over to another, slightly larger wagon, this one with tin wind-chimes dangling from the eaves that flashed in the sun. Sitting on the folding steps, glowering, was a late-middle-aged human with thick black curls and moustache. The only detail that registered with Landros was the red vest with the gold braiding. Everything else was swallowed by the swiftness with which the slightly overweight man stood, flicking his dark brown eyes between his son, his grand-daughter and the stranger walking beside them.

"Ox," he began warily, his eyes lingering on the smaller elf beside his son.

Ivan's answer was to hand his daughter over. Anji helped by gurgling as she was passed, changing the focus of the Captain's attention.

"Captain," Ivan began, which told his father this was official. "I bring you my baharen. His name is Kestrel, for all world calls him Landrosallenthyoia."

Landros offered his hand and arm. "Landros will do for less a mouthful."

Petrov did not reach for the hand, eyed it a second before using the baby as an excuse. Landros did the polite thing and nodded, accepting it.

"Are you reason my caravan is about to embroil in politics and petty local squabbles?" he asked sternly. Though not as aggressively as he no doubt wanted to, because he eyed the baby as he spoke.

"No," Ivan answered for him. "That would be Illyana's fault." The eyes flashed to him, angry for his daring to use a real name before this man who was not Romeri, baharen or not. "He is merely agent by which it will be done."

Petrov glared between the two of them, then turned his shoulder to Ivan, cutting him out of the conversation and looked down into Landros's eyes. "Tell me, *baharen*, why Illyana would dare to ask of us this risk?"

Landros sought desperately for the words, knowing he was far from the diplomat. That was Adrick, pompous though he was. But judging from the few examples of this clan that he had seen, perhaps formal and diplomatic was not the best approach. He decided on pragmatic.

"The Romeri have difficulties most places they travel. You are tolerated only so long as you are useful, and rarely trusted."

Petrov gave an expression of 'tell me something I don't know', and sat on the step again with the baby.

"But what if you didn't have that. Here at least? Not all of Tembia feels that way. But if those who oversee the country, who make the laws, were to see you as helpful in their most desperate hour, they might make it illegal to harass you. There is something to be said for having a king in your debt."

Petrov could not argue that point. "This is truth. But risk in gaining this debt is too great. Could shut us out of Tembia altogether."

"Ah, that is where you miscalculate. You haven't all the facts," he added, realizing even before he saw the flash in those eyes that telling a Captain he is wrong was dangerous. "The risk is mostly mine. So long as I succeed, the debt is assured."

"Only mostly," he growled.

Landros nodded. "Yes, but I can mitigate even that. I have the right to approach the king."

"Then why do you need us?" Petrov grumped. His surly tone was ruined by the faces he made at the baby.

"Speed." He was thrown a glance. "There is an army coming to 'rescue' Portswain. This army is led by the man who allowed the siege, made certain no one broke it before he was ready to charge in like a hero. He wants to be king. And he will be no friend to the Romer."

"Like current king *is*?" he sneered.

Ivan interrupted. "Current king is one who removed need for travel papers, made it easier for us to roam through."

Petrov mumbled an acknowledgment and Landros continued. "I do not have time to travel to the capitol, get into the palace and gain an audience with the king, then bring him to the city in time to stop what is happening. Not by traditional means. I cannot even ask you to gate us into Portswain itself, because since it has been known that a Romeri in the city is gaining aid from outside, even that method has been blocked."

He looked to his son for confirmation.

"Is true, father. I have tried to get to her. Gruma could not affect gate within city walls."

"But you expect me to roll whole caravan through besieged gates?" he grunted, glancing beyond them to the old woman lingering there.

"Following a rescuing army inside once the siege is broken should be like stealing apples," Landros said with a grin, glancing at Ivan, who chuckled.

"Would be as crowded as full market. And with king amongst us, who is going to tell him no?" he added to his father.

Petrov had missed something, growling in anger in Romeri at Ivan. *"You would have us work with man who accuses us of stealing? Even apples? This is man you have risked everything for?"*

Ivan laughed. *"Is merely parroting my words back at me, father. I compared task at hand to stealing apples in crowded market. Blame me."*

This mollified the man slightly, shifted back to Tembian. "I am still reluctant to put this caravan at risk. Our whole clan. Can this not be done with single wagon?"

Landros shook his head. "That would be a greater risk trying to get in, not to mention the risk to the king. One wagon is easily overwhelmed. A whole caravan not so much."

Old Ruby stepped forward now. She stood over her son-in-law and stared for a moment before speaking. "Is more at risk than clan, than city. There is Mushyan." She spat into the nearby fire and Petrov hastily circled his fist over the infant and spat himself. He had paled considerably. "This witch has her claws in our little Lark and this is only way to stop her."

"Why would this witch be interested in our songbird?" he snarled. The baby began to cry, forcing him to lower his tone and soothe her. "This is why I wanted her to leave that place. I knew I should have forced her!" he managed to growl in a singsong voice at great dissonance to his words.

"She was given something of great power. Witch wants it. Sagavis," she said simply. "Yani was drawn to it simple as that. And to more. But is best for us Yani beat witch to it. Now, give me child and get us moving. Need to be at forest of Kellvetch by nightfall."

Petrov handed her the infant and stood, sighing. If his daughter was involved, he had no choice. And the existence of a Mushyan was reason enough. He began giving orders.

Ivan led Landros away with Ruby, calling over two men he had not yet met. He was introduced when they arrived at his wagon. "My younger brothers, Bear and Weaver," Ivan threw out casually. "Gruma fetched them after she sent me to you."

The larger and older of the two was very bearlike indeed. Hairy, with a thick moustache and, while a few inches shorter than Ivan, he was definitely broader. Taking Landros's arm in greeting, he learned very quickly that the layer of fat that surrounded the man was corded through with iron muscle. "Aptly named," was all he could manage.

He felt stupid the moment the words left his mouth, but the man grinned, pulling him in to whisper: "Keir means dark bear."

He then gave the elf a pat on the shoulder that felt more like a pound and spun him at his other brother.

This man was definitely smaller, built more like their sister, and the callouses on his hands were very different than even his own. "I weave," he shrugged with a grin, fingering the brightly woven pattern of his vest. "Luca means nothing."

"It means light-haired, you dainty oaf!" snapped Raven, rolling up with a swagger. "Though what Pomona sees in you, I have no idea."

Landros took note that the man's hair was slightly more brown than that of his brothers, but then Weaver had let him go and seized the younger man in a headlock, ruffling his hair violently. "My face? Nothing. My hands? *Every*thing," he grinned. "But at least my name does not mean 'Eager', *Emilian*. Or rival!"

Using his true name in front of Landros actually angered the boy, enabling him to escape the hold and shove his brother back, snarling in Romeri. "*My name is my gift to give, Luca! Ivan may have accepted this pointy-eared gegenta, but I have not yet.*"

Landros was clueless as to the exchange beyond the anger of the words. But there was no mistaking Ivan's rage as he descended upon his younger brother and pinned him back against the wagon.

"*You would stain clan name, and mine, by refusing to respect rite of baharen? To insult him is to insult me, Raven.*"

Raven seemed a little cowed by the reaction and the words, but he remained sullen. *"I take insult back, but not my words. My name is mine to give or not. And this* baharen," he said the word carefully, barely managing not to sneer it, *"has not earned enough of my respect to be gifted it."*

Ivan put him down and Weaver looked sheepish. *"I apologize, Raven. You are right. That was your choice. I forget that you are man now."*

The boy seemed partially mollified, but his cheeks retained their high colour as he straightened his clothes. When his eyes caught his grandmother standing near the 'pointy-eared gegenta', his colour darkened and he turned away.

The others recollected themselves, stifling their embarrassments. Landros was polite enough to not inquire. Ivan took his daughter from Gruma and turned to his wife. He gave her a passionate kiss before handing the child over, gazing at both with adoration a brief moment before he turned to two small boys, twins who had hopped out of the wagon now that the commotion was over.

Landros stood back, watching with interest as Ivan turned to his sons and gave one of them orders to get the wagon moving with the caravan and to obey their mother. The other was told to help Gruma. That boy looked almost disappointed until the old lady began giving him instructions on what she wanted done, and it dawned on him that he would be unsupervised for most of it. He watched the sense of intense pride wash over his face before he nodded and ran off.

"Gregor is here," Jena called as she adjusted the baby in a sling against her body so she could work.

Ivan looked up, grinning, led Landros and his brothers over to meet their half-sister's new husband, introducing him as Fiddle. Standing amidst so many taller men, Landros was beginning to feel that he might not be taken seriously. But his reception with the Romer was as earnest as the two middle brothers and he made that voice in the back of his head fall silent.

Ivan took them over to the back of his wagon and began rooting through a chest of clothing. Weaver he tossed an embroidered tunic and a velvet hat. Himself, Fiddle and Bear, he dressed more like bodyguards. Raven, whether it was to further chastise him or just because it was what they had in his size, was dressed as a page, but had the grace not to say anything.

As they changed, Weaver looked down at what Landros was wearing, forester's gear, well-worn and stained with the days of fighting and living rough. "What about Kestrel?" he asked.

Ivan grinned. "Messenger, of course."

Landros grinned a little sheepishly, pulling his hood up to shadow his face. He adjusted his bag to try and look more like a harried messenger than a weary adventurer.

It was not long before the old woman returned to lead them off into the near-by forest to open the gate.

Lark sat in the corner of her cell, arms wrapped around bent legs, forehead pressed to her knees. She was not asleep. The darkness did not bother her, not any more. Once the effects of the necromancy used on her had completely worn off, and her attention had been diverted from her panic, she could see as easily in the pitch as she could in bright light. Sudden illumination would cause her undoubted problems, but for now she was all right.

Mentally, not so much. The cold here was not at all like that of the warren, where it was just chill enough to be comfortable if you had sleeves. Here there was also the weight of despair and isolation, the sensation of being buried alive. Not being able to see the sky, to feel the wind on her cheek, or the sun on her face was her greatest fear. It drove a terror within her, threatening her sanity with every passing moment.

FitzWaller spoke to her frequently, distracting her, trying to maintain his own sanity. It was his silences that hurt the most; times, like now, when he was likely sleeping, and the walls felt like they were closing in, and the air grew stale with her own breath. Panic fluttered like a trapped bird in her chest.

Her head came up. The fluttering of feathers, both feel and sound, rippled in the air around her. She looked, but saw nothing, just the dim outline of the door, where the stone gave way to wood. She closed her eyes and focused. Saw the city beneath her, familiar buildings, Lily's stable. The chirruped question of where was she, echoed in her mind.

"It is all right, my friend. I am... alive. Find one of children. You cannot come here."

Hovering in his mind, seeing from his eyes, she flew with him, searching the streets for any of the army. Finally they found one, squatting on a roof, keeping an eye on a group of soldiers. They landed a foot away, caught the boy's attention with a flip of his wings and very softly whistled the call the children had come up with.

His eyes flicked immediately to the mockingbird, recognized him as Lark's and nodded. He crumbled up a few grains from the stale crust of bread he was chewing on for the bird and went back to his watch.

Lark left him then, telling Nightingale to go with Mouse.

Having partaken of a bit of sky and sweet, sweet freedom, however vicarious it had been, she felt a little more grounded. The panic abated for a little while. She did not get up or move, but she did start singing.

FIVE

Landros was still a little disturbed walking through the gate. Sure, teleporting the priest's way was violent on the belly and equilibrium. But stepping from a near silent, needle-carpeted forest floor through an arch made by a fallen tree into a marble tiled palace room with the cacophony of hundreds of busy people nearby was as unbalancing as suddenly walking out of the wagon had been earlier. It didn't matter than he could see it before walking through, smell the food, hear the noise. What could be heard through the gate was nothing to being in the midst of it. Or rather on the edge of it. Thankfully, the archway in question was unobserved at that moment.

They walked into the next room as if they had every right to be where they were. Landros followed the directions Lord Colwyn had given him, speaking softly to Weaver who walked beside him. Raven followed a half step behind and the three 'guards' brought up the rear, looking about suspiciously, even as Weaver played up the bored noble talking with a messenger.

Things fell out as Colwyn had said they might. Everyone of any significance was in the banquet hall, and every available servant was dancing attendance there. There weren't many guards here, and those few they passed did not acknowledge them.

Landros opened the door at the top of the staircase and held it for the small party. He glanced around for a brief second before he followed them in. Closing the door behind him, he had to stop and lean back against the steady wood.

It was dark at first, but Weaver had activated a magical stone around his neck, casting the room in a soft glow, allowing them to see the wonders they had walked in on.

The room was not huge, barely the size of his whole apartment at the Cygnet, but it was opulent. The curved ceiling was an easy twenty feet high and elaborately painted with a sunrise and a view as if standing on a high tower looking over the countryside. There were even wooden crenelations surrounding the dome. No windows graced the walls, but there was a large fireplace with a fire lain ready, which Raven was lighting, and a scattering of very comfortable chairs and velvet couches. A few dark paintings graced the spaces between bookshelves that were absolutely full.

Rows of dark, leather-bound volumes rose high above his head, halfway up the walls. Stacks of portfolios that might have filled Lark's wagon with no room to move filled shorter, deeper shelves and cabinets. There were twisted, iron statues in the shape of sinuous, fey maidens holding sprays of bell-like flowers whose petals were blown-glass shades protecting crystal stamen. These hung their bounty over the backs of certain chairs as if they were reading lamps. He assumed they had to be magical. He could see no way to light them if they were not. Though he did find a twisted humour in the fact that fey things had been sculpted in iron.

Once Raven had the fire going, they settled back to wait, making themselves comfortable. Weaver perused the shelves, finally settling in the chair nearest the fireplace to read what he'd chosen. Raven parked himself onto a couch, lounged back and promptly fell asleep. Bear nudged him over, managed to squeeze on without waking the boy and dozed off himself. Ivan sat in the most comfortable chair and stared up into the glass flowers, trying to figure out how they worked. Gregor found something to keep him occupied near the door, keeping his ears open. Landros merely paced like a caged animal.

Lark stirred, began pacing the tiny room. Something was happening beyond the prison. Her stomach rumbled, reminding her that they had not been fed or brought water in some time. Actually, Lark could not remember having been fed at all. She couldn't really say how long she had been here, but she supposed that was part of the point.

Before these thoughts could poison her current peace of mind, she tried to reach out, to contact the cardinals. It was difficult. She knew they were out there, that they were somewhat safe, but it was as if there was something interfering with anything reaching outside these walls.

She touched Nightingale. That was a connection that thankfully transcended whatever barriers were currently up. His report was a volley of over-excitement to the point she could understand little. She had him fly up, to let her see for herself, but he refused.

Before she could get upset with him over the refusal, he let her see from where he was: high on a rooftop with Mouse watching a great deal of commotion on the far side of the city walls. It was night, and whatever was happening was creating a great deal of light and fire and explosions. She felt her heart rise in her chest.

Mouse turned to look into the bird's eyes as he chirped, and smiled. "Hello, Standard. I know the cats got you. I am glad they have not eaten you."

She relayed through her familiar, "Not yet. What is happening?"

He shrugged, looking back over the walls a few dozen streets away. "I think the army you said was coming is here. They've stopped lobbing fireballs at us. But then, they stopped that almost as soon as we merged. Not much point then, eh *daskvi*?"

"*Sesket,*" she smiled. Her smile did not last. "Won't be long now. Whatever is plan, is soon."

"I agree. We will be prepared, Standard, come what may."

"Get some rest, North," she urged. "Trouble comes with sun, am thinking."

She saw him nod, offered Nightingale a seed. "Goodnight, Standard. Tomorrow night we will sleep free or we will be dead."

As she left her familiar's mind, she mused over the boy's words. It had been fairly morbid for a child. But she could neither question or doubt his conviction.

"What news, my lady?" came the Mayor's voice.

"Army has come. Enemy fights its own siege now. One way or other, all ends tomorrow."

There was a deep breath beyond the stone, slowly drawn and released. "May the crone walk readily amongst our enemies but keep her back to us."

"And may Mother keep us safe," she whispered. She had never been one for prayers or religion, but it felt a little hypocritical now not to invoke. Not when she herself stood Maiden, and now Mother as well by virtue of Eshanai's soul.

They had warning before the door opened. The footsteps of soldiers on the staircase outside was heard, though only barely. Gregor suddenly animated and moved away from the door. The others melted into the background as best they could, so when the guard entered the room to check its security, it was only Landros who was obvious, standing before the fire in an otherwise dark room, waiting patiently.

The guard closed the door and drew his sword. "Name and business here," he demanded.

Landros glanced at the man's chest, made certain the tabard was white and not the yellow the firelight made it appear. There was a crest, discreetly embroidered in gold over the left breast. He moved slowly, holding up his hands to show them empty, then pulled off his left glove, wiggled a finger to indicate a ring he knew the man could not see at that distance.

The guard kept his sword out, but moved slowly closer, the

point held lower than before. He eyed the others in the room, came around the side of a couch to stand a few feet away from the elf.

Landros lowered his hand, to let the firelight play over the surface of the copper band on his finger. He slowly turned it over, to show the etched falcon.

The guard suddenly nodded, took a step back and sheathed his sword. "Your pardon, squire," he said with a half bow. "Your friends?"

"Merely my assurances of getting here safely. But they are involved with the business at hand and may be privy if His Majesty allows it."

The guard bowed again and retreated. Before leaving the room, he paused at the sculptures and whispered something in the graceful iron ears. The crystal stamen began glowing, providing a soft light that was more than enough for reading or seeing the contours of the room. Then he left, closing the door behind him.

Raven was peering curiously at one of the lamps a minute later when the door was once more opened and someone entered. Landros immediately knelt. He was aware that the Romers had stepped back to the edges of the room almost instantly, and that none of them bowed.

The king ignored them and crossed to him. He saw a hand appear near his face. "Your ring, squire," came the mellow voice, but there was authority in it.

He felt his heart tumbling into his stomach, but obediently removed the ring and set it in the royal hand. He felt the king move past him to the fire, waited, quietly panicking until that voice told him to rise.

He obeyed, turned to face the man who held the ring back out to him. He was younger than his lord, perhaps Weaver's age, maybe a little more. It was hard to tell with the close cropped beard he wore. The king was dark-haired, with dancing brown eyes and high cheek bones and a decided tilt about his eyes that spoke, perhaps, of elven blood somewhere a long way back. Except for the beard, he was almost beautiful, but with a rugged edge. He wasn't quite

Ivan's height, but he was tall, and moderate of shoulder. His coat was richly embroidered and of heavy damask cloth. His hair fluttered in short waves around the base of the gold band, half hiding the rose-cut rubies that ringed it. The crown had what looked like golden sword points rising above the nest of soft curls.

He looked both soft and rugged at the same time, and Landros found it a little disturbing.

He accepted the ring back with a bow. "Thank you, your majesty."

The king smiled, turned towards the largest chair, beneath one of the iron ladies and sank into its comfort, sighed. "Please," he gestured for Landros to sit opposite him. "And your friends. And tell me what message Lord Colwyn sends in such a clandestine manner."

Landros sat, waited as the Romeri gathered around and sat as if this were a casual evening chat around a campfire rather than a private firelit meeting with a king. "Actually," he began. "I merely bring to you what they have already discovered," he gestured to Ivan, "through Ox's sister."

"Oh?" he asked, turning to look at the man in question.

Landros found himself blurting out, even as the thought occurred to him, "Wait, why do you think Lord Colwyn sent me?" He was shocked by his own outburst the moment the words were out of this mouth.

But the king merely smiled, looking back at him benevolently. "You are his squire. I assumed...."

He frowned, and, emboldened by the monarch's reaction, dared to ask, "But how did you know I was his squire?"

The king actually laughed. "It's inscribed on the inside of your ring," he finally managed. "I shall have to have words with him. He is apparently neglecting very important elements of your training."

He flushed immediately, leapt to Colwyn's defence. "No fault of his own, your majesty. One, I came to him a fully trained Pathfinder, an adventurer in my own right. Two, the war has left us very little time."

That sobered the king quickly. He sat up straighter. "What war?"

He took a deep breath and began to explain, "The city of Portswain has been under siege for months."

Between Landros and Ivan, they filled the king in on everything that had been happening on the other side of the country, including what Lark had been able to discover. By the end, the king was pacing before the fire in a livid state.

"And you have no physical proofs?" he raged. "Nothing I can use to silence any supporters he might have?"

"They have been quite clever, your majesty," Landros grumbled, angry at the situation himself. "However, we, too, are clever, and if your majesty will trust me, you might hear the villain's confession with your own ears."

"How? Portswain is more than a week away by rapid horse. And you say the battle is eminent!"

Ivan stepped forward, "By trusting us. We got into your palace without walking through doors... from Kempmere."

That caught the king's attention. "That's ... nearly a month away!"

Ivan grinned. "Romeri have ways of travelling quickly from place to place. We do not use often, and are limited in how is used, but we have. Our plan is simple. You come with us, ride disguised as Romer when we play camp-follower and slip in after army. No doubt will be big show for people to greet 'rescuer', and sister says his plan is to malign you, to speak lies."

The king's eyes lit up with delight, and it was a frightening thing, when Landros thought about it. "And if I am in the audience listening, it's as good as a confession. But are there folk enough in Portswain still loyal to me who will arrest them on my order?"

It was Landros' time to smile. "Many, your majesty."

The king clapped his hands gleefully. "This might be fun. To a point. Adventure at last!" he crowed. He turned to Raven. "Young man, would you be so kind as to open the door and tell my sargent that I need to speak with him?"

Raven frowned, about to say something, but Gregor nudged him. "Are supposed to be page, remember?" At which point he grumbled and stood, straightening his tunic and doing as he was asked.

When the man entered, Raven dropped immediately back into his normal, slouchy grouchy mode and slumped onto a divan. The king was already shedding his coat, revealing a soft, but only modestly embroidered shirt and plain trousers. Landros realized the sargent was the guard from earlier.

The man bowed. "Your majesty?"

"Sargent Fitz, your breastplate and tabard, if you please?"

If the man was confused by the request, he did not show it, but immediately began removing his tabard. "Is his majesty going gadabout?" he asked delicately. "And who do you wish to attend you?"

"Oh, no one will be in attendance but the squire here and Lord...?" he turned suddenly to Weaver, prompting him for a name.

"Weavermire, your majesty," he grinned, actually performing a small bow. He was clearly enjoying his role of noble.

"Lord Weavermire and his men, along with Lord Colwyn's squire will be in charge of my personal safety," he said as the guard began to help the king into his padding before buckling on the breastplate. "As for any visitors or other individuals of import, I am simply unavailable at the moment. I'll send word if anything changes. Please inform the Lieutenant as soon as you get to my rooms, and have him inform the Captain first thing in the morning."

"Of course, your majesty. Am I to tell them everything?"

The king thought that over a moment, even as he helped the guard into his own coat and adjusted it for proper effect. "The Captain, yes. The Lieutenant, only that I am 'gadding about' as you put it, and that you are to inform the Captain. Oh, and have him send my ship with adequate support and all due fanfare to Portswain as soon as possible."

"As if your majesty were aboard?" the sargent asked.

"Yes. Excellent idea, Roben. Enjoy the night in my bed," the king grinned.

The man smiled, perhaps because of the invitation, perhaps because the monarch had called him by his given name. "The crown, your majesty?" he said, flicking his eyes to the ring of gold.

"Quite right, Roben. Thank you," he said, taking it off and placing it to effect on the man's brow. "Perfect."

The sargent reached out and made an adjustment to the king's attire, the set of the sword belt on his hip, mimed to him to ruffle his hair to erase the indentations of the crown, then stood back and gave a nod of approval. "Remember to ease your stance, your majesty, if you change your guise. You have your signet?"

The king held up his hand, showing the identifying band of gold embossed with a diamond. The guard handed the king his gloves. "Then you are ready, Sargent Stefan. Enjoy, but return safe."

The guard then turned to Landros, with every attitude of a king. And, in fact, he would easily have been mistaken for the man from a distance, perhaps even up close if one had never met him. "Squire...," he began, in an asking tone.

"Landros, your majesty," he answered, bowing automatically.

"Squire Landros, it is unto you that I place the care of my guardsman, Sargent Stefan. Should anything untoward happen to him, it will be you and Lord Colwyn who will answer for it." He gave a nod to Luca, "Lord Weavermire as well."

"I understand, your majesty," he answered, bowing again.

The 'king' then nodded once more, walked to the door and left the room, closing it behind him.

Gregor listened at the portal. If the guards noticed the switch, none of them had said anything to give it away. He turned to the king-turned-guardsman. "Do this often, Stefan?" he chuckled.

'Stefan' grinned, pleased that they would take up the charade so effortlessly. "Not often enough to please me, but often enough there is a strict protocol for it." He laughed. "My father hated the fact that my grandfather would do it frequently. Though Grandfather's reasons were far less... noble? savoury?" He did not need to clarify.

Ivan bent to the fireplace, to encourage it to die quickly, even as Stefan pulled on the gloves and turned to his new companions. "So, we'll wait a few minutes more and then leave. How are we managing?"

Keir piped up, grinning as he pulled a small stone from his pocket. It glowed faintly in his hand. "Can use this door. Gruma is just stone's tap away."

The Romeri laughed softly at his joke, though neither Landros nor the king quite understood it.

"Are you prepared for this, Landros?" Stefan asked while they waited.

"Anxious, y... Stefan," he said more carefully. "It feels good to be doing something at last. We had wondered why you had not sent us aid."

The king shook his head. "I still don't understand how I have not heard anything of your plight. Portswain is not a small town! Perhaps I rely too heavily upon advisors to keep me informed of goings on outside of my castle. ...I still cannot believe no one asked me about it, ...or said anything!" He turned back from his sudden pacing to look at Landros. "You see now why I need my falcons more than ever."

He bowed his head. "I do."

Stefan got his emotions corralled and refocused on the adventure at hand. "So, gentlemen, what am I to call you?"

Landros made introductions, carefully using only their gegenta names. By then, Bear was telling them the gate was ready.

"It's going to be a little disorienting at first," Landros warned. He had almost said 'your majesty' again. He resolved not to call the king by any name or form of address from here on out unless he had to. He did not trust himself not to slip up when it mattered.

The king grimaced. "I have teleported once before."

Landros laughed. "All right, not *that* bad. Just... weird."

Then Bear was opening the door onto a crossroad at the edge of a broad, dark forest, and nothing more needed to be said.

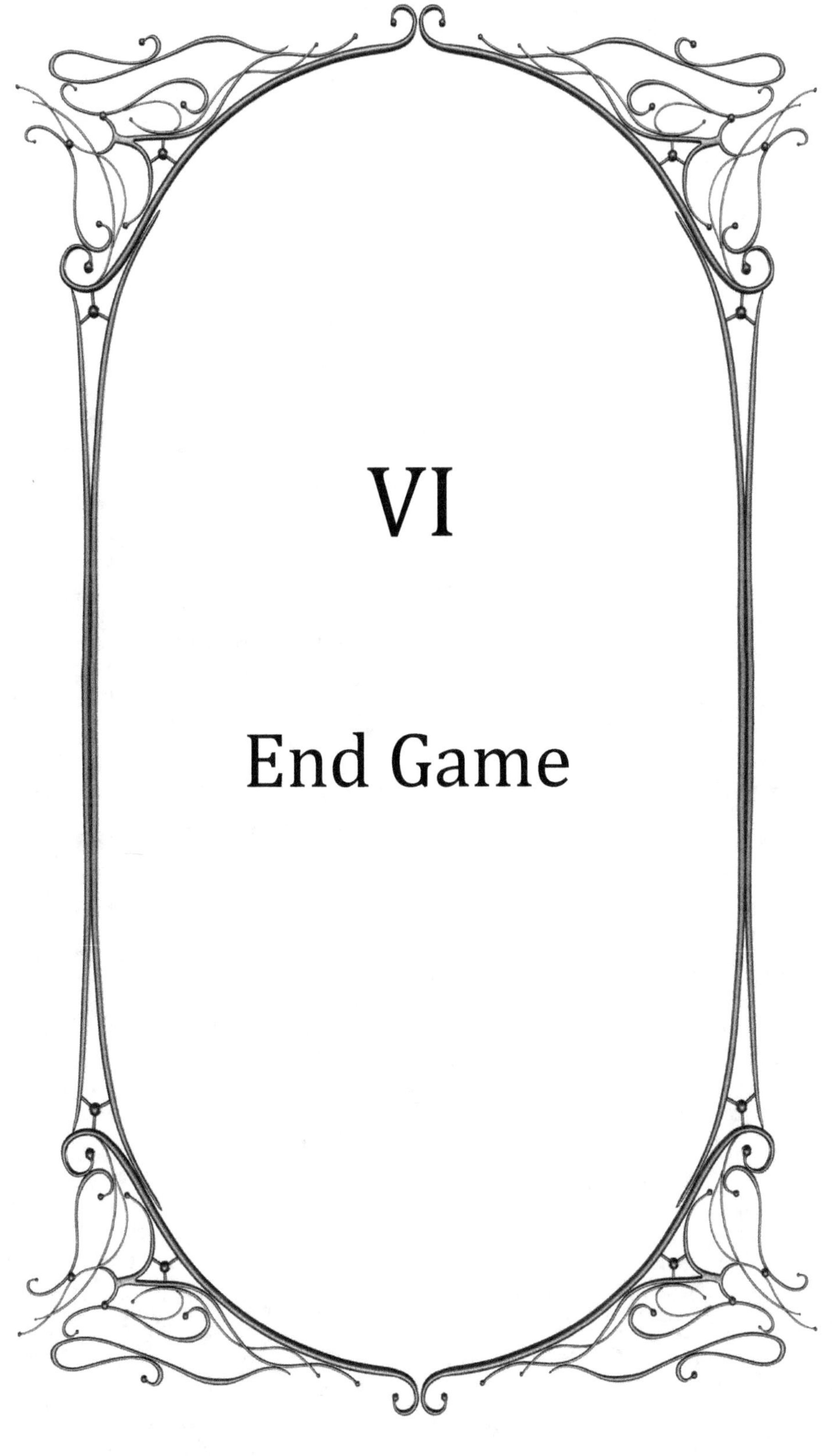

VI

End Game

ONE

Dawn found the Rushavska caravan rolling into Tent Town in the wake of the conquering army. There had been issues at the East Gate, but when told and shown that they carried foodstuffs for the city, they were directed around the walls to the northernmost gate that led into the shantytown grounds.

The king frowned; first, to see the once beautiful fairgrounds relegated to a camping slum; second, to see the poor and dispossessed forced to live here being run out to house the army encampment. Some of whom were clearly recovering from illness. Soldiers moved about, ripping down tents and destroying any ramshackle structures weak enough to be easily uprooted. What few shacks were sturdy enough, were cleared out and repurposed for the use of officers and supplies. Everything not immediately usable was thrown onto a huge bonfire.

The officer in charge of the encampment told them to set up the wagons, as tightly packed as they could, in a pre-cleared area on the other side of the well, nearer to the wall. Old Ruby, getting down from her wagon, looked around, spat, then began to chant a blessing in a strange, singsong voice.

The king and Landros, both dressed to blend in with the caravan, joined the rest of the people in a ring around the chanting old woman. Neither could explain afterward why or how the area felt different, but it was palpable. Ruby ordered the women to burn sweetgrass when campfires were lit, and everyone scattered to begin setting up.

The king approached the Romeri Captain as he was guiding the supply wagon to be parked against the wall and shielded by all the others. It was only then that the king noticed something odd about it: that it was stacked only half as high as he had remembered.

"Did the soldiers take from the wagon?" he asked, growing angry, forgetting why he had approached in the first place.

Petrov laughed. "No. Was never as full as seemed. Was ruse to guarantee entry. There *is* food here, to trade, help. Just not so much as seemed." When the king appeared upset by this news, he set his hand on his shoulder. "Was little time to gather enough, and had not trade goods for more. Will suffice. More can be arranged. Word is already out among family that trade in basic needs and foods will be good here. Many will come. More than Rushavska."

They were interrupted by Raven leading over a harried looking soldier carrying a writ.

"You are in charge of this train?" the man asked.

Petrov stood taller. "I am Captain Rusk," he answered.

The man handed him the paper. "I was told to give you this. It is a writ to be handed to the Magistrate, detailing what you are providing so you can be compensated. Two hours before noon, there will be a public gathering in the square. Instructions as to where to take the writ and the supplies will be given there. You may wish to get there a little early. It's going to get crowded."

The Captain took the paper, thanking the man for his politeness, which seemed to make him uncomfortable. He left quickly. Petrov handed the writ to Landros. "Use if give trouble, to get close enough. Don't bother submitting."

The king frowned. "You aren't going to turn all this over to the city requisition?"

He laughed, deeply and unkindly. "No. I have no intention of giving to Magistrate who has harassed my daughter. Him I do not trust. No, food will be given to those were run out of here. *Priviet.*"

"Priviet?" the king asked, confused.

Raven chuckled. "Privately," he explained, and meandered off to find something to do before something less pleasant was found for him.

Landros cleared his throat. "I may be of some assistance there, Captain," he said.

Petrov turned to him, waited.

"I know someone who would know who needs it the most, probably knew everyone here. I'll send him to you."

"How will know?"

He grinned, held out his hand at hip level. "Little elven boy, yea-high. Name of Mouse."

An eyebrow quirked, but he nodded. "Will tell clan to look out for. Best you take Ox, Stefan and go. Rest of us will do what must."

"Take care, Captain," he said, offering his arm. "I will bring your daughter back to you."

Petrov seized the arm and pulled him in. "You better, Kestrel. Even baharen can be made goshaska."

Landros paled a little, but nodded. "It won't come to that, sir. If I don't bring her back, it'll be because I'm dead."

With a nod of reluctant respect, Petrov let him go, turned to the king-in-disguise and offered his arm, which the king accepted. "I will hold you to your promises, Stefan. You have ridden with us, eaten with us. This demands kindness for kindness."

The king grinned. "We have shared hazards, Captain. That carries its own onus. I will not forget what you have done, are doing. The Trinity keep you and your people safe if we do not meet again."

Petrov nodded, then grinned. "For all you look Romeri man, still you stink of crowns. Best take steps to guard that profile before stepping into crowd," he warned.

The king's hand automatically went to his head, then he grinned. "If I might borrow a cloak, then? I have traded shirt for shirt, and what little remains to me is not mine to trade."

He nodded, letting go and gesturing to the caravan at large.

"You may ask." He ran his own hand down the front of his and grinned. "Is very nice shirt."

It was only then that Landros realized that, sometime during the night, the king and the Captain had traded. Shaking his head, he clapped the king on his shoulder as he would have any comrade, subtly guiding him away. "Come on, Stefan. Maybe Fiddle will loan you his."

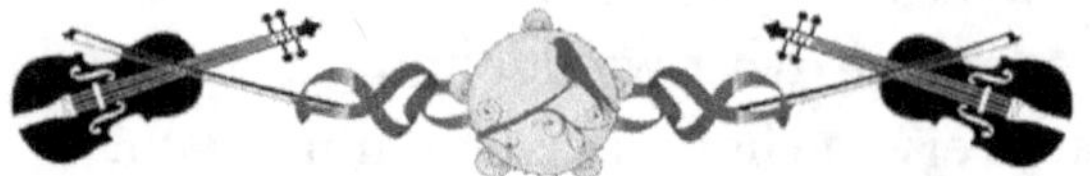

It took Landros a little longer than he wanted to spend to find Mouse. His whistle just outside of Tent Town had eventually brought a private, who promised to pass the message. They were at the square jostling for position before Tamlain, the East Cardinal found him.

"You have a message for North, General?"

Landros blinked. "Where is he? I expected he'd be near his quarter at the very least."

Tamlain shook his head. "Been coordinating with me and South all morning, relocating folk."

"From the 'evacuation'?" he asked with a snarl. The king just stood nearby with Ivan, merely tightening his fist at the subject.

"Aye," came the matter-of-fact response, carefully omitting any mention of it having been a plague zone not so very long ago. "What word?"

"The word is, that there is a caravan of red-roofed wagons in Tent Town with fresh supplies. They would like to be met outside of the grounds to give to the people who were evacuated."

Tamlain looked around, ogling the crowd like everyone else hoping to catch a glimpse of why they'd been told to gather. "I've let him know," he said casually. And continued, even though Landros gave him an odd look. "Someone will slip in and meet with the caravan to give them advice on how best to share the bounty. Now that you are here and ready for anything, are there any instructions, sir?"

"Just see everything. If things go to hell, interfere if you can but don't get caught. Or hurt."

"Will do, sir. Any message for the Standard?"

Landros surged, bumping into the lanky boy's shoulder as if he had been shoved or was moving to reposition himself. The second he was in close enough, he hissed. "How can you get her a message?"

Tamlain, grabbed his shoulders as if helping someone he'd fallen into. "Same way I gave your message to North, sir. Things have changed while you were gone. I pray we have the opportunity to explain later, but now is not the time. The message?"

He stammered, adapting quickly, taking a lot on faith. "That I love her, and that I am here, and I've done as her mother asked. And tell her.... Tell her *'sagavis'*."

Tamlain grinned at that, blushed a little as he brushed the shoulders of Landros's cloak of imagined dirt. When he spoke, it was slow and deliberate, as if making sure to pronounce the words correctly. "Sono mas, kima vas." And then he was gone, melted into the growing crowd.

Landros felt like someone had hit him with a hammer. He took a staggering half-step back, impacted with the king who reached out to steady him. He turned to Ivan's hooded form. "What does *'sonomas kimavas'* mean?"

Ivan smiled, "Oh, my sister has it bad!" he laughed.

Landros lightly punched him in the shoulder as he had seen the brothers do, "Come on, Ox! Spill!"

"It means 'you are woven in my heart'. *Sono mas* is 'we are one', and *kima vas* is weaving of vas..."

His heart skipped, then started again, catching the word, "*Vas*? Like the lifebelt?"

"She explained *vas*?" Landros nodded. "She show you hers?"

"Yes. I've seen it hanging in her caravan. It's been a while since we... sat in there and ...talked," he added, rubbing the back of his neck.

He was saved from any further response by the thickening of

the crowd, and folks elbowing and pushing for real.

"Save it," said Stefan, sounding almost king-like for the first time all night. "Something is clearly about to happen."

They turned, moved closer to the broad stone apron that extended from the front of the city's main government building. A row of eight knights blocked access to the flight of steps that led up to the platform, each standing, fully armoured, behind a tower shield embossed with a golden rose in the upper right corner, above their own devices. It occurred to him that, if those in control were so inclined… this would be the perfect spot for a massacre.

The three of them gathered as close as they dared. While Stefan said he was unfamiliar with any of these knights, it did not mean that none of them would recognize *him* if they got a good look. They exercised caution.

The knights themselves only spent a few seconds studying those in cloaks and hoods. And there were many. Only those nearest to them held their interest for long. It was a chill day, despite the hour and the amount of people. The sky was heavily overcast, likely lingering smoke from the battle the night before and the bonfires outside the city burning the remains.

It did not take long before armed guards walked out of the building to take up stations and the magistrate walked out. He was followed by the Hierophant D'Meysen in his most officious and ostentatious robes who stood off to the side, under the shadows of the roof. The crowd remained still, holding its collective breath. Apparently the outcome of the battle was not widely known yet. The magistrate stopped almost at the edge of the top step and held up his hands to the crowd for a silence he already had.

"Good citizens of Portswain," he bellowed, his voice carrying a bit farther than it normally would have. Landros assumed magic was involved. "For long months we have suffered. An unknown enemy with unknown intentions camped upon our very doorstep, locking us in our own harbour. As you have no doubt surmised, we are besieged no longer! The king's army has finally reached us and broken the back of the enemy!"

A riotous cheer rose up as the whole city seemed to scream its relief. It took several moments to quiet.

"We have suffered more than just privations, starvation and bombardment. We have suffered betrayals by the very souls we trusted to save us."

At this, as if on cue, the doors opened again and a small group of about a dozen prisoners were brought forth. One of them everyone knew. The reaction to the former mayor's squinting, dishevelled face was a disparate mixture of discontent. Many outright booed him, some even threw things. Some perhaps were protesting the arrest and accusations. But it was hard to tell which. No one was happy, that much was clear.

Landros ground his teeth at the sight of slightly crushed red velvet and wrinkled, grimy motley skirts being led out in chains in the middle of the group.

Lark had prepared herself for the sudden light. They had kept them in a dark, windowless room just off the entrance before dragging them out onto the wide portico of the Hall. They had even put out all lights on the trip up from the dungeons but for the lanterns the guards carried for their own use. They wanted them to be caught blinking and cringing when the sun struck them, to make them look more villainous and guilty. Lark refused to allow that. She had closed her eyes, concentrating on turning off that which allowed her to see in the pitch. She cracked her eyes the moment the doors were open to start the adjustment.

The result was her stepping out in the line, chained to the prisoners on either side of her, with a calm serenity she wasn't sure she fully felt. Well, she wasn't sure if it was her own confidence in coming events or the dragon's assurity, but she could feel the presence of the Cardinals scattered in the crowd.

It did not take long for her to find her familiar who stayed obediently with Mouse, crouched on a nearby roof. Or Landros, hooded near the front. Finding him let her pick out Ivan with ease, led her to assume the cloaked man between them to be the king. She nodded solemnly to them before casting her gaze out over the rest of the crowd. Things were going to plan then.

She found Portholus, not far away and in a hidden position well suited to cause mischief if called for, as well as Rog, Adrick and Rue. Just off to the side of the portico, right up to the very edge were three figures in cloaks of blue, purple and black respectively. The crowd was kept back from them, not by the soldiers who had moved away from them, but by the half ring of priests and priest-esses who stood behind them with their backs confidently to the crowd.

Lark smiled at them, felt heartened by the looks the triumvir-ate gave her. Mother Mylenai gave her a stately nod, Maid Jeliana merely winked with a smirk, but the Crone, whose name she did not know, had a very smug look on her face.

She realized, then, that the magistrate was talking, droning on as he introduced a lord.

Landros stood silently beside his baharen and his king, trying not to lose his temper at the man's words, or look overmuch at the dishevelled state of the woman he loved. That she stood there so calmly in spite of the chains he knew always induced panic, helped him to not act just yet.

Lord Harsus Malius stood centre stage on the apron of the por-tico, basking in the early sun. He looked resplendent in clothes that were fitting for both a high noble and a soldier. His rich brown hair lay back across his scalp in oiled waves, and his face was conven-tionally attractive. His smile was broad and believable and tinged with sadness and regret when appropriate. He had spent a moment to bask in the gratitude and adulation of having broken the siege, but then turned his acceptance to apologies.

"I welcome your thanks, but alas I should, in truth, be begging your forgiveness. We should have been here sooner, months ago, but the king did not believe that anyone would dare, and would not allow the armies to be deployed or for any to investigate." A tense silence captured the crowd. "I sent my own scouts, gathered my own intel. When I learned of the horrors being suffered at our most treasured coast, I secretly gathered my own men, men loyal to the kingdom if not this callous crown, and marched to relieve you of your burden! This should not have been allowed to get this far!"

On a whim, Lark cast a small spell. She drew a rune on the ground with her bare toes, imbuing the very stone of the portico with an enforcement of Truth.

The Crone grinned, cackling softly to herself, and Lark clearly saw the lines of magic intensify as all three of the triumvirate began to reinforce what she had done. She glanced towards the hierophant, standing beside the magistrate, saw the look of startlement, then panic on his face.

He whispered frantically to the magistrate who immediately tried to stop the speaker. The lord shrugged him off, full of his self-aggrandizing words and self-righteousness.

"If the king were half the man his father had been, he would have led the charge the moment word had reached us! But I am loyal to the idea of this kingdom, as it stood under the hand of the late king, Randalst IV. I will do everything in my power to bring us back to those glorious golden days! I will take the traitor FitzWaller back to the capitol in chains to confess before the king. These others, deluded by him, I will leave to the mercies of your own justice."

"Lord Malius," the magistrate tried to insist. He was once more shaken off, this time with a hard word and a glare.

Lark saw her brother's head tilt towards his companion. The hood tipped up just enough to project the voice while still obscuring the face. **"Did the king truly abandon us?"**

She smiled as the magistrate pulled at the lord's arm even as he answered without thinking: "Of course not. He had absolutely no knowledge of the siege." He choked immediately upon his words, even as the crowd began to murmur.

"I am trying to tell you, there is a spell at work," the magistrate hissed loudly.

"How could he not have known?" demanded a woman

near the front.

The lord tried not to answer. He really did. He went so far as to clamp his hand over his mouth to force himself not to say the words that eventually were mumbled.

The woman shouted at him to say that again. Someone else bellowed for him to speak up.

"Because I prevented it!" he blurted.

His face turned red and the Magistrate pushed him back away from the edge of the crowd and shouted. "There is a spell at work! Foul magic designed to force words from our mouths to elicit a specific response!"

"It's called the Truth, you pompous jackass!" bellowed the former Mayor. This caused a spattering of laughter amid the growing mutter.

"Did the Lord Mayor really betray us?" Landros shouted. This was something he dearly wanted to know.

"No." His eyes bugged and he added hastily, "I will answer no more questions. This assembly is ended!"

The crowd surged in response, angry at being left hanging with so many questions still unanswered. The soldiers moved to push back, brandishing their weapons.

FitzWaller took a step forward, ignoring the sword the guard aimed at him, or the fact that the motion pulled at the chains of the others attached to him. "Why did you frame me for treason?"

"Because you were in the way!" the magistrate screamed. "You were more interested in the reasons for crime than punishing it!" He immediately closed his mouth, refusing to say more. Apparently his will was only a little stronger than Lord Malius.

The hierophant stepped forth, letting his voice boom out over the about-to-riot crowd. "There is a spell in effect, interfering with the purpose of this assembly!" he shouted. The masses quieted a little. The man commanded a bit more respect than the magistrate, apparently. "Until such time as we can determine the nature, source and purpose of this spell, do not believe the words of anyone standing up here!"

As he was speaking, the man between Landros and Ivan moved towards the steps with the pair of them flanking him. There was a brief moment at the foot of the steps, as a knight sought to prevent him, then he saw what the hood hid, shifted and fell to his knee. His nearest fellows followed immediate suit. The three of them strode up onto the stage and the king dropped his borrowed cloak.

"Then believe me!" he intoned.

The crowd looked, fell to a hushed murmur as those who recognised the face upon their coin informed those near them who did not. Those on the portico with him had very different reactions. The guards of the prisoners lowered their heads, but maintained their vigilance. D'Meysen paled, but bowed. The magistrate also bowed, but inched closer to the edge, in the shadows of the overhang. Lord Malius went white, and it was clear he was straining to keep his mouth shut.

The king turned to the hierophant. "You are?" he asked, only a trace of disdain in his voice.

"I am the Hierophant of the Temple of Three, if it pleases your majesty."

Landros heard the Crone grumble, "It doesn't please *us*," and grinned.

"Ah, a man of magic," the king smiled. "Do you know the effect of the spell in play?"

"I... there has not been time to fully assess..." he began carefully.

"I did not ask if you had assessed it. I asked if you knew."

"I do, your majesty." His face began to turn slightly red.

"And...?" he prompted sternly.

"It's... a truth spell."

"So," the king grinned, "you are saying that everything said up here has been the absolute truth from the moment the spell went into effect?"

His face grew redder. "Yes, your majesty."

"Ah, good. So why are you trying to suppress these truths?"

The man sighed, giving up on any deception. "Because it was in my best interests to do so until the damage could be assessed."

"The damage to what?"

"My reputation, my power base. I wanted time to twist things to my advantage. That is all, your majesty. I believed the lies we were told about your not caring. At least mostly," he confessed. "I am guilty of ambition, but not treason, your majesty."

The king waved him back, and the man obeyed without hesitation. Though he did glance down at the three women of the temple who glowered at him. Only then did the heirophant show any signs of fear.

As the king turned to Lord Malius, Landros crossed to the back of the portico and seized the magistrate by the shoulder, preventing him from slipping down and into the crowd. He smiled to see his brother, Portholus, standing there with a sword in hand, waving the man back onto the platform.

Portholus leapt up onto the raised stone after him, taking the man from his brother. "Go get her," he grinned.

Landros did not need any further urging. He crossed to the head of the guards and took the keys from him even whilst the king interrogated Lord Malius. He unlocked Lark first, pulling her into an intense kiss that caused a roar from the crowd.

The king glanced over with a wry grin, but a warning eye. Chagrined, the elf bowed his head and turned to unlock the other prisoners, starting with the former Lord Mayor.

"I am sorry for the hand I had in your..." he began.

FitzWaller clapped him on the shoulder, interrupting him. "Water under the bridge. You were used. I would not have had you do anything less with the knowledge you had. I am only sorry for the torment you must have suffered under such a heavy burden, battling between loyalty and betrayal."

He nodded his acceptance, too full of emotions to give voice to any of them. He turned back to start undoing the other chains, only to find that Lark had opened all of them with her runes. She stood beside him, smiling with relief. Taking his hand in hers, she turned to listen to the king.

That was when Felise appeared on the platform out of nowhere, at a respectful distance, startling quite a few. "I have evidence to give, your majesty, that will confirm this lord's intentions."

The king turned and Felise bowed. The lord looked like he might take the opportunity to bolt, but the knights that moments before were protecting him from the press of the people now faced him, weapons at the ready.

"You can attest that this man planned treason?"

Felise shook her head. "Not directly, sire. But I overheard the plan between conspirators: a Mushyan witch and an unknown who claimed to be close to your person. However, you are free to ask him if he was involved in these plots and his answer will be honest. If he is guilty, will he not incriminate himself?"

The king smiled broadly. "So he will. Please, illuminate us."

Felise began to recite the plans that she had overheard, including the intent to assassinate the king, blame it upon FitzWaller and place Lord Malius upon the throne in his stead.

Of course, Malius could not truthfully deny the charges, though he did try to twist his way out of some of them with clever wording. The king was not having it. "You stood here and spoke of betrayal and broken trusts, all the while you were the most guilty of that crime. I trusted you because my father trusted you, swore by your administrative skills. Did he know how underhanded and devious you are? That you would take his son's life and throne?"

Lord Malius had apparently had enough. "Your father hated your ideals, your wild egalitarian notions! He thought you were weak and ill-suited to be his successor! He trusted me to keep the kingdom in line and running smoothly!"

"So you raised tolls and import taxes and withheld them from the royal coffers?"

Lark did not think the man could get any paler.

"What, you thought I would not discover your duplicity? I had hoped it were not you, but... once I had the first thread, the rest unravelled nicely. Guards, take him into custody. Find him some dark hole to abide in until I am prepared to leave."

The former Lord Mayor stepped forward, bowed. "I know just

the place for him, your majesty. For him and yon magistrate both."

"Lord William!" the king exclaimed, smiled to recognize the man, then frowned at the state of him. "I take it to be the same hole they stashed you in?"

FitzWaller's grin was feral. "Aye, sire. It is the most secure hole in the province."

"Hmm, yes. But first bring this magistate forth. I would interrogate him on his involvement whilst this wonderful spell is still in effect."

Lark cleared her throat. When she had the king's eye, she gave a shallow curtsey and a grin. "Your majesty may take his time. Spell is in very stone. No lie may be spoken here, now or ever. Though compulsion to answer, this will fade. That was not me." She glanced towards the holy three at that, found her assumptions confirmed.

The king looked impressed. He smiled at her, then turned to FitzWaller as Portholus dragged the magistrate to the front of the apron. "Lord William, would you like to do the honours? Seeing as you were the one to suffer the most at his hands. Not to mention this being your city."

"My city again?" he asked, his eyes damp, and not just with the bright.

Lark grinned at him. "Your city *still*." The crowd sent up a roar at that, proving her words.

His eyes spilled. He took a deep breath, bathing in the cheers of a city glad to have their hero back, and eager to have him confront the villain.

"Alright, Timmons," he growled.

Lark was a little startled. She had never heard the man's name before, never known him as anything other than 'the magistrate'. She shuddered at the thought of losing oneself so far into one's job that you lost all other identity.

Felise slipped up to the other side of her, opposite Landros who had wrapped his arm around her waist and had yet to let go. She passed the wood-sheathed sword to her. "*Daskvi,*" she said softly, grinning.

Lark blushed as she accepted her scimitar. "Am thinking I prefer Standard."

"Too late. I think it's ingrained in th' others. Those of us without our own like th' idea of having one."

She sighed. "Is not like need army any more."

"Dare I ask?" injected Landros.

"Not yet," she whispered, nudging him to pay attention to the interrogation.

"How long were you working with the enemy?" they heard.

There was a growl from Timmons. "In the beginning I was just taking advantage of opportunities to undermine you!"

The Lord Mayor growled dismissively at that. "That I understand. You've always been petty. At what point did you actively ally yourself with the enemy?"

The eyes glittered. "Ah, but I didn't. I was allied with Lord Malius. His factor came to me, explained what was truly going on. I saw an opportunity to make this town better than it ever was. Clean it out of the undesirable, re-codify the laws, and if I helped a more suitable man ascend the throne, so-be-it. I kept the majority safe. I always made sure that any breaches were covered by my own men, so the enemy never really broke through. I did what I thought was best for this city!"

FitzWaller sighed. "And that is the greatest tragedy of all." He looked out over the crowd, saw the rage and betrayal on their faces. He turned to the king. "Sire, while a great deal of his crimes were against this city, he agreed to help a man overthrow your majesty. Therefore, in the interest of justice and his own safety, I think it best he join Lord Malius at your majesty's pleasure. I believe this lot would rip him apart, and I think they have suffered enough."

The king set a comforting hand on his shoulder. "It is your city he has betrayed, he is your vassal. If this is what you wish, I will honour it."

"Thank you, your majesty," he bowed. "Now, if it is all the same," he added with a wry expression, "I do not know about those poor souls in the higher cells, but the lady Lark and I have not been fed since she was arrested a few days ago and, like most of this city, we could use a mouthful of bread."

Lark's stomach growled loudly at that, but she ignored it for a moment. "Other prisoners should be freed. Have friends in those cells no more deserving of arrest than I."

He nodded, turned to one of the guards on the platform. "See to it, Sargent, that any who were arrested under Timmons' orders since my own incarceration are freed. I will want the records gone through this week of all who have been jailed, to make certain they are justly held. Also make certain every soul in that prison is accounted for and their crimes known. I will begin dealing with that myself starting tomorrow until I can find a new magistrate."

Landros bowed his head, "Your majesty, your lordship, if you would follow me to the council table, I might be able to take care of that, for us and perhaps for the prisoners."

Lark looked at him. "Are sure?"

He shrugged. "The Warren is fed. The Lambs are fed. And these people have suffered." He ran his hands through her hair on either side of her face, rubbing at a bit of dirt on her cheek with his thumb. "Have you suffered?"

She broke him with her smile. "Intermittently."

Nightingale dropped to her shoulder now that it was clearly safe to do so, began to nuzzle and fuss at her. She laughed as she stroked his feathers. "Am well, dirty, but hale. You've had adventures, I hear."

The bird gave a sudden, deep exhale and settled in a tired fluff of feathers on her shoulder.

They laughed as a guard escorted them to the great council room. Landros pulled his blanket out of his satchel and spread it. She set a hand on his as he leaned in to whisper the magic words. He looked up, saw her smile and stepped back, allowing her to bend, stroking the fabric and whisper the command.

He was shocked when the blanket began to provide enormous amounts of food, more than it ever had before. Lark began sliding dishes off of it as quickly as they appeared. Felise was there, helping, then Mouse and Portholus. Gathering his wits, he began to do the same, even though his eyes were bugging nearly as much as those who had stopped in the entrance of the room to stare in awe. The king was first and foremost, and no one was willing to push past him, but even the guards were gawking.

Finally, when the table could hold no more, Lark whispered again to the cloth and it stopped its provisioning.

Once more attached at her hip, Landros whispered, "How did you..."

She gave him a tired little smile, even as she picked up an airy roll filled with creamy cheese and fruit. "It might need to rest day or two, but will be fine. Will tell all tonight."

They moved back from the table, bowing to allow the king to approach the feast. He stood before the spread, frowning. "If you had this ability, why are so many hungry?" he asked, still too shocked to speak more eloquently.

"The blanket has never provided so much, your majesty," Landros answered. "And I have used it every day I have been in town to make certain that the orphaned and homeless children of this city did not starve."

The man seemed mollified, but still gestured his hand to the palatial spread before them. "And now?"

Lark blushed. "Merely enhancement, your majesty. But taxes both of us, blanket and self."

He chuckled, waved to the roll in her hand. "Eat, my lady. We can talk later." He turned to those who were filtering into the room in his wake following the intoxicating smells. "Please, every soul, eat. Prisoners first, then the most vulnerable outside." He began to issue orders, designating people to oversee the banquet and other matters.

Lark moved aside, quietly eating her roll. She would have stopped there, but both Landros and FitzWaller fussed at her to eat more than that. She conceded with a large chunk of ham, realizing as her stomach took possession of the roll that she was really hungry.

As she sat in one of the council chairs along the wall watching the steady stream of the starving, Ivan dropped down beside her. Landros stood guard nearby, as if afraid to let her out of his sight again. She leaned against her brother. "Have fun?" she asked.

He just laughed, putting his arm around her shoulders. "Most in years. You are great deal of trouble, Yani."

She grinned tiredly, "Would you have any other way?"

"I wouldn't," Landros growled.

Lark smiled up at him.

"You are doomed, brother!" Ivan crowed.

"Yup," Landros agreed happily.

Lark pushed at both of them, smiling all the while.

They were distracted by the approach of the Mayor. He actually bowed before Lark, which made the two other men frown in confusion.

"Well, my lady," he began.

She interrupted politely, "Oh, am no lady, your lordship. Merely lowly Romeri entertainer."

He chuckled, "Were we still upon the steps of the Hall, young lady, I doubt those words could leave your lips. Lowly? Most certainly not. *Merely an entertainer?* My lady, you are not *merely* anything," he insisted, shaking his head. "If you are staying..."

She shrugged, "Is my caravan now. What choice is left?"

He nodded. "Then to have the freedom to do what you must, to make the decisions you will,... you will need be among the rank and file." Lark groaned at that. "What man of authority would listen to you otherwise?" he asked with an arched brow. "Besides myself, of course?"

"Lord Colwyn," she began.

He laughed. "Well, one man is not enough. I would have you named and ranked, that you might move as you choose and give orders where you need. If it would not offend your clan?" he asked, just realizing the man sitting beside her, glowering at him, was her kin.

"To have one of our own named and landed like gegenta?" he

huffed, puffing himself up. Then, just as swiftly, he deflated with a chuffing laugh. "Will have to ask father. Has never been done."

"And Gruma," she added.

He nodded ruefully.

The Mayor shook his head, "I will give you time to think, talk it over. But to have a say at the Council Table, you will need a title at the very least." He started to move away, turned back, pulling something from around his neck. "Oh, I would return this to you. And thank you for it's use. It helped."

She shook her head. "Keep. Is not like am needing it now."

He hesitated. "You are certain?"

"Insistant," she smiled.

Finally, he nodded and walked away, allowing room for the others who wanted her attention.

The moment he was gone, she was attacked by Dane, hugging her for all he was worth. "You're all right!" he exclaimed.

She returned the embrace, but looked up at his mother, more patiently waiting her turn with her brother-in-law standing protectively behind her. "Why is allowed to come?!" Lark demanded. "Could have been dangerous!"

Neneis grunted. "I couldn't stop him, so I kept him to the sides and back. There was a young man who stood with us, promised me should anything go south Dane would be whisked to safety faster than I could get him there."

"Tam," Dane said. "We were right by a tunnel," he explained, reaching back to hug his mother as well.

Lily clasped her friend tightly, letting her son draw her into the three way embrace.

"Am so sorry got you into this," Lark began.

Lily shook her head. "No you don't. Things would have been so much worse without you, so don't... don't even try... Oh, goddess! I am just so glad you are all right!"

Daskvi, came the thoughts of Billy, ***there are others who want to see you, too.***

Warren? she asked.

Tent Town. I'm not going to cross that old woman!

Lark laughed, confusing those who were gathered around her. "Come," she said. "I would see my other family now. Worried sick must be!" She squeezed Dane a little tighter before letting him go. "You, too," she said.

Without a word to anyone else, the group of them slipped away, and out into the city.

TWO

Tent Town had been utterly transformed by the time that Landros and Lark reached it. Gone were the gathering tents of soldiers and the detritus of years of squatters. The red-roofed wagons were no longer clustered against the inner wall, but were now centred in the old Fairgrounds in a loose, open circle near the tree where Lark's own wagon once stood. A large fire had been lit in the middle, and the women of the caravan were gathered around a smaller one serving food to the long line of ragged people who wound their way in.

It seemed to Landros that there were more wagons here now than there had been when he had left just hours ago. The men were sitting around the main fire, playing music, smoking, drinking coffee and watching the children at play.

As they crossed the weak and worn grass, Landros and Ivan fell back, allowing Lark to go alone, though they were not far behind.

She felt everything she had always felt as a little girl approaching her father, especially after there had been trouble. Petrov stood, waiting for her. The musicians paused, waiting to see what would happen. She stopped just a few feet from him, looking up with wet eyes, and fear at what would happen now. She was prepared to be declared *genti*, but it would hurt.

Then he was pulling her into a fierce hug, crushing her against him, weeping himself.

Everyone pretended nothing was happening, even though the air of intense relief was palpable.

When he finally let her go, Lark saw Gruma standing nearby, hugged her far more gently, though there was strength in the old woman yet. No sooner had she stepped back than she was swarmed, and not just by the children of the camp. It seemed the entire Warren had found their way here, including Analie and Navarel. She was highly surprised to see Keltree lingering by one of the wagons, flirting with a young lady.

Catching her eye, he kissed the girl's hand and found his way over to her. "Welcome home, my lady!" he grinned.

Landros came over, clasping Keltree's wrist and clapping his arm. "Good to see you up and about!" he crowed, then gestured to the fairgrounds. "Any of this your doing?"

Keltree's eyes twinkled. "From what I hear, this is ninety percent your fault."

Landros growled good-naturedly, but did not deny it. "I mean, where are the soldiers? When Stephen, Ox and I left here this morning, it was crawling with them."

The taller man laughed, an easy sound. "Oh, that," he said casually. "A higher ranked lord than our 'sainted deliverer' ran them out, issued orders for them to camp outside the walls and make certain that the gates were kept safe and clear. The rest of this..." He gestured off towards Old Ruby, sitting next to the fire chatting with some of the Warren children. "Let us just say, that lady there wields some unquestionable power and leave it politely at that."

Landros glanced that way and his expression was all that needed to be said.

Once the initial swarm was over, and the food line had dwindled, Lark sat with her family around the main fire. Ivan had given her his own seat, choosing to sit at his wife's feet surrounded by his sons and cradling his infant daughter. Landros had accepted a stump near Lark, and in the shadows of the old oak, Keltree and

Portholus lounged and listened, content to prop up the great, twisting trunk.

"You have story to tell us, daughter," her father said. "We gleaned bits from Ox's baharen, but I am told there is much not known."

She nodded, took a deep breath to put herself in the tale-telling mindset. She began with the story of Eshanai, and how the Mushyan witch had killed her and murdered her children seeking the power of life. From there, she wove the tale in with some of her own adventures, those that pertained to Eshanai and her own calling. During her telling, the audience grew. A fact she noticed when friends who had been part of those adventures made a laughing comment or injected something into the narrative. Many of them were injured. It warmed her soul to see them here, though she wondered how they had known to come.

She told then of her return to the Warren during the last bombardment, the evening that led to her joining with the dragon and gifting her children to the Cardinals.

The faint sliver of the waxing moon was high in the sky when her tale was done. Though it had sounded the purest fantasy, no one doubted a word of it. In the silence that reigned after, Lark slipped her hand into Landros', even as she scratched the ears of the over-fed racoon sleeping in her lap.

She waited, fearful of what her father would say, waiting for the explosion as he railed at her for throwing away her hereditary place as head of her clan to be a stationary ranie of a gegenta city.

It took him a long time to answer. He only looked to Old Ruby once. It seemed the old woman, too, was waiting to see what he would say.

Finally, "Some how I knew. As I did not get to keep my beautiful Danine, neither could I keep my daughter who was so much like her." There were tears in his eyes. Rosita, standing behind him, bent and pressed a kiss to the top of his head, squeezed his shoulder gently. "What greater glory is for us, but to defeat Mushyan?"

"Is... all right with this?" she asked, cautious still.

He threw up his hands in exasperation. "My daughter is dragon! What choice have I?"

Laughter shattered the tension in the camp.

Lark began laughing and crying at the same time, feeling pride welling up within her. Landros, bubbling over with relief, pulled her to him and kissed her, displacing the now-grumpy racoon. She melted, returned his passion in kind. She had been without him for so long she had not realized until now that it had physically hurt.

And then the roaring came.

They turned, saw Petrov rising from his seat in near apoplexy. "What is this!?" he bellowed.

Lark pulled Landros behind her, shielding him, even as he was trying to do the same. She could feel his panic feeding her own.

"I love him, Papa!" she cried, twisting her bare feet into the earth in case she needed to move it. "I am ranie in own right. Even you have accepted this! I can love where I please!"

"Ranie or not! I will not have member of my clan running around with gegenti!"

Ivan stood, his crying daughter now in her mother's arms. "He is my baharen!" he shouted.

"Baharen or not, he is not Romer!" He stepped towards her, towering over both of them. "No," he bellowed. "I forbid my daughter to run about kissing gegenta elf unless she is married to him!"

Lark was roaring with anger now, closed the gap between them. "I am ranie in my own right! Can make own choices, lie where I choose! Are in *my* caravan, you pompous...."

"Sweet-heart," Landros said, pulling her back. The calm in his voice catching her off-guard, but she ploughed on heedlessly.

"NO!" she snarled, blinking away tears. "Have seen that future, cannot live what I have seen if cannot have you!"

He gave her a soft, lop-sided grin, cradled her cheek in his hand. "So? Marry me then, *simoya ellinoia.*"

Somehow, that got through. But she could not have heard what she thought. "What?"

"Marry me."

"But father..." She half-turned to look at him, saw him still puffed up, but waiting to hear what she would say. There was a laughing light in his eyes. "Father..."

"You will set own traditions, my child, but first must respect your mother's," he growled. "Well, are going to answer him or leave hanging like poor Gregor?"

She looked up into the golden eyes of the man she loved, still not quite believing this was real.

"Please don't leave me hanging like poor Gregor," he begged. "I've heard stories...."

"Yeees?" she began. Nightingale scolded her from the eaves of the nearest wagon, where he had flown when things had exploded. "*Sesha*!" she wept, letting him crush her against him.

"About fucking time," Portholus exclaimed, just as cheers erupted around the camp.

Ivan sank back to the ground like he had been hit by a hammer, groaning. His head was still reeling.

Finally, she pulled away, turning in his arms as he refused to let go of her. She wiped her eyes as she looked at her father. "Why? All this time, this fear you would hate me for loving him..."

Petrov sighed. "My daughter, my joy... Too much like your mother, you are. Once... once upon time, yes, would have railed, forbade ...this. But... too close to losing you. Am seeing is this or nothing, and," he glanced towards Old Ruby, "am being told is what *must* happen. He has proven himself to have Romeri soul, would move earth and sky for you. Besides, to see you glow so bright, how can say no?"

She let him envelope her in a great, bear-like hug, both of them too overcome with emotions to trust to further words right now.

Landros glanced towards Ruby, happened to notice the reedy little girl that had helped the night of the baharen ritual standing beside her, watching everything with dark eyes that were at once sad and happy. Something was different about her, but it was nothing he could place. Scraps was lurking nearby, drawn to her, but afraid of the old lady. He called the animal to him, luring him with a bit of dried apple.

Scraps happily clambered up into his hood, snatching the apple on his way.

Lark was beside him again, poking the raccoon's rounded belly through the hood. "Will explode, you eat much more," she teased.

Landros laughed, lighter in his heart than he had been in a very long time. "He'd die happy," he smirked. Turning slightly away from the person in question, he softly asked, "Who is the little girl by your grandmother? The fifteen-year old with the sad eyes?"

Lark peeked, frowned. "Vadoma? Is youngest sister. And is eleven."

He pulled back. "No, she's at least fifteen if she's a year!" he exclaimed, glanced to confirm his suppositions.

She just laughed at him. "Are doing again," she said, poking him in the ribs. "Human children age faster," she reminded. He groaned, "Come, I will introduce you to Magpie." She dropped to a whisper as she wrapped her arm around his, "Whatever you do, do not call her 'Maggie'. Quick with curses that one," she grinned. "And very creative."

"Great, another family member I don't want to cross!" he groaned.

She laughed. "Especially not Vadoma. Now that I have my own caravan, is she who will one day stand ranie as I was supposed to."

"One day sooner than all would like," Ruby grunted.

"Gruma, no! Do not say such things. I will not speak of losing you fortnight from my wedding day!" Lark protested.

"A fortnight?" Landros asked, shocked by the time frame. Trouble was, he wasn't sure if it was too long or too short for his comfort.

"*Sesha*, Kestrel," Vadoma grinned. "Romeri weddings are held on full moon. Will take this long for word to spread and family to gather."

Lark looked from her grandmother to her sister. "You have met?"

The girl grinned. "I helped with his birthing!"

He blushed to have it described in quite those terms, which only made her giggle.

"Magpie, be nice," Ruby grunted.

Vadoma backed off, though she sniffed. "Needs to get used to being treated like brother. Is not like this one will run off, like Arturi did."

"That was too easy," Ivan grunted, meandering over. "That one was only wanting to be king one day. He was not worthy," he said, handing his now sleeping daughter to Vadoma. "Would put in cradle, please, little sister?"

She took the baby, but protested. "Why me? Where's Jena?"

"Over by fire, enjoying music of blind fiddler. Deserves some peace, that woman! And you are not ranie yet, Magpie!"

Gruma chuckled. "Even after, will be stuck with mewing babes. Is part of job. Shoo." She sent the girl off with a light swat, all without waking the infant.

"Dane is playing?" Lark asked.

"Winning hearts," he crowed. "Father is talking with his mother about taking for year."

Landros groaned. "That's going to be a hard sell."

Lark shook her head. "Not so much. Maybe more now is no siege, but had agreed before this. Now is just..." she sought for the right words.

"Negotiations?" he grinned.

"*Sesha!*"

Ivan deftly used the hand still on the elf's shoulder to turn him towards the main fire, near where the musicians were playing. "But I came over to tell you there is visitor for you. ...Both."

"Visitor?" they asked together. When they saw who was standing in the gathering circle, they both felt a heavy weight dropping onto them.

'Stephan' was back, flanked by several very uncomfortable looking knights in plain clothes. He was handing his cloak back to Gregor, chatting with him amiably. Landros also noticed Lord Colwyn as part of the entourage. He, alone, looked perfectly at ease in the simple tunic and coat.

Without much more urging, the three of them crossed the distance and waited politely to be acknowledged. Landros restrained himself from bowing, or otherwise behaving any differently than he had all day. The king was still just 'Stephan'.

Ivan did not observe such niceties. He strode up, offering his arm in friendship and shared a familiar laugh. A fact which caused several of the knights in his retinue to bristle at the informality. Colwyn glared pointedly at them, and they restrained themselves further.

"Am sorry to steal my brother-in-law, Stephan, but Fiddle and I have bet to settle. In consolation, I have brought you my sister and her," he glanced back at Landros. "Is word? *Intend*? I cannot say man who will become my brother, as he is already that."

Lark saw the confusion on some of the knights' faces, as well as the perverse delight Ivan took in it. Let these men think the worst. Their opinions did not matter.

"Then you are most readily forgiven, Ox, my friend. These are the very souls I came to see. I hope to see you again some time!"

"If you see red-roof-tops from your ivory towers, come down and dine with us!"

"Music to my ears!"

Ivan began dragging Gregor away, and Lark overheard him whisper, "*What bet are you talking about, Ox?*"

Then the king was standing in front of them and she felt a sense of formality in the air, even though no one's manner had changed.

"First," Stephan began, "allow me to congratulate you both."

They all but mumbled their thank yous.

"No, it is I who should thank you," he insisted. Just as quickly, 'Stephan' was gone and King Feremon stood before them. "Were it not for the pair of you, I would very likely have been assassinated within the week. I have also been informed of everything you and others have been doing for this city for several long months, and I feel that should be recognized." His eyes flicked to Landros, then he turned to Lark.

"My lady, I have spoken at length with Lord FitzWaller, and he has explained to me your unique... situation? For you to take the place both your people and my city need you to, as indeed you are apparently destined to...."

"Sire," said Lord Colwyn softly.

The king glanced back.

"Too many words for your audience, your majesty," he said gently. "Neither of them are much for courtly rhetoric. May I advise plain speaking?"

While some of the knights clearly thought Lord Colwyn deserved to be smote for his daring, the king thought differently. He nodded, turned back and smiled at her again. "Forgive me. I am over-used to pomp and circumstance in these situations. I am honoured to have finally met you, Lark. I have heard much of you in the last twenty-four hours. In order for you to do as you must, as I clearly need you to," he chuckled, "you must have a title. I am here to give you one."

Lark felt her whole body flare: in panic, in awe... a whole tapestry of emotions erupted in flames in a matter of seconds with those words. The unhappy shifting of men behind the king was lost on her, but not on Landros. He met the gaze of the worst of them, daring them to act on it.

"I know, I know," the king continued. "'It is not done'. The Romer hold no land and bear no title and are beholden to none but their own. But the caravan you have claimed as your own is also beholden to me, and isn't, I pray the Trinity, going to start wandering the world."

The laugh this elicited made the pair of them aware that this little meeting had the attention of the entire encampment.

"I am aware this belonged to the dragon first. But I am hoping you are willing to share it with Tembia?"

Lark finally found her voice. "We are. But as for titles, I cannot be ...noble as they expect nobility," she said, gesturing to the men behind him. "Know nothing of lands and cities and taxes and laws.

I know people, how to take care of people. I cannot be bound to hall or desk."

The king smiled. "I have recently been educated in the political system of your people. I think we can work with this. Besides, do you really think they're going to listen to you if I don't?" he asked, jerking his thumb behind him.

She had to concede that fact, glanced towards her family, who watched with interest and equal trepidation.

"And so, I hereby dub you Rana of Portswain."

Her head came up, her midnight eyes locking on his. Beside her, Landros squeezed her hand, bursting with pride for her. "How do *you* mean Rana?" she asked. She had to wonder how much he had been taught, and who had done the teaching.

"The Lord Mayor is the Captain of this caravan," he said, shrugging lightly as he explained. "For the most part, all those 'noble things' you say you are not suited to do... he does. For all intentions, he rules the city. But you, my dear, you alone save myself, have the power to overrule him. I trust you will use it wisely and sparingly."

There was an explosion from behind the king, as one or two of the more pompous knights objected. The king did not even look back, though Colwyn set his hand on his hilt, in case it was needed. "You are welcome to relocate, Lord Falwell. I am sure I can grant you a more suitable fief closer to ...Kerestan perhaps? Or maybe Evandair?"

The man stilled, but Lark could tell he was undecided yet which punishment would be worse.

"And if next Lord Mayor is like him?" she asked, waving towards Falwell.

He smiled deviously. "Well, my dear, then you had best help me choose a good one."

Any protests were drowned out by the cheering shouts of everyone else; both Romer and the dregs of the city who had come to be fed and stayed now that the atmosphere was more wholesome. Lark flushed even as she felt the surging of the dragon within her, very much pleased.

"Other than the fact that you may be formally addressed as either Lady or Rana," he continued as the noise abated some, "life will go on pretty much as it has."

"But with less arresting," Portholus injected.

Landros nearly jumped out of his skin, having not heard his brother slip up behind them.

That alone made Lark feel more comfortable with the idea. In her mind she heard the chimes of the Cardinals, tendering their own congratulations.

The king laughed and actually bowed before her, holding out his hand for hers. Drawing herself up, she accepted both, let him lightly kiss the back of her hand. "All that remains is for you to choose the name that will wear that title."

Now that there was so much noise that no one would hear but the two of them, Lark leaned in. "Are aware that in my tongue *rana* means queen, *sesha*?"

He grinned. "Only you and I will know the difference, my *queen*. And your kin... Now, if you will excuse me, my lady, I want to see if there are any of those baked apples left." He then walked away, not caring if any of his retinue followed or not.

Lord Colwyn did not. He crossed to the pair of them to offer his own congratulations, for everything. Lark did not think a man could grin quite so widely. Landros nodded his head as he accepted his handshake. He was a bit startled to feel his knight's fingers tap a very specific pattern on the inside of his wrist.

He blinked up at the man.

Colwyn smiled. "Perhaps the lady might stay with her family tomorrow night?"

"Which?" she grinned, guessing it was Falcon's business that passed so silently between them.

"Any of them. Alas, I have some repairs to do to the caravan."

She felt a stab of pain at that. "What? How bad?"

He shrugged. "Just some minor roofing. It will be right as rain overmorrow. Say, where is your feathered shadow? I haven't seen him since he left with Landros."

Lark smiled, lifting the bulk of her hair to show the bird snuggled up below her ear, sleeping soundly.

"How did he sleep through all that?" he asked, incredulous.

"Same way sleeps through everything!" she laughed.

He walked off then,shaking his head, followed the king.

"Let us go home, my heart," she whispered. She was full to bursting with everything that had happened in the last few days. While she desperately wanted sleep in a comfortable bed, there were other needs making her tetchy, and she wasn't sure how much more she could take tonight.

Landros nodded, turned to tell his brother to make himself scarce, but he had already vanished. Without another word to any-one, the pair of them strolled out of the Fairgrounds towards the Cygnet, arm in arm.

THREE

It was early morning when Landros slipped into bed with his princess. The warmth of her body nestled against his after the cooling night air was grounding for him. She purred against him, even as she drew his arms around her like blanket.

"Mmm, how go night with king?" she asked, her voice a little muzzy with sleep.

"How did you know the king was involved?" he asked.

She chuckled, waking up a little more. "Was gathering of Order Falconis. King, Head Falcon himself, is in town. You really think would not be there? So how go?"

He pulled her tight, drinking deep of the scent of her and her hair. There had been subtle changes to it in his absence, but somehow it was just more... her, intensified. "Hmmm, deduction. Here I thought someone had tattled."

She scoffed. "Nightingale? Out at night?"

"Or your mother," he added.

"Oh, I talk *to* her. She does not talk to me. Well, if she does, I am unable to hear her."

He idly played with the large emerald on her finger. "I didn't know if your new... tenant... came with... those kinds of powers."

She sighed. "I would not call her 'tenant'. She and I are one now. I have all of her essence and power and knowledge, but am still myself. And no, her powers were of life, not death. Not even Il-anil could speak with ghosts. Eshanai is more enhance my own powers than give new ones."

"Ilanil?" he asked, caught by the elven name and it's familiarity.

"*Sesha.* An elven woman who's name mean star was last keeper of Eshanai's heart. When died ...oh, year ago, am thinking... is when Mushyan began hunting, dragon-baiting."

He closed his eyes, remembering meeting the most ancient of his kind several years ago, when he had first come to Portswain. "Il-anilayana," he breathed. "It means 'the earth-bound star'."

Though Lark had never heard the name before, she felt a wash of love and loss at the sound of it; knew without a doubt they were speaking of the same woman. "Long brown hair, dark golden skin, eyes like new grass," she offered.

"Well, when I met her she had silver hair, and her green eyes had paled some, but, despite being the oldest elf who ever lived, she was still strong and handsome, wrinkled or no. Sadly, I was out of town on an adventure when she passed. Every elf in several hundred miles came to the funeral."

"Must have been quite impressive sight," she breathed, toying with his fingers.

"It was. And a sombre one. They held her in state under a great oak tree in the grove outside the city for nearly a week. Then one morning her body was just gone."

She frowned. "Did they look for it?" she was half-worried that the Mushyan had done something with it.

"No," he sighed. "The druids assured us all was as it should be."

Lark smiled then, realizing that she must have been returned to the Warren and the earth, to slumber as she awaited... her. It was not lost on her that her name and the name of her predecessor were only a handful of letters away from each other. They were only a step away in meaning, too, for Illyana meant 'light' or 'light-bringer' if you were being literal, and 'joy-bringer' if you were being poetic.

Finding something different on his hand brought her back around to her original question. "So how go? Is not squire's ring am feeling. Has more weight."

He smiled, held it up so she could see it in the dark. This new dark-vision of hers gave her a distinct advantage between them, but he would have fun trying to compensate. The ring was a simple band of gold, but bore a deeply embossed falcon in flight. "By the king's own hand," he said proudly.

"Nice. Gold is pure. Inscription is code, *sesha*?"

He frowned. "How the hells.... All right, knowing it's pure gold, I'll give you. Dragon. Whatever. How can you see the inscription? It's on the inside."

She smiled, twisting in his arms to face him, her hands immediately wandering to places that were highly unconducive to prolonged conversation. "Can taste gaps," she purred.

"What is **that** supposed to ...**Woman**!" he exclaimed as her fingers found very sensitive places. He growled as he rolled over her, pinning her to the mattress. He was tired of being the subject of physical teasing he would much rather dish out.

Lark spent a great deal of her time at her father's caravan, getting ready for the wedding. It was not unusual for her to arrive and find Gruma arguing with a bevy of women of various ages that Lark had never seen before. Most of them gave her furtive glances whenever she came up to greet her grandmother, but few would say anything until she had left. Always, the whispers after had a different tone than before her interruption.

Finally, near the end of the first week, Lark found Ruby alone but for Vadoma, who was busy embroidering something by the fire. "*No circle of squabbling biddies tonight?*" she asked as she kissed the old woman's cheek before sitting beside her.

"*No,*" she said curtly. "*They will come or they will not.*"

"*What are they all arguing about?*"

Vadoma all but growled as she pricked her finger with her needle in the dim light. *"They are arguing about whether or not you deserve Romeri wedding!"* she snapped.

Lark cast a were-light and hung it in the air over her sister's shoulder. The soft light illuminating a red-velvet vest which the girl was embroidering with golden thread. *"What?"* she exclaimed when she realized what was said.

"Thank you, Yani," Vadoma said, referring to the light.

"Welcome. But why? Is horseshit having to do with him being blood-brother and not blood-Romer?" she snapped.

Her grandmother snorted. *"More that is not human. Also, you give up rule of your clan for gegenta city. Some claim you are more genti than Gypsy."*

Lark could feel the slow burn of anger beginning to simmer within. But her sister was grinning, and not entirely kindly.

"When told you do this to thwart Mushyana, begin to change tune. Some because mad respect, others," here her grin grew wider, *"because fear to insult woman of such power."*

Ruby cackled. *"Helped you showing up when you did."*

"Like you didn't time that perfectly," Vadoma snorted.

Ruby ignored her. *"All but weakest ranie could smell your strength and magic. Heh, one even said could smell dragon."*

Lark felt mollified, but only a little. She did laugh softly as she remembered the look on the women's faces. Knowing what she did now explained quite a few of them. She poked the fire a bit, checked the pot of tea brewing over it. *"So will come?"* she asked as casually as she could manage.

"Most," Vadoma said, trying to act as grown up as she could. She knew that one day she would be counted among them, and more powerful than most. The Rushavska clan was among the largest, not to mention had just secured safe and easy passage, as well as legal protections, within the kingdom of Tembia. That carried a lot of weight that she felt she had to live up to. That and being a seventh child.

Lark watched her, smiled. *"Do not let it change you too much,"* she advised.

Magpie looked up, startled that her thoughts had been so easily read. *"How..."*

Lark laughed. *"Dragon. Apparently blood ties have advantages. When you come to power I will try to give you gift."*

She narrowed her dark eyes. *"What you mean 'try'?"*

"I mean, hope will have figured out how by then. Want to see if can imbue you with ability I have with my children."

Her sister gave her a look that made her laugh even as she explained about the dragon's children and her new connection to the Cardinals who had joined with them. *"But, do have gift can give you now,"* she said, crossing over to sit beside her. She pulled the emerald ring from her finger.

Magpie's eyes grew wide and her jaw hung slack as her sister slid the ring on. She drew in a slow, gasped breath. *"But mama... gruma...."*

Lark cradled her cheek tenderly. *"Was given to me because was eldest and heir. Is Rushavska heirloom, should go to Rushavska heir, which is you, little one. I am not exactly Rushavska any more,"* she added softly. She had expected her sister to protest that, for Ruby to growl something at her. Goddesses knew that her father would. But none of that happened.

Vadoma looked up at her knowingly, almost shyly, from admiring the heavy emerald that hung a little loosely on her thumb. *"I... I know. Are something new, something different. Mother said will take new name on wedding day. Have you decided, yet?"*

Lark shook her head. She had a couple of ideas, but nothing concrete.

A blush crept up on her sister's cheeks as she shifted the fabric on her lap, passing it to her. *"Maybe this might help,"* she said.

Lark slowly accepted it, looking over the garment. It was like all her other vests, a rich red velvet that laced up with ribbon to make a snug bodice. Only, instead of embroidering flowering vines, etc, along the edges of the garment, she had created a band that was centred on the shoulder and ran straight down, almost to the hem, front and back. She had already started a matching band on the left side. What caught her eye the most, was not the precious thread of gold, or the delicately twisting vine border, but the stylized dragon that wound its way through roots and branches and tiny, underground creatures. A glittering red bead had been sewn for the eyes. The dragon had been draped over the shoulder, with its tail weaving through the roots on the back, and its head stopping somewhere near the top of her breast, watching benevolently.

The work was breath-taking. It was clear her sister had taken a great deal of time making sure it was perfect. "*This... is this for...*"

"*I know every clan has to have own identifier, pattern or colour. I thought... might use this? Red, to mark origin, and gold for dragon?*" When her sister said nothing to this, she babbled nervously on. "*Don't have to use it. But thought... might look nice to trim wagon? Would not be insulted if just wanted for wedding... I...*"

Lark pulled the girl into a hug. A few seconds later both were teary-eyed.

"*Am sorry to put this burden on you,*" Lark whispered.

"*Was always little jealous was supposed to be you,*" Vadoma answered to her surprise, as they pulled back from the embrace.

"*What?*"

"*Sesha,*" Vadoma confessed, wiping at her eyes. "*Was more than little mad you walk away from this. Seemed were throwing away what I would have killed for.*"

Lark brought her finger up threateningly, tapped her sister's slightly reddened nose. "*Never say that. Never kill to become ranie. Is bad for all, even in thought.*"

"*I know,*" she protested. "*But you understand my meaning. I understand now why had to.*"

"*Sagavis,*" they both said at the same time. The synchronisity made them laugh.

"*Well, you may one day be angry with me again for saddling you with. But truthfully, when choice was made... was only able to make sacrifice knowing you would succeed me. That you were here for them as I could not be. Rule wisely, little sister."*

"Don't forget us, big sister," she countered, grinning.

Gruma sat on her stool throughout the exchange, smoking her pipe and staring into the warmth of the fire with a knowing smile.

"Request, though," Lark began, going back to the vest. *"This second band, do opposite? So dragons look toward each other?"*

"Can do that. I drew pattern out, so can paint on wagon if want."

"Would be lovely. Know someone who likes this kind of work," she grinned. *"Maybe use gold silk laces? Gold ribbons are good markers too."*

Portholus was helping Landros with his end of the wedding. Ivan had explained what was needed, what would be expected, was helping with the Romer matters. Portholus had decided to take him to get wedding clothes made, and of course, Landros had insisted on going to Bianca.

"You sure you should be wearing Elven wedding finery and not Romer stuff?" Portholus asked him while watching the woman laying various ribbon trims over the shoulder of the sleek, dove blue coat to test them.

"Ox said that the groom comes in as from his own clan. He joins hers after, so yes. He said Elven fashion was appropriate. There's going to be enough resentment among the clans of my ...non-humanness... that we might as well go for broke."

He shrugged. He couldn't disagree with the argument. "So... your big plans," he fished. His brother flicked his eyes in his direction. "What, you thought I didn't know about them? That you *had* big plans?"

Landros sighed, glanced down at the two trims that Bianca was deciding between and touched the woven ribbon with tiny dragons flitting like butterflies through vines of morning glories. "That one, I think."

She smiled. "You are absolutely right. The purple of the flowers will draw the eyes without clashing with the base fabric. I'll be right back."

When she left the two of them alone, he turned to him. "I may have to leave that up to you, little brother. I do believe my life is going to be quite full soon."

He laughed. "Never a dull moment?"

"Goddess, no!" he exclaimed with a grin.

Portholus sobered, leaned back against the only bare portion of wall as he regarded his brother. "Well, there will be time enough to get back to it, I suppose. When you're older...." he hedged.

Landros was adjusting the fit of his cuff, glanced up, "What do you mean by that?"

"Well, she's human. You're an elf."

The amber eyes grew a little harder then, darkened. "Your point?"

"On the tip of your ears," his brother smirked. "No, seriously. We live on average three, maybe four hundred years? Five if we're lucky. Humans average maybe fifty? Eighty if they're careful? What are you going to do when she... when the Crone calls."

To his brother's surprise, he popped a crooked grin and went back to inspecting the coat in mirror. "Oh, I think you may want to ask her that question, not me."

"That makes no sense," he frowned, taking exception to the smirk. "What, is she going to haunt you like her mother's been watching her?"

The eyes flicked, "You know about that?"

"We've talked," he growled, "while you were off warring. I caught her talking to her mother once."

"But no. I have a feeling she'll outlive me."

"How do you come to that conclusion?" he asked, moving out of the way as Bianca returned with more of the ribbon wound on a wooden spool and went to work.

"Do you remember Ilanilayana?"

Portholus blinked in shock, confused by the change of subject.

"The oldest elf in history? Used to live in Portswain? How does one forget? She was, what? Eight hundred something?"

"Try a bit past a thousand," he said casually.

Portholus whistled. "That is... truly venerable. What about her?"

"Lark is her successor."

It took his brother a few minutes to understand what he meant by that. "She was the one who drove the Mushyan out the first time?" Landros nodded. "Ok, so...?" he asked, still missing the point.

Then the point hit him right between the eyes. "OH!"

Landros laughed, stepping off the small pedestal and letting the seamstress ease him out of the coat full of pins.

"You'll be pleased as punch with these, I promise you," Bianca chattered. "Almost makes up for the lady not coming to me for her gown..."

He smiled at her. "Her bridal clothes are being made by her family and are probably not quite as fancy. We are observing both traditions. But I promise to bring her by for something interesting later. The siege was very hard on her wardrobe."

Her fist went to her hip as anger made her cheeks flush. "I should say it has!" she snapped. "I saw the state of that poor child when they brought her out in chains! Disgraceful! The Lord Mayor was wise to let the king sort the magistrate out. No telling what the people of this city would have done to him!"

He gave her an indulgent smile. "I am just glad she said yes."

She melted immediately back into the happy, doting woman from before. "I am so glad the two of you got together! You're such a sweet couple! Now go on, both of you. I have a lot of work to do," she said, shooing them out of the workshop. "And do tell her I said hello, and that she is welcome to stop by any time, whether she is shopping or not!"

"I will," he smiled, walking out into the sunlight with his brother grinning like a satisfied tomcat. "What are you grinning about?" he half-snarled, not quite reaching his normal level of surly.

"You. I'm starting to realize just how much the thought of marrying this girl has mellowed you."

Landros frowned at him quizzically.

"I've never seen you smile this much."

"Getting everything you've ever wanted and more apparently does wonders for one's demeanour," he replied jauntily.

A few days before the wedding, Lark was relieving her nerves by performing at the Cinnamon Tree. Dane was playing with her, for her while she danced, and the Tree was busy. Lily had needed to hire extra help to serve everyone, and even so, was still run ragged by the sheer number of customers. Every chair and stool was full and there were even people standing, which was causing traffic issues for the servers.

It was a good night all around, until the pair of them took a short break. Dane headed into the kitchen while Lark settled their instruments safely behind the stool beside the hearth. Her only warning was Ivaska's snarling.

She turned in time to see Coolie kicking at the dog. She swung her scabbard to block the blow, stepping up between him and the wolfhound. She glared up into his face, not a bit afraid of him.

"Leave dog alone," she said coldly.

"Dangerous animals have no place in a tavern," he snarled.

"At least does *his* job," she said, then demanded, "What want, Coolie?"

"You may have fooled everyone else with your fake title..."

She put a fist on her hip. "So what king himself gifts is fake?" she chuffed. Behind him, she had noticed the nearest portion of the crowd growing dangerously silent, but no one made a move yet. They were subtly watching.

Coolie snorted, "One, Rana ain't a Tembian title. Two, he only made you a 'lady' to placate those too stupid to know what a conniving, thieving harlot we both know you are."

On the mantle, Nightingale made a low whistle of warning and put the corner of the chimney between him and them.

The ass jerked his chin towards the now hidden bird. "See? Even feather-head knows."

Lark laughed to keep from erupting. She set a hand on Ivaska's head as he started growling.

Someone at a nearby table muttered, "That just means trouble, dumbass."

She thought she recognized the voice.

Coolie ploughed ahead. "You're about as noble as that dog."

Her smile was genuine as she stroked the shaggy head. "Would not be so sure of this. Brother assured me Ivaska had impressive pedigree. Besides, was Romeri princess before was Tembian Rana. Not such big step."

He scoffed. "Everyone knows that king and queen of the gypsies bullshit is just that: bullshit to bilk the rubes."

"Actually impressed you know word 'rubes'," she said calmly.

"I've dealt with your kind before."

"Mmm," she nodded, beginning to understand a little. "Surprised you came away uncursed, if behaved with any of my people as have with me. Honestly, I was little afraid of my own power, or would have cursed you already. But by all means, keep going. I might still."

He leaned in, getting a mean look on his face. "Go ahead. I'll have all I'll need to hang you, bitch. Or didn't you know that it was illegal in this kingdom to cast a spell on an unwilling person."

She was aware that more than just the nearest tables had quieted. She decided to treat this as any other performance. "Oh, am certain there are exceptions for self-defence or defence of others. Doubt is soul in room who will not agree you provoked."

He turned, giving a contemptuous laugh. It was clear he was not one hundred percent comfortable with having everyone's attention, but it did not shake his confidence in the slightest. "I doubt any of them are fooled by your duplicity. After all, what 'lady' performs in a tavern?"

An elven woman stood up somewhere in the middle of the

room. She was attired as befitted a high noble 'dressing down', but there were still jewels at her ears and the very subtle cornet of a countess holding back her russet braids. "I have been known to grace a tavern or two with my voice. And danced on a public green at a harvest faire. Granted, I have taken no coin to do so, but there is nothing to say I cannot."

He clearly had no idea whom he was being addressed by, and less respect for her race. "My lady," he began, though his use of the words were less respectful than they should have been.

A man stood up beside her, hand on his hilt. "That is Countess Ashanastiliera. You will be respectful of her rank and person or you will be reminded of your manners most aggressively."

Coolie paled just a little. The name was not unknown to him, though it was not general knowledge that the countess of the north-eastern wilds had arrived with the king's ship. He actually bowed, though shallowly. "Forgive my ignorance, my lady. I did not know your identity."

Her man sat down, mollified, but she did not. "Ignorance does not excuse ill-manners. Now, what was it you were going to say to me?"

"Nothing of significance, my lady," he deflected, beginning to realise that he might have lost control of the room entirely. If he had ever actually had it. "Knowledge of your identity makes my words... moot."

She gave him a look of disdain. "I sincerely doubt they ever held any value. But you have yet to answer the Rana's question. What was your purpose in approaching her?"

He glanced back at the bard, waiting placidly with her arms akimbo. "Just..." he was clearly unsettled by the scrutiny. "That I am watching her. I don't trust her, and I know her for a liar and a thief."

"Thief?" Lark exclaimed. "What have stolen beyond hearts?"

This earned a laugh from the patrons.

"You took mine the first night you danced here," someone piped.

"And mine when you danced upon my table and fiddled like a

fae-thing," confessed a woman slightly farther from the hearth. Her cheeks were flushed as her companions ribbed her about it, though good-naturedly.

"She stole mine when she said she could teach me to play," called Dane from near the kitchen. Lark felt her eyes water when she saw him standing there, a pie in one hand and a knife in the other, ready to defend her even if he could not see his target.

"And mine when she gave my son a trade, and myself a friend," said his mother, stepping up behind him and deftly disarmed him. She passed the knife to Heleda standing beside her, who clutched it in her fist as if ready and willing to use it.

"She stole my son back from the enemy," a man called from nearer the bar.

"My daughter!" shouted another.

"She stole my sister's whole family from a vampire on Evandair!"

"She stole my best friend!" Adrick's presence was a shock, but the grin on his face as he raised his mug to her, warmed her heart.

"She twice stole me from the brink of death."

Lark's head spun, finally picking the speaker out of the crowd. Keltree sat at a table with Navarie on his knee, near the middle of the room. Vanessa was with him and another man, similar in face but broader of frame, and bearded.

Keltree leaned back in his chair, his arm stretched out in front of him on the table with deceptive casualness. Navarie just sat on his knee shooting daggers at the bully with her eyes.

"So, ...Coolie, was it? I think you can see that no one here gives a flying..." A sharp look from Vanessa altered his choice of words. "...harpy-fart about what crimes you think she has committed. Or what authority you may think you hold. Many here believe that what the king gave her was an empire less than she deserved. But it is what she would accept," he said with an exaggerated sigh. "I think I speak for all of us, that you have disrespected her person, her rank and her race. Not to mention insulted your king. Who is still in town, by the way..."

The room filled very quickly with angry murmurs, and the sound of shifting chairs.

"I think you owe the Rana an apology at the very least," Keltree finished.

Lark saw Coolie's face go red as he realized how deep he was in. He turned stiffly, bowing with the proper deference to her, and she could see the fear in his eyes as he offered his apology. "I beg your forgiveness, your ladyship, and take back what I said."

She drew herself up, emboldened by the response of the tavern. "You may leave," she said. "Though if is repeat of this evening, will not be so lenient next time."

He bowed again and hurried towards the door. There was a roar from the room, and a great many catcalls as he wove his way through the hostile crowd. Lark had no doubt he would try again if he could catch her alone and unawares.

Oh, I wouldn't worry about him, *Daskvi*, came Mouse's very pleased voice in her mind. **The cats got him.**

Cats? she asked, though she was smiling.

Were waiting outside. They told him that the king wanted a word.

Does not bode well for Coolie. She could feel the boy's delight through the connection. **Did my little mouse have ought to do with this?** she asked.

Someone must have told the cats he was speaking treason.

She sighed. **Come round through kitchen. Heleda will feed. Has meat pies.**

With cardamom?

And cinnamon. She knew he needed no second urging and her attention was being captured by Keltree waving her over. She set Ivaska to guard the money and the instruments, though she had serious doubts anyone would dare right now.

"And how are doing tonight?" she asked when she reached them.

"Oh, fine and dandy, my lady. Are you quite all right after that unpleasantness?" he asked, kissing her hand.

She could not help but smile. "Can honestly say was best part of night. Does Gypsy heart good, to hear such kindness. And to know he has dug own grave. Mouse has told me was arrested just outside." crowed his appreciation of the fact. "That is the sweetest music I've heard all week! And you and that boy have played some sweet melodies!"

"Evening, Vanessa," Lark smiled, turning to Navarie's mother. "Enjoying family outing?" she asked.

Vanessa returned her smile. "Yes. We've been hearing about this place all week, and when we were told you were playing here again, we had to come. My husband wanted to meet you. Rus, this is *Lady* Lark," she smiled. "My lady, my husband Rustan Danhaven."

Lark met his reverent bow with a smile. "Actually," she corrected gently, "is officially Rana Illyana Rushanai. But simple Lark is fine when not being 'official'. Which will be as rare as can make," she chuckled.

Keltree took her hand and kissed it gallantly. "You will always be 'my lady' to me," he grinned.

She swatted him lightly with a playful scowl. "Am pleased to meet you, Rustan," she said.

"Rus, please," he said. "I wanted to meet you to thank you for everything you have done for my family. From bringing my daughter back to me to saving my reckless brother's life," he added with a grin towards the idiot in question.

"He's been told lots of stories," Navarie grinned.

"Will bet he has, between two of you..." Lark teased the girl.

She giggled.

"Those two are thick as thieves," her father sighed fondly at the pair of them. "Both of them take after our father."

"While you took after mother, stable, steady..." Keltree grinned.

Lark looked the three of them over, beginning to suspect, as anyone would, that there might have been a little... infidelity involved. But she got no sense of it at all, even as she was surprised that she expected to be able to tell. Focusing, she could see the familial ties and the emotional ones. Keltree was indeed deeply in love with Vanessa, easily as much as Rustan was, but he loved his brother as much and had not broken that trust. Nor did Rus suspect he had. Navarie gravitated naturally towards the uncle who was so much like her. Vanessa... she was solely in love with her husband. Though she was quite fond of her brother-in-law, she loved him as just that: a brother. Lark could see she was also pregnant. Early stages yet, but there. Information was absorbed faster than she could read it, sinking into her with a general 'knowing'. Advantages of earth dragon energy, she guessed.

She smiled, shaking her head in apology as she realized she had been asked something she had not heard. "Please forgive me. Magic has grown, shifted. Am getting used to. I should go, though. So happy to see again, and to meet. Will come visit, bring my husband."

Keltree lit up. "Husband? Is there something I should know?"

She laughed. "Not yet. Few days."

"Was worried for a minute," he grinned.

"Expect you there," she growled, poking his shoulder. "Make sure others come. Family, too!"

"Landros has Adrick already. Rue knows and will make sure Lithgorin makes it. He was hurt pretty badly in the last surge. Took a manticore spike dagger to the hip in the joint. Healing is taking time. Rog, I'm not sure where to find."

She smiled. "Rog is usually at Sleepy Dragon."

He nodded. "I'll make sure he makes it."

"Thank you. Am sad Ebastian won't be there. We lost too many."

He covered her hand with his. "Everyone has someone to grieve for. But a wedding will be good for all of us. It keeps us living."

She squeezed the hand before slipping out of it's grasp, bent to kiss the top of Navarie's head. "And you... you are welcome in Warren any time." She smiled over at her mother. "Is safe adventures, teach to keep even safer. When come to caravan for wedding, make sure to see Old Ruby. Tell her I sent, bring her small gift... tea or tobacco she likes. She will give you blessing and tell more about treasure you carry," she grinned and walked back to the hearth.

As she tested the tuning of her new fiddle, she half-watched their table as confusion ruled for several minutes, and then realisation dawned. She saw Vanessa's hand go to her belly and the eyes grow wide. Seeing the faces light up with tearful joy made her heart lighter. The tune she played was spritely, and sent up a cheer from the whole tavern, setting the tone for the rest of the night.

FOUR

By the time the moon was full, so were the fairgrounds and the surrounding fields and forest. Anywhere a caravan could fit comfortably, one was camped. One could hardly throw a pebble without hitting one of the brightly coloured wagons. The city, even those who resented or mistrusted the Romer, found themselves grateful for their presence. For with them came trade goods and desperately needed foodstuffs and other luxuries that were sorely missed the past season.

While the main Rushavska caravan was set up around the great oak on the fairgrounds, several of them had moved to the clearing where Colwyn's camp had been. After, of course, it had been thoroughly cleansed by no less than Old Ruby and six Rushavska ranie. Her father's wagon was opposite a blue and white striped pavilion, and the rest interspersed with tents where Landros's 'clan' were staying. Her own wagon had been brought here, set on the eastern arc of the circle, halfway between them. People had been decorating it for the last two days.

Lark was amazed by the amount of people who had shown up. It made her heart full to see the support, even those who only came out of fear of showing disrespect. She knew the Rushavska clan was one of the most powerful because of her mother's line, and worried that her leaving it would weaken it somehow. Watching her little sister following Gruma around, being introduced as the heir, lessened those worries. While Lark had mostly charmed the clans with her cheery manner, her music and her spirited dancing, Vadoma was both charming and terrifying. There was just something about her, a wildness, that bled out of her even when she was being happy and excited. She would grow into a dangerous woman to cross, and everyone knew it.

She laughed to think that some might one day wish that she were still the heir. But she, herself, was not worried. She knew that Gruma would temper the girl, help her control her quickness to anger and make her think before she acted.

Gruma had finally shown Lark how to open the 'Gypsy Gates'. She was almost ashamed of herself for not having figured it out herself, it was so simple. But she understood that there was some kind of mental lock on the ability and the knowledge. It was something only a ranie could do. Lark would not have been surprised if she were told it had to do with an ancient bargain. The Romer were well-known for their bargains and sense of debt nearly as much as the Fae. How much you were respected deeply affected the subtext of said agreements. The less you were liked, the more teeth either had.

Lark used a gate the morning of the full moon to bring the children to the camp. The clans loved having so many children underfoot enjoying themselves, and the kids were excited to have new playmates and new games to learn. She expected that she might have slightly less of them when it was time to return to the city. The Romer were known to adopt unwanted children. And, while Lark may have wanted them, she knew she was not a good substitute for a close family, nor could she offer them the array of choices they would be exposed to among the Romeri.

Mouse was a special case. Landros introduced him to Nalenil, who had shown up with Kerola.

"He is one of the wild ones Lark told you about," he explained. "Who can teach you the Ways of the Grove."

The boy's eyes grew wide, and he seemed to smile with his whole body. Then a worried, sad look crossed his face and he turned back to her. "I want to go, but I don't want to leave you, *Daskvi.*"

She smiled, knelt to his level. "Will going make happy?"

He nodded vigorously. "And sad, though."

She took his hands in hers, touched his fingers to her temple. "Always, you will be here, if need. Children grow, fly away from nest to make own lives. If you happy, I happy. Go, grow, be. Come home to visit. But stay for wedding," she added, dropping into a warning, maternal tone.

He laughed, threw his arms around her neck, "Yes, momma." They hugged tightly for several minutes before he pulled back, carefully tucked a curl back into her scarf from where he had dislodged it. "And don't worry about the cats any more. You're bigger than them."

"I know," she laughed. "Now have to watch for rats."

He shrugged. "It's always something."

She sighed heavily as he walked away with the elf for a long talk before joining the other children. Landros set a hand on her shoulder, smiling proudly at her. "He's in good hands."

"This I know. I remember Savaren's people. Is was my idea. But... I understand my father little bit more today than yesterday."

She let him help her up and gave him a quick kiss. "Now go, you are not supposed to be spending time with me today. Have long time for that. Will get sick of me," she teased.

He pulled her in for a more passionate kiss. "I highly doubt that, princess."

Their embrace was abruptly ended when Ivan found them. He and Vadoma physically pulled them apart. "Told you they were misbehaving," she snarked, began dragging her sister in the opposite direction.

Laughing, though reluctant, they allowed themselves to be separated, and dragged off to different duties.

Lark remembered Yarmine's wedding, not that long ago. Today

was not much different. Though, instead of wandering camp to greet various people or avoid them as she liked, she was the one who had to stay at her own fire and be greeted. At least she was not alone. Yarmine, Vadoma and Ruby kept her company, fitting her with bits and pieces of her wedding finery, plying her with food and drink.

Eventually, Ivaska, run ragged by the hordes of young ones, flopped down at Lark's feet and slept like the dead.

It was a good night. She met many whom she had not seen in years, or since she was small. Even Arturi put in an appearance, though very reluctantly. His wife practically dragged him. She was not a ranie, but she was very round in all the right places and demanding enough to have been one had she any power. Lark found her pleasant enough, though she could tell Arturi was kicking himself for allowing Ivan to run him off. She greeted him politely, as if they had never once shared a kiss beneath a barren pear tree.

In retrospect, Lark should have taken that as an omen. She smiled politely, shared conversation and put him from her mind. Though his presence did make her wonder what Landros was up to.

While Lark was wined, dined and serenaded, Landros was being schooled. Granted, there was a great deal of alcohol and food in Colwyn's tent, and people of all races coming and going, but still he was beset with brothers (Lark's) telling him what would be expected of him as a ranie's husband.

"Don't you mean a Captain?" he asked.

Raven laughed meanly. "Just cause wife is Rana does not mean get to be Captain!" he crowed. "What am hearing, Mayor Fitzbottom is 'Captain'!"

"FitzWaller," someone corrected.

Raven tossed his hand dismissively at that.

"Oh, all right," Landros replied, trying to decide if he was relieved or not. In the end, he decided he was better off without the headache.

Finally, once they were certain he knew what to expect tomorrow night, they dragged him out to visit Petrov's fire. There they wined him and fed him some more and teased him unmercifully.

Thankfully, with Portholus for a brother, he was well-prepared to handle this part, and more than held his own. Before the party began to wind down, a few hours til dawn, he had managed to earn a little much-begrudged respect from Lark's father. And not just by the stories he told, or the come-backs he fired off, but by the nature of the non-Romeri who came to pay respects.

Even 'Stephan' made a brief appearance, bringing a couple more shirts and a tunic or two he had hoped to trade for the very comfortable Romer styles. He did not go home empty-handed.

Ivan and the rest of Lark's brothers made the rounds of the whole encampment, collecting the gifts for the new couple. From many, it was useful things, but there was also an awful lot of money. Not as much as they announced, but multiplied, of course, for luck. Lark knew most of it would likely be spent on the children, making the Warren more comfortable for those who had to take refuge there. And to help rebuild for the souls that had been forced to eke out a beggar's living in Tent Town.

Eventually, the camp grew quiet. Visitors from the city either stumbled home or found some place to curl up and sleep off their heads. All of the Warren found their way in with the Romer children, snuggled in piles in, under, and in one case, on top of wagons.

The second day started late, mostly due to an over-exuberance the night before, and the city itself had declared a state of holiday. Few complained. There was now enough food to warrant it, and the initial assessments had been made. Everyone was more than willing to have a day off before the hard work started, and most had an excuse to drink.

All the taverns would be full but for one. The Cinnamon Tree was closed. Lily and Heleda spent all morning baking the light, fluffy bread the Tree was famous for, and Neneis gathered up all the beer he had been brewing since the siege started that was ready.

The entire bar was going to the wedding. The bread was allowed to be a gift, but Petrov had insisted on paying for the beer.

Lark had been right about families coming to find her about the 'loose' children. As soon as the initial round of coffee had been consumed, women began trickling in with various children from just about every clan, asking her if they could take someone with them when they left.

Always, Lark would consult the child, double-checking to make certain they were not being taken merely for extra labour. Where she found love and acceptance, and the child's agreement, she allowed the orphans to be adopted.

Magpie sat beside the fire, tending the porridge and doling it out as needed, watching it all. Lark had taught her the secret to making sure the pot was never empty until it needed to be and she was having fun practising.

"That is something don't see every day," she commented after the latest happy family left.

"What? Romer taking older child?" she asked, moving to get a small bowl for herself. "Kibbie is lucky. And are good match for Foret clan. He is good with horses."

"No," Vadoma laughed. "Though yes..." she added hastily. "Meant... watching dragon give away horde."

"What?" Lark asked, confused.

"Well, are dragon now," she explained with a small wave of her hand. "And is obvious horde is children. You do have lot of them, Mahren."

"Ooo, you!" she growled playfully, once her initial shock and speechlessness had passed.

She ain't wrong, *Daskvi*.

Lark looked around, found Billy lounging by a tree, invited him over to breakfast. It did not take long after that for all of the dragon-children to find her fire. And she spent the majority of the day enjoying their company. Terri even showed Vadoma some of the magical cooking secrets her mother had taught her: how to season and stretch ingredients much farther than they ought to be able to go.

Before they knew it, the moon was rising and it was time.

The sun was no longer in the sky when they gathered before the basin that had been set up in front of Lark's wagon, but there was still a great deal of light left. Though the forest canopy was open here, most of the sunset colours were hidden. It left the light a vibrant purple and orange, filled with a fae haze as the moon rose, fat and golden, to shine down upon the host below and the couple standing before the vessel of herbed water.

Ruby and Lyuba stood beside the young ranie from the Dalascu clan: a girl named Florin (who preferred Nettle) that had just, unexpectedly, come into her power. She was only sixteen.

Lark paid them only little mind. Her eyes were only for the elf in front of her. He was dressed in a new, dove-blue elven coat, his hair held back by a simple circlet, cascading over the tips of his ears like ripples of polished gold. She had seen more handsome men, elven men so beautiful as to make you weep. But in this moment, he was the most beautiful sight she had ever seen. She did not think that she could be happier than she was right now, staring across the water into those amber-coloured eyes.

She was a vision in red and white. Her midnight eyes glinted like sapphires in the moonlight beneath ebony waves crowned with gold and white wildflowers. The scent of orchids and cinnabar drifted his way, intoxicating him. The white blouse shone starkly against her olive skin, the simple embroidery only serving to enhance the effect. The layers of silk swirled from her hip to her calves in an ombré fade from deep red to nearly purple. It was all held together by a red velvet bodice, laced in gold ribbon and embroidered with bands from mid-back to front hem in a thread that glinted like real gold.

Glamour or truth, he did not care. She was the most mesmerizing creature he had ever known, and he was hers. He found he did not even care about the dragon any more. It was just one more layer of mystery, though one they would discover together over the next few centuries, Goddesses willing.

It was not until a drop of water touched their held hands that they even realized that someone was speaking. They turned to face Lark's father, who held a length of wet silk in his hands. "*Illyana Petrovna Rushavska, my daughter, my joy. I who helped give you life now give you husband. Take him in love, be faithful, be fruitful, be happy.*"

He then wound the tasselled cloth over their clasped hands, and up their arms nearly to the elbows, leaving the ends dangling. He set his hands on their joined ones. "*Now are one, both blood of my blood, daughter and son.*"

Landros then pulled her to him by their bound hands and kissed her, deep and passionate. The camp went wild with shouts of joy.

Off to the side, one of the other clans asked, "I*sn't it 'be faithful, be obedient?'*"

Raven snorted, "*Have you met my sister?*"

They were both distracted by Old Ruby stepping forward, holding up her hands for silence as the basin was removed. The crowd obeyed immediately. She spoke in Romeri, but every soul gathered understood her. "Yes, we gather for wedding. But is more than this. Is birthing, too. Tonight, under goddesses' eye, we witness birth of new clan. No less important than our own for all it does not move, for all it is mixed of blood.

"No longer is our beloved Illyana, whom we named songbird from her first chirp, of Rushavska." She set her gnarled hand upon their joined ones, and both of them felt the electric surge running through the connection. "I present before you Queen Illyana Petrovna Rushanai and her consort, Landrosallenthoia."

If the shouts before had been loud, these could probably be heard to the walls of the city.

The musicians began to play, and several children started a scarf dance, weaving in pairs around the still-bound couple. The two of them joined the dance, turning, stepping as far away as their arms would reach, when children would wind in between them, and then together again in turn.

They were laughing, mostly because Landros felt a little awkward. Dancing with hands bound was not easy. "How long do we have to..." he wiggled their arms, making the tassels bounce and the miniature bells ring.

"Until is dry, at least."

He tried to pull her back in, close enough for a kiss, but the kids kept cutting in between them. He growled, but he was still in a good mood.

They danced, ate and drank, mingled with what felt like the whole world until well after midnight.

Lark had a clue what was coming. She knew the traditions from countless weddings in the past. Landros hadn't a clue. Somewhere in the woods there would be a bower set up, provided they even made it that far. Any time too many people clustered around them, she would grow suspicious, but would be wrong.

The moon was well on his own way to bed, and Lark had been conversing with Lily and Rue and Vadoma, trying to keep Landros in sight. It was only the three of them until Yarmine joined them, chattering about the prestige of having a king at a Gypsy wedding. Before she realized it, they had drawn her far enough away, and he had been surrounded by enough friends and relatives to hold even him back.

The moment it dawned on her that they had 'gotten' her, they dropped the pretence and began to drag her away from the ring of wagons. Others came to help them, whisking her off, while she laughingly called out his name.

They just about had to sit on him when he realized what was going on. At the last minute, she tore the wreath from her head and threw it towards him, watched it spinning like a chakram through the air to land in the grass near his brother's feet. The last thing she saw was Portholus snatching it from the ground and dangling it tauntingly just out of his reach.

Then she was beyond the majority of the partiers and Kerola pointed out a direction. "That way, about three hundred yards,

End Game

there's a natural bower. Stream, a small waterfall. There are witch-lights in the tree."

"Thank you," she said, clasping as many hands as she could. "All of you," she said, and then darted off into the night.

Landros was upset at first, before he realized this was a game. One that was likely to have a very satisfying end. That did not mean he was going to make it easy. He surprised the hell out of those who didn't already know better, how much strength his slight frame hid.

Finally, when they figured she had enough of a head-start, they let him go. He jumped, snatching the wreath from his brother's startled hands and pelted off into the night in the direction the women had gone. The people he passed laughed, dodged and cheered him on. He had to admit, this was a fun way to get the bride and groom away from everyone for a little private time. Elven weddings went on for a week, with a great deal more ceremony and less time alone together until the very end. Privately, he was very glad they had followed her traditions instead. He didn't think either of them would have had the patience for an elven ceremony. And honestly, what would have been the point? He did not live in elven society, and had no family that would have been scandalized by the lack of it.

He paused, looking around. He was well away from the last of the wagons, though he could just hear the sound of the music and people who were still drinking and dancing. Otherwise, the wood was quiet and still. Crouching, he cast about for signs of her running this way. The light was dim, only starlight and fireflies but, for his own cat-like vision, it was more than enough.

He grinned. The fireflies should have been abed by now. Something had stirred them up. It did not take him long to find her trail and he found himself wondering what surprise she would have in store for him. The last time they had spent the night alone in the woods, she had seduced him with a very provocative dance where the layers of her clothes slowly melted away. He could not even imagine what she might have up her sleeve tonight.

Reaching a large rock that a very stubborn hawthorn tree was growing around, he paused. A little ways down the gentle slope, he could see a natural bower by a small stream where someone had lain bedding and a basket. Tiny, fae-like witchlights hung among the foliage, no doubt the cause of the increased firefly activity. But there was no one there. Her trail clearly veered away from this, above the hawthorn.

He crouched at the apex of the hillock, searching the wood for any sign of her, and the hairs on the back of his neck began to stand up. The air was filling with the smell of something acrid and sharp, as well as the fragrance of cinnabar. There was light ahead, an acidic green that pulsed softly.

He crept in that direction, painfully aware that if something was wrong, he was unarmed. He did not get very far before he found the source.

The woods opened up near the bottom of the slope, a place where an orcish encampment had been. He recognized the area. He, Nalenil and his band had slaughtered them practically in their sleep. The ground here was soaked in blood. There was something else here, too: the source of the glow.

Within a few feet of him, ran a line on the ground. He bent to examine it. Someone had mixed blood, pitch and a phosphorescent fungus into a paste and drawn an enormous magical circle with it. Only without the circle. He did not know much about the details of magic, but he did know that lines of symbols radiating from a centre point like the blades of a spiked chakram had intent. Usually fairly deadly intent. And that ritual circles like this were enclosed for a reason.

He shifted his position, remembering a very good spot to do just that: a tree thirty feet south of him. Moving with swift silence, he left his wedding coat at the base and scaled the trunk, crouching in the central crotch where just a few weeks ago, he had observed the orcish encampment.

In the centre of a very nasty looking set of symbols, stood his wife, her red skirts rippling like flickering flames around her legs. Her hair was loose and just as wild. There was a very tiny circle of short, green flames around her, no more than two feet wide, and the symbols radiating outward from it were slowly lighting up, like a trail of lamp oil after a spark.

Standing in another circle painted on a jut of rock not a hundred feet from her, stood a withered hag. She was dressed in a ragged dress of black and purple with a blouse of the most acidic yellowed-green he had ever seen. A strand of gold beads hung around her neck, nearly as low as her breasts, and what was left of her coarse, grey hair was covered by a turbaned scarf in the same acidic fabric.

He had once seen, with his own eyes, the oldest person in the known world. If this was the woman Lark had told him of, she was older still, and she looked every year of it. Ilanil had not looked nearly so haggard. She had been graceful in her wrinkles, almost other-worldly. This woman was terrifying.

He felt frozen, paralysed by the knowledge of what was about to go down, and that he was powerless to do anything. He did not even have a boot-knife with him. And so he listened. He did not understand most of what he heard, but he listened.

Lark was livid. The wind snatching at her hair and skirts was her own doing. It had risen with her temper when she had found herself caught in the witch's circle. The old bat had taken the time to gloat, stalling, really. The bitch would have known that Landros would not be far away, come hunting his bride. It was a tradition even the twisted Mushyan followed, though it more often had darker undertones. A fact the witch bragged about, along with what she would do with him when he fell into the net himself.

What the witch did not know was that Lark was neither helpless nor alone. And she, too, was stalling.

"You really believe that this twisted ritual will resurrect your clan, dead more than thousand years?" she sneered. *"Are dust by now."*

The old woman cackled. *"Oh, that I know. But this is important night, as would know if were worth one ounce of your power! But no, were so much in looove, so much in huuurry,"* she drawled in a singsong tone, *"that could not be bothered to read significance of day,"* she sneered.

"What, Witch's Harvest?" Lark snorted. *"Is only dangerous if fall on new moon."*

The old woman's laugh was far more sinister now. *"Yes, but other things can be done when moon swells on cusp 'tween harvest and winter."*

Lark felt the pulsing of the intended magic as it raced through the symbols. She studied it, subjecting her senses to the flavours and odours of it. Her conclusions left her cold and numb. Only the presence of the children in her mind allowed her the warmth of heart and confidence not to show the horror she felt at what the witch planned. The way things were running, it was not likely she even needed to kill her to use the dragon's heart as she wanted. She would simply use her as a living conduit to fuel the exchange.

When the moon fully set, the souls of the Mushyan clan would rise from whatever hells they burned in, and Eshanai's magic would be used to seal them into the very living bodies of every Romeri clan across the continent. What would become of those dispossessed souls? They could very well burn up come sunrise.

"She is absolutely mad," whispered Terriserra from beside Landros.

He nearly jumped out of his skin, and might have fallen had she not grabbed his shoulder and steadied him. Still trying to get his heart to slow down, he managed to whisper back, "What the hells are you doing here and how did you get up here without me hearing you?"

"Gate," she smiled, and put what looked like the grip of a bow in his hand.

It was a beautiful piece of Elven craftsmanship. Smooth as pearl, with dragon heads of Elven silver at each end. It seemed to hum in his hand.

She smiled. "It likes you. Good. Wait for your shot."

"What? What shot? And how will I know?" Things were happening too fast and he did not have time to process everything.

Terri set her hand on his, where he gripped the object. "Have a little faith." Then her lips quirked. "And you'll know. This all begins with us, but it ends with you." Then she fell backwards out of the tree and was just gone.

He turned back to the war of wills in the clearing, tightening his fist on the bow grip. He was not imagining the vibrations. It did not feel like a warning. It was comfortable, anticipating. Magic, then.

Lark put up protections, drew runes in the air to lessen the witch's draw upon her, sent out little bolts of lightning to slow her down. But the witch had defences of her own, and the lightning did nothing but shower sparks around her. She cackled in delight and danced a little jig in place, began a singsong chant with great, swirling gestures of her arms.

The time for stalling was over. The children were in place, had drawn a circle around the witch's ritual made of good, clean earth and raw stone, the twisting knobs of tree roots. It was as easy as remembering how a favourite song went.

Lark folded in on herself, as if in excruciation. In truth, she wasn't comfortable. The circle was drawing power from her, building it up in the bowl of the earth as if she were a well-spring. A mist began to rise in the forest around them, a strange vibration in the air.

Landros watched, horrified, as his wife bent in agony and the witch redoubled her chanting in triumph. He wanted to act, tried to will the object in his hand to do *something*! But powerful magic items, elven items in particular, had a thing about timing. And apparently, now wasn't it.

Then Lark began to twist and writhe, her body swelling. For a full second he feared the witch was doing something unspeakable to her, and then he saw amber scales on her back where they tore through her bodice. The rest of her clothes shredded as an eighty foot long, wingless dragon rose up where she had been standing, stretching for the heavens, one foot still within the tiny circle. Then the other foot came down... outside the circle and the witch's voice rose in protest.

"You can't DO that! I've bound you by blood and pitch!" she screamed.

"You forget, Tavora," the dragon spat, her voice booming as if in a canyon and not a forest clearing. *"So long as part of me touches earth, I can be* anywhere *I want!"*

The witch paled, her chanting faltered.

There came a sound, not so much heard as felt, like the dropping of a pin, the moment the moon left the sky.

The witch snapped out of her shock, fell into a crouch and slammed her hand upon the stone. A visible wave of green light burst outward from where the dragon stood, rippling through the fog. Odd shapes began to appear, moving in contorted jerks.

Landros did not know what had just happened, but it could not be good. He stood, walked out along the largest, most horizontal, of the branches and held the grip out as if ready to aim. From the dragon's mouths, the horns of the bow spewed forth, forming a recurve made of moonlight. He made to draw the string, felt it, as thin as cobweb, as strong as wire. An arrow of starlight glittered into being as he pulled. He held the shot, taking aim at the witch, waiting for the right moment.

Just as she began to laugh in triumph, the wave she had sent out came rolling back, amplified by the magic and wills of five more dragons, though their scales were darker, more earth-brown than honey-gold. Golden streaks of light followed it, silencing the howling, screaming tide. The dragon vanished in a column of earth as the wave struck the witch, drowning her shrieks. It swirled about her, consuming her.

Landros heard the tiniest ting of a crystal bell and loosed. Time seemed to slow down. He watched the arrow sailing, twinkling through the silent air, an inch a second, or so it seemed. The dragons slithered downward, became children, to circle the maelstrom, holding hands with Lark. Out of the mists he saw women descending into the clearing from every direction. They formed a secondary ring around the first, all of them chanting. The first ring in Draconic, the outer in Romeri, and it was like a song, melody and counterpoint.

He saw something stripping away from the old woman at the heart of everything, peeled off by a magical force he could feel. It was beautiful and terrifying to watch.

Then the arrow reached her, slid through her bared heart like a gannet diving into the sea. There was no time for realization, or terror beyond what had registered before he had loosed. There came not a single sound, but a great boom was felt, seemed to shake reality itself. Then the edges of her blackened and rotted until all that remained upon the outcrop was a pile of dust, a glint of gold, and some very nasty paint.

The sudden sound of the woods at night was painful after that soul-crushing silence. Landros gasped for breath, felt like he had been holding it for minutes. He jumped from the tree, running towards the group of women, not even noticing when the bow became a mere grip again.

The ring of ranie had parted enough to allow Lark and the children out, and bent to dispose of the remains in their own way. Lark did not even complain when Landros pulled her from her feet, wrapping her in a crushing embrace. The Cardinals said nothing, merely waited until they were standing still before closing the ring again in a massive hug.

He held her face in his hands, looked into her eyes to make sure she was all right before kissing her as if it were the last time he would ever get to.

It took Billy poking him and joking about 'coming up for air', to prompt him to let go.

Not in the least bit embarrassed, he looked around at the lot of them. "Is everyone all right? No one's hurt?"

"Tired," Mouse mumbled.

Terri nudged him, "Staying up late will do that, too," she teased.

He shoved back fondly. "I smelled a cat."

"More like wood told you someone was up to no good," Lark

told him, running her fingers through his tousled hair.

"Maybe. Nalenil said I'll learn a lot, figure out more, maybe be teaching them by the time I'm grown. Cause Earth Dragon."

That made Landros look at her. "Speaking of dragons..."

She laughed, realizing what he was thinking. "No. Did not, can not ...without significant spell... turn into dragon."

"It was an illusion," answered Tamlain. "Pretty cool, huh, General?"

"Had th' witch convinced," grinned Felise. "I didn't think Eshanai ever knew th' name of th' witch who killed her."

Lark shook her head. "Didn't. To manage that spell, witch had to embed true name. We read it when we read intent," she said with a shudder.

"Do I want to know?" Landros asked.

Billy didn't wait for an answer. "Mad whumper wanted ta raise th' souls of 'er dead clan an' stick 'em inna bodies here fer th' weddin'," he snarled, jerking his thumb back towards the camp. Landros felt his soul shiver at that. "When mum found th' circle, she tole us ta tell her gruma an' take th' short cut 'ere. Guess Gruma tole ever' ranie in camp."

"Where's everyone else?" Landros asked, confused as to why Rog, Keltree, Colwyn and the others weren't charging through the wood right now.

Felise answered. "Cause th' menfolk were told to protect th' camp. Lord Colwyn had already taken 'Stephan' back to th' city, so you can stop worrying about that. He had a good time, though," she added, smiling at him. "He'll likely sail for th' Capitol at first tide tomorrow with a very sore head. Said something about it being a wedding present."

Even Lark frowned at that. "How so?"

Mouse laughed sleepily. "He took the cats with him! Your present is them gone when you get back."

Lark pressed a kiss on the top of his head. "Oh, you! You know, cats are very nice creatures."

He gave her a soft smile as he stifled a yawn. "*Moyin* are, yes," he answered, using the elven word for 'cat'. "When they wants."

She ruffled his hair. "Go to bed, sweetling."

This time he didn't bother to stifle the yawn, and promptly vanished mid-way.

Landros blinked. "When did they learn to teleport? Can you teleport?"

"No. I meant what 'dragon' said. If touching earth, can be anywhere touching earth. Sort of teleport but with limitations. Is taxing, though."

Terriserra tapped Landros for his attention, held out the bow-grip when he turned. "You dropped this."

"Oh. Sorry. I was so...," he couldn't find the words he wanted, so he just gestured at Lark to explain. "Thank you for the loan. It's a very nice weapon."

Terri laughed. "Understatement! But, uhm... it wasn't a loan. It was one of your wedding presents."

"One of...." his mind just shut down on that thought. "Who would... give a powerful magical weapon like that... to *me*... as a ...wedding present?" he stammered.

"Maid Jelliana," she answered, still holding it out to him. "Rue delivered it yesterday. She's the one who told me to get it to you."

Landros shook his head as he reached out to accept the bow. He needed to learn not to question the strangeness of the goddess-touched.

The moment the grip touched his hand, he yelped as it shocked him.

Terri just grinned smugly at him. "That's what you get for dropping it." Then she walked away without further explanation.

Billy tugged the other two away, to walk back to camp with Terri, and bride and groom turned to watch what the ranie were doing behind them.

Some of the women had already left, though a great many were still at work.

"How..." he tried. "I mean... was it the bow? What she tried to do? How was it ...it seemed so easy in retrospect."

Lark chuffed, "Far from *easy*. But we had advantages. She did not know about children. When Ilanilayana was graced, children were not part of bargain. They came when called. Witch did not close circle because wanted magic to flow out. Children closed circle, like beaver dam. When came flooding back, it tried to consume her instead. Arrow's flight gave us opening, time to revoke curse upon her, which allowed arrow to kill her."

"She was cursed?"

"*Sesha*. With eternal life, invulnerability. She watched whole clan die, but herself could not. So, we revoke. Thousand years catch up fast."

He laughed at that, though still in shock. "By all that is holy, what have I gotten myself into?"

She slipped her arms around him, bent to whisper into his ear. "Whole, scaly, noisy, sexy mess."

A shiver ran down his spine as he felt her breath at his neck. "Scaly?" he asked.

She shrugged. "Who knows. Mebbe. Will have to check thoroughly. Every night."

He took a deep breath, slowly exhaled. Then took a step back from her, looked her over from head to toe, making sure there was no physical damage.

She let him, waiting.

Then he bent and she was over his shoulder as he stalked off towards the bower. "No time like the present, princess."

THE END

Other Books By
S.L. Thorne

Love In Ruins
The Speaker
Mercy's Ransom
Fang and Bone
(an anthology)

The Gryphon's Rest Series:
Lady of the Mist
The Gloaming

SHIFT Books 1 & 2
Stag's Heart
Dragon's Bride

PORTSWAIN Books 1 & 2
Midnight and Amber
Sagavis

All Available in hardback, paperback and e-book
at:
Thornewoodstudios.com/books
through Amazon.com
and other outlets near you